D0465058

RENEWALS 458-4574

DATE DUE

GAYLORD			PRINTED IN U.S.A.

SUPERMARKET

SUPERMARKET

SATOSHI AZUCHI

TRANSLATED BY

PAUL WARHAM

THOMAS DUNNE BOOKS

ST. MARTIN'S PRESS ✄ NEW YORK

This is a work of fiction. All of the characters, organizations, and events portrayed in this novel are either products of the author's imagination or are used fictitiously.

THOMAS DUNNE BOOKS.
An imprint of St. Martin's Press.

SUPERMARKET. Copyright © 1984 by Satoshi Azuchi. English translation copyright © 2007 by Paul Warham. All rights reserved.
Printed in the United States of America. For information, address St. Martin's Press, 175 Fifth Avenue, New York, N.Y. 10010.

www.thomasdunnebooks.com
www.stmartins.com

Library of Congress Cataloging-in-Publication Data

Arai, Shin'ya, 1937–
    [Shosetsu supamaketto. English]
    Supermarket / Satoshi Azuchi ; translated by Paul Warham.—1st u.s. ed.
        p. cm.
    "Originally published in Japan as: Shosetsu supamaketto by Kodansha Co. Ltd."
    ISBN-13: 978-0-312-38294-0 (alk. paper)
    ISBN-10: 0-312-38294-4 (alk. paper)
    I. Warham, Paul. II. Title.
    PL845.R246S56 2009
    895.6'36—dc22

                                                            2008044585

This book has been selected by the Japanese Literature Publishing Project (JLPP), which is run by the Japanese Literature Publishing and Promotion Center (J-Lit Center), on behalf of the Agency for Cultural Affairs of Japan.

Previously published in Japan as *Shosetsu Supamaketto* by Kodansha Co. Ltd., Tokyo.

First U.S. Edition: February 2009

10   9   8   7   6   5   4   3   2   1

SUPERMARKET

PROLOGUE

It was nine forty-five in the morning when the PA system sparked to life and the voice of Manabe, the store manager, came over the speakers. All employees to the cash registers on the first floor, please.

Something was obviously up.

Ôtaka Seizô, the man in charge of the fresh produce section at the flagship store of the Ishiei Stores supermarket chain, was putting the finishing touches to the tomato display when the announcement was made. He stopped what he was doing and headed toward the cash registers. Normally, the four floor chiefs ran their own morning assemblies. The fact that they were summoning the whole staff together like this meant they had a special announcement to make.

A number of employees were already there by the time he arrived; looming above the crowd was the hulking form of Ichimura Juichi, the general manager of the company. Next to him stood Ishikari Seijirô, the managing director. Manabe the store manager was hurrying about like the athlete he was, busily corralling people into position.

Eventually, the employees formed a circle around the two directors and the store manager. There were nearly a hundred people in attendance.

"Good morning, everyone," Manabe said in his powerful baritone.

The employees returned his greeting in a slightly out-of-sync chorus.

"As you can see, we are joined today by Mr. Ishikari and Mr. Ichimura from the head office. So without further ado I'll turn things over to them and ask you all to listen carefully to what they have to say."

Ishikari nodded vigorously and stepped forward to face the crowd.

"Morning, everybody." Despite its slightly nasal tone, his voice carried well. "Results for the last quarter have just come in. And I'm happy to say that thanks to all your hard work, the results are excellent once again." He paused and scanned the crowd of employees surrounding him.

"In particular," he went on, "I want to thank all of you here at the center store, where results were outstanding. This store is setting an example for the rest of the company to follow—a model for the way we want the company to develop as we move forward into the future. I have to confess to you that the decision to invest in a big store like this wasn't an easy one to make. It was a huge gamble—one that might easily have put the future of the whole company at risk if it didn't succeed. Mr. Ichimura here still makes fun of me about it, but there was a time when I was so worried I literally couldn't sleep. I felt that I had the future of all the company's employees on my shoulders. Fortunately, I needn't have worried. Everything has turned out better than we ever hoped. I want to take this opportunity to say again how grateful we are for your hard work. But now it's time for the company to take the next step forward. We want to build on what we've achieved, and use the success we've had here as the launching pad for an ambitious new expansion program. We're looking at opening new outlets on a regular basis, with the aim of having a total of thirty stores up and running by 1975. This will mean an average of five new stores every year."

Everyone listened intently to what Ishikari was saying. The only discernible movements were a few gentle nods of agreement from Sashima Kôji, head of the fresh meat section, and an occasional flick of the hand from Sugai Keinoshin, distractedly running his fingers through his hair.

Ôtaka would have liked to know how this optimistic talk was affecting Také Norio, the young fellow in the fresh meat section who had shared his concerns about the department with him the previous evening, but from where Ôtaka was standing he couldn't see Také at all. It was hard to reconcile what Také had told him with the rosy future being painted now.

"And these new stores are not going to be small-scale affairs like most of the outlets we've had in the past. Our plan is to continue to develop bigger stores like this one. Even bigger than this one, in some cases. Of course, this is easier said than done. We're going to need the whole company to pull together if we're going to have any chance of success. Unless the whole company works together as one; unless every single one of us works as hard as we can—every hour of every day—to develop that all-important 'care for the customer,' then our plans will come to nothing. I know I can rely on you all to do everything you can to help, and I look forward to seeing everyone working harder than ever to help us achieve our goals."

There was still something of the young man in Ishikari's voice as he brought his speech crisply to a close. You almost felt you ought to applaud.

Ichimura stepped forward next, a broad grin on his face. "Morning, everyone," he said.

The energy in Ichimura's voice was contagious, and the employees boomed his greeting back: "Good morning!"

"I've been a businessman all my life, so I'm not very good at making speeches. But as far as business is concerned I'd back myself against anyone. People often ask me what the most important ingredients are for success in business. I always tell them the same thing. One: you've got to learn to bow your head. And two: never lose sight of the bottom line. It sounds easy—but believe me, it's anything but."

Ichimura's speech was seasoned with anecdotes from his days as a food wholesaler: a man who had forgotten to bow and lost thirty million yen worth of business as a result; another man so obsessed with bringing in new business he didn't realize he wasn't making any profit at all. They were entertaining stories, and Ichimura told them well.

"What it comes down to is using your head. And that goes for all of you here, whatever your work involves. Ask Sashima-*san* here, for example."

Sashima was the smug-looking head of the fresh meat section. He sprang to attention at the sound of his name. His chubby cheeks gave him a mischievous air that made him look like a bit of a comedian at times.

"Look at how Sashima's department works. As soon as meat starts to lose its color, he makes sure it's marinated in seasoning. Old meat is worth nothing if it's left to go bad, but once Sashima has ground it up and added flavoring, it's back on sale before you know it—and at a higher price than before. That's what I call good business sense. If Ishiei Stores are to continue to develop and expand in the future, it's this kind of business sense that we need."

Again, Ōtaka would have loved to see Také's face. For it was the same Sashima, now being extravagantly praised in front of his colleagues, who was the cause of Také's worries. Did a man who made a habit of walking off with company property really deserve to be held up as an example for everyone else to follow?

After the assembly came to an end, the daily announcement that marked the opening of business for the day sounded: "Thank you for visiting Ishiei Stores today." It was the recorded voice of a woman that rang out like chimes over the PA system. The doors were pushed open, and the first customers stepped into the store.

ONE

THE COUSINS

It was early afternoon on Sunday, January 5, 1969, and a man in his mid-thirties walked briskly from the railway station into the center of Sawabe city, along a main road that was still unusually quiet after the New Year holidays. The man wore a dark green suit and carried a leather travel bag, a coat draped over one arm. It wasn't a look that would have been right for everyone, but the man was tall and fair and carried it off with aplomb.

After a while, the road entered a shopping mall known as the Center Arcade. Near the entrance to the mall was City Hall, where construction work was going on. The man looked around to get his bearings and turned onto a road opposite the mall. He was walking toward a plain, two-story concrete building.

The sign on the building looked far too distinguished for such a nondescript structure. It read:

ISHIEI STORES
Head Office

The man stepped inside, a trace of a smile on his lips. A couple flights of stairs later there was a glass door. He opened the door and found himself in front of a low counter, over which he could see across the entire office.

It was a room of about 250 square meters. Desks were scattered about the room like islands. Above the desks, signs hung from the ceiling: ADMINISTRATION, ACCOUNTS, and so on. The man stood at the counter, studying the layout.

The first person to notice him was Misaki Yoshiko. Strictly speaking, she was Ishikari's secretary and worked in administration, but since she happened to have the desk closest to the door, she tended to act as the receptionist as well.

"Good afternoon, sir. Can I help you?" she said, smiling attractively.

"Hello, my name is Kôjima. I have an appointment to see Mr. Ishikari," said the man, slightly disconcerted by the sudden vision in front of him.

"Certainly. Just a moment, please."

Yoshiko spoke into a telephone and turned back toward the visitor. "Follow me, please," she said, flashing him another attractive smile as she showed him the way.

Yoshiko had barely sat back down at her desk before she found Kuroba Motoko of the development department standing beside her.

The development department was responsible for finding locations for the new outlets the company was planning to build. But they obviously weren't very busy at the moment (or maybe supervision there just wasn't as strict as in other departments), because more often than not Motoko could be found wandering the office in search of gossip.

"Hey, Misaki-*san*, who was that?"

"One of the boss's cousins, I think. Works for one of the big banks in Osaka."

"In town for the holidays?"

"Could be. But there's more to it than that, I think. The boss was talking about him this morning as *a very important visitor.*"

"'A very important visitor'?" Motoko repeated. She stood silent for a few moments, deep in thought. Then she erupted, "I've got it! He's going to quit the bank and come work here."

At Motoko's words, Yoshiko felt something flicker inside her. For some reason, she'd been thinking the same thing herself.

"Has to be," Motoko went on. "What other explanation could there be? Cool. So finally the company is going to have a dignified, good-looking gentleman of its own. It's about time." Motoko had already convinced herself that the decision was made and the move was imminent. "Tall and handsome . . ."

"Maybe."

"What do you mean, 'maybe'? There aren't many men in this company who could get away with wearing a suit like that."

"I guess," Yoshiko said as she got up and started toward the kitchenette.

"You making them coffee?" Motoko asked.

"Hmm."

"When you serve them, do it really slow so you can hear what they're talking about. Then come back and tell me all about it, OK?"

"Whatever. Anyway, Kuroba-*san*, didn't you see the ring on his finger? I bet he's totally devoted to his wife."

"Who cares? I'll make him take it off."

"Listen to you!" Yoshiko laughed, as if scandalized.

Motoko was in her late twenties, but still didn't have a boyfriend. She was bright and cheerful enough, and not bad looking. Probably it was her personality that was to blame. A lot of men nowadays wouldn't know how to deal with an assertive girl like Motoko. The fact that she was tall and on the large side didn't help. At times she could come across as just a little formidable.

Motoko was obviously getting tired of her situation, but to Yoshiko it seemed an enviable existence. Motoko was still enjoying the carefree life of a single young woman. For Yoshiko, those days were gone forever. She remembered it as a time of hope and possibility, like the moment just before a game begins. After a failed marriage that had left her with a young son to bring up by herself, it was a time she would never know again.

She knew that self-pity would overwhelm her if she allowed herself to dwell on the past. Banishing the thoughts from her mind, she quickened her pace as she walked toward the kitchenette.

•   •   •

Ishikari's office looked out of place amid its drab surroundings.

His large desk was neat and tidy. There were New Year decorations—an arrangement of pine branches, red buds, and chrysanthemums. His bookcase included several art and calligraphy books as well as a set of encyclopedias and business and management texts. On the glass coffee table, which was the center of the comfortable office suite of leather furniture, were a large crystal lighter and ashtray.

Here, in this well-ordered office, managing director Ishikari Seijirô and Kôjima Ryôsuke sat facing one another, struggling to find words to communicate the rush of nostalgia they were feeling.

It had been a long time.

The two men were cousins, but for two years a quarter of a century ago, they had lived like brothers in the same house. The Tokyo residences of the Ishikari and Kôjima families had been destroyed in air raids during the war, and for a time the two families shared the Ishikari family home in Nagano prefecture. The Kôjima side of the family had been Tokyo born-and-bred for generations and had no home in the countryside to flee to, so it was agreed that they would move in with the mother's family in Nagano.

At the time, Kôjima was still in the lower grades at his national primary school. Ishikari Seijirô—a taciturn boy with intelligent features—was already in the fourth year of middle school. His brilliance in class was the talk of the school almost as soon as he arrived. Kôjima took a liking to him, this strange new "big brother," immediately.

Seijirô's school uniform suited him. Unlike most boys his age, he was always neatly dressed, and he had a confident, grown-up air about him. And he was happy to play with Kôjima, never showing any impatience with the younger boy's company. Seijirô had an older brother of his own, but he had never had a little brother to play with, and he soon developed a real fondness for this new "little brother."

Even after their Nagano days came to an end, Seijirô would often send Kôjima immaculately written postcards, and would take him out for dinner whenever he visited. Once Kôjima graduated from college and started work, though, they had drifted apart, and they had hardly met since. But as they sat across from one another now, the years seemed to fall away, and the warmth of those long-gone childhood days was rekindled in their hearts.

"Looks like you're doing all right for yourself, Ryôsuke. You've got that air about you that says: *This man has a good job with one of the big banks.*"

"And look at you: The picture of success and prosperity. I'm going to have to start calling you 'sir.'"

"I think we'd better stick with 'elder brother,' don't you?" Ishikari smiled.

It was the same smile Kôjima had always loved as a boy. Relaxed and careful, and slightly bashful.

"So how's work, Ryôsuke?"

"Banking's great. Something you could devote your whole life to and not feel you're wasting your time. Sometimes I think it's the banks that are driving the whole economy."

"You're probably not too wrong there. But if you love banking that much, there's no way you'd consider an offer to come join a little supermarket chain like ours."

"I have to admit I was pretty surprised when I got your letter. It wasn't something I'd ever thought about."

There was a knock at the door, and Misaki Yoshiko entered carrying a tray with two cups of coffee.

"It probably wouldn't make sense for you to give up what you've got and come to a business like this, I suppose," Ishikari asked.

"No, it's not that. I mean . . ." Kôjima searched for the right words.

"It's all right, Ryôsuke," Ishikari said. "Don't force yourself to take the offer seriously just because I asked you to. If it's not right, it's not right. You can just refuse. It's not a big deal."

"It's not a question of refusing. Your letter came just before the holidays, so I had some free time. I started to think maybe this was the ideal opportunity for me to reconsider what I want to do with the rest of my life," Kôjima said, and took a sip of coffee.

There was the sound of the door closing as Yoshiko left the room.

"Not bad looking, eh?" Ishikari said mischievously, lowering his voice.

"Not bad at all. I got quite a shock when I saw her at the door. You don't expect to find a beauty like that out here in the sticks."

"You're right. But she's had a tough ride, that girl. Married some loser, who left her high and dry. I offered her the job when they split up. I thought it might help keep her going till she got married again, but I don't know how we'd cope without her now."

Kôjima relaxed as the discussion turned to talk about the office sweetheart. "To be honest," he said, picking up the thread again, "one of the things that attracts me to Ishiei Stores is precisely the fact that it's not a big business. Of course, even small businesses can end up as subcontractors for the big guys in a well-developed market. Not much romance in that. But the supermarket business is still almost new. There's plenty of room to grow. A small- to medium-sized company within *that* sphere of business, with all kinds of potential for growth and development . . . it reminds me of an ambitious young man with a head full of dreams."

Ishikari nodded.

"After I thought about your offer, I wasn't sure what to do. So I figured, why not come up, have a look at the store, and listen to what you had to say face-to-face. Tell you the truth, I'm getting tired of life in a big company."

"I thought you said you couldn't be any happier," Ishikari said, surprised.

"It's got nothing to do with this bank in particular. Just big companies in general. There's something about them I don't like anymore."

"So you like your work at the bank, you just don't like big companies? Half of me thinks I know exactly what you mean, the other half hasn't a clue. Either way, I'm happy to hear there's a chance you might come work with us." Ishikari leaned back in his chair and stretched, satisfied.

"Now it's my turn to ask you a question," Kôjima said. "Why are you looking for a successor anyway? You're still young. You've got it all ahead of you. I'd understand if you were looking for some kind of assistant."

Ishikari smiled, slightly embarrassed. "The truth is that I've been . . . enlightened. I've come to realize that I'm not cut out to be a manager."

"I don't understand. You've been successful enough, haven't you?"

"The company is certainly doing all right, that's for sure."

"So what's the problem? Or are you telling me that Eitarô is responsible for all the success?"

Ishikari Eitarô was Seijirô's older brother, president of the Ishiei Trading Company food products wholesale business; he was also the president of Ishiei Stores.

"No, my brother leaves the running of the company entirely to me. I almost wish he would take more of an interest sometimes."

"So what's the problem?"

"The main reason Ishiei Stores is doing so well is one of the guys who works directly under me. Ichimura. He's a natural businessman, and any success we've had is mostly thanks to him. One thing for sure, it's not due to any talents of mine."

"You're amazing," Kôjima said, laughing. "Just as modest as ever. You haven't changed a bit."

"It's not modesty, I'm afraid. I know myself better than anyone. And I know that I'm not suited to being a manager. I don't enjoy it. And rather than spend the rest of my life slaving away at a job I'm not suited for, I'd rather . . . Well, I'd rather do that. . . ." Ishikari raised his eyes and gestured at the wall.

It was a framed piece of calligraphy, with four Chinese characters that read: *Follow heaven, abandon selfishness.*

"I'd like to open a little calligraphy school, make a living doing what I love," Ishikari said. "Not right away, obviously. I have to find someone to take over the company and show him the ropes first. But I'm thinking, maybe three years from now."

"If it's a successor you want, then why not ask him, that manager who's so good?"

"Ichimura? Well, he's talented enough; no doubt about that. But he's a businessman. And the best businessmen don't always make the best managers."

This was the answer to the most important question Kôjima had in his mind as he was riding the train from Osaka. It was an odd kind of answer, but it struck him as typical of everything he knew about his cousin.

· · ·

"So what were they talking about?" Again, Motoko was over at Yoshiko's desk almost before she had a chance to sit down.

"Nothing, really."

"No secrets allowed. You must have heard something."

"No, they just sat there in silence the whole time I was in there," she said. Yoshiko wasn't telling her friend what she'd heard. Confidentiality was a secretary's first duty.

"Figures. They must have been talking about something secret, and they didn't want you to overhear."

"Hmm."

"But if that Kôjima guy has nothing to do with the company, then anything said between him and the boss would have nothing to do with the company either. So then it wouldn't matter if you overheard it, right?"

"You think?"

"Definitely. So I think he's going to quit his job and start working here. And then we'll have our very own handsome man here at last."

Motoko let herself get carried away. If Kôjima really did join the company, she was speculating, what position would he take? If he was related to the company president and the managing director, then he would be the perfect candidate to be groomed as a successor. Then again, with his banking background, perhaps he would end up in charge of accounts. . . . Motoko stood, considering the various possibilities out loud to Yoshiko, then suddenly turned and hurried away.

Yoshiko watched Motoko sashay off across the office. But once she was alone, she found her own thoughts drifting back toward Kôjima too. One thing was for sure: he was not the kind of man they had ever had at Ishiei Stores before. Yoshiko thought of the kind, honest impression he had made on her at the door, and found that she was already starting to feel warmly toward him.

Ishikari gave Kôjima a capsule history of the Ishiei Stores Company.

It was ten years now since his brother Eitarô had taken up a friend's suggestion and opened one of the self-service stores that were starting to become popular at the time. His friend alerted him to a plot of land for sale in the main shopping district of Sawabe.

None of the shops the Ishiei Trading Company did business with were located anywhere near Sawabe. This was an essential condition for a wholesaler thinking of expanding and opening a supermarket of his own. It had taken Eitarô years of painstaking effort to build up his customer base, and there was little sense in alienating that base now.

The store in Sawabe, opposite the Center Arcade, was soon attracting plenty of customers. The store didn't make much money at first, but it was holding its own.

At the time, the driving force behind the company was a man in his sixties by the name of P., who was the managing director of the Ishiei Trading Company. P. believed that the key to making a supermarket profitable was to increase the number of outlets as quickly as possible and to boost sales by any means available. And so the company proceeded on an expansion course of one new store a year, despite the fact that it was struggling to stay in the black—all because P. had persuaded Eitarô that this was the only way of making the new business pay.

Ishikari Seijirô joined the firm in 1963, after Ishiei Trading opened its fourth store. He had approached his brother for advice after the steel company he had been working for went bust, and was offered a job with the new supermarket chain, dubbed Ishiei Stores.

Ichimura joined the firm soon after.

In quick succession, P. suffered a brain hemorrhage and died. It was almost as though he had been waiting for these two men to come along and take over. Despite the company's struggles, his ambitious plans for expansion remained in place, with locations for several new stores already negotiated.

Eitarô wasn't sure what to do. The business wasn't doing as well as his wholesaler friend had led him to expect, and it was eating up a fair bit of capital. But a crisis did not appear imminent, so he decided to give it a couple more years and see how things went.

He was in this wait-and-see period when Ishiei Stores suddenly started to turn a profit. Apparently Ichimura, whom he had hired on the recommendation of his wholesaler friend, was starting to produce results as the head of sales. If Ichimura could make the business profitable, then there was nothing to worry about.

Ishiei Stores continued its policy of aggressive expansion throughout the sixties, under Ishikari Seijirô as managing director and Ichimura Juichi as general manager. By 1968, there were ten stores and annual sales of 2.2 billion yen. The stores were generally small-scale, one-story affairs, with a sales floor area of around 650 square meters. They were entirely self-service—an innovation from the U.S. that had taken hold. The first thing you saw when you entered a store was the fresh produce. Meat, fish, and other fresh foods occupied the main aisles, with processed foods and sundries in the middle. There was no clothing, apart from items like hosiery and underwear.

But three of the stores differed significantly from this basic model. Two were three-story buildings; the other had four stories. All had been built from the ground up. These stores were not only much larger than the basic model; they also included whole departments of non-food items, such as bedding and clothes for men, women, and children. The range of sundries in these stores was much wider too: shoes, toys, sporting goods, furniture, and small electric household appliances.

At present, the largest store in the chain was the Sawabe Center Arcade store (or the "center store," as everyone called it). Essentially an extension of the original store, it had sales floor space of nearly four thousand square meters distributed over four stories.

It was the success of these larger stores that was behind the recent upturn in company results. Clothes and sundries were making the bulk of the profit. The company made money on processed foods (canned goods and confectioneries), but fresh produce, meat, and fish (the three "natural food" departments) were always massively in the red. Across all stores, processed foods covered the losses of fresh food, while the sundries and clothing departments made up the bulk of the company's actual profits.

In 1968, operating profit was forty-five million yen—a little over 2 percent of sales. For a supermarket chain, these were healthy figures indeed.

The company had Ichimura to thank for the new range of products that were now reaping such impressive profits. Before Ishiei Stores he had worked for a food wholesaler, so he did not have special experience with this side of the business. Nevertheless, he had managed to pull it off.

There was a loud, impatient-sounding *rat-a-tat-tat,* and the office door opened suddenly before anyone had a chance to reply.

A large, stocky man entered the room, his swarthy face covered in pockmarks. His head was enormous; it looked comically oversized even on top of his bulky frame.

"I'm sorry, I didn't realize you had a visitor," the man said when he saw Kôjima. He bowed respectfully.

But to Kôjima, something in this man's demeanor seemed false and calculating. It had to be Ichimura, the "natural businessman" he had heard so much about.

"Perfect timing," Ishikari said. "This is my cousin, Kôjima Ryô-suke. He works for the Saiwa Bank."

"Pleased to meet you," Ichimura said, bowing again. "I've heard a lot about you. Mr. Ishikari is very proud of his talented young cousin."

Kôjima and Ichimura stood facing one another, with Ishikari between them. Ishikari himself was of medium height and build, but next to these two giants he looked tiny.

Kôjima and Ichimura looked intently at one another the way two men do when they meet for the first time, each one trying to figure the other one out. If they ended up working together, would they be friends or deadly rivals?

"I hear you might be coming to join us, Kôjima-*san*?"

So Ichimura had heard the news too, Kôjima thought. Probably not much went on within the company that he didn't know about.

"It may not be as simple as that," said Ishikari with a smile. "He'd be quitting a job with a big bank to come and work for a small supermarket chain. I told him I wanted him to learn a bit about the business before he made up his mind. I wanted him to see exactly what he's getting himself into."

"Makes sense. It's only fair. He would be giving up a lot if he came to join us here. I don't know if you've had a chance to look at the store yet?"

"Not yet; he's only just got here."

"I'm just on my way to the center store now. I could take you over and show you around if you'd like."

"That's not a bad idea. That all right with you, Ryôsuke?" Ishikari looked over at Kôjima.

"Perfect."

"You can tell me what you think later tonight. My brother should be able to join us too." Then, as if an afterthought, he asked, "How's Takako these days, by the way?"

"Same as ever, thanks."

"You think she'll like it if you do decide to join us?"

"She'll support me whatever I decide. I can't imagine there'll be a problem." As Kôjima said this, an image of his wife came to mind. Deep down, he knew there was no way she was going to approve of his change of career. But that was something he would have to deal with on his own. No one could help him with that.

"Just a second, and I'll take you right over," Ichimura said to Kôjima. He stepped aside with Ishikari, and began to confer in a low voice, presumably dealing with whatever business had brought him into the office in the first place.

Kôjima looked on as Ishikari, almost hidden behind Ichimura's huge head, listened attentively, occasionally giving a grunt of assent. Kôjima couldn't help remembering the "elder brother" he had known twenty-five years earlier. He'd only been in middle school then. But he'd always been a good listener.

Until he saw it with his own eyes, Kôjima hadn't imagined what was involved in running a large supermarket.

His first impression was that it was a whole lot bigger than he had expected.

"We call it an 'SSDDS'," Ichimura said.

"What's that?"

"Self-service discount department store."

"Does something this big still count as a supermarket?"

"Good question. In America I don't suppose they would call this a supermarket at all. There probably wouldn't be any supermarkets in Japan if it hadn't been for the American example, but things have developed differently over here and the word has taken on a different meaning."

"What does the word mean in America, exactly?"

"Basically, it's a self-service grocery store that offers discounts."

"So strictly speaking, a supermarket sells food and not much else. In which case, this isn't really a supermarket, is it?"

"It's a little different, I guess."

A jumbled mass of bicycles stood in front of the store, along with an occasional wheeled shopping cart. Customers entered and left the store via automatic doors. Large stacks of fruit caught the eye as you entered.

"Things are quieter than normal right after the holidays. There are probably only about a third our usual number of customers today," Ichimura explained. "As you'll see, the sales area is still a bit of a mess—the after-effect of the end-of-year sales frenzy."

Ichimura led Kôjima farther into the store.

There seemed to be plenty of customers around. If this was just a third of the number who normally shopped here, then the place must be packed the rest of the time, Kôjima thought. "Wow, this is amazing," he said, not hiding his surprise. He had little knowledge about the supermarket business, but his experience told him that turning this income into a reliable profit was not as easy as it might seem.

"The very first store is right next door. The four-story building you see now is basically an extension of the original store. We bought up the land a couple of years ago and really went for it. The new store has opened up a whole new future for the company. In total numbers, we get three times the customers we used to get, and sales are about five times what they were."

"A big success, then."

"In terms of results, no doubt about it. At the time I could hardly sleep, I was so worried. Your cousin was worn out from the stress too. I remember getting a late call from him on the night before the groundbreaking ceremony. He was saying, 'Let's just do the first and second floors for now, and think things over again when that's finished. We can leave the third and fourth floors for another time.' It took me half the night to talk him out of it."

Kôjima was charmed by the story. It sounded just like Seijirô. He'd always been a worrier. He and Ichimura seemed to complement each other perfectly. Ichimura, the businessman—calculating, driven, and ready to take risks; Seijirô, the more cautious and responsible half of the partnership. It was clearly this alliance of differences that was behind the company's success.

But what role was *he* going to play if he joined the company?

"Let's start on the first floor and work our way up," Ichimura said, leading Kôjima slowly toward the center of the store.

Kôjima was about to see what went on behind the scenes in a supermarket for the first time. He'd been in a supermarket countless times with his wife, of course. But everything looked very different now that he was seeing it from another angle: the sales area was huge—the size of a gymnasium, a large theater, a factory. Not an inch of this space was wasted. Flyers and posters covered the ceilings and walls; they were plastered onto the shelves and sales bins up and down the aisles. Fluorescent lights were built into the ceilings, with additional fixtures dangling from the ceiling every few feet. Pools of light focused on items for sale.

All of the necessities of life were to be found here—fruit and vegetables, tofu and pickles, butter, meat, ham, canned goods, cakes, bread, toilet paper . . . Many of the items Kôjima couldn't even recognize. There was color everywhere.

Kôjima's eyes blinked in the face of this jumbled mass. Everything seemed to be competing desperately for attention. And then there was the noise. Instrumental arrangements of old pop ballads blared from low-quality speakers. On top of this, which was little more than noise, came a constant stream of announcements in a booming male voice. Definitely these could be categorized as noise too: New Year's greetings, reminders of special offers and promotions, and announcements to staff.

In the midst of all this noise and color, the customers, who were almost all women, went calmly about their business, apparently quite at home. The cash registers marked the finishing point of their supermarket circuit. They reminded Kôjima of the tables at public bathhouses where the caretakers sat; the thought brought a smile to his lips.

Only four of the twelve cash registers were open, operated by teenage girls, but they were enough to deal with a constant stream of customers. The girls were amazingly fast with their calculations. You would have thought someone was standing behind them with a stopwatch. They were mechanical, almost automatic. There was none of the human interaction you got at the bathhouses.

"These are called 'gondolas,'" Ichimura said.

"What?" They were standing in front of a display cabinet full of processed foods.

"I'm not sure why they call them that. That's just the word for them, I guess."

"A gondola is one of those flat-bottomed boats, right? I think it's the same word that's used for the flat-bottomed compartments under blimps, so why not for flat-bottomed shopping displays too?"

Ichimura was impressed. "Wow, you're the first person who's ever been able to explain the origin of the term to me."

"I don't know if I'm right. I'm not even sure I know what *groceries* are, never mind gondolas."

"Groceries are basically food products. In Japanese supermarkets, at least, it refers to any food product that's not fresh. Anything in bottles or cans, as well as dairy and confectionery. The department responsible for all these kinds of products is called the 'groceries department'."

The two men walked a little farther.

"These flyers we call 'pops,'" Ichimura said, coming to a halt in front of a poster that read: TRY OUR DELICIOUS HOMEMADE PICKLES TODAY! "It's an abbreviation," he went on. "Point of purchase. An ad placed where the customer can buy the item being advertised, in other words. For a supermarket, it's an important promotional tool."

For Kôjima, the unfamiliar jargon was coming thick and fast. Steady products and unsteady products; regular prices and special prices, show cards, price cards, face, loss leaders, jumble displays, flat displays, price zones, dummy cases, caster cases, gondola ends, mass displays . . .

"Would you like to see the back too?"

"The back?"

"The area behind the main sales floor. The storerooms and work areas."

"Sure."

Kôjima followed Ichimura through the work areas for the various fresh produce departments, then out to the groceries storeroom. Everything he saw fascinated him, but he was struggling to make sense of it all.

One thing that took him by surprise was how young the employees were. At the Saiwa Bank they would have struggled to get anyone to take them seriously. Yet here was a young man in his twenties, apparently in full control of everything that went on in the fresh fish department. He exuded the confidence of a man who knew that he held the whole department under his sway. He wore a waterproof apron and rubber boots, and wielded a long knife in his right hand. In a bank an employee would spend long years working his way up the ladder before he was given anything like this much responsibility.

"What's your policy on long hair?" Kôjima asked, having noticed several male employees with hair down to their shoulders. "Isn't there a danger that might create a bad impression with customers?"

"I'm sure it probably does," Ichimura replied. "But what can we do? A small company like ours has enough on its hands just attracting workers. We can't afford to dictate their hairstyle to them. That's one of the differences between us and the big boys."

Kôjima detected a hint of sarcasm. But most of the employees he observed seemed to be dedicated and hardworking. Employee attitude had been one of things he was keen to ascertain in the course of this tour. This was something far more important than the size of the company or the bottom line. Management could achieve nothing without the right employees.

As employees saw Ichimura approaching, they greeted him. Occasionally Ichimura would exchange personal remarks with his staff, stopping from time to time to ask after somebody's wife or a father who was recovering from illness.

Relations between management and employees were clearly much closer here than at the bank, but whether this was because of the nature of the two businesses or their size Kôjima had no way of knowing. It could be simply due to the personality of Ichimura himself.

The second and third floors were devoted to clothes. Ichimura was in charge of this department, which apparently was responsible for the upturn in the company's performance. Ichimura's explanations became more enthusiastic now, and he began to speak in greater detail. Kôjima was struggling to keep up.

For one thing, Kôjima was unable to recognize many of the things on sale beyond the familiar confines of the menswear department. He just about knew where he was with flared skirts and tight skirts, but a box skirt? Culottes? He couldn't begin to imagine. And then there were the unknowable abbreviations; they might as well have been secret code. *Lin-fan* seemed to be short for "lingerie" and "foundation," but since he didn't really know what either of these words translated into, he was still left perplexed.

And what exactly was a jump skirt? It seemed to have something to do with a jumper-skirt, but again, what that was, he had no idea.

The jargon didn't end there. A lot of the terminology had been borrowed from English and other languages. Everything seemed to carry a mysterious moniker of its own—things were *basic* or *traditional*, *feminine* or *chic,* for *infants* or *toddlers.* Some words he didn't even understand in Japanese. Early spring plum blossom ranges . . . wholesale inventory prices and point-of-purchase prices . . . consumption-based inventory stocking systems . . . It was beginning to overwhelm him.

"I think maybe we'd better call it a day for now," he said. "I don't know how much more I can take in."

Ichimura then took Kôjima into the second-floor storeroom, where the store manager and the floor manager were unpacking cardboard boxes.

Manabe, the store manager, was about thirty, with an impressive athletic physique. He had thick eyebrows, a strong jaw, clear eyes, and a well-defined nose. When Kôjima was introduced to him, he snapped to attention and bowed deeply.

Seems like a decent guy, Kôjima thought.

Sugai, the floor manager, made a different kind of impression on him. When Sugai's large eyes looked up at him, he couldn't help feeling slightly uncomfortable. It was the embarrassment you feel when confronted with unexpected beauty.

Sugai had well-defined features and a slim figure. His long legs were clad in narrow, tight-fitting trousers, and a sky-colored turtleneck sweater that was visible above the collar of his uniform stood out against his pale, soft complexion. In spite of Sugai's good looks, however, Kôjima sensed something unhealthy and dark about the man.

"Two of our very best," Ichimura said. "A good deal of our success at this store is thanks to them. We're planning to send them on a study trip to America this March."

"Fantastic," Kôjima said. "Is that common practice nowadays?"

"I'd say so. The whole industry started from the American supermarket model, after all, and groups have been going over for study tours for several years now. If anything, it happens too often, if you ask me. We'll have to get you set up with a trip of your own if you decide to join the company."

A trip to America wouldn't be bad, Kôjima thought to himself. He'd been with the Saiwa Bank for ten years, and he hadn't been out of the country once on business. "So what did you make of the beautiful Mr. Sugai?" Ichimura said as they walked on.

Obviously Kôjima wasn't alone in being struck by Sugai's good looks.

"Every woman who joins the company goes nuts for him, but for some reason he never seems too excited about it. Maybe if you're that good-looking it's no big deal after a while. He's nearly thirty now, though, and still single. Maybe he's just spoiled for choice."

"You've got to envy him, really," Kôjima said with a laugh. "I bet Manabe does all right for himself too. That's a nice baritone he has."

"You noticed? Yeah, he's got the best singing voice in the whole company. But I bet you're not so bad yourself."

"I can't sing to save my life. I can play the piano a little, though, so if a star ever needs an accompanist, I can fill in."

"Great! I'll look forward to that."

Ichimura really did sound surprisingly enthusiastic about the idea.

Maybe the guy was not as aloof and calculating as he seemed. Maybe once you got to know him, he was a straightforward, unaffected guy after all.

By the time Kôjima settled into his seat on the crowded bullet train back to Osaka he had all but made up his mind. He was going to quit his job at the bank and leap into the unknown world of the supermarket trade.

He still had his doubts. He was sure there were all kinds of dangers and difficulties down the road, but the appeal of the new job was enough to sweep all of his worries aside. The possibilities seemed practically limitless, and the business was young and full of opportunity.

He began to believe that this change of careers would give him a chance to do something meaningful with his life. Here was none of the predictable, stagnant atmosphere that plagued life at one of the big companies. He was tired of a world where people spent their days going around and around in circles, memos and minutes in hand. He wanted to escape from a life dominated by cautious self-interest, where everyone constantly kept one eye on rivals and the other on the boss.

It didn't matter what hardships his new life might bring. The risks didn't concern him. Life was always unpredictable. It was foolish to think you could ever be certain of anything. And yet this illusion was what the big companies used to keep people in their places—to keep men sitting obediently at their desks day after day following orders till death or retirement carried them off.

The only real question was whether Ishiei Stores had a future. If he could arrive at an informed judgment that it did, then there was no doubt about what he ought to do. He ought to jump right in and do everything he could to help the company fulfill its potential.

In Kôjima's lap were the company's financial reports for the last three years, showing profit, loss, debt, and expenses. He had skimmed through the numbers once already since boarding the train, and he looked them over again more carefully now. A detailed analysis would have to wait till he got home, but so far as he could tell, everything seemed to be in order.

"We might even be listed on the Tokyo stock exchange by the end of the seventies. . . ."

Seijirô had been full of optimism at the dinner given by Ishikari Eitarô, Seijirô's elder brother, the company president. And Ichimura, who seemed to take it for granted that this dream would turn into reality, was similarly full of passion and enthusiasm, excited by the bright future ahead. Ishiei Stores would enlarge their current stores, he said, expand aggressively into clothing and other durable goods, and push into unexploited markets where the population was booming.

"Hang on a minute," Ishikari Eitarô interjected, his drink-flushed face breaking into a laugh. "You're going to put him off. He's going to start thinking it all sounds too good to be true. You'll need huge amounts of capital if you're going to expand even half as much as that. And since that money is going to come out of my pocket, I got to thinking. What this company needs is a cool-headed banker. Someone to make sure the company stays on the straight and narrow financially. So naturally when my brother suggested recruiting Kôjima-*san*, I was all for it."

"You make it sound like you want Ryôsuke to keep an eye on us."

"Right. That's exactly what I had in mind all along."

Kôjima listened with a smile to this give and take.

As wintry fields streamed by the window of the train, Kôjima returned the financial reports to his lap and closed his eyes.

Saiwa Bank was going to go on with him or without him. If he quit, someone else would take his place—someone who had been to the same kind of school, with the same kind of abilities—and the work he was doing now would be carried on by someone else without the slightest inconvenience to anyone.

With Ishiei Stores, things were different. The decision he was making now might well affect the future of the whole company. That was it. He counted for something.

The company had potential; it had no serious short-term difficulties.

Kôjima's mind was made up.

At first Takako thought her husband was joking when he told her about quitting the bank and going to join his cousin's supermarket company. When she realized he was serious, she mumbled, "How can you even think of such a thing?" and then lapsed into a shocked silence.

Takako's mind was like a finely calibrated machine, and Kôjima could picture what was going on inside it. The machine was processing every scrap of information related to the present discussion (and some that wasn't related to it at all). The circuits were flashing furiously, the machinery whirring faster and faster.

It was not the first time he had seen her like this. It had happened once before, during the third year of their marriage, when Takako had come across a packet of letters documenting his love affair with a woman named Hirose Yoko. The letters were written while he and Takako were engaged.

Kôjima had been careless. He should have burned the letters when he moved out of his tiny bachelor's dorm room. Instead, some lingering sense of attachment had led him to bundle them together and bury them in a desk drawer along with other correspondence.

Takako had been furious. That he had been deeply in love with someone else and had kept the affair secret far outweighed the fact that he had stayed with her and married her. Perhaps part of the reason she was so upset was the simple regret that theirs had been an arranged marriage rather than a love match. She hurled Yoko's letters in front of him, then picked them up and ripped them to shreds. Then she gathered the scraps together in a heap and broke down in convulsive sobbing. How could she ever have left home to live with such a cruel and faithless man? She cursed the day they had met.

Nothing Kôjima said was going to get through to her. All he could do was wait for her to calm down. Part of him was fascinated at this glimpse of an unknown aspect of his wife's character. But he sympathized with her as well. He could see how things would look pretty bad from her perspective.

Kôjima probably loved his wife more at that moment than ever before, but the moment didn't last long. Without warning, Takako had gone the following day to the Saiwa Bank, where she asked for a meeting with her husband's boss, a man by the name of Oki. She demanded that he immediately transfer a certain Hirose Yoko from her husband's department.

At first, Oki was taken aback by Takako's sudden visit, but it didn't take him long to figure out what was going on. He calmed Takako down and sent her home with the most consoling words he could muster, then called Kôjima into his office and told him with a wink and a grin what had happened.

"Looks like we're in a bit of a pickle here."

And that was all Oki ever said about the subject. Kôjima was touched. Most of the bank's other managerial staff would probably have subjected him to a pointless sermon. Thanks to Oki's sensitivity, the incident passed without serious consequences.

He could understand how Takako felt. She had been brought up to expect a certain kind of treatment. And he had only his own stupid carelessness to blame. But confidence and trust in the workplace were the salaryman's most valuable assets, and Takako's jealousy had come perilously close to shattering his reputation. He could sympathize with her to a certain extent, but in his heart he found it hard to forgive what she had done.

"And what about Kayoko?" Takako was saying now. "Have you thought how this harebrained scheme of yours might affect her when it's time for her to get married?" Takako was struggling to control the emotion in her voice.

Kayoko was their five-year-old daughter, currently walking hand-in-hand with her mother on the apartment block where they lived.

"This has nothing to do with—"

"Don't tell me you don't understand. Surely you realize the difference between having a father who works for the Saiwa Bank and one who's the manager of a little supermarket in the middle of nowhere?"

Kôjima said nothing.

"We'll never get any decent marriage proposals. Don't you understand that?"

26

"Why would somebody decide not to propose to her just because I happened to work for Ishiei Stores?"

"You don't understand anything. A friend of my father's, a big land-owner, built a block of luxury apartments on the outskirts of Tokyo. But he's having trouble selling them, and do you know why?"

"Of course not. How could I?"

"The supermarket. He followed someone's stupid advice and put in a supermarket on the first floor of the building. Now no one wants the apartments—all because of the supermarket."

Kôjima was speechless.

"It doesn't matter how much you go on about 'distribution revolutions' and the 'business model of the future.' When it comes down to it, a supermarket is just a glorified butcher shop."

She was making no sense. The situation was hopeless. He could rebut everything she said and beat her down with logic, but it wouldn't solve anything in the end.

Acute to any tension between her parents, Kayoko kept raising her small, pale face and looking from Kôjima to Takako.

"You've never considered my opinion in anything. Not once in all the time since we've been married. Not since the day we met. So I'm sure this time will be no different. You'll just make up your own mind and do whatever suits you. You don't even stop to consider what I might think."

"That's not true. I have thought about you. And I don't see any reason why it should upset you at all if I want to change jobs. I'd be earning more money, and we'd be able to live in a proper apartment instead of this box in a housing complex. Seijirô's given me his word. I'm not asking you to make any sacrifices."

"Fine. So maybe everything will start out great. But what about the future? Who knows where this little supermarket chain of yours is going to be in a few years' time? We might move into a nicer apartment and have more money now, but if the supermarket goes bust we'll be left with nothing. How is that a better deal than staying where you are and working your way up?"

"You make it sound like I've not considered this at all. This is my life we're talking about, remember. I have looked into all this. Their finances are good. Their future prospects are good. There's a good chance the company will be listed on the stock exchange ten years from now."

"If it's a listed company you're looking for, you'd be better off staying right where you are."

"But I want to help bring the company up to that level by my own hard work. Not just by my efforts alone, of course. I want to have the satisfaction of giving myself to a company and watching it grow. I'll never have that if I stay where I am now. In that big bank I just feel more and more helpless. This isn't an impulse thing. It's an accumulation of the frustration and disappointment that comes from being just another faceless worker bee in a big company. Can't you at least try to understand?"

But Kôjima knew that what he was saying would make no sense to a woman. Day in, day out, a woman spent her life preparing meals for her family, doing the housework, and looking after the children. It might not be the most inspiring life in the world, but however dull and unsatisfying she found these chores, a woman had to resign herself to her work and get on with it. Now here was a man whose work was already considerably more interesting than her own saying that he wanted to give it all up and move somewhere else in search of something more satisfying. Perhaps it was to be expected that she should accuse him of thinking only of himself. Their conversation was doomed to travel endlessly down parallel tracks.

They climbed the stairs to the fourth floor of Building 58 and entered their apartment. The curtains were drawn, and the room was dark. Takako broke down and started crying, quietly at first, then with gathering force.

Kôjima said nothing. He pulled the curtains back. The previous day's newspapers were scattered across the coffee table. He listened to his wife's sobs as he tidied them up. *I understand how she feels,* he said to himself, *but my mind is made up. I will do what I can to calm her down and bring her around. And if she still can't reconcile herself to it after that, then there's nothing further I can do.*

The following day Kôjima called Ishikari Seijirô and told him of his decision.

"And Takako approves, does she?" Seijirô asked.

"Of course. She would never stand in the way of anything I really wanted to do."

"Great. Well, sort things out with the people at the bank and then come down and start as soon as you're ready. We're really looking forward to having you join us."

"Me too. I'll be there as soon as I can." And with that, Kôjima put down the receiver.

TWO

BIRD FOOD

Ôtaka Seizô, head of the fresh produce section, was moving the day's fruit and vegetables out onto the shelves at the center store. In an ideal world this would have been done before the store opened at ten, but in reality this was almost impossible.

He simply didn't have enough staff. If he really wanted to get the displays ready by the time the doors opened, he would need to hire two extra part-timers—and even then he'd have to ask everyone to come in at least half an hour earlier.

It wasn't worth the effort. Only two kinds of customers came to the store immediately after doors opened: hard-core bargain hunters and a few people wanting a bottle of milk. It wasn't till eleven thirty that people started thinking about the evening meal. So as long as things were on the shelves by then, Ôtaka figured, everything would be fine.

Suddenly he heard Ichimura's voice behind him. "Ôtaka here has an amazing feel for color," he was saying. Ôtaka stopped what he was doing and turned to find Ichimura and Ishikari examining one of the fresh produce displays.

"It's beautifully done," Ichimura said. "The red strawberries here at the front, then the green of the grapes, and then a touch of red again here with the apples. Next to that, the yellow citrus fruits. Something really fresh about the picture, don't you think?

If we had a few more people capable of work like this, then maybe our fresh produce sections might finally start to make a profit." Ichimura smiled at Ôtaka like a parent admiring a favorite child.

Ôtaka wasn't used to being praised in such terms—certainly not by Ichimura, and he felt a little embarrassed by the attention. Not that it was unpleasant.

"Where did you learn to do this?" Ichimura asked.

"I'm not really sure," Ôtaka replied. It was hard to know what kind of answer they were looking for. "I definitely picked up some ideas at that cooperative seminar for fresh produce managers."

"Hmm, it sounds like those seminars really were useful," said Ishikari. "If these are the kinds of results you get, we should send more of our people to them."

"That's the aim," Ichimura said.

"Nothing more important than skills development—that's my motto."

"Absolutely," Ichimura answered reflexively. He was looking over into the corner of the fresh produce section.

Ôtaka heard him cooing softly in surprise. It was a sound intended to attract attention. *Uh-oh*, Ôtaka thought, *this is going to be awkward.*

Ichimura was standing in front of what Ôtaka called the "discount corner." At the moment, it was full of rotten-looking cabbages cut into halves. They'd been able to sell less than 50 percent of the stock they had ordered. A mass of unsold cabbages now languished on the floor, withered and yellow; some had started to develop ugly black blotches.

Ôtaka had been at the point of throwing them all out yesterday, but he couldn't bring himself to do it. It was such a waste. If he was going to throw them away, he might as well try selling them off cheap first. He had put them on special offer at ten yen each.

At that price, the cabbages started to sell. Not all of them, of course, but the slashed price dramatically reduced the number of unsold stock. Ôtaka had been feeling pretty pleased with himself.

The feeling lasted until just before closing time yesterday, when Kôjima Ryôsuke, a "special trainee" who had been floating around the store for the last several weeks, came around asking questions. For reasons known only to himself, Kôjima was fascinated by these rotten cabbages.

"Were these cabbages selling well?"

"They weren't before. That's how they got to be the state they're in now."

"And now? Are they selling now?"

"Sure. They're only ten yen each. What can you buy for ten yen these days?"

"And what do you think people do with them when they get home?"

"How would I know?" Ôtaka said. "Pickle 'em? Put 'em in their miso soup. I don't know, there're all kinds of things you can do with them."

"Make them into pickles, you say?" Kôjima seemed lost in thought. "Would they taste good pickled?"

"I don't know. If they're no good as pickles, you could always use them as bird food."

"Bird food?" Kôjima said, a smile appearing on his lips. "Of course, I hadn't considered that possibility. They would be ideal for bird food."

Ôtaka was starting to feel like an idiot. "You're interested in the most unusual things," he said to Kôjima. "Is there anything else I can help you with?"

"There is, as it happens. Tell me—how many of these halved cabbages are left?"

"About fifty?"

"About twenty more than what's already here, you mean?"

"More or less." Ôtaka was starting to find Kôjima's persistence tiresome. He had picked a number off the top of his head, and now it turned out Kôjima had counted them while they were talking. And Ôtaka was twenty short.

"When did you reduce the prices?"

"About an hour ago."

"How many were there then?"

"Maybe two hundred or so?"

"So you've achieved an extra two thousand yen worth of sales by putting them on special offer?"

Ôtaka wasn't sure if he was being praised or scolded, but he knew he didn't like the way the conversation was going. "I like to think about profit more than sales," Ôtaka went on. "Profit would go down if we just threw the cabbages away."

"I see. I remember someone told me once: If a grocer buys twenty thousand yen worth of produce in the morning, he has to make sure his sales for the day reach at least twenty thousand yen. If he has sold twenty thousand yen worth of produce by three in the afternoon, everything after that is profit. So the price of each item is not so important. Is that the idea here?"

"More or less. I'm sorry, can you excuse me for a minute? There's a customer who—"

"Sorry. I was getting carried away. Thanks for your time," Kôjima said, giving Ôtaka a friendly smile. "Just one more thing. Could you join me for a drink after work tonight?"

"I'm afraid tonight's no good." This was the truth. Ôtaka already had plans to go out with Také, the young guy from the meat section who wanted to talk about what was going on in his department.

"How about tomorrow then?"

"I'm afraid I've got plans for tomorrow too." This was a lie. For some reason Ôtaka felt like refusing just for the sake of saying no.

"Busy, huh? How about the day after tomorrow?"

"No good either, I'm afraid." This one was true. He had a date with Misaki Yoshiko, Ishikari's secretary. If things went well, it could turn out to be one of the most important days of his life.

Kôjima was a cheerful sort of guy, but even he was starting to look a bit deflated after being turned down three times.

"I'm sorry. I'm just really busy this week. Let's do something next week. I'll let you know."

"All right. Next week then."

After Kôjima left, Ôtaka got back to work on the yellowing half cabbages. But something was gnawing away at him, something that felt almost like guilt. And now Ichimura was standing in front of his discount corner too.

Ôtaka had the feeling he was going to be subjected to another painful interrogation. But Ichimura's reaction could hardly have been more different from Kôjima's.

"Look at this. Amazing. Exactly what we're looking for," he said to Ishikari.

"A real businessman. Don't you think? He could easily just have thrown all this away. Instead, he makes an extra effort and turns waste into profit. Ten yen each—it's not much, but every little bit counts."

"This is the man you were talking about before? The natural-born businessman?"

"Right," Ichimura said, a broad smile on his face. He patted Ôtaka on the shoulder. "Although of course, a real businessman would never have left himself so many unsold items in the first place."

It was a pretty neat parting shot.

"I'm sorry, sir. I'll try to do better in future." Ôtaka bowed his head, relieved to see the back of the two directors as they walked away.

It was just after lunch the next day, and Ôtaka was sorting through some old bills and receipts at his desk when he heard Kôjima's irrepressibly upbeat voice behind him.

"Hi, Ôtaka-*san*. You busy?"

Another Q&A session with Kôjima was the last thing Ôtaka wanted. He would have wriggled out of it by claiming to be snowed under with work, but it was plain to anyone with eyes that right now all he was really doing was having a smoke. He was going to have to be pleasant and give him a few minutes at least. Besides, rumor had it that Kôjima would soon be joining the company's board of directors. Maybe he was being groomed to take over Ishikari's position as head of the company. No point going out of his way to piss the guy off.

Not that he had any intention of cozying up to him. Things like promotion and professional advancement didn't really interest Ôtaka. Work was a necessary evil. As long as he was putting food on the table, that was enough for him. Fighting to get your foot on the next rung of the ladder only brought you more stress. What was point of that? People who wanted to get ahead were like the red-faced goons you saw screaming in the mah-jongg parlors.

Experience had taught Ôtaka how futile it was to bust a gut for something as meaningless as work. His first job after high school had been in Niigata, his hometown, at a small supermarket. Really the place was just a local grocery store that was starting to expand. His teachers at school could probably have found him a better job somewhere else, but the store was run by a distant relative of his father's, and met his basic condition: that he not have to move away from home.

Ôtaka was put in charge of fresh produce, where he worked more or less contentedly for six years. It wasn't the kind of work a man could get passionate about, but he had always fulfilled his duties enthusiastically enough. By the mid-sixties the company had three outlets, and Ôtaka was the rising star of the fresh produce division. By the time he quit, he was vice president, with great things expected of him.

He'd started to believe that work made life worth living. If things had continued the way they were, he would probably have settled down in Niigata and would have been a model employee there to this day. But then, out of the blue, disaster struck. There was no other word for it. It was the spring of the year he turned twenty-five, and he was alone at the store working late one night. Everyone else had long since gone home, or so he thought. Suddenly, the boss's wife was standing next to him, and before he knew what was happening, she had all but forced him into sleeping with her.

Ôtaka was young and naïve, and this was his first experience with a woman. Had he been just a little older and wiser, the disaster would never have happened. He'd have understood that he was being used by the boss's wife to fill the void left by her husband's absence. The boss was in the hospital, having an operation for gallstones.

The affair that began the unusually warm spring night lasted two months. It drove him completely out of his mind. Finally, he could take it no more. He set out one day like a medieval knight to call on his boss, his heart swelling with an absurd sense of chivalry and pride. His boss was recuperating at home now, nearly well. He confronted him with the facts, and asked him to give up his wife. The idea had seemed heroic at the time, but of course the whole thing turned into a catastrophe.

His boss flew into a rage and his wife denied everything, laughing at him scornfully. News of the incident reached Ôtaka's father, and he soon found himself reviled by the whole family. He was a reprobate, a fool.

Scarred and ashamed, he left his hometown in disgrace. His dedication had come to nothing. His reputation was worthless. He left for Tokyo, bitter and disillusioned. What was hard work good for, beyond the occasional pay raise?

"I want to ask a favor," Kôjima was saying. "There's a little experiment I want to try."

Everything was just fun and games for this guy. "An experiment? What kind of experiment?" Ôtaka replied for the sake of something to say. He had no interest in any plan Kôjima might have.

The fact was, there were several things about Kôjima that Ôtaka didn't like. First of all, Kôjima was tall and handsome. Ôtaka was neither, and people had been calling him "shorty" since his earliest days in school; he wasn't much taller than five foot three. They might as well have belonged to different species. On top of that, Kôjima had gone to one of the best universities in the country, and was related to the people who owned the company. Ôtaka didn't like him at all.

"I've got a new idea for a way to reduce the amount of unsold food we end up throwing away. If it works, I think we should be able to increase profits for the department by several percent." Kôjima went on to explain his so-called experiment. "I've noticed something interesting over the past few weeks I've spent looking at the fresh produce sales and work area."

Kôjima was looking around the work area as he spoke. Suddenly, he walked over into a corner and picked up a stalk of celery lying there. It was one of several that had been put on display a few days ago and had failed to sell. "There are cracks here in the middle of the stalk, where it's starting to turn black." Kôjima put down the package and picked up the next one in the pile. "This one doesn't look too great either." He moved on to another package. "And these here are missing leaves at the top of each stalk."

Ôtaka struggled to contain the anger welling up inside him. When it came to selling fresh produce, he would have backed his own knowledge against anyone else's. And now this twerp who knew nothing about supermarkets was proposing to lecture him on how to sell celery?

"It's clear enough why these didn't sell. Customers didn't like the look of them. The price is the same for all the celery on display, but from the customers' point of view these don't offer the same value for money. And so they don't sell, and we either have to give them away for next to nothing or throw them. My guess is that this kind of thing is responsible for most of the losses in the department."

Ôtaka listened in silence. *So what do you want me to do about it?* he was thinking. Gradually, Kôjima's calm, reasonable tone of voice soothed some of the resentment he was feeling.

"And then it occurred to me: If we're going to flog the stuff for next to nothing anyway, why not offer imperfect produce like this at a cheaper price from the start?" Kojima pulled out a large notebook; it was black, leather-bound, with SAIWA BANK engraved in gold letters. Folded between the pages was a small piece of paper. "I thought we could call this the 'special price seal.'" It was an oblong sticker about two inches by one inch, with the words *special price item* in the upper left-hand corner. The center of the sticker was blank; presumably this space would be filled in with the discounted price of the item.

"Here we write the price, say, twenty or thirty percent off the regular price. And then stick the seal so that it sits just on top of the regular price tag. And cross out the regular price with a simple diagonal black line." Kôjima stuck his "special price seal" onto a package of celery with a flourish. "That's all we have to do. As long as we get the prices right, the customers are going to buy items with this seal first. And since we end up practically giving it away otherwise, the numbers are going to come out looking a whole lot better if we can sell them at a discount of twenty or thirty percent. The only reason customers avoid this kind of produce is the little superficial defect—a crack here, a tiny bit missing from the top of the stalk. There's nothing wrong with the produce in terms of freshness and flavor. So the customer's going to think twenty or thirty percent off the regular price is a real bargain."

There was obvious excitement in Kôjima's voice as he outlined his scheme. "Once the discounted produce has sold out, what's left on the shelves will be the preferred produce—without superficial defects. By the end of the day, we should be pretty much all sold out.

"What I'd like you to do," Kôjima went on blithely, "is to choose one or two items you think we could use for a trial. I'll take the responsibility if things don't work out. Let's give it a week or so; that should be long enough to give us an idea whether it's going to work or not."

"Fine, fine. We can start tomorrow if you like."

"Really? That'd be great. Thanks a lot for your help. I owe you one." Kôjima seemed genuinely pleased. He flashed Ôtaka a grin, revealing a mouthful of beautiful, straight teeth.

This brought on another twinge of jealousy in Ôtaka. His only wish now was to get Kôjima out of his work space as quickly as possible.

Later that afternoon, Sashima, who was head of the meat department, came over to invite Ôtaka to join a group of people for drinks with Ichimura that evening.

Ôtaka said yes right away. This coincided nicely with the fictitious engagement he had used to excuse himself from Kôjima's company yesterday. And the prospect of getting closer to Ichimura was tempting. What he didn't like was that it was Sashima who was inviting him.

The previous evening was still fresh in Ôtaka's mind. He'd been out with Také, a gangly and pale young man from the meat department who still looked like an awkward college kid. In his earnest, fumbling way, Také had blurted out what was on his mind: "Cuts of meat are disappearing from the refrigerators. Expensive cuts of Japanese beef worth anything up to ten thousand yen."

"Has this been happening a lot?"

"Yes. The first time I noticed something was wrong, I went straight to Sashima-*san* and asked him what we should do. Maybe that was a pretty dumb thing to do—but how was I to know? He told me not to worry, that I was probably just imagining it. For a while nothing happened. But then meat started disappearing again. It's happened several times again since then."

"That's no reason to accuse the guy. It might be different if you actually saw him taking the meat, or if you had some kind of positive proof."

"That's the thing. I do have something close to proof."

It had happened two days before. Také had been the last in his department to leave at the end of the day. He was about to go home when he decided to check that all of the meat was secure in its proper place in the refrigerator. Officially, this wasn't one of his responsibilities, but his recent suspicions made him want him to double-check just to be sure. Everything looked fine.

He was out of the store when he remembered he'd left something behind in his locker. It was only a songbook, but he couldn't do without it. He was going to perform at a friend's wedding reception, and he needed to practice. So he made his way back to the meat department.

And as he did so he bumped into Sashima, on his way out with a large leather bag over his shoulders. Sashima looked surprised, flustered. His lighthearted conversation sounded forced. "Just popped back for something," he said. "What are you doing here at this hour?"

Také told him about the songbook.

"Looks like our department's full of forgetful people. See you around." And with that, Sashima hurried off.

The doubts in Také's mind kicked in. The first thing he did, even before collecting his songbook, was to take another look inside the refrigerator. As he suspected, all was not as he had left it. Two whole blocks of *wagyu*, the Japanese beef, were missing from the second shelf, one a sirloin roast, the other a tenderloin—two of the most expensive cuts of all. Také's first impulse was to run after Sashima and demand to see what was inside his bag. But in the end a sense of deference toward his boss held him back.

Hearing this, Ôtaka wasn't sure what to think. It was hard to believe that Sashima would be stupid enough to risk his reputation over something like that. But one thing was for sure: there was something about Sashima he didn't like.

The man had intelligence, but he was self-centered. Other people's feelings didn't interest him at all. He used his glib way with words to charm his bosses, and seemed to have the people at head office eating out of his hand. And his appearance matched his personality—plump and flabby, with cheeks like a hamster's and a belly that looked ready to burst.

But the fact that Ôtaka didn't like the guy didn't make him a thief. It couldn't be true . . . or could it? Také didn't seem to be making the story up.

And now Sashima was inviting him to join him for drinks with Ichimura.

"This is a big day for us," Sashima had said. "Who knows, this could be the turning point. The beginning of a secret group of Ichimura's supporters."

"What? You're starting a secret society?"

"No one's going that far just yet. I'm just saying that's what might end up happening. No one who cares about Ichimura can ignore the crisis confronting him now."

"Crisis? What crisis?"

"You really don't understand what I'm talking about, do you?" Sashima seemed genuinely surprised. "You've seen this Kôjima guy hanging round the place, right? Pale, pasty-looking guy, always got that big shit-eating grin on his face. Fancy university. A real jerk-off if you ask me. Anyway, rumor is the Ishikari family wants him to take over the company. For reasons best known to themselves."

"I've heard the rumors."

"Well, it's obvious. If Kôjima's being groomed to take over, then Ichimura's lost his chance. Think about it. This company only got where it is today thanks to him. He's running the whole operation. You really think the company would have expanded into clothes and stuff if he wasn't on board? The center store wouldn't even exist if it wasn't for him. The company itself might not even be here today if not for him."

Sashima seemed to become intoxicated with the sound of his own words as he spoke. "Why should we stand for it? It's outrageous. Who knows what the Ishikaris are thinking? They may be the owners, but that doesn't mean the whole company is theirs to do what they want with. It's not their private property. It belongs to all of us. And of all of us, one man has contributed more than anyone else to the company's success. Ichimura's sweated blood to make the company into what is today. He's the one who deserves to have the biggest say in deciding the future of Ishiei Stores."

Sashima gushed excitedly for several minutes longer, before finally returning to his own department, leaving Ôtaka standing exhausted behind him.

Ôtaka was forty minutes late. The get-together was in a private room on the second floor of a sushi restaurant, and by the time he arrived the party was in full swing. The room was full of laughter and conversation. This was clearly a group of men with a few drinks inside them. Sashima spotted Ôtaka through the open shoji screen as he approached and stood up to greet him.

"Hey, Ôtaka, you're late. We've been waiting for you."

There were seven people there. Ichimura and Sashima he had expected, of course. Also in attendance were Manabe Saburô, manager of the center store; Sugai Keinoshin, head of the clothing department; Kikuchi Tsuyoshi, deputy head of the sundries floor; Karaki Daisaku, who worked in the fresh fish department; and, for some reason, Kishiwara Takao, who ran the clothing division at the head office and was responsible for choosing the clothes that would be sold in the chain's various outlets.

As the man in charge of buying clothing for the entire chain, Kishiwara worked closely with people at each of the company's stores. But for Ôtaka, who had been expecting to find only Ichimura and his center store deputies, his presence still came as something of a surprise.

He was also surprised to find so few people there. And it wasn't clear to him how these people had been selected either. The store head was there, but not his deputy. The head of the clothing department was there, but what about the heads of all the other floors?

The food floor was made up of four separate sections: fresh produce, fish, meat, and groceries. There was no sign tonight of the men in charge of the fish or groceries sections—and yet Karaki, who worked in the fish department at a lower level, *was* here.

"Go and pay your respects to Mr. Ichimura then sit down over there," Sashima told him. It was practically an order.

"Come on, Sashima," Ichimura objected. "There's no need to be so formal. Let's just relax and have a few drinks." He was sitting with his shirtsleeves rolled up, waving his arms in the air like a man conducting an orchestra. Apparently this was something he often did when he'd had a few drinks.

Conversation seemed not to have strayed yet from the usual small talk: baseball, the recent company bowling competition, the obligatory talk about women.

Ôtaka sat down next to Manabe, the store manager, and listened to what the others were saying. In a lull in the conversation, he turned to Manabe and said in a low voice, "How did they decide who got invited to this?"

"I'm not really sure what the criteria were," he said.

Sugai, who was sitting on the other side of Manabe, overheard Ôtaka's question and leaned over. "Sashima's mah-jongg buddies, basically. That and Ichimura's fan club."

"And which category do you fit into? Are you an Ichimura fan?"

"Me? I'm more of a Manabe fan. But Manabe practically worships the ground Ichimura walks on," Sugai replied, a faint smile on his face.

What a jerk, thought Ôtaka. He was aware of his tendency to form strong likes and dislikes when it came to the people he worked with. But with Sugai it was something else. It was more like physical revulsion. There was no denying the man was good-looking. But there was something creepy about him. He had no personality, no human warmth. Even when he smiled, his eyes remained cold and inexpressive. For Ôtaka, it was like seeing through a mask, catching a glimpse of the calculating aloofness behind the smile. There was more to Sugai than met the eye; he was sure of it. This alone was reason for Ôtaka to dislike him. The world would be a better, simpler place if people were more like himself—honest and uncomplicated.

Everyone seemed to agree that Sugai was doing an excellent job. He was obviously an extremely talented manager. And it had all gone to his head. Probably that was what made him look down on everyone. That would explain that cold, aloof attitude of his.

The man certainly had a brain. What was that remark he had made just now? Sashima's mah-jongg buddies and the Ichimura fan club?

Not bad for a spur-of-the-moment crack. Probably not far from the truth either. Witty, pithy, *and* perceptive.

The problem was, Ôtaka himself was none of these things.

At length, Sashima stood up to speak.

"If I could have everyone's attention for a few moments, please. There's something I want to say before too much sake goes down the hatch. The reason we're all gathered here tonight—"

"Just try to finish some time today, OK?" someone shouted. It was no secret that Sashima liked the sound of his own voice, especially when he had an audience in front of him.

Sashima brushed the heckling aside. Basically what he had to say was a restatement of what he'd told Ôtaka earlier in the day. The crisis facing Mr. Ichimura. The responsibility of those who cared for Ichimura and respected him. How Ishiei Stores would not even exist today if it wasn't for him. And now it was all under threat. Thanks to some grinning, snotty-nosed kid called Kôjima—a pasty-faced buffoon of a man with stuck-up college-kid ways. There were tears in Sashima's eyes as he spoke. When he came to the bit about Ishiei Stores not being the private plaything of the Ishikari family, a murmur of agreement and sympathy swept through the audience.

Ôtaka's eyes were on Ichimura's swarthy, pockmarked face. How would he react? It was impossible to guess what he was thinking. He sat motionless with his eyes closed and his head lowered in thought, arms folded across his chest.

But as soon as Sashima started criticizing Kôjima, Ichimura opened his eyes and spoke up. His voice was calm, but resonated with an effortless authority. "Don't speak ill of other people, please," he said.

"I'm sorry," Sashima said, taken aback by the interruption.

"Carry on," Ichimura said, resuming his silent and unmoving position.

Ôtaka felt strong emotions welling up inside. Presumably the same was true of everyone else. There was hardly a dry eye in the house by the time Sashima finished his speech. Ôtaka lowered his face to hide his tears.

Sugai was the first to speak up. "You can depend on us to support you, sir!" There were no tears in *his* eyes.

Suddenly, everyone began to speak at once. The exact words may have been different, but the gist was the same: they would do everything they could to support Ichimura.

Sashima got to his feet again. "Thank you all for your support. Now I'd like every one of you to sign this oath, and seal it with your blood." He took out a sheet of paper with some writing on it. He was holding a thick-bladed Stanley knife in his other hand. He was expecting people to cut their fingers and sign the manifesto with their blood!

Ôtaka felt a shiver run down his spine. His mind flashed back to the time he had his tonsils out as a child. The operation itself hadn't bothered him at all, but when the doctor showed him the lump of flesh and blood that had been removed from his body, Ôtaka fainted. Just the thought of making a cut in his finger, however small, made him feel sick.

A rumble of surprise ran though the group and the atmosphere changed. Sashima had gone too far.

Sashima either didn't notice, or had been expecting this reaction all along. Hardly pausing for breath, he read what was in his manifesto:

> "Item one: We the undersigned respect and admire our managing director Ichimura, whom we regard as the guiding light of the Ishiei Stores Company.
>
> "Item two: We all want to see Ishiei Stores continue to expand and prosper. To this end, it is our hope that Mr. Ichimura will continue to enjoy good health, and that he will be entrusted with the seniority within the company that his talents deserve.
>
> "Item three: United by these aims, we will continue to do anything and everything within our power to ensure that Mr. Ichimura remains where he belongs, and that he continues to be the guiding spirit of the Ishiei Stores Company.
>
> "Signed on this day, April 1969, and sealed in blood by the members of the Ichimura Support Committee."

Sashima paused and looked at the faces around him, anxiously trying to gauge their reaction. For a few moments there was no reaction at all. Nobody seemed to know quite what to make of what they had just heard.

It was Ichimura himself who eventually broke the silence. "Thank you, Sashima, that's enough," he said. "Thank you. I will never forget what you've just said. I don't think I have ever felt this much happiness before in all my life. Unfortunately, though, the world isn't as simple as we might like it to be. And I'm really not as special as you make me out to be."

There was another tearful intervention from the floor at this point. It was Kikuchi, the deputy head of the sundries floor. "I'm with you all the way, sir. I admire you."

"Listen. Wait a minute." Ichimura stood up. His huge features subdued the chattering crowd and reduced everyone to silence. "Forget about it. Give it up. The things you have said tonight will remain engraved in my heart for the rest of my life. But that's enough. There's no need to draw up pledges and sign them with blood. You've made your feelings understood. What more do you need? I will continue to do whatever I can for the Ishiei Stores Company and for the people who work there. Isn't that enough? What more do I need? Why should I want to become president of the company? I'm sure Mr. Kôjima will do an excellent job if and when he inherits the position. If that's what the Ishikari family wants, that's good enough for me."

"It's not good enough," Sashima shouted, but Ichimura's voice was more powerful.

"Now come on, let's drink. Let's all just relax and enjoy a drink together. You only live once. We should appreciate what we have. Let's drink to that. Let's live life to the full and do what we can to help the people around us. Work hard, and play fair. Right, Sashima? Right, Manabe? Right, Kikuchi? Come on now, let's drink."

Everyone was quiet for a few moments, and then voices were raised in agreement. Before he knew what he was doing, Ôtaka found himself raising his glass of beer and joining in the chorus.

Before long an atmosphere of drink-sodden rowdiness dominated the room, and Ôtaka lost all sense of time. Suddenly he noticed that everything had gone quiet. And then he heard the voice of Manabe at his side.

"Come on, Ôtaka. Quick, you're next." Hurriedly, he passed Sashima's rejected oath to Ôtaka. Several people had already sealed it with their blood.

"Quickly. We want to get everyone to do it before he comes back," Sashima stated in his no-nonsense tone. Every word he said was like an order.

Ôtaka made a small incision in the soft padded part of his little finger and pressed it down onto the paper. The booze was obviously working its magic, because this time the sight of his own blood hardly seemed to affect him at all. But that didn't mean he approved of what was happening. Ichimura had gone to the bathroom. What would he think when he got back to find the oath he had expressly told them to forget about was being passed around in his absence? Maybe there would be nothing worse than a mild expression of annoyance. But maybe he would be outraged. Ôtaka could almost hear his voice now: "Didn't you understand what I said?"

As it turned out, his reaction was exactly the opposite. It was Ôtaka who had misinterpreted the entire situation. Tears welled in Ichimura's eyes when he sat down and was shown the oath signed with the blood of everyone present. "This makes me very happy. I don't think I've ever been as happy in my entire life. Thank you. To think you would do all of this just for me. I don't know what I have done to deserve anything like this."

Several of the men were crying too.

It should have been a moving scene. But this time Ôtaka wasn't moved at all. He no longer felt a part of what was going on. He looked over at Sashima, who was standing next to Ichimura with the oath in his hands and a look of triumph on his face. Were there tears in his eyes? Probably, but apart from that, his chubby features showed no sign of excessive emotion. He looked like a man in control. Suddenly, an awful thought ran through Ôtaka's mind: "Ichimura's being taken for a ride."

He glanced round at the faces around him. No one else seemed to be the least bit embarrassed by what was happening.

I'm thinking too much. Now even I'm starting to get too complicated about things. Get a grip. You're supposed to be a down-to-earth guy, he said to himself.

The atmosphere of drunken good cheer returned. People were taking turns refilling Ichimura's cup with sake. When it came to Ôtaka's turn, he stood up with the sake bottle in his hand and made his way over to where Ichimura was sitting.

It was the morning after the party, and Ôtaka was struggling with a miserable hangover. He was trying to concentrate on getting the displays ready for opening when he heard Kôjima's chirruping voice exchanging morning greetings with the part-time girls.

Kôjima was a big hit with the girls. Ôtaka had heard them talking about him, singing his praises to the sky. He was "so nice and kind," "so genuine," "thoughtful," "approachable." Why did they always have to say the same things? At first he'd been annoyed by their tedious predictability, but now it was Kôjima himself who was getting on his nerves.

" 'Morning, Ôtaka-*san*. We're going to go ahead with that experiment we talked about yesterday. I'd be grateful for your help."

"Experiment?"

"Don't tell me you've forgotten. The special price seals. Remember?"

"Sorry. It slipped my mind." His head ached and he felt like throwing up. His first thought when he woke up bleary-eyed and heavy-headed this morning was what a fool he had been to let himself get into this state on the very day of his big date with Misaki Yoshiko. He had forgotten all about Kôjima's little experiment.

"I'd like to give tomatoes and green peppers a try first, if that's all right with you."

"Whatever you like."

"Great. I really appreciate it." Kôjima was almost beside himself with excitement. "There will be a reduction in price, of course, while we use these new seals. We'll balance things out later on when it comes to doing the budget. I've spoken to Mr. Shinkawa, the head of the accounts department, and he's fine with it."

Ôtaka nodded and mumbled something in reply, struggling to keep his headache and nausea under control.

The first results of the new scheme became clear early that afternoon.

The tomatoes Kôjima had chosen for the first trial came in packets of two. Kôjima had attached his stickers to a half dozen or so of the one hundred packets toward the front of the display shelf. Twenty yen off. The price per packet was 150 yen, so it was a discount of more than 10 percent.

As his hangover dissipated, Ôtaka pretended to work on the adjacent cucumber display. He wanted to see what kind of vegetables Kôjima had chosen to stick his stickers onto. Kôjima, in the meanwhile, was now staring at the green peppers, oblivious to everything else.

In a packet of tomatoes marked with Kôjima's stickers, one of the tomatoes was still very green. In another, both tomatoes were ripe, but one had a tiny black blotch on the skin. Neither of these "problems" affected the vegetable; they were minor blemishes at the most, but things like this were enough to put customers off. Another discounted packet contained one tomato that was much bigger than the other.

When Ôtaka went back to the display a half hour later, four of the five discounted packets had been sold. The last unsold packet contained a ripe tomato and an unripe one.

"We're going to have to reduce this packet a bit more, I think," Kôjima said.

Ôtaka hadn't noticed Kôjima standing behind him. He would have taken off if he'd seen him coming. Ôtaka smiled to hide his embarrassment. Whatever happened, he wasn't going to give Kôjima the satisfaction of knowing he was interested in the experiment.

"Seems a shame to put a good red tomato in the same packet with an unripe one like this, don't you think? It's a perfectly fine tomato, but if it's lumped together with a green one, it's not going to sell. Or only at the same lower price for the unripe one."

"I'm not so sure," Ôtaka said. His first reflex was to disagree with whatever Kôjima said; he could worry about justifying his objections later. "Some customers like that. They don't want all their fruit to be at the same stage of ripeness."

"Eat one today, and save the other one for tomorrow, you mean?"

"Right." But even as he spoke, Ôtaka knew that he was talking nonsense. This green tomato wasn't going to be ripe for another three or four days. Not many people pushed carts around supermarkets thinking *We'll eat this one today, and the other one next week once it's ripe.*

Kôjima didn't push the subject any further. Perhaps he had noticed the absurdity of what Ôtaka had said. Instead, he made a new "40 yen off" sticker for the one remaining unsold package, and stuck "20 yen off" stickers on four more.

Ôtaka went back to the display to check again after another twenty minutes. The relabeled "40 yen off" package was gone, and only one of the other four discounted packages was left.

Ôtaka couldn't help being impressed. A small reduction in price really did make a difference. Without these stickers, there was a good chance that some of these packets of tomatoes would have ended up being thrown away. He didn't say anything to Kôjima, though, and continued to go about his work in silence.

The second result of the new scheme became clear toward early evening.

The store had had more customers than usual that day. Sales had been brisk across the board, but for some reason tomatoes and green peppers seemed to have outsold almost all other produce. That in itself was maybe nothing to get excited about. But there was something else. Ôtaka noticed it when he went to look at the tomato and pepper displays just before the evening rush hour: Every one of the tomatoes and peppers looked like top-quality produce. The overall impression was quite pleasing. The displays of the vegetables seemed to sparkle. It was something that he had never seen before.

Why?

Right away, Ôtaka knew the answer. No blemishes. Thanks to Kôjima's stickers any items with marks or defects had already been sold earlier in the day.

For the first time in all of the years he had spent selling fruit and vegetables, Ôtaka understood the effect a display of blemish-free produce could have. This was the second effect of the stickers: they gave the displays an extra sheen.

This could really make a difference, Ôtaka thought. He looked closely again at Kôjima, the man whose idea this had been. And for the first time at the store, he felt something like fear run through him.

It was more than an hour since Ôtaka had picked up Yoshiko in his Toyota Corolla and driven her to a restaurant in the suburbs of Tokyo. They'd had a couple of beers—even Ôtaka, who was driving (just one or two won't hurt, they had agreed)—and had just finished their meal. Now, sitting with empty coffee cups in front of them, Ôtaka was feeling anxious. He had let a whole precious hour pass by and he still hadn't been able to steer the conversation in the right direction.

They had started out by chatting about everyday things. Then talk of the special offer stickers had led them to conversation about today's experiment, and from there to a discussion of Kôjima the man himself. Whenever Kôjima's name came up, Ôtaka noticed a twinkle in Yoshiko's eyes and a smile on her face. It couldn't help rubbing him the wrong way.

"Kôjima won't last long at Ishiei Stores, if you ask me," he said.

Yoshiko looked shocked. "What do you mean?"

"Simple. Basically, it was Ichimura who built the company from the ground up. And he's the one keeping it going today. Lots of people in the company revere and respect him. They're not going to take it sitting down if he gets pushed aside and Kôjima takes over as the next in line. These people are going to have plenty to say about that." And before he knew what he was doing, Ôtaka found himself telling Yoshiko about dinner the night before.

Yoshiko showed no emotion as she listened, but it was only with great effort that she was able to keep up her calm, unruffled appearance. Inside, she was struggling against a chaos of confused emotions.

When Ôtaka came to the end of his spiel, neither of them said a word for what seemed like an age. The refined, sophisticated atmosphere of the restaurant was spoiled by the heavy cloud that now hovered over their table.

"Have I said something wrong?" Ôtaka said. "I'm sorry if I hurt your feelings. Please forgive me."

"No, it's all right," she said, and then fell silent again. She was lost in thought. She wasn't sulking, she wasn't trying to push him away; she hardly seemed to know he was there. As she'd listened to Ôtaka go on, all she could think about was a girl named Saijô Sakiko.

Sakiko, who was nineteen at the time, had been employed in the personnel department. She was a good worker, and her fair-skinned good looks made her popular with her male colleagues. This didn't endear her to most of the other women in the company, but Yoshiko liked her. Something about Sakiko reminded her of herself when she was younger.

Perhaps Sakiko had been a little careless. Sashima had asked her out on a date. They drank a lot of whiskey, which Sakiko normally didn't touch at all, and then went for a ride in Sashima's car. Things from that point on went the way they usually do. Perhaps the whiskey was responsible for what had happened. Or perhaps Sashima had been planning the whole thing all along. He drove her to a deserted suburban street and raped her.

Sashima then took Sakiko back to her dormitory—an act, in the mind of many, sufficient to prove the sex had been consensual. At 2:00 A.M., Sakiko rushed over to Yoshiko's apartment. She had nowhere else to turn. She was a high school graduate from a small town in Tohoku and was living alone for the first time in her life. She had been a virgin.

Yoshiko could still see the way Sakiko looked that night: her pale, haggard face, her shock, her exhaustion. She put Sakiko to bed, and in the morning she went to the office and, thinking it best to go straight to the top, told Ishikari what happened.

Ishikari was shocked, and called Ichimura immediately. From this point on, all discussions took place behind closed doors, out of Yoshiko's sight.

Ichimura summoned Sakiko into his office. She was to keep silent, he said. This was for her own good, for there was little doubt that what had happened would hardly be considered rape. Surely she understood that the evidence suggested she had been willing? Ishikari would, of course, keep a close eye on Sashima, and he would take it upon himself to see the two of them properly married, if that was what she wanted. After all, a man had to face the consequences of his actions.

Sakiko responded immediately, "No way."

"In that case there's nothing more I can do." With these words, Ichimura removed an envelope from his inside pocket and laid it on the table in front of Sakiko. "Take this," he said. "Take a week off from work, and go for a nice trip somewhere."

Sakiko understood there was money inside the envelope. She felt misery welling up inside her like nausea. She felt insulted, abused. She pushed the envelope back across the desk. One week later, she resigned from Ishiei Stores. She told no one about the rape, and there were no rumors about the real reasons for her leaving. But Yoshiko knew, and she watched to see how the company would deal with Sashima.

One day not long after, Ishikari called her into his office: "About the unfortunate incident with young Miss Saijô, I thought you'd like to know that everything has been taken care of. So there's so need for you to worry about it any longer. Miss Saijô herself was most understanding. Naturally, something like this can come as a considerable shock to a young lady, and I'm afraid she could see no alternative but to resign. We were very sorry to see her go."

"What about Sashima? What's going to happen to him?"

"Mr. Ichimura is keeping Sashima under close supervision. Sashima himself genuinely regrets what happened. If he treats this little incident as a wake-up call, then maybe some good might come of this after all."

Yoshiko could not believe what she was hearing. "Some good" coming out of "this little incident"! This was rape! Sakiko was going to have to live with this for the rest of her life. The company was treating it as a minor infraction, nothing to get excited about. As if Sashima were the victim! But Yoshiko chose to say nothing more. If she tried to take matters further, it would come down to an argument about whether Sakiko had given her consent. That would be adding even more insult to injury, even if Sakiko never found out about it.

Six weeks later, Sashima was appointed head of the meat department in the center store.

So when Yoshiko heard Sashima's name again now, and heard that Sashima was to form a secret group to support Ichimura, Yoshiko felt sick to her stomach. This was the way the grubby, sweat-soaked world of men worked.

"I'm sorry, I'm boring you. Let's go," Ôtaka said, standing up. "Stuff like this can't be of interest to a woman." He was thinking hard, trying to revise his strategy. He was hoping that once they got in the car it would feel like they were on a date again, and he could say what he wanted to say.

"No, sit down. You wanted to talk about something. Let's talk."

"Sure. If you want." Shit, this wasn't coming out right at all. How was he supposed to start? Maybe he was still hungover. Sashima, Kôjima . . . screw those guys. They had put him off his rhythm.

Ôtaka wrestled with himself silently, struggling to find the right words. He should have held her hand while they were still in the car. He should have parked the car somewhere by the side of the road, with the moonlight streaming in. He should have seized the moment right then and there. He should have looked into her big eyes and whispered, *I think I'm in love with you.*

It might have worked. The romance of the moonlight, the gentle silence of the late-night streets, a sudden confession of love . . . Who knows, if he'd been bold enough he might be kissing her now. But come on, he wasn't a kid anymore, and she was married before. The best thing to do was declare his feelings in a calm, businesslike manner:

"Misaki-*san*," he began, "will you marry me?"

Yoshiko's eyes bulged. She stared at him open-mouthed, speechless.

"I've always liked you. I'm sure I can make you happy. Please say yes. Say you'll marry me."

"You'll give me a heart attack, springing surprises on me like that. Please, I can't take much more shock." Instantly, Yoshiko had understood. What Ôtaka blurted out had been haunting him for a long time.

She felt grateful to him for his sincerity, but it happened like an outburst, and she was struggling to keep a straight face.

"I'm serious," Ôtaka persisted. "I don't mind that you're older than I am. Or that you have a kid. I know you've been married before." But as he spoke, he realized that this wasn't coming out right. He had spent weeks rehearsing what he was going to say, and now all he could come up with was this stream of incoherent babble. He had planned it all out in his mind, had marshaled all his arguments, rebuttals, and counter-objections. But she'd barely said a word, and here he was reciting a catalog of reasons why her objections didn't make sense.

"It doesn't matter what the future holds," he finally got around to saying. "As long as you're by my side, I don't need anything else. Please, I beg of you."

"Ôtaka-*san*, thank you. What you've just said makes me very happy. But please, no more."

"Is there no hope for me at all?"

"Please, no more."

Ôtaka felt every sinew in his body pull tight. His mouth clamped shut. He felt numb, like an actor who had forgotten his lines and was stranded on stage.

"I'm sorry." Yoshiko herself could think of nothing else to say. Probably it was better this way.

They left the restaurant and got into the car, neither saying a word. The car sped faster and faster through the night. The accelerator seemed to have a mind of its own.

Yoshiko was frightened, but kept quiet. She felt sorry for Ôtaka, and she didn't want to make things even worse. But there was something she felt she needed to say: "You know, this group that's formed around Ichimura. I don't think it's a good idea. And Kôjima—he's really not such a bad person."

Ôtaka said nothing. His hands tight on the steering wheel, he was staring straight ahead at the road in front of him.

Yoshiko looked at his face in profile. He looked like a man who was carrying the weight of the world's sorrows on his shoulders. She regretted so much. She ought to have been more considerate. "I'm sorry," she brought herself to say. "I'll always cherish the feelings you have for me."

"I'm the one who should be apologizing to you. Thank you for coming out with me tonight." With these words Ôtaka fell silent, and thrust his foot down on the accelerator again.

THREE

FOXES AND BADGERS

"Don't you think we've seen enough, sir? This heat is killing me."

Kôda Kôtarô could hardly get the words out of his mouth. He was panting and out of breath, and his blue shortsleeved shirt was drenched in sweat.

Kitô Jun'ya, head of development, continued to thrash his way through the undergrowth as if he hadn't heard a thing.

"Please, sir, this is hopeless. There's nothing but trees and bushes and brambles up here. We're not going to find any sign of life in a place like this. Let's call it a day."

"What are you mumbling about down there?" Kitô's breathing was strained, but his voice remained cheerful and full of energy. Unlike Kôda, he seemed to be enjoying the experience.

"If we go all the way to the top, we won't find anything but trees and brush. And that's if we're lucky. We could get there and find nothing but wilderness. Just wooded land as far as the eye can see."

"Stop talking nonsense, Kôda. There's not a square foot of untouched land left in Japan. One thing there is plenty of, though, is untapped potential. And that's what we're looking for. Unexploited markets. Now stop whining like a woman and follow me. The first thing to do when checking out a site is *walk*. Most of our customers still get to the store by foot, even today. We're going to keep on walking till we get a sense of what the site might be worth. And it's no good just wandering around empty-headed. You've got to be thinking the whole time. Ask yourself: What kind of people live here, and where do they go for their daily shopping?"

Continuing up the path, Kôda knocked a branch away from his face. "What do you think I've been doing all this time? Actually, it all just came to me."

"Here we go again. What is it now?"

"I'm serious. Remember that field we went through? The one with the little statue of the rice god Inari? That's it. That's where they go. Night falls, and the inhabitants of the village gather in a circle around the statue to lap up lantern oil with their long red tongues. And as they drink, their necks get longer and longer."

"What are you talking about? You can't even get your legends straight. You're getting fox spirits mixed up with the *rokuro-kubi*. They're the ones with the long necks, you idiot."

"Same thing. But imagine if you did start a store around here. You'd open the store and you'd notice that all the customers were these amazing-looking women. Think how shocked the store manager would be. Where are all these beautiful women coming from, out here in the middle of nowhere? And then the guy in charge of groceries comes running up to him one day in a mad panic. The only thing these women are buying is fried tofu. They're all fox spirits!"

"Whatever."

"Wait, it gets worse. When they open the cash registers at the end of the day, there's nothing in them but leaves! The store's like a madhouse. The deputy manager catches a shoplifter and takes her to the police, but she puts a spell on him, and before he knows what's happening he's taking a bath in the middle of the field and getting drunk on horse piss. He's so bewitched, he thinks it's sake."

"Enough."

"The store manager freaks out. He calls the head office for help. It's terrible, he says, all our customers are fox spirits, we can't carry on like this much longer. So the guy from the head office says, OK, we'll send someone down right away. And guess who they send?"

"I give up. Who?"

"Ichimura! They send Ichimura! So the store manager sees him coming and his eyes nearly pop out of his head. It's even worse than I thought, he says. It's not just foxes. Now there's a badger here too!"

"Very funny," Kitô chuckled. "But enough. You'll get in trouble if Mr. Ichimura finds out you're talking about him like that."

Eventually, the men reached the top of the gentle slope of trees. Ahead, the path headed downhill again almost immediately. Suddenly the view opened up all around them.

"See, what did I tell you?" Kitô said triumphantly. "Look over there!" On the other side of a bamboo thicket at the bottom of the hill a small village of thirty or forty houses stood glinting in the midsummer sun.

"You're right. Who would've thought—a real live human settlement in a place like this! Do you really think people would trek all the way to the supermarket site from here?"

"Absolutely."

"How can you be so sure?"

"Where else are they going to go? They'd walk miles if they had to. It's no distance at all with a bike or a car."

"If you say so. Come on, let's turn back. I'm tired. I'm not going any farther in this heat. Not even if it's an order."

"Yeah, we've probably seen enough for now." Kitô wiped away the sweat pouring from his brow.

"I still can't see how it would be a profitable site. Even if you add these houses to the catchment area," Kôda said.

"I think we could be onto a real winner with this place."

"Really? But the store the company is thinking of buying is about to go bust? That doesn't sound too promising to me."

"It's not going bust because of a lack of business."

Kitô recounted the history of the proposed site:

The owner was a man by the name of Ogawa, who'd been a dry goods wholesaler until a few years ago, when he'd decided to expand and turned his store into a supermarket. The supermarket had been a big success. Three years ago he opened a second store, followed by a third last year.

But Ogawa had no self-control. And when large amounts of money suddenly come the way of a man without self-control, it's not good news. Flush with cash, Ogawa started spending serious money on women, and before long found himself supporting a full-time mistress. He liked to boast how his life was expanding: he set up his second store at the same time as his second wife.

The fly in the ointment was his woman's gambling habit. The bulk of his profits now went to feeding her addiction. It was like pouring water into the desert. Things went downhill fast. By the time he was building his third store, he was borrowing from some pretty shady characters. He had no choice but to sell off the new store almost as soon as it was built.

Ishikari Eitarô had known Ogawa for years. Ogawa's store was a little outside the company's territory, but there was every indication that the site would do well. Eitarô passed the news of Ogawa's misfortune onto his brother Seijirô. And that's why Kitô and Kôda were standing in the heat today.

But Kôda wasn't convinced. A supermarket needed to attract at least two thousand customers a day to break even. Where were those customers going to come from in a remote spot like this? And with average income here 20 percent lower than in Sawabe, spending per customer was going to be lower too.

"As it happens, Mr. Ichimura agrees with you," Kitô admitted. "He described this as another of the president's mad ideas. Told me my job was to make sure we nipped the scheme in the bud."

"No way. The badger really said that? I guess he's heard what everyone in the company says about Ishikari."

"What's that?"

"The three vices of the company president," Kitô began to sing, as if it were a jingle. "Number one: he's greedy. Number two: he doesn't trust his employees. And number three: he looks out only for his own cronies."

"That's pretty harsh."

"Don't tell me you've never heard that before? And his brother? You know what people say about him?"

Kitô did not respond. Of course, part of him wanted to hear the dirt. But it wasn't right. He wasn't a lowly rank-and-file employee anymore. This kind of talk wasn't seemly; it went against everything he believed in.

"The three vices of Ishikari Seijirô," Kitô began to sing again, undeterred. "Number one: he can't make decisions for himself. Number two: he doesn't understand that ten thousand yen today is worth more than a million tomorrow. And number three: he takes forever on the toilet."

"What the hell is that supposed to mean?"

"He's so indecisive. Can't bring himself to let go."

Kitô had to stop himself from laughing out loud. Things were so clear and obvious when seen from below. These people didn't miss a thing.

Before joining Ishiei Stores, Kitô had worked for a large trading company, where the attitude had been much the same. The only difference was that the employees at Ishiei Stores were younger. The company hierarchy wasn't as strict either, and people tended to be a little more outspoken in their criticism of the management. Maybe it was better this way. People were honest, open, and straightforward. Given the right leadership, these were qualities that could be turned into a powerful force. But at the moment it was hard to see where the leadership was going to come from.

A lot of people seemed to have high expectations of Ichimura in this regard—not least the man himself. But Kitô had his doubts. Perhaps a good business instinct was incompatible with leadership. Maybe you either had one or the other.

All over the country, people were jostling for control of the business that seemed destined to dominate the trade and commerce sector for years to come.

What would become of Ishiei Stores? The company was making decent profits, and the number of outlets was growing. The mood within the company was optimistic, especially since the success of the new center store. But Kitô could not shake a nagging sense of doubt. He worried that people were getting carried away, and that the company's bright prosperous future was nothing but an illusion.

He couldn't have said why he felt this way. The lack of a unified leadership was one thing that worried him. Things were too relaxed. If people weren't sure of the direction they were supposed to be pulling in, they sometimes ended up not pulling at all. But something else worried him more. It was the sense he got when he put himself in the shoes of the customer. Given a choice, would he shop at Ishiei Stores? He didn't think so. Ishiei Stores was second rate.

If he wanted a snack to have with a drink at home, he could find almost nothing on the shelves to tempt him. And whatever he did bring home never tasted very good. He'd make a valiant effort not to waste the food, but on several occasions he told his wife just to throw the stuff away.

His wife was more critical than he was. She had a long list of complaints: "Why are the cucumbers from Ishiei Stores always so soft and soggy? The ones from the market are much crunchier. . . . They trick you with the meat. They put the fresh-looking cuts on the outside of the package, then when you get home and open it up there's cheap, stringy junk meat underneath. . . . The clothes have absolutely no style, and the quality is just awful. I bought a skirt the other day. It's itchy around the waist; there's something that feels like thorns on the belt. And forget about the stuff they sell at bargain prices. You wash them once and you'll never wear them again. . . . The girls on the cash registers have no manners. And they're always adding things up wrong."

"That's what supermarkets are like," Kitô had told his wife. All of them were the same.

But was it true? Were all supermarkets really as bad as one another? All he knew was that having to make excuses like this to his wife was not helping his faith in the company.

"Look!"

Kitô's musings were interrupted by a sudden shout from Kôda.

"It's Mr. Kôjima and Také from work!"

Kôjima and Také were standing ahead of them at the entrance to the Shimo-Shinden branch of the Ogawa supermarket chain.

Kôjima looked up and laughed. "You two are absolutely drenched. Whoever said the development team had it easy?"

"Tell me about it," Kitô said, wiping his brow. "When I first saw this site a while back, I thought it looked promising. But when we presented it to the board, Ichimura acted unimpressed, so we came to have another look."

"And what do you think now you've seen it again?"

"Personally, I still think it might work. Kôda's not convinced, though, and I have to confess, I don't think it's a sure bet myself anymore. How about you?"

"I don't know yet." Kôjima smiled broadly; even in this pitiless heat, he was as unruffled as ever. "Ever since I joined the company it's like I've been thrust into a whole new world. It's fascinating, but there are so many things I still don't understand. I need you to help me figure it all out."

"Oh, I don't think there's much I could teach you," Kitô started to say.

"Leave it to me," Kôda butted in. "I'll teach you anything you need to know—as long as I get something cold to drink!"

Kôjima laughed out loud. "Come on," he said, "let's go get something to drink."

The four men turned and wandered over to the slightly scruffy-looking coffee shop next to the entrance of the supermarket.

Také Norio listened intently as the three men discussed the merits of the prospective site. They were making an effort to keep their voices down. The store they were thinking of buying was just next door, after all. But they needn't have worried. Apart from the old woman who had brought them their lukewarm iced coffees and then disappeared to the back of the store, the coffee shop was empty.

Také owed his presence among the group to a request Kôjima had put in that morning for someone from the development department to go with him to the site. There was talk of buying the site, store and all, and he wanted an expert's view on the state of the building. "They transferred him to us a month ago from the meat department. He doesn't know much about construction yet, but he's the only one in the department not busy with other things today. He'll do as a driver, at least."

"Sorry, I should have given you more notice," Kôjima said. "But this young man and I have met already. Také taught me a lot during my time at the center store. I'm sure he'll be a great help today."

Také lowered his head.

"From the meat department to development—sounds like a big jump for you. Did you ask for a move?"

"No. They gave me the sack."

He had meant it as a joke, but his dark tone betrayed his true feelings.

"We'll leave around ten," Kôjima said, changing the subject. "Bring the plan for the Shimo-Shinden site with you."

It was an hour and a half from Sawabe to the proposed site, on the other side of the prefectural boundary. This was far beyond the company's regular sales territory.

Kôjima talked about nothing else all the way there. He wanted to know in concrete terms what effect being so far away from the head office would have on the store. Given Také's background, most of Kôjima's questions involved ways the distance might affect the meat department.

Také didn't have answers to all of Kôjima's questions, but he did his best to respond as accurately and thoroughly as he could. He was impressed by Kôjima, who had a way of attacking a question from as many different angles as possible. He almost never gave a hint of his own opinion. His only responses to Také's remarks were a satisfied-sounding "of course" or an occasional thoughtful sigh.

They parked a few hundred yards from the site and after a quick bite carried out an inspection of the surrounding area by foot. They had been just about to go into the store when they bumped into Kitô and Kôda.

As usual, Kôjima did more listening than speaking once they took their seats in the coffee shop. First he wanted to hear Kitô's reasons for supporting the proposed site, then Kôda's reasons for opposing it. And how similar were Kôda's objections to Ichimura's? The only time Kôjima showed any sign that he had an opinion of his own came after yet another of Kôda's blurted indiscretions:

"It doesn't make any difference really what we think, Kôjima-*san*. It's already been decided. If Ichimura's against the proposal, it's got no chance. The only point of these board meetings is to bring everyone around to Ichimura's opinion."

"How do you mean?"

"Take this case. Ichimura might start out by listing all the good points of the site, so it seems like he's all in favor of the idea. Then some other board member, who's been primed by Ichimura before the meeting, comes out with the opposite point of view. They argue and make compromises and then finally Ichimura comes out with what was his real opinion the whole time. The way he does it just makes it look like he's prepared to consider other people's opinions."

"But that would mean the whole thing was just a meaningless piece of theater."

"Right, with a badger playing the lead."

"But Kôda," Kitô interrupted, "you can't make accusations like that. It's all in your imagination."

"It's not my imagination. It's true. A guy who Ichimura tapped to play the dissenting role told me about it one night after a few drinks."

Kitô scowled but said nothing.

"I see," Kôjima said. "This kind of thing happens in companies all the time. But we could do without the management behaving like that in our company, I think. Tricks like that are one thing for a big established company, but I don't think they're appropriate for one like ours that's still trying to find its way." Kôjima spoke slowly and precisely, choosing his words carefully. "I know I still have a lot to learn, but personally I don't think a decision like this should be made subjectively. You've got to depend on the empirical data you collect, and then come to a more or less objective decision.

"I wonder, Kitô-*san*, if you'd mind if Kôda came to do some work for me for a while? There's some data I'd like to have him draw up."

"As you like. Of course, we've collected a fair bit of data already." Kitô's pride as a manager showed in his face.

"We'll make full use of that too, naturally," Kôjima said. "In fact, I'm sure that will be more than enough on its own."

Kitô looked relieved.

"Come on then, let's take a look around the store. The manager is expecting us. But remember: as far as he's concerned, we're just here for a tour to see how companies get things done. I don't want him to know the real reason we're here, OK?"

"Wow, this is pretty bad," Kitô said in a whisper.

They'd all been thinking the same thing.

"Maybe we should have used a different excuse. No one would come for a tour of a dump like this," Kôda joked.

"Not so loud," Kitô hissed.

But there was no denying it: the store was a mess. A few fluorescent bulbs cast a faint, mournful light. Movable gondolas lay scattered on the floor; there was dirt from vegetables and scraps of food in them. Many of the shelves were empty, and what little merchandise there was on display was covered with a film of dust. The place looked abandoned. Cardboard boxes littered the aisles, where a few long-haired assistants stood jabbering to one another and pretending to work.

It was barely three in the afternoon, but the fresh food section had almost nothing left in stock. Management was obviously worried about being stuck with unsold stock at the end of the day. There were only a few blackened cuts of meat and some fish that had seen better days. The place stank, literally.

At the service counter, where fish was on special clearance, the stench was overpowering, like blocked drains.

"Wow, when you see a place like this, the future for our company starts to look pretty rosy, huh?"

"Shut up. He can hear you," Kitô said, trying to keep Kôda under control.

But the store manager showing them around didn't seem to mind at all. After leading the group casually through the meat and fish sections, he led them to the work area at the back of the store.

Kôjima was taken aback by the size of the area.

"I don't know why it's so big. It was designed by some hotshot consultant. A big waste, if you ask me. And look, there's no real division between the work area and the sales floor. This consultant said the biggest problem for supermarkets in the next few years was going to be rising labor costs, and this was supposed to be part of the solution. You could do all your loading and unloading by putting stuff on carts with little wheels. This whole setup was designed so that caster-wheel carts could move anywhere within the store. But does it look like it's working?"

For some reason, Také was quite taken with the plan. If all of the lifting and shifting could be done by loading produce onto wheeled carts, you could cut down on the heavy labor—and the back strains.

Kôjima seemed interested too. "What was the name of this consultant?" he asked.

"I'll ask. But I'd stay away from him if I were you. A screwy store that looks like this isn't what you're going to want."

"Was the lighting his idea too?"

"What, those? Nope. The consultant was telling us we needed to install some ridiculous expensive system. But the boss didn't want to spend the money; he said lights weren't that important. So he went for the cheapest he could find. He wanted to get everything finished on schedule."

The store manager next introduced the group to the regenerator fridge.

"This was another one of the consultant's big ideas," he said, opening the door of the huge refrigerator for them. "I mean, look at the size of the thing. This is for fruits and vegetables. Might make more sense if it was for meat or fish or something, but who needs something like this for vegetables?"

"Did the consultant give a reason?"

"Oh, he had all kinds of reasons. He was going on about how cooling stuff meant you dried stuff out too. So if you had this expensive 'regenerator' thing, stuff wouldn't dry out. At least that's what he said."

"And what's different about this refrigerator?"

"It's supposed to keep the vegetables humidified or something. Get this—the word he used was the vegetables would be *reborn*! Revitalized, you know? Can you believe it? Anyway, he was going on about how if you had some spinach that came in dry and withered, you could put it in the regenerator and, bingo, it would come out all crisp and fresh like it was just picked. That's where the crazy name came from."

"And does it work?"

"Who knows?"

"Even when you used the recommended temperature and humidity?"

"Huh?" The store manager looked at Kôjima, perplexed. Who was this strange man asking these questions, and why was he so interested in this stuff? He shook his head. "His name—the consultant—was, I think, Inoue. Can't remember his first name. A real piece of work. He can tell you whatever you want to know—temperature, humidity, lighting system, whatever."

"Thank you."

"Look at this pillar! It's all bent out of shape!" Kôda shouted.

"Be quiet, you idiot!" Kitô hissed.

The group had left the store manager in the work area and were back on the sales floor. Kôjima walked over to take a look at what Kôda was making all the noise about. Sure enough, a steel pillar in the middle of the sales floor seemed to be bending under stress.

"This steel pole is about five inches in diameter," Kitô explained. "Normally, with a building of this size, you'd want to use something bigger and thicker than that. In fact, the whole place looks like it was put together pretty cheaply."

"What would happen if the pillar was too weak? Would it just suddenly snap one day?"

"I don't think so. Probably the bend will worsen gradually over time. It might take years, but one day the whole roof could come crashing to the floor."

"What about the other pillars?" Kôjima asked.

Kitô and Kôda took a quick look around the rest of the store. "They seem to be fine. It's possible this pole was bent before it was put in place."

Kôjima mumbled dubiously and beckoned to Také. "This looks like pretty slipshod construction. Let's look everything over carefully."

Také nodded in agreement. Things were looking pretty bad.

Board meetings at Ishiei Stores were held every Monday morning.

There were normally nine directors in attendance, and the meetings were chaired by Ishikari Seijirô. Ishikari Eitarô, the owner and president of the company, put in an appearance every few months or so.

"I prefer to leave the day-to-day running of the company to my brother," was what he liked to say. In fact, this was not quite true. He simply didn't like the work. The decision to expand into the supermarket business had been his alone, so it was ironic that he should hate the work so much now. But there was nothing he could do about it.

He never really liked the idea of selling radishes and mackerel in the first place. His aim was to stack a few shelves with tins and see how it went. He'd hoped to leave the serious business of meat and fish selling to the vendors, but in the end he found himself opening a fresh food section of his own.

Another thing he didn't like was that most of his customers were women. Any company that dealt primarily with women was a second-rate business in his opinion.

He had been brought up to believe that a businessman needed two basic skills: a gift for face-to-face negotiations and the ability to predict market trends. These were the things one lived for as a businessman. Bowing and smiling to an indeterminate mass of women and trying to sell them a bunch of products that didn't even turn a real profit was not his idea of a respectable way to make a living.

And as if that wasn't bad enough, the work was surprisingly difficult.

"It's easy work, and you'll make a killing," his wholesaler friend had told him. In fact, the opposite was true: the work was hard as hell, and it made him almost nothing.

He'd been ready to wash his hands of the whole business when the steel company his brother worked for collapsed and Seijirô joined the company. It was only then that they'd started to make any money. He didn't know the details, but it seemed that Ichimura, who had been hired on the recommendation of another wholesaler acquaintance, was now essentially in charge of managing the stores and was starting to see results.

It didn't make sense to pull the plug just when the thing had finally started to make some money. He decided to let Ichimura run the business, and put Seijirô in nominal charge above him. Seijirô chaired the board meetings, but Ichimura did most of the talking. And it was certainly Ichimura who had the biggest influence over the decisions that were passed at the end of the day.

The usual procedure was for Ichimura to summarize the argument and propose his own opinion for Ishikari's approval. Ishikari would give a nod of his head, and Ichimura's motion would be passed. But at this week's meeting the members of the board were in for a surprise. The subject under discussion was the proposal to take over the Shimo-Shinden branch of the Ogawa Supermarket Company. Things had started moving toward Ichimura's view that the proposal should be shelved when Kôjima suddenly started to argue the opposite point of view with considerable force. The board members swallowed hard and looked on in amazement. This wasn't the kind of thing they were used to.

"I can't speak with much confidence, of course," Kôjima began. "I'm no expert on supermarket locations after all . . ."

It was several months now since he had joined the board. In that time he had hardly spoken at the board meetings, and the hesitant and self-deprecating manner in which he began now ensured him a sympathetic audience.

"It seems there are two main objections to the proposal. First: that there are only a small number of households within the site's potential catchment area. And second: that average income levels within the catchment area are a good deal lower than at any of our other stores to date. As I understand it, the argument is that if we can attract only a relatively small number of customers, and if average customer spending is also relatively low, then we could struggle to achieve the kind of sales figures we would need to make the store viable."

Several board members nodded their heads in agreement.

"To tell you the truth, that was my gut feeling too, the first time I saw the site. So I decided to look for evidence that might shed light on these two points, using data from the stores we already have in operation. Surprisingly, the results I obtained were exactly the opposite of what I had expected. The data suggest there would be a more than sufficient customer base to support a store on the Shimo-Shinden site, and that per-capita sales there would also be more than adequate."

There was a mix of emotions on the faces of the board member as they listened. How was Ichimura going to react?

"First of all, we need to look at the number of households inside the catchment area, since this determines how many customers we can expect to attract to the store. Obviously, this figure will vary depending on where you set the borders of the catchment area. I know many of you thought the three-kilometer figure given in the original proposal was unrealistic. In fact, however, it turns out that several of our stores already depend on catchment areas that are even larger than this."

Kôjima had started out in a low voice but his enthusiasm soon got the better of him. He spoke clearly and persuasively, occasionally pausing to scribble something on the blackboard. "Next, I want to talk about average sales per customer." He gestured to Kôda, who stood up and attached a graph to the easel.

"This graph shows all the existing Ishiei Stores outlets, ranked by sales per customer," Kôjima went on. "The data shown here reveal several surprising facts. It turns out that the most important factor influencing customer spending is the presence of other stores in the area that allow customers to shop around for the best deals. The less competition there is, the higher our average sales. The second most important factor is the amount of parking space available, followed by the range of goods on sale. Each of these factors has a bigger influence on customer spending than local income levels."

Kôjima paused for a few moments and looked up to gauge the reaction of the other board members. He went on:

"In terms of the present proposal, my analysis suggests that the average sales volume at the Shimo-Shinden store would be in the region of seven hundred yen per customer. This is as high as the figures for any of our existing outlets, and a good deal higher than most. If the store could attract twenty-two hundred customers a day as the development report suggests, then we would be looking at sales figures of a little over one point five million yen a day, and annual sales of around five hundred forty million yen.

"In summary, then, our forecasts suggest that a new store on this site could be expected to become one of the company's highest-earning outlets, and would most likely start producing a profit right away."

The reaction was mixed.

Asayama, the director responsible for the fresh produce, and Katsumura, who was in charge of personnel, both seemed convinced, and were nodding their heads vigorously in approval of Kôjima's lucid analysis. But not everyone was so impressed.

Odagiri, the director in charge of groceries, had looked uncomfortable throughout Kôjima's report. A smug, self-conscious character who liked to think he had seen it all, he had glanced over anxiously at Ichimura several times while Kôjima was talking. Everyone in the company knew that Odagiri was one of Ichimura's most loyal yes-men.

Shinkawa, who was in charge of the nontrade side of the business and therefore ultimately responsible for the development department that had drawn up the proposal, also looked uncomfortable, but for quite different reasons. Shinkawa was over sixty, with a head of thick white hair. He had been at Ishiei Stores for five years, having been picked up by Ishikari Eitarô at the end of his regular career and put in charge of accounts. His life as an ambitious businessman had come to an end long ago. Now his only concern was to avoid trouble, to live the rest of his life in peace. The last thing he needed was unnecessary quarrels and disagreements.

There was a prolonged silence as Kôjima came to the end of his presentation. Finally, someone spoke up: "This may be all very well in theory . . ."

It was Matsuo, the director in charge of the clothing department and an intimate member of Ichimura's faction. He was an emaciated-looking man with a long, thin face and a supply of indigestion pills never far from hand. Originally from Osaka, he still spoke with a strong accent. He liked to boast that he had spent his college days doing nothing but playing baseball, and was fond of imparting to others the precious lesson he had learned as a result: theory was useless. The words were never far from his lips, and his fondness for this trite aphorism was a company joke. Everyone laughed, grateful for relief from the tension building in the room. No one wanted to be the first to speak.

The silence was finally broken by Konno. Konno was responsible for the company's stores, and therefore the immediate superior of each of the store managers. The look on his face during Kôjima's report suggested he was rather enjoying the prospect of trouble ahead. This would certainly have been in perfect accordance with everything he said and did on a daily basis.

"Everything you say seems to make sense," he said. "I really hope your contribution will be taken on board." He was doing his best to be ironic.

Of course, Kôjima's arguments stood no chance. Everyone knew that Ichimura and his clique would get their way in the end. But Konno thought he'd amuse himself with a joke or two first. There was a hint of mischief in his chubby face, and his eyes darted from side to side as he spoke.

His words had their desired effect. No sooner had he spoken than Odagiri, Ichimura's most faithful lieutenant, and Shinkawa, who wanted to avoid responsibility at all cost, were both openly scowling.

"This isn't going to be easy," said Ishikari, distressed by this unexpected turn of events.

"Differences of opinion are healthy. Nothing was ever achieved without differences of opinion. But what can you do with two opinions as diametrically opposed as these, especially when they both seem to have logic and facts on their side?"

"I have an idea," said Kôjima. "I'd like to hear both sides of the argument. I would like to hear the objections to the case I've just laid out, in concrete terms. With questions like this—the size of the catchment area and the projected sales per customer and so on—it should be possible to back up your arguments with solid facts. Whether people agree with me or not isn't important—I'd like to see concrete data."

"But what if the data simply doesn't exist?" said Matsuo, who didn't want to be led astray by theory.

"There are always areas where we won't have all the facts, but otherwise I think we ought to be able to decide things like this with a good degree of certainty."

"I'm not so sure." Suddenly Matsuo fell silent and shook his long, thin face nervously from side to side. It had occurred to him that it might not be a good idea to get on the wrong side of Kôjima. He was related to the owner of the company, after all, and people said he was in line to take over one day.

The atmosphere in the room was tense and uncomfortable.

It was Ichimura himself who came to the rescue. Beaming a smile that radiated good humor across the room, he looked from face to face as he spoke. "Kôjima-*san* is right," he said.

This was not what everyone had been expecting. The group stared at him in disbelief.

"You've convinced me," he continued, looking over at Ishikari. "Our opinion was based on intuition. This is different. Kôjima-*san* has come to his own conclusion after a process of logical deduction, and his opinions are backed up with hard, solid facts. I think we should assume that we'll go ahead with the proposal, and take the discussion forward from there."

"Are you serious?" Ishikari seemed to be struggling to come to terms with the dramatic shift in Ichimura's stance. There was relief on his face too. At least it looked now as though conflict was going to be avoided.

"Of course I'm serious. How can you insult Kôjima-*san* by suggesting otherwise?"

"OK. So let's put this to a vote—"

"Wait a minute." It was Kôjima. "I don't know how to say this. This isn't what I wanted at all. What I was really hoping for was not that people would agree with me, but that we would start to discuss the issue seriously."

"Come on, that's enough," Shinkawa said. He could see his peace and quiet going up in smoke before his eyes.

Odagiri and Matsuo spoke up in support of Shinkawa, and even Konno, not normally regarded as a member of the Ichimura faction, seemed to agree that the discussion had gone far enough.

Kôjima couldn't afford to push it any further. "All right," he said. "But there's one thing we absolutely need to check up on first."

Here he goes again, Ishikari thought.

"I'm sure I'm not the only one who's noticed. One of the central support pillars in the Shimo-Shinden building is crooked."

Konno nodded vigorously, as if to signal to everyone present that he had noticed the same thing himself a long time ago.

"I think the development department should run a check on the whole building before we agree to any purchase."

Shinkawa was the director in charge of the development department. He agreed with Kôjima's proposal, but not without reservations. "That's fine, Kôjima-*san*. But you know, a supermarket doesn't really need to be all that impressive as a building."

"It's a stage prop—that's all," Ichimura added. The discussion was closed.

Maybe, Kôjima thought, *but you still need to make sure it's safe.* The words rose to his throat but he managed to swallow them in time. He didn't want people to think he was getting carried away with the sound of his voice just because one of his ideas had been accepted. Besides, he was well aware how little he knew about what a supermarket building was supposed to look like.

With that, the subject was closed, and Ishikari announced that they would move on to the next item on the agenda.

It wasn't long before word got out that Kôjima and Ichimura had been in disagreement at the board meeting, and that Kôjima had eventually forced Ichimura to back down.

The source of the rumors was Kôda from the development department, who had sat in as an observer.

It was the lunch break immediately following the meeting, and Kôda was sitting in a coffee shop near the office giving a vivid account to his coworkers of what had gone on at the meeting, complete with wild exaggerations and over-the-top gestures.

His audience consisted of Misaki Yoshiko, Ishikari's secretary, and Kuroba Motoko and Také, both from development.

"That's so cool," said Motoko, thrilled by the news. Ichimura was a boss for whom she felt little affection or admiration, and now he had been beaten down by Kôjima, whom she had been heard to refer to as "that wonderful man."

"It was amazing. I wish you could have seen it. They were practically eyeball to eyeball."

"Wow."

"And they're both big guys, right? It looked like a fight was going to break out at any second. You could tell Ishikari was kind of freaked out by what was happening. He was standing between them with his arms out, trying to calm them down. He looked like a sumo referee or something. But he just made them more pumped up than ever. He was jumping around between them waving his fan around and shouting 'Face off, face off!' "

"Yeah, like I'm going to believe that."

"I'm serious. At first it looked like the fight was going to go Ichimura's way."

Kôda was enjoying his story, and his audience was lapping it up. What really happened had no effect on them; they were not responsible for what went on in these meetings. For them, it was just a tale to be told.

"Then finally, Ichimura steps forward. He's looking pretty calm, but you can tell his heart is beating like crazy. 'I'm sorry,' he says. 'Accept my apology. All of you. As a result of my own stupid incompetence and my own misguided ideas, the whole company was nearly led down the road to ruin. Forgive me,' he said, and then he knelt down with his hands on the floor in front of him, and touched his head to the ground."

"Can you believe it? And this man is the father of two children?" Motoko was holding her sides, laughing out loud.

Yoshiko was smiling too, but in her heart she couldn't treat the story as just a silly joke.

Kôjima was proving quite a hit with the younger members of the company's staff. Finally someone had appeared who could provide the leadership the company needed, Kôda said. It was about time they had someone who could take the place of that old badger. Kôda had even taken to referring to Kôjima as his "big brother."

Motoko's admiration was also starting to spin out of control. Her latest obsession was to dream out loud of being held in Kôjima's arms—even if it had to be for just one night. She fell in love easily. As a result, her life had been a long succession of unrequited crushes. She had limped from one hopeless infatuation to the next, and now found herself nearly thirty and still on the shelf.

A couple of years ago Yoshiko had acted as go-between for Motoko and had approached a man Motoko had been feverishly besotted with. He was married now, and worked as store manager of one of the Ishiei Store branches.

"Motoko's fine," he'd said. "But it's hard to think of her as someone I might want to marry. She's just not appealing in that way, you know."

That was the last time Motoko had had even a sniff of romance.

It was clear that Motoko was still no nearer to uncovering whatever hidden charms she may have had. Instead, her makeup got heavier. And then, just when she had resigned herself to giving up her dreams forever, along came Kôjima, a handsome and successful man just the right age. And as if that wasn't enough, someone had started a rumor that all was not well between Kôjima and his wife.

People said his wife had been dead set against the idea of joining Ishiei Stores. The company had rented a big apartment for them, but Kôjima lived there alone. Apparently the divorce was just a matter of time.

Motoko couldn't contain her excitement any longer. "And guess who's going to be his second wife? Me!"

Kôda dismissed the idea scornfully. "Yeah, right. Why would he want someone like you?"

To Yoshiko, though, this was no laughing matter. These were nothing more than distant events in a world that had nothing to do with her, but for some reason Yoshiko felt that that she alone really understood what Kôjima was going through. She had no evidence for this, of course, but the feeling was there all the same.

If the rumors were true (and Yoshiko for one believed they were), then Kôjima's wife had been opposed to the idea of her husband switching jobs. Having been married once herself, she thought she understood only too well the reasons for his wife's disapproval.

Ishiei Stores and Saiwa Bank were both private companies, but there the similarities ended. In terms of their records, their reputations, and their stability, the two companies could hardly have been farther apart. Yoshiko would probably have opposed the move too.

And to make matters worse, Kôjima's position within the company was still far from secure. If he failed to establish his leadership position within the company, he would ultimately have no choice but to leave. Even if he did manage to carve out a niche for himself, that on its own was no guarantee of success. He would constantly have to prove himself by coming up with a never-ending string of successes. That would not have been the case at the Saiwa Bank.

Yoshiko sometimes thought she sensed loneliness in Kôjima's eyes. Some of his usual good cheer seemed to have faded recently, and more and more often she could see dark brooding clouds of loneliness and isolation in his features. It worried her to hear that Kôjima and Ichimura had had a disagreement at the board meeting. If Kôjima had been forced into this position by all the pressure he was under, it was bound to end badly for him.

For Motoko, things were simple. For her, Kôjima was nothing more than prey to be hunted. "I want to go to Kôjima's apartment," she said.

"What's stopping you?" Kôda replied. "Just turn up on his doorstep and tell him what you feel. 'Here I am. Take me, I'm yours.'"

"No way. I couldn't go on my own. Hey, we could all go over together!"

"Not a good idea," Yoshiko said, but there was no dislodging the idea from Motoko's mind.

"I'll try to mention it to him if I get a chance," Motoko said. "If he says yes, then you'll all have to come with me, OK?"

"Well—" Také started to say something, but Motoko would accept no refusal.

"You too, Také," she said. It was an order. And with that, the matter was closed.

FOUR

THE DARUMA DOLL

Asayama Tomita, director of fresh foods, stood in
front of Kôjima's desk, a smile spreading across his
wrinkle-worn face.

The two men exchanged morning greetings and
got down to business. This wasn't the first time
Asayama had been to visit Kôjima at his desk; recently, in fact, he'd been stopping by almost every
day.

"Today's the big day, Kôjima-*san*. You haven't forgotten? Today's the day Kameyama Tsurunosuke is
coming to see us."

"That's right. Ten this morning, right?"

"So what do you think? His name sounds
promising—*kame* is turtle and *tsuru* is crane; you
can't get more auspicious than that. I wonder if he'll
live up to your expectations, though."

"I guess we'll just have to wait and see."

Kôjima had to smile. Asayama was being a little
coy. The idea had come to them a month ago, when
the two men were having drinks at a yakitori stall.
Asayama had been confiding to him about troubles
at work.

"We're losing money across the board. Meat, fish,
fruit, and vegetables—every single section is constantly in the red. I'm ashamed of myself. Some
days I can barely bring myself to show my face at
work. . . . No one ever tells me what I'm supposed to

be doing. . . . They only put me in charge of food because I used to work for a ham and sausage company. I don't have a clue. . . . I'm starting to think the whole thing's hopeless. Maybe there's no future in selling prepackaged food self-service style like this. . . . I've tried talking to Ichimura about it. All he does is ramble on about the character of the true businessman. . . ."

"Do you think things are any different for other supermarket chains?" Kôjima asked.

"Nope. The situation must be more or less the same for anyone trying to sell food this way."

"Don't you know anyone in the business you can trade stories with?"

"Sure. But those guys are just full of hot air. You never get the truth out of them."

"That's too bad."

"Everyone's fighting for a piece of the same pie. Always trying to stay one step ahead by second-guessing the other guy."

"Right. But can't you talk to the Self-Service Association, or the editor of the trade journal or something?"

"They wouldn't be able to tell me anything. What's the editor of the trade journal going to know about selling meat and fish anyway?"

"Sure, but they might be able to put you in touch with a company that has managed to overcome the same problems you're talking about. Maybe they'll know someone who could give us some advice."

"Maybe. Is it really likely, though? That would be like asking someone to give away his secrets. Besides, it wouldn't do much for our reputation if we had to show them what a mess things are in here."

As it happened, Asayama took himself down to the Self-Service Association the very next morning. The person he spoke to gave him an answer right away: "You need to talk to Kameyama."

Kameyama Tsurunosuke was the president of Banrai Stores, a five-store supermarket chain based in northern Saitama prefecture. Asayama arranged for him to come to Ishiei Stores the following month.

"Yes," Asayama was saying to Kôjima, "we probably shouldn't expect too much. Let's just see how it goes." He was starting back toward his own desk, when he turned around and said, "You know, Kôjima-*san*, it's amazing the way those special offers are selling."

"Things seem to be going OK so far."

"Everyone's saying it's due to your new guidelines."

"There's more to it than that, I'm sure."

"No, it's all due to that new sales strategy you set down. One: set clear targets. Two: work together for synergistic results. Three: concentrate on what's important; don't try to cover everything at once. Four: look carefully at other companies' results when drawing up sales plans. Five: give your sales promotions a storyline. Six: draw up attractive, eye-catching promotional materials that customers will want to pick up and read. Seven: uh . . . there was a number seven, wasn't there?"

"No, I think that just about covers it. I'm impressed. You've memorized everything."

"You're right, I have. You've only been here a few months, Kôjima-*san*, but in that time you've brought in ideas we'd never heard of before. The things you come up with are amazing. So I like to commit the really important stuff to memory."

"That's great. I'm glad to hear it."

"But it won't help much if I'm the only one who knows them by heart. That's why I'm making everyone in my department memorize your guidelines too."

Kôjima stood, his heart filled with gratitude, and watched Asayama return to his desk.

It was one minute past ten when a woman from Asayama's department came over to Kôjima's desk.

"Mr. Kameyama is here, sir."

"Thank you."

Kôjima stood up from his desk and made his way into the reception room.

When Kôjima got there, Kameyama Tsurunosuke was sitting opposite Asayama. Kameyama reminded him of a stubby little *daruma* bodhisattva doll, the kind that were sold at temples for good luck: red, chubby face, slightly blue, close-shaven cheeks, thick eyebrows, aquiline nose, cleft in his chin, and a sharply protruding jaw. He looked to be about sixty.

"You're going to have to do something about the restrooms," Kameyama started right in.

"Excuse me?" Asayama had no idea what Kameyama was talking about.

"The restrooms. There's no soap—at the head office of a company trading in food products! And no paper towels either. That won't do at all."

"Normally the restrooms are well supplied. They must have just happened to run out today, that's all."

"What difference does that make? If salmonella microbes *just happen* to get into your food and cause an outbreak of food poisoning, that's the end of the company."

"You're right, of course, but—" Asayama was fighting hard to keep his emotions under control, but you could tell by the way his left hand was twitching on his knee that he was insulted.

Suddenly, Kameyama burst out laughing. The sound he made was like the noise of a motorbike engine revving up. "I'm sorry," he said. "I'm always getting off on the wrong foot. I'm the kind of guy who says what he thinks. But that's the whole reason I came here today, right—to tell you what I think? So I'm not going to hold back. If at any stage it gets to be too much and you think you've heard enough, then just say the word and I'll be on my way. *Ga ha ha ha ha ha!*"

At the sound of his laughter, the girl who had brought them their tea nearly dropped her tray, but by the time she left, she was struggling not to burst out laughing herself.

"Please, don't hold back," Kôjima said, bowing his head low. "We'd be very grateful for your impressions."

"Why don't you start by showing me around the store," Kameyama suggested.

Together the three men walked the short distance from the head office to the center store. They had phoned ahead to let Manabe know they were on their way, and the store manager was waiting for them at the entrance when they arrived. Manabe's relaxed, dignified manner always seemed to put people at their ease, even on a first meeting.

During the time he'd spent in training at the center store, Kôjima had noticed the respect that Manabe's employees had for their boss. Even when they were out drinking, Manabe never lost his positive outlook, always remaining dignified and in control. He was an impressive figure. Kôjima had taken to him right away, and it seemed the feeling was mutual. Their relationship had continued even after Kôjima finished his training and moved to head office. Manabe often passed on information he thought might be useful for Kôjima's new sales job, and Kôjima now made it a habit to give Manabe a call whenever there was an aspect of the business he needed help with.

"Well, you seem to have found yourself a good store manager, at least," Kameyama said after they had been introduced. Once again his remarks were accompanied by a gale of laughter. But he wasn't joking. The man really did seem to say whatever was on his mind.

"I've come to have a quick look around your store, if that's all right," he said.

"Feel free. I'm sure you'll be able to set us straight on all kinds of things. Follow me." Manabe started off into the store, but Kameyama stood still outside by the automatic doors.

"Is there something wrong?" Kôjima asked.

"In itself, it's nothing. The problem is how it links up with things inside." Kameyama was mumbling mysteriously to himself. He strode through the doors and stopped in front of the fruit and vegetables displays, his eyes glinting. He circled the displays slowly, examining them from every possible angle. He crouched to get a closer look at the produce. Several times he stopped to pick up a piece of fruit in his knobby hands. This went on for fifteen minutes or so. The three men supposed to be showing him around stood, watched, and waited.

"I'll have a quick look at the work area too, if you don't mind," Kameyama said, striding over toward the fresh produce work area without waiting for a reply, as though he were in one of his own stores.

Ôtaka was preparing lettuce to go on display. He looked up at Kameyama suspiciously as he entered. Asayama hurried up behind him. "This is Mr. Kameyama, president of Banrai Stores. He's come to give us a few pointers."

"Oh yeah?" Ôtaka said. The news hadn't done much to improve his mood.

"Hello! How's it going?" Kameyama all but shouted. The professional gleam was gone from his eyes now. He looked more like a kindly father who had come to give his son a pep talk. "I'm sorry to be in the way when you're trying to work. Do you mind if I have a look at that knife you've got there?"

Ôtaka handed over the knife with a look of deep suspicion.

"Vegetables don't like metal. Ideally, of course, you'd use a bamboo slicer for cutting vegetables." He held up the metal knife in his right hand, and turned to Asayama, Kôjima, Manabe, and Ôtaka. "But it's not always practical to work with a bamboo knife. Sometimes we have no choice but to use a stainless steel one."

Kameyama touched the fingers of his left hand to the blade of the knife. "Unfortunately, this knife won't do at all. Look how blunt the cutting edge is; look at the nicks. Any vegetables you cut with this will discolor soon after they've been cut. Your knife needs to be razor sharp, and then you need to cut your vegetables with one smooth slice. You see what I mean?"

Kameyama's tone softened as he came to the end of what he had to say, and there was a hint of a smile in his eyes as he turned his rosy-cheeked face to Ôtaka. Ôtaka fidgeted uncomfortably, unsure how to react. "*Ga ha ha ha ha ha ha!* So now you know—always sharpen your knife before you start. OK?"

Kameyama turned to Asayama. "I take it you don't have a freshness preserver yet?" he said.

"A freshness preserver? You mean a regenerator fridge? We've been looking into getting one, actually. It was Kôjima's idea."

"That's good. They did call them regenerators once, but I don't think the name is used much these days. They don't *really* bring things back to life, after all. But whatever you want to call it, it's an absolute necessity. Once you give them the proper level of humidity, you'll find your vegetables will stay as fresh as when they were growing in the fields. Come and take a look around one of my stores if you like. I can give you all the information you need."

"Thank you very much."

"All right. Now, you're not going to like this much, but I'd like to remove a few items from your displays that I think might cause you some problems. If you don't mind?"

"Please. It'd be a great help. You don't mind, Ôtaka?"

"Be my guest."

Kameyama led the way back to the displays. He gestured for Ôtaka to join him by the cucumber racks and handed him an empty shopping basket. "Cucumbers," he began, "should have little spiny prickles on them, almost painful to the touch. When were these delivered?"

"Yesterday," Ôtaka said.

"What about this morning?"

"There was a delivery of fresh ones this morning, but we still had some left over from yesterday, so I put those out first."

"But that way you just end up putting out old produce every day. These weren't delivered yesterday, though—look at them."

Kameyama was holding a packet of three cucumbers. A layer of white mold was growing on the bottom of one of them. Kameyama prodded the mold with his finger, turning the cucumber to mush and revealing the flesh inside. "And this is not the only one that's affected," he said, pulling one distressed cucumber after another from their hiding places and putting them into the shopping basket.

By the time they moved on to the tomatoes and lettuce, the basket was practically full with unsatisfactory produce. "Here, take this." Asayama handed Ôtaka a fresh basket.

"It's all right, there's still room in this one," Ôtaka protested. His wounded pride was making him stubborn about the most ridiculous things.

Kameyama turned his attention to the cabbages. This time, his inspection didn't reveal anything that was seriously bruised or damaged, though he did turn up a couple of specimens with yellowed leaves. Several more were showing signs of discoloration in the stems where they had been cut. "Ideally, these shouldn't be out for sale either,"

Kameyama said. "But if we carry on like this there'll be nothing left on display. Do them again later with a sharper knife."

Ôtaka nodded silently.

Kameyama continued his painstaking inspection of the produce on display. He found unsatisfactory items everywhere he looked. Over-ripe tomatoes, eggplants with wrinkly skins, dried-out pumpkins with molding seeds, brown green peppers, blackened okra, wilted parsley, bruised yams. On and on it went. Kôjima looked on in astonishment as the pile of rejected items grew higher and higher.

Kameyama held a gingko nut to his nose and sniffed it gingerly. On the outer shell of the nut was an almost invisible speck of black mold. Kameyama bit into the nut; it was withered and shrunken inside, utterly inedible. Next he opened the seal on a polyethylene bag of *nameko* mushrooms. A sour smell of rot and decay assaulted his nostrils.

Once they'd finished with the vegetables, they moved on to the fruit. The diagnosis was no better here. Kameyama tapped at one of the watermelons. "Would you mind cutting this open for me?" he said. Ôtaka took the melon back to the work area and sliced it open. Inside, the fruit was overripe, the flesh soft and mushy. As a piece of merchandise, it was worthless.

Asayama had been viewing the proceedings in dismay at first, but the more he saw of Kameyama's supernatural powers at work, the harder it was to contain his admiration. "Amazing," he said. "But your standards are way beyond us. There's no way a bunch of amateurs like us could ever learn that."

"*Ga ha ha ha ha!* Not a bit of it. Anyone could tell you these items are not fit to be put on sale. I'm sure your wife would never buy stuff like this."

"But how do you know what a watermelon is like inside just by tapping it a few times?"

"It just takes a bit of practice, that's all."

"Yeah, I can do that too, to a certain extent," Ôtaka said. He should have kept his mouth shut.

"Then why did you put these things out on display in the first place?" Asayama asked, exasperation in his voice.

"I—" Ôtaka started to reply, but soon ran out of words.

Kameyama reacted to his discomfort with another cackle of laughter. "Now I don't want to start any trouble. And you can't really blame all this on poor Ôtaka here. You won't get rid of the problem unless the whole management team agrees that the company will never sell anything but the freshest produce. Until the fresh produce chief and his bosses, the store manager or whoever it may be, are united behind that aim, the problem will never go away. The same applies for most of the other problems you might face: running out of stock or over-ordering, for example."

Kameyama looked around the store again. "Speaking of which, I didn't notice many items that were out of stock."

"Finally, you've found something good to say about us!" Asayama said, with a look of real relief on his face. But the moment didn't last long. Kameyama turned aside and spoke to him quietly in a voice only he could hear.

"Actually, it's nothing to be so pleased about. In fact, it's a major problem."

"What? Not running out of stock? Why?"

"I'll explain later."

Kameyama had one more observation to make before they left the fresh produce area. "This is no good. You'll never get anywhere while this is going on." He pointed at the discount corner that had recently been such a talking point at the store. On display at the moment were reduced bundles of spinach for ten yen each, and packets containing five eggplants selling at twenty yen a bag. "Don't tell me: You figured you were just going to throw them away anyway, so you might as well put them on sale for next to nothing. Customers know they're buying damaged goods, and anything you make back on them has got to be better than nothing, right? I assume that was the thinking behind this scheme?"

"Kind of." Asayama smiled bitterly. He'd heard almost exactly the same words from Ichimura. Only that time the theory had been presented as "the fundamentals of good business."

"This is really bad," Kameyama went on. "For lots of reasons. There's no point trying to explain this kind of thing away. The ques-

86

tion is simple: Is it really acceptable for Ishiei Stores to sell such stale, poor quality produce? Never mind how low the price is. At Banrai Stores, we make it a point never to sell any produce we can't be proud of. It doesn't matter that many of our customers would probably be happy to buy it. And it doesn't matter how low we might set the price."

"That makes sense," Kôjima said with a smile.

"I'm glad you agree."

And with another gust of laughter, Kameyama made his way to the next section.

Kameyama's eagle eyes found problems everywhere. The meat department, the fish department, and the processed food department were all exposed as miserably inadequate, along with their respective work areas.

Some people might have taken this as public humiliation, but neither Asayama nor Kôjima felt real discomfort. Partly this was due to the amiable tone in which the old man delivered his pronouncements and his simple likability as a person. But more important still was the fact that every criticism he made was obviously and incontrovertibly true. Only one of the section chiefs showed any displeasure at Kameyama's appearance: Sashima, of the meat department.

When the group showed up, he gave Kameyama a reception that was almost over the top: "Welcome! I'm so grateful to you for taking the time to visit. Please feel free to let me know anything that catches your eye. I hope you'll forgive the mess. Things are usually much neater than this." The grin that filled his face while he spoke these words made his chubby cheeks even more pronounced. His voice burbled out of him like the self-satisfied chirruping of an over-plump songbird.

Kameyama wandered slowly through the work area. He hardly spoke, except to utter the same damning refrain: "This is dirty. Really dirty."

Dirty, dirty, dirty. The word was constantly on his lips. Almost every part of the work area failed Kameyama's inspection: the sales area floor, the joins between the display cabinets and the floor, the floor by the exit from the work area into the sales area, the empty display shelves. There was dust around the desks in the work area and dirt inside the refrigerators and freezers and carts. Several pieces of merchandise were covered in dust, and old labels and advertising flyers littered the shelves and aisles.

"I'm sorry," Sashima said. "One of our part-timers suddenly called in sick this morning. We haven't had time to clean up properly yet."

Kameyama didn't flatter him with a response.

"I'm sure everything will be much tidier the next time you come by."

"Don't try to tell me this is just one or two days' dirt," Kameyama said. He almost spat the words out. His voice was low and controlled, but Kôjima was startled by the anger in his tone. It wasn't so far from what was really meant: *Don't lie to me. I can't stand liars. You're a disgrace to the business.*

How much of this had been communicated to Sashima? It was hard to say, but something was getting through because his flippant attitude was no more. Offended, he fell silent. Anger and resentment at this meddling intruder welled up inside him. Sashima was not a man who could hold things in for very long, and his attitude was now one of naked hostility. There could hardly have been a more dramatic contrast with the jovial tone he had adopted just a few minutes earlier.

Kameyama tried to suggest that there was a little too much fat on his sirloin steaks. That was how they liked to do things here, Sashima responded. And when Kameyama expressed his doubts about several packets of sukiyaki beef in which old and discolored bits of chuck steak lay hidden under a thin covering of top-quality sirloin, Sashima had an excuse at the ready again.

"Ideally, we'd do things differently. But it's Mr. Asayama here you need to talk to. He's the director in charge of the department, and he's always pushing these really tight budgets on us. That makes it almost impossible for us to do things as we'd like."

"I don't remember ever forcing budget limits on you," Asayama said.

"Last month, for example. You said we needed to guarantee a gross profit of twenty percent on fresh meat, didn't you? That's what I heard from the floor manager."

"That's not the same as actually forcing it on you."

Asayama seemed unsure how much more he should say.

"You don't usually make twenty percent on meats?" Kameyama asked.

"Seventeen or eighteen percent on average."

"It's because of the beef," Sashima explained.

"Company policy is that since this is the company's flagship store, we have to have beef on sale at all times, whether it sells or not. And it has to be *wagyu*, Japanese beef, the most expensive stuff of all. That's why it doesn't sell."

"I don't remember ever saying anything of the kind," Asayama retorted.

"The order came from the top. Mr. Ichimura. Check with him if you don't believe me. But Japanese beef is not easy to move, I can tell you. I don't know how things are where your Banrai Stores are based, but around here in Sawabe, it's hopeless. We always end up with unsold beef. We have to either throw it away or end up selling it cheap. That's why profits are so low."

It was clear that Kameyama had no desire to continue the conversation. His face was serious; he was clearly pondering something privately to himself.

"Shall we move on?" Kôjima asked.

But Kameyama still had one more surprise up his sleeve.

"Would you mind showing me your refrigerators?" His attitude had changed completely. The jovial roly-poly figurine features had vanished without a trace—and so had the infectious *rat-a-tat-tat* of his laughter.

Time sped by. It was a little before two when Asayama and Kôjima led Kameyama into the restaurant next door to the center store. As they ate, Asayama and Kôjima threw out some of the questions they had jotted down during their tour.

"Your range of processed foods isn't right," Kameyama said. "You've got plenty of space to play with, so it's natural that you should want to increase the number of items on display. The problem is the way you have done it. There's no point getting carried away if all you're doing is selling a range of identical products with different names on the tin. From the customer's perspective, you haven't increased choice at all. It's meaningless."

"Makes sense," said Kôjima, remembering something he had been meaning to ask. "You stopped and said something as you were about to enter the store this morning."

"What did I say?"

"Something about a problem with how it linked up with things inside."

"Oh that? I meant the wind."

Kameyama began to explain about innovative new display cabinets for meat and fish that were set to revolutionize the industry. One of the defining issues for supermarkets in the seventies was the conversion to the new technology to make the best use of these new stand-alone refrigerated displays. The new displays used an air curtain to stop warm air getting into them. It was essential to avoid any wind blowing into the premises from outside.

If things happened the way Kameyama said they would, then it would not be long before wide-open doors like the ones at the center store would be obsolete. It all made perfect sense.

Kôjima felt his eyes opening to a new world. It was the same excitement he had felt that day at Shimo-Shinden when he had seen the regenerator (or the "freshness preserver," as Kameyama wanted them to call it) for the first time. He sometimes found himself filled with a sense of gloom about the company's future. *If we're not careful we're in danger of being left behind,* he thought. Kameyama was like a savior reaching down a hand and promising to lift the company up toward a brighter future.

"There was something I wanted to ask you," Asayama said. "About the fresh produce department. There weren't many items that were running out of stock, and you said that could turn out to be a problem, rather than a good thing?"

"Absolutely, a major problem."

"Why?"

"You allow the department chiefs to set their own retail prices, right?"

"Sure. The head office issues rough guidelines, of course, but other than that—"

"You might want to check some time. Just to see whether those guidelines are actually being followed."

"As far as I'm aware, it's been working fine. Stock purchasing is done at the head office, but with more than ten different outlets scattered over a wide sales area, it's not surprising that things vary a bit from one store to the next. The competition is different, for one thing. So sometimes a store might not be able to keep to the guidelines. But we've always regarded that as something that can't be helped."

"That's not the case, though. The reason they're not keeping to the guidelines has nothing to do with the local competition."

"What is the reason then?"

"They're using the retail price to adjust for miscalculations made buying stock."

"What do you mean?" Asayama looked at Kameyama, eyes open wide in surprise. The hand holding his coffee cup stopped suddenly in midair, inches before it got to his lips.

"This is how it works," Kameyama explained. "The department chief calls the head office and tells them how many of each item he needs to be ordered for the following day, right? The next day, the new stock is delivered to the store and goes on sale. But if the chief realizes he doesn't have enough of a certain item, he'll just raise the price, regardless of what the original purchase price was. When he raises the price, the item stops selling. If he has too much of an item, on the other hand, all he does is give it a lower price, again regardless of what the company paid for the item in the first place."

"And that's why things never run out of stock?"

"You got it," Kameyama said, a friendly smile returning to his face. "This can cause all kinds of problems. First of all, your orders are no longer accurate. Then, department chiefs start adjusting prices to make up for the inaccurate ordering, and it becomes almost impossible to put together a coherent sales strategy to appeal to your customers."

"What would happen," Kôjima asked, "if a store in that position were given instructions from the head office to increase profits? How would the section chiefs react?"

"In order to increase overall profits, the section chiefs would have no choice but to cut down on products that were harder to make a profit from. The section chief will order less and less of the item. If he thinks he can sell one hundred, he'll order eighty. And then he gives them a price high enough to make sure they won't sell out. If the retail price is set in-store, then the section chief can fix his own prices without worrying about the price originally paid by the head office or the pricing guidelines he's been given. Inevitably, the retail price will climb higher and higher.

"And what happens then? Because the price is too high, the item doesn't sell. The amount of new merchandise ordered by the section chief falls even further. And before long, sales figures start to shrink lower and lower."

"That's pretty bad," Asayama said, holding his head in his hands.

"It's not just fresh produce. The situation is the same for meat and fish too."

"Ichimura and I have told them time and time again: always look at things from the customer's point of view. Obviously we're not getting the message across," Asayama said despairingly.

"I don't think you can blame the employees," Kôjima interjected.

"I know. I'm not blaming them. If anyone, we're the ones who should take the blame. But why did things go so wrong in the first place?"

"We can talk about that later," Kameyama said. "I know you've had to face up to some pretty unpleasant facts today, Asayama-*san*. But look on the bright side. This might be just what you needed to help you figure out why your section isn't making a profit."

"You're right, of course. I can't thank you enough."

"It's been a pleasure. I'm glad you're taking it in the right spirit. From what I hear, your new clothing department is doing well. Maybe what you need to do is to treat your success there as a springboard, and use it as an opportunity to get your food sales—and particularly your fresh produce sales—firing on all cylinders as quickly as you can. It's not a bad position to be in really—I'm quite envious of you, in fact."

Kôjima expected this remark to be punctuated by another explosion of laughter, but the laughter never came.

Something's on his mind, Kôjima thought. *And I bet I know what it is: the meat department.*

Kameyama wanted to be shown around the new clothing department at the center store. Banrai Stores had branched out into clothing themselves about three years before, but things had not gone as well as they had hoped.

"I've done what I can to figure it out," Asayama said. "But selling clothes is a whole different ball game. It's nothing like selling food products at all."

"In that case, maybe we should ask Ichimura to come along; he's one of our directors," Kôjima said.

"Ichimura's away on a business trip to Gifu," Asayama said.

"Please, don't go to any trouble on my account. I probably wouldn't understand anything too technical anyway. I'd be grateful if one of you would take the time to show me around quickly, though. There are a few things I'd like to ask about sales promotions as well. Would you mind showing me around, Kôjima-*san*?"

"With pleasure," Kôjima said.

"So you won't be needing me anymore?" Asayama asked. His head was in a spin. He was suffering his first bout of what he and Kôjima would later refer to as "Kameyama shock."

"Come on, follow me," Kôjima said to Kameyama. He had a feeling there was something Kameyama wanted to discuss with him in private.

Once they were alone they made their way up to the small children's play area on the roof of the center store.

"You're still pretty young for a director, Kôjima-*san*. Are you the son of the company president?"

"Not quite. Cousins."

Briefly, Kôjima talked Kameyama through the events that had led him to switch careers and move to Ishiei Stores.

"So your position is a little different from most other directors. I'm not suggesting only owners and their relatives can be trusted, of course, but I still don't really know much about Asayama-*san*, so I thought . . ."

Kôjima waited for Kameyama to continue.

"I'm ninety-nine percent certain that what I'm about to say is right. Something is going on in the meat department—one of the employees has been embezzling. And I have a strong feeling that the central figure in the theft is the man we just met—the department chief. . . ."

A vague feeling that had been nagging at Kôjima for some time suddenly clicked into focus at Kameyama's words. Of course. It made perfect sense. But how could Kameyama have figured it out just like that?

"Several things led me to think this," Kameyama went on, leaning against the railing and marking a somber beat with his fingers. "First of all, I noticed that your *wagyu* fillets and sirloin steaks were priced unusually high. The fillets I saw today were five hundred fifty yen per hundred grams; the usual price would be about four hundred fifty yen per hundred grams. Obviously, a difference of hundred yen per hundred grams is going to dramatically reduce the amount you sell. My guess is your department chief set the prices high on purpose."

"So you think he's trying to use a high retail price to make up for mistakes with the ordering. Like what you were talking about with the fresh produce department?"

"No, I don't think that is it. It looks like the same phenomenon at first glance, but this is something quite different."

According to Kameyama, the biggest difficulty for meat retailers was how to juggle the natural imbalance of supply and demand that existed between different cuts of meat. Each of the cuts corresponded to a different part of the animal—rump, flank, rib eye, chuck, brisket, and the rest—so a fixed proportion of each cut was produced from each animal. The demand for the various cuts, however, was constantly changing, depending on the time of year, the region of the country, and market trends. When the market price of beef was high, there tended to be a surplus of the more expensive cuts. The opposite was the case when the market fell.

A constant imbalance therefore existed in the demand for various cuts of meat. For less competent butchers, this imbalance could easily become a headache and lead to all kinds of other troubles. Unsold surplus, insufficient stock, debt: in most cases these problems could be traced back to the same cause. In order to avoid this, some butchers bought their meat not as a whole carcass but in parts. This helped reduce the risks, but also meant that most of your sales advantage was lost too. "For a butcher who knows what he's doing, on the other hand, this is what makes the job interesting. And by careful planning and calculation, a good butcher is able to increase his profits considerably."

But there were also dishonest men in the business, who would twist the situation to their own advantage: unscrupulous types who would deliberately manufacture a surplus of those more expensive cuts of meat that could be easily removed from the premises and sold for personal gain.

But what made Kameyama suspect embezzlement was the way the meat was being prepared for sale. A butcher had considerable leeway when turning his meat into a product ready for sale. A cut of the knife here and there could make all of the difference in terms of price. A sirloin steak with its fatty ends trimmed, for example, was worth about 10 percent more than the cuts they had seen in the store with the fatty bits left on. With sliced meat, it was even easier. All you had to do was to add a cheaper meat into a package marked "sirloin"; and it was the simplest thing in the world to manipulate prices.

Most of the meat at the center store was fatty, low-quality meat that was being sold from a mixture of cuts. Almost certainly, this was because someone was trying to squeeze extra profit out of the cheaper cuts to cover up the fact that the high-quality stuff was somehow disappearing—by embezzlement.

"But surely there's another explanation," Kôjima argued. "Surely there must be some other reason for all this besides theft? Maybe Sashima just doesn't have the proper skills. Maybe he just needs more training on how to price his products and how to process the meat—"

"It's not out of the question. I considered that possibility myself. That's why I wanted to see inside the refrigerators. A good way to measure the standard of a butcher's processing is to look at the waste left over: the parts of the animal that are unsuitable for human consumption: fat, muscles and tendons, lymph nodes, and so on."

"They keep all that waste in the refrigerators?" Kôjima asked, realizing that he was revealing his ignorance. It was embarrassing, but he had no choice.

"There are specialist companies that come and collect the waste products. You must do the same thing at Ishiei Stores. The waste is kept in the refrigerator until someone comes to take it away."

"So when you saw the waste, what did you think?"

"There was almost nothing of commercial value mixed in with the waste. I'd say there was nothing wrong with his processing work; in fact, I'd say he's probably better than average in that respect."

"And you don't think there's any chance the problem might lie with his pricing?" Kôjima knew even as he asked the question that it was meaningless. But the last thing he wanted was to be forced to believe that an employee was stealing from the company.

"Not really. He seems to be deliberately pricing his high-quality cuts too high, but the rest of his cuts were on sale at more or less the standard prices. Like I said, the quality of the meat is low. It's too fatty and there's poor quality meat mixed in with the good stuff, but the prices are low too. In terms of price per hundred grams, most of his stuff is probably cheaper than the competition. He's taking ten percent off the value of the meat and then offering a five percent discount. It's all so neat there's hardly any way it could be happening by accident or incompetence."

Kôjima simply didn't have the knowledge to argue against Kameyama's theory. He didn't want to believe it, but it was starting to look as though he had no choice. "How is he doing it, then—assuming it is actually taking place?"

"Could be any of a number of ways, it's hard to say for sure. Sometimes the employee is in cahoots with his supplier. Then when the supplier comes to make a delivery, he has him take away the stock of high quality meat he has kept over from the previous delivery. This is more difficult if there's a rigorous system of checks in place, though it is not impossible. For a nonspecialist it's not easy to tell the various cuts apart by sight, so they might still be able to get away with it if they're lucky. But there's another, simpler way that's much harder to detect. The chief simply carries the meat out with him when he leaves at the end of the day."

"But the meat's so heavy. He couldn't carry much out like that, surely?"

"It wouldn't be as hard as you think. As you know, top-quality *wagyu* is one of the most expensive of all food products. Depending on the cut, the price can be as high as five thousand yen per kilogram. All he has to do is bring a decent-sized bag to work with him in the morning and he can carry off merchandise worth ten thousand yen at the end of the day. It would be easy enough to put a stop to this kind of thing, of course. All you have to do is carry out an inspection of employees' bags as they go home."

It was something, in fact, that Kôjima had proposed during his period of training at the center store. Ichimura had laughed. "None of our stuff is worth that much. I don't really think it's worth doing. If anyone was stealing, I think we'd find out about it pretty fast. But we've got to trust our employees, don't you think?" Kôjima had wanted to reply that checking people's bags didn't necessarily mean a lack of trust, but he held back and said nothing. He assumed it was standard operating procedure for supermarkets.

But wait—was it possible that Ichimura was caught up in this too? Sashima claimed that Ichimura had personally ordered him to have *wagyu* on sale at all times. Now it looked like something funny was going with *wagyu*. And Ichimura was the one who decided not to implement checks.

One terrible thought led to another, leading to a whole host of fantastic ideas. If Ichimura really was the ringleader of the scam, then his activities were almost certainly not restricted to the meat department at the center store. The same kind of thing was probably going on all over the company. It was unthinkable—or was it? Different scenarios raced through his mind.

"Kôjima-*san*? Are you all right?" Kameyama said, looking at him with concern.

Kôjima tried to smile, but the smile wouldn't come. "Let's move on to the clothing department. At least we're making a profit there. It might bring a change from all this gloomy talk."

But even as he said that, Kôjima felt a chill of foreboding. For if Ichimura really was involved in what was going on in the meat department, then who could say for sure that there wasn't something going on in the clothing department too?

Kameyama apparently had his suspicions too.

He hardly said a word as Kôjima showed him around the sales areas and storerooms that took up the second and third floors of the store. He took in everything around him seriously, occasionally bending forward to take a closer look at something that caught his interest.

Employees bowed and nodded silent greetings as they passed, a little anxious at the sight of this unexpected visitor.

"Do you mind if I have a look in a few of those?" Kameyama asked suddenly. He and Kôjima were in storage area on the second floor, which was used as a kind of backstage area for the clothing department. There were shelves, a desk, mannequins, old display racks, and empty cardboard boxes. Kameyama was pointing to a shelf piled high with boxes.

"Of course. Let me help," Kôjima said, bringing down several large white cardboard boxes.

They were full of women's clothes: blouses, skirts, cardigans, and dresses. Kameyama picked up several pieces, looking at them carefully before folding them neatly and returning them back to their boxes. There was a long silence.

Finally, Kameyama spoke. "This could be worse than I thought," he said quietly in a low, flat voice. "These are winter clothes. Stock left over from last season. Or even farther back. It's at least two years since turtlenecks like this were in fashion."

Kameyama didn't have to spell things out; Kôjima knew instantly what he was thinking.

"How many of these are there?" Kameyama asked.

Kôjima did a quick count. "I'd say at least a hundred." But almost immediately Kôjima realized that the true number could easily be twice that. There were more boxes piled up to the ceiling along the corridor that led to the machine room.

"And how many pieces are in each box?"

Kôjima randomly chose a box to open. Skirts. Printed miniskirts in bold colors, and beneath them long, pleated skirts that seemed a bit out of fashion. Altogether, he figured there were about a hundred pieces of clothing in the box, price tags still attached. Average cost: two thousand yen.

He did the math. Each box of merchandise was worth roughly two hundred thousand yen. Multiply that by two hundred boxes. It was forty million yen! Forty million yen of bad stock!

How could that be? Maybe the other boxes had less valuable merchandise. Kôjima opened another box, hoping against hope. Formal dresses. The price tag on the first dress read "17,800 yen." Kôjima felt his head start to spin. He sent for Manabe, the store manager, who arrived on the scene a few minutes later.

"Unfortunately, Sugai, the head of clothing, has his day off today," he said stiffly. "I don't know very much about this department, but I'll answer any question I can."

"Have you ever looked inside these boxes?" Kôjima asked.

"No."

"No?" Kôjima felt the wind go out of his sails.

There really wasn't any reason why the store manager should know about something like this. The way things were run at Ishiei Stores, each floor manager and department chief was pretty much autonomous within his area of responsibility. The store manager didn't normally pry too much into the details of what went on in their departments.

"We'll have to talk with Sugai when he gets back then," Kôjima said. "But since you're here, could you take a look at what's in these boxes?"

"OK. It's women's clothes. Is there some kind of—"

"Yes, it's all bad stock. Look at it—all leftover merchandise without any sales value whatsoever."

"But these are all winter clothes. They're just in storage for the summer. We'll put them out on the floor next winter."

"That doesn't sound right to me," Kameyama interrupted. "These clothes are out of fashion. And they're limited to certain sizes and colors. The market for this merchandise is past, whatever season you try selling them in."

"I see. I'll talk to Sugai about it as soon as he gets in tomorrow."

"No, that's all right," Kôjima said. "I'll speak to Sugai myself."

"As you like," Manabe said, a look of worry crossing his young face.

"I don't know how to thank you," Kôjima said, lowering his head in a formal bow. "I feel as though the scales have fallen from my eyes."

"Not at all," Kameyama replied, the grave expression on his face unbroken. "I'm afraid I've had to say all kinds of things I would rather have left unspoken. And I've probably shown you things you would have been better off not knowing." For a few moments, Kameyama fell silent as he searched for the right words. "To tell you the truth, I think the company has serious problems. And I'm afraid it might be up to you to solve them."

"If I can . . . ," Kôjima said.

"If there's anything I can help you with, please let me know. I'll be happy to do whatever I can to help."

"Thank you." Kôjima bowed his head low again.

A trace of a smile broke through the gloom on Kameyama's face. "It's not going to be easy," he said.

Even after he was gone, his parting words lingered heavily in Kôjima's heart.

"It must be some kind of mistake," said Ishikari Seijirô as Kôjima got to the end of his report.

Kôjima had decided to pass on the discoveries that had come to light following Kameyama's visit: the suspicious goings-on in the meat section and the bad stock in the clothing department. He had considered going straight to the company president, Ishikari Eitarô. After all, embezzlement and bad stock were probably the two things any company owner feared most. But in the end he had decided that for now, it could wait.

For one thing, Kôjima had no idea how Ishikari Eitarô would react. The company president was a difficult man to understand. When it came down to it, Kôjima didn't know him very well at all. They were cousins, of course, and had lived together in Nagano for a while during the war—in this respect, his relationship with Eitarô was just the same as his relationship with his younger brother Seijirô. But there was a big age difference between them. Kôjima had been a child at the time, and Eitarô was already practically an adult.

But there was more to it than that. Eitarô was a typical business-man: affable, respectful, and optimistic. He liked to talk, but his con-versation rarely seemed to touch on anything meaningful or profound. Nothing he spoke of ever showed evidence of special knowledge or cultural refinement. The man was clearly no fool. Somewhere within him lurked the talent and drive that had enabled him to build a pros-perous wholesale company amid the wreckage and chaos of the post-war years. Yet, to Kôjima, his cousin Eitarô was a mystery.

Kôjima opted to go to Ishikari Seijirô instead.

"It's a mistake. It's got to be a mistake," Seijirô said, a friendly, intelli-gent smile on his face. It was a smile Kôjima remembered from the time they were children. "Who is this Kameyama person anyway, Ryô-suke? What do we really know about him?"

Kôjima explained the sequence of events that had persuaded him to invite Kameyama to visit the company.

"So he's running a rival business? Even if we're not in direct compe-tition right now, we could be at any moment. Why would one of our competitors want to tell us the truth?"

"But everything he said makes perfect sense."

"Does it? How can you really be so sure? You . . ."

Ishikari did not say what he was on the verge of saying, but Kôjima knew what he meant: *You know nothing about the supermarket business. How would you know whether what he said made any sense or not?*

"But the prices we're charging for the best cuts are way too high, and there is poor quality meat mixed in with the sukiyaki beef. Add to this the fact that we're not making anything like the profit we ought to be making, and it's hard to avoid the conclusion that someone is mak-ing things disappear."

"What do you mean by 'the profit we ought to be making'? How much do you think we should expect to make?"

"Shouldn't we be able to make at least twenty percent?"

"And this is according to Professor Kameyama?"

"Yes."

Ishikari smiled. "I've got an idea. For a few moments, why don't we stop indiscriminately believing everything this great expert of yours says. There's more than one side to everything, you know."

"I'm not being one-sided. It's just—"

"It's perfectly respectable to mix several cuts of meat together, especially with the thin slices you use for sukiyaki. It's not cheating at all. It helps give the meat the proper flavor. Some thin slices of lean topside mixed in with some of the fattier skirt or flank steaks create the balance of flavors the customer wants. A Japanese dish like sukiyaki is different from Western dishes, where the different cuts tend to be prepared separately. 'Mixed cuts,' they call it. It's a common term."

"All right," Kôjima said. "I admit I haven't checked all the facts yet. But I wanted to let you know what was happening as soon as possible. I'll try to find out exactly what's going on."

"Fine. But really, Ryôsuke, it might be a good idea if you stopped suspecting people without any evidence."

"You're right."

Kôjima gave the reply he knew his cousin was expecting. But in fact, he had been preoccupied since halfway through the conversation. Také had come to mind. Také, who had been working in the meat department at the center store back in April when Kôjima was doing his training there, and was then suddenly transferred to the development department in the head office. "They gave me the sack" was how Také explained it, trying to make it sound like a joke, although he could not entirely mask his disappointment.

Maybe Také knows something, Kôjima thought. Maybe that's why he was moved from the meat department. Maybe someone had him transferred. Someone in a position of authority, with the power to shift employees from one department to another on command. That someone being . . .

Ichimura.

•   •   •

"Is that all, Ryôsuke?" Ishikari asked, preparing to stand.

"No, there's one other thing. I'd like you to have a look at the stock in the clothing department."

"What for?"

"I want to confirm whether what's in the boxes really is bad stock."

"You should have Ichimura take a look at it. He knows more about that merchandise than I do." Ishikari picked up the telephone on his desk.

"Wait a minute," Kôjima stopped him. "Perhaps it'd be better if we didn't tell Ichimura about this just yet."

"What do you mean?"

"I know you'll probably tell me not to be so suspicious again, but . . . Well, even if there is just a miniscule chance that it might be true, maybe we should just assume the worst—"

"Do you really mean to suggest, Kôjima, that one of our top directors knows all about this? That for some reason he has been turning a blind eye to embezzlement and bad stock? Or do you think he's the central figure behind it all?"

Ishikari stood up brusquely from his chair, a look of shock on his face, as if stunned by a sudden earth tremor. Neither he nor Kôjima noticed that he had referred to Kôjima by his family name.

"This is not a joke," Ishikari said, quietly but forcefully. Deep wrinkles appeared on his brow. He shook his head from side to side, like a superstitious person who has heard a taboo word. He stepped away from his desk and walked over to the leather furniture suite he used to receive visitors.

What was he going to do now? It took a few moments for Kôjima to realize that Ishikari had gone to fetch a cigarette. This came as a surprise: so far as he knew, Ishikari didn't smoke. Ishikari sat down in the leather chair and brought the cigarette to his lips. He lit it with the crystal lighter and gestured for Kôjima to come sit opposite him.

"Listen, Ryôsuke," Ishikari began, returning to the more familiar form of address and looking Kôjima directly in the eyes. "The world we live in is made up of relationships between people. Relationships based on trust. Once you start doubting people there's no end to it. It's not easy to put your trust in someone. You have to learn how to trust them, and how far to . . . Of course, only a fool would trust everybody. But not to trust anyone at all would be more stupid. Maybe you've become suspicious of people after your years working in a bank. Maybe in that world it makes sense to assume people are guilty until proved innocent. But a supermarket is the exact opposite of a bank in that respect. Our business depends on trusting other people. How could it be otherwise? It's a self-service store."

Kôjima felt like screaming. That wasn't how it was at all. Ishikari was blind to what was happening. How can he resolve a problem if he can't even see it? But it was on this man's invitation that Kôjima had given up his job at the bank and entered the unknown world of supermarket trading. He had trusted him enough to accept his invitation and switch careers. And he had no one else he could rely on now.

He knew what he would have said in this situation if he still worked at the bank. *I have made my report. It's up to you to decide what happens next.* Or maybe he would have responded with another question of his own. *What will you do if Ichimura is proved to be involved?*

But he wasn't at the bank. And the situation was not going to be resolved if he backed down or if he confronted his cousin further.

"Grant me one favor at least," Kôjima said forthrightly. "Don't mention any of this to Ichimura yet."

"All right. I won't mention it to Ichimura yet." He stubbed out his cigarette and immediately lit another.

"If we're going to tell anyone about this, I think it should be your brother."

"Are you out of your mind?" Ishikari almost never raised his voice, but he was practically shouting now. "I could never go to my brother with something like this. Not if my life depended on it. If he found out, he'd . . ."

He'd what? Kôjima never found out because Ishikari never finished his sentence.

"Let's give it a while and wait till we have a clear idea of what is really happening. We can take it to Eitarô if and when it becomes absolutely necessary," Ishikari said, then slumped back in his chair, a look of exhaustion on his face. His eyes flitted aimlessly about the room.

"Will you at least come with me to the storeroom?" Kôjima asked.

"When?"

"Right now."

"That I can't do," Ishikari said. He looked at the clock and stood up.

"I've got to run. There's a Rotary Club meeting today. I'd forgotten all about it."

"How about first thing tomorrow morning, then? Please."

Ishikari gave him a noncommittal nod, and got ready to leave.

FIVE

MALICE

"Ah, Kuro-*chan,* perfect timing. We need the benefit of your expertise."

Horiguchi Gen of the sales and promotions department was addressing Kuroba Motoko, who had wandered over on one of her excursions from the development department. It was one of Horiguchi's habits to refer to all subordinates with the diminutive *chan* suffix. From anyone else, this might have sounded disrespectful, but Horiguchi had an innocence that allowed him to get away with it.

"Expertise? Take as much as you want. I've got so much I hardly know what to do with it," Motoko replied cheerfully.

It was no coincidence that Motoko happened to turn up at this exact moment. The head office wasn't particularly big, and Motoko spent much of her time drifting from one department to another in search of gossip. When she overheard the boisterous conversation and laughter coming from the far corner of the sales department, she was powerless to resist the temptation to find what was going on.

"Suppose there was a single guy you'd never really been interested in," Horiguchi began.

"Impossible. If he was single, I wouldn't care who he was."

The men around her burst out laughing; she had beaten them to the punch with a joke at her own expense.

"It's a hypothetical question. Imagine that, just once, such a man did exist."

"All right, hypothetically speaking . . ."

"And imagine that he's in love with you."

"I like the way this is going."

"What we want to know is this: What should he do to get your attention?"

"What—? That's it? But that's so easy." Nevertheless, she had to think it over for a few moments before she gave her answer. "Let's get the least effective methods out the way first," she said.

"This should be good," someone shouted.

"The most annoying thing would be if he came up to me one day and said, *I know you don't get asked out on dates much, but I don't mind going out with you if you want.*"

Everyone laughed.

"And forget any long love letters."

"Why's that?" Horiguchi asked.

" 'Cause she can't read," someone shouted. Again, everyone laughed.

"Hey, that's not fair. I have two years of college, you know."

"I had no idea you were so highly qualified."

"Obviously if a love letter came from a guy I was interested in I'd read every word a hundred times. I'd sleep with it under my pillow."

"Wow."

"But if it was from someone I wasn't interested in, I probably wouldn't even look at it."

"So what should he do then?" Horiguchi asked. He seemed to be taking this quite seriously.

"Probably the direct approach. He should ask me out for a drink or dinner. I wouldn't want him to come on too strong. The dinner idea should come up naturally in conversation. Then once we're out on a date he has the perfect opportunity to show me that he's interested. I'd notice that, right? And then I might start to think, well, I've always thought this guy was a bit of a loser, but if he's got enough sense to be interested in me then maybe he's brighter than I thought."

Several men laughed out loud.

"But what is this anyway? This has nothing to do with work."

"It has everything to do with work," Horiguchi explained.

The buyers for the various departments had gathered in the sales and promotions department to discuss the flyers announcing the opening of the new Shimo-Shinden store at the end of September. They had assumed they would run the same kind of campaign they had used for every other store opening. But at a meeting a week ago, Kôjima had given them some surprising new instructions.

"This opening is going to be different from all the others," he said. "Until recently, this store was a branch of the Ogawa chain. And as those of you who saw it know already, standards were pretty low. The facilities were fine—outstanding, even—but the produce was pretty much just allowed to rot on the shelves. The place was filthy. And the staff was rude and lazy."

"You mean it was even worse than one of ours?"

"Very funny. Look, we have plenty of room for improvement ourselves. But compared to Ogawa Supermarkets we're superstars. Our stores are much, much better in every respect." Kôjima was talking louder than usual. "That's the thing. Every time people walk past that store, they are automatically going to be reminded of the terrible produce and the shoddy service they got at Ogawa Supermarkets. A lot of them won't even notice that the store is under new management or that everything on the shelves and all the people working there are different too. On a subconscious level, they're going to remember the bad taste in their mouth."

"Actually," Horiguchi said, "I've heard we're going to be taking on quite a few of the part-time Ogawa staff."

"That just makes it even more important. Ogawa Supermarkets lives on in the memories of our potential customers. We've got to put an end to that. And we need to do it in time for the opening. Big discounts and special offers won't be enough. No doubt, Ogawa Supermarkets used to offer plenty of discounts too. We need something else—something that will get the message across loud and clear, that the supermarket is under new management, and that from this day forward everything at the store is going to be completely different."

"You mean having this in the flyers?"

"Not just flyers. Everything. I want you to think about all the things we can offer our customers."

The instructions were simple enough, but the assignment was turning out to be more difficult than they had expected. An initial brainstorming session had turned up a few potential slogans, but nothing that really seemed to fit.

Changing for the better.

Greetings from a supermarket reborn!

Yesterday's store no more.

But things soon spiraled out of control, and before long the group was producing phrases that no one could really make any sense of.

Let us make it up to you.

Soon to rise on this site: the customer's friend, Ishiei Stores!

"Why the hell should we be apologizing for another company's mistakes?" Horiguchi had said, irritated and frustrated. "We need to get back to basics, to first principles." And it was at this point that Motoko appeared.

She had a quick mind, and understood everything as soon as the story was explained to her. "The straightforward approach is best," she said. "Tell it simply, and then show results, consistently. That's the only thing that's going to change the way they think. It might seem a slow way of doing it, but it will turn out to be the quickest in the end."

"Hey, that's good," Horiguchi said, genuinely impressed. "Strange that such a quick-witted woman can't find a boyfriend," he muttered.

"What did you say, you fool?" Motoko mugged, pretending anger.

Everyone burst out laughing again.

Horiguchi was enjoying himself, working under Kôjima for the last three months.

Odagiri, the previous head of sales and promotions, was in his early forties. He was a smooth talker with an urbane air. He impressed people with his energy and attention to detail. But after working under him for several years, Horiguchi knew what an empty suit the guy was. Sure, he was attentive to detail—to the point of pettiness. He would obsess about the tiniest details, sticking to the rules, observing the formalities. His prime motivation was to avoid trouble at any cost. There was little evidence that he ever considered what was good for the company.

Suppose one of his subordinates made a mistake, for Odagiri the important question was not how the mistake might cost the company or how it might be avoided in the future. The question was how the lapse should be dealt with in disciplinary terms. He liked to claim that "everything that goes on in a company should be judged on its results." As far as Horiguchi could see, even this attitude came from Odagiri's all-consuming self-interest rather than from any noble business philosophy.

Horiguchi was starting to feel his passion for his work fading when Kôjima took over and Odagiri was made director of groceries. What a difference he made. Kôjima exuded an air of calm authority. Whenever he couldn't understand the workings of something, he would mutter reproachfully under his breath, "Wow, what a mess I've made of this." Somehow, because he stated it out loud, the remark didn't make him look weak at all. Generally speaking, he was a generous and laid-back character—but when he needed to be tough, boy, he could be.

Not long after Kôjima was put in charge of sales and promotions, Horiguchi committed a major gaffe.

He was proofing the flyers for the next day, and for some reason the price of eggs—the special promotion of the stores—was printed as "28 yen" instead of "88 yen." He had read through the material as carefully as always, but somehow he had missed the typo in the big numerals at the bottom of the ad.

Specials on eggs were one of the most powerful marketing tools in their armory. Sometimes eggs were offered at less than cost. When this happened, there was a risk that restaurateurs and people from rival stores would buy them up in bulk. For this reason all ads were printed with the words ONE PACK PER CUSTOMER. OFFER APPLIES TO FIRST 1,000 CUSTOMERS ONLY. The same restrictions were printed on this day's ads too, but because the center store was so large, the sale price was guaranteed to the first two thousand customers. Yet, even with these safeguards in place, an inadvertent drop in price from eighty-eight to twenty-eight yen per pack of eggs meant a huge shortfall.

It was Kôjima who discovered the mistake. He had just arrived at work and was reviewing the day's leaflets. "Hey, Horiguchi," he called out, "are eggs really that cheap?" It was typical of Kôjima to put the question so delicately. But pretty soon, all hell broke loose.

Horiguchi was mortified. "I'm sorry," he said, bowing. "It is my fault."

Kôjima replied with another question: "Even at eighty-eight yen per pack, do they sell well?"

"Sure. That's already fifty yen cheaper than the usual price."

"How long does stock normally last when we're selling one thousand packs at eighty-eight yen each?"

"In some stores, right up until closing time, but in others we run out by early afternoon."

"Hmm. That's not good . . . ," Kôjima said, losing himself in thought.

"I'm so sorry," Horiguchi said again. "I have no excuse, and I've cost the company six hundred and sixty thousand yen."

"What will happen when people find out eggs are on sale at twenty-eight yen per pack?" Again, Kôjima responded to Horiguchi's apology with a question of his own.

"There'll be long lines outside the store before the doors open."

Kôjima's eyes looked ready to pop.

"Even at eighty-eight yen there are usually at least a dozen people outside at opening time."

"That's terrible. So at twenty-eight yen, there's a good chance some stores will sell out during the morning?"

"More likely, we'll be sold out everywhere by lunchtime."

"All right. Come with me." Kôjima stood up and led Horiguchi to Odagiri's desk. Odagiri greeted the two men warily. The tension they had brought with them was palpable.

Kôjima explained what had happened, and apologized on behalf of the sales and promotions department. "I'll be responsible for explaining everything to Ishikari later," he continued, "but for now I want you to call our egg suppliers and ask them to deliver twice the number we normally put on special to each of our stores. These prices are going to bring the crowds flocking to us, and we need to be prepared."

"What?" Odagiri stood up, surprised.

Horiguchi likewise found himself struggling to make sense of Kôjima's request. If they did what he was asking them to do, they'd only increase the company's losses.

"Imagine how it would look if we ran out of eggs before lunch!" Kôjima exclaimed. "Our customers' faith in us would be shattered! We have to avoid that at all costs."

"I understand how you feel," Odagiri said. "You're young. You've only just started your new job. Of course you're shocked and upset by what's happened. But we mustn't panic."

"You have any better ideas?"

"Plenty. We don't have to do anything. We leave things the way they are. So the item on special offer goes out of stock. Whether it happens at five in the afternoon or eleven in the morning doesn't make much difference—it comes to the same thing in the end. People will notice, but it won't be the end of the world. We've said it was limited to a thousand customers, two thousand at the center store. That's good enough."

"Is there another way we can deal with it?"

"Let me see," said Odagiri, frowning. "We could just tell the truth and apologize. We could include an apology and explanation of what happened on the POP ads: *Owing to a misprint the special price for a pack of eggs was written as twenty-eight yen. In fact, the correct price is eighty-eight yen per pack.*"

Kôjima's cheeks flushed and his eyes narrowed. Anger was seething inside him; he tried to keep it under control. "I can't approve either of those suggestions."

"But we'll lose a fortune if we double our order and sell them at twenty-eight yen each," Horiguchi said.

"I know. More than three and a half million yen altogether," Kôjima said.

"What—?" Horiguchi was shocked to hear the full extent of the damage.

"We are a business, Kôjima-*san*," Odagiri interjected, "not a charitable organization."

"I'm sorry," Kôjima took the lead in apologizing. "This has all been brought about by our mistake." Horiguchi bowed humbly at his side. "We'll take full responsibility for what has happened. I'll speak to Ishikari and Ichimura. But for now, please call the suppliers and put in an extra order."

"I'll do it if you insist. But we're probably wasting our time requesting an additional order for delivery today." Odagiri's hand reached for the phone, but stopped midway. "That's funny," he said. "The flyers were delivered to stores yesterday morning. Why hasn't anybody called us about the misprint?"

"That does seem strange, now that you mention it," Horiguchi said.

"Wednesday is my day off, so I wasn't in yesterday. Maybe people were trying to call while I wasn't here," Odagiri said, picking up the phone to call the center store.

Nishida, the grocery department chief, answered. "The eggs? Yeah, I thought the price was too low to be true, so I called Yamaguchi. But he's away on his honeymoon. I'd forgotten completely. I even went to the wedding reception the day before yesterday. Everyone was laughing, saying Yamaguchi must have put the eggs on super-special to celebrate his wedding. Anyway, there it was in black and white on the flyers, so we figured it had to be true. And it's sure gotten a response. There's still a half hour before opening, and people are lining up outside."

Odagiri hung up and reported what he'd learned to Kôjima.

It was nine twenty-five.

"Odagiri-*san*, we really must ask the suppliers to do what they can," Kôjima said urgently.

Odagiri picked up the phone again. He spoke into the receiver and then listened silently to the reply. Kôjima stood by grimly, saying nothing, awaiting the verdict. Horiguchi bowed low before him in apology. "I'm sorry," he said. "This is all due to my carelessness."

Finally, Odagiri put down the receiver. "I told you it wouldn't be easy. I've arranged to have another four thousand packs delivered to the center store, but that was all they could provide."

"Thank you. We'll have to make do with that." Kôjima said, pondering their options. "Do you have any ideas, Horiguchi?"

"How about vouchers?"

"How do you mean?"

"We can issue a voucher to anyone who wanted to buy eggs today. The vouchers are redeemable for the rest of the week, allowing customers to buy eggs at the special price of twenty-eight yen per pack."

"That's not a bad idea. At least that would stop the customers running riot if we run out early. But where are we going to get the vouchers printed in time?"

"That's one thing we don't have to worry about," Horiguchi said, sounding a lot more confident now. "We have a supply in the storeroom."

Kôjima examined the vouchers and immediately gave instructions for them to be distributed to all the company's outlets. He would deal with the center store himself.

Before long the entire staff of the sales and promotions department, a grand total of four people, set out for the stores with the vouchers. They didn't have the personnel to get the job done on their own, so they borrowed staff from the groceries department and the general affairs division.

As he was leaving, Kôjima spoke to Horiguchi: "I want you to take these vouchers and stay at the Ikenoshima store the whole day. Hand them out to the customers personally. You may run out of vouchers after a while. If that happens, I want you to apologize personally to every customer who comes in to buy eggs."

Horiguchi bowed deeply.

"I'll be at the center store till closing time," Kôjima went on. "If anything comes up, you can reach me there." He raised his right hand

and sent Horiguchi on his way, like a college student wishing his friend good luck.

Horiguchi spent the rest of the day at the Ikenoshima store, much of it with his head bowed low.

The store was packed with people. Whole families were there together, immune to any attempts to corral or control them as they thronged in front of the checkouts, each person excitedly clutching a carton of eggs. Endless lines of expectant faces waited in front of the cash registers.

By eleven in the morning, all one thousand packs had been sold, and by one thirty the two thousand vouchers were all gone too.

All the store personnel could do now was to bow apologetically to angry customers and endure their sarcastic complaints.

As Horiguchi stood with his head bowed low in apology, it occurred to him that he wasn't apologizing just to the customers standing in front of him. He wasn't apologizing just to the customers who lived in the vicinity of an Ishiei Stores outlet. No, he was apologizing to every customer the company had ever had or would ever have—even in areas where the company didn't yet have a branch. "I'm sorry, I have let you down," he repeated a thousand times. Tears came to his eyes. "Forgive me, please forgive me."

"You're just a bunch of cheats and rip-off artists," a plump middle-aged woman grumbled loud enough for him to hear.

As he bowed abjectly once more, Horiguchi noticed that the store manager was standing next to him, his head bowed low too. Horiguchi turned to him and bowed. "I'm very sorry to have caused you this trouble," he said.

"Don't let it get to you too much," he said, in a rather kindly voice. "This kind of thing is always happening in our store."

And sure enough, now that he mentioned it, there was a well-rehearsed air to the way he bowed.

When Horiguchi saw Kôjima the next morning, he apologized again.

"No use crying over spilt milk," Kôjima replied. "Or broken eggs.

We can't help what's already happened. The important thing is we don't make the same mistake again."

"I'll take extra care with the proofing from now on," Horiguchi said. "I've never made a mistake like this before. I promise it won't happen again."

"Good. I'd like you to run even stricter checks from now on. We all need to pay more attention to detail. But there's something more than that—something over and above basic carefulness. What bothers me about what happened yesterday is a lack of self-confidence in way the department relates to the public."

"How do you mean?"

Horiguchi was worried. Was he now going to be branded as forever incompetent just for this one stupid mistake?

"Don't worry, I'm not talking about you," Kôjima reassured him with a smile, as though he had read his mind. "It's as much my own approach as anything. Those flyers represent a kind of formal offer from Ishiei Stores to our customers. If the other party accepts the offer, then the company has to stake its reputation on fulfilling the terms of the agreement. It's a fully binding offer. Those flyers are important contracts for us. And yet not only did the head of the department not sign them before they were issued—he didn't even look them over! That's what I'm talking about. Do you see what I mean?"

"I think so."

"This might sound a bit extreme, but from now on I want to personally sign every single flyer we put out."

"Huh?" Horiguchi was staggered. He had never seen a personally signed supermarket flyer in his life. He had never even heard of such a thing.

Kôjima laughed at the boggle-eyed effect his suggestion had had. "We could print a few words in the corner of every leaflet. *Please address any questions or concerns about this leaflet to Kôjima Ryôsuke, Head of Sales and Promotions, Ishiei Stores.* I would add my signature to the bottom of every leaflet as the final stage in the printing process. That would give me an opportunity to look over the flyers at the same time. I would try to examine them from the point of view of our keenest-eyed customer. I would personally guarantee the quality of the products named on the leaflets, and make sure that the words we printed on them were suitable. I would treat them as seriously as if I had spoken them with my own lips."

"I understand what you're trying to do, but I think it's impossible," Horiguchi said. "Of course, we can arrange for you to check the flyers during the printing process. But there is no way you can guarantee the quality of the products, or stand by the words printed on them as though you had spoken them yourself."

"Why not?"

"Because we're not the ones who choose the products. We can only put on offer what the merchandise department sends us. And sometimes some of the things they send us are . . . well, not exactly perfect. We do what we can with what we get.

"And there's no way you could take responsibility for all the copy printed on the leaflets either. There are so many of them, for one thing, and each department makes its own. Even the advertising copy sent out by the manufacturers contains things that are not one hundred percent reliable. It would be impossible for you to check all the slogans and hype against the quality of the merchandise. All we can do is make sure we print the text without any typos or omissions."

"Look," Kôjima said. There was a frightening expression on his face. "You spent all day yesterday apologizing to customers. Do you think they forgave you for your mistake?"

Horiguchi shook his head.

"That's my point. The customer is like a god. But he's a narrow-minded and unforgiving god, whose heart yearns for vengeance and retribution. He is not a forgiving god. And you can be absolutely sure that he doesn't give a damn about the internal politics of the Ishiei Stores." Kôjima spoke calmly and quietly. "It came to me as I stood there all day yesterday bowing. This isn't my opinion; it's fact. The sooner we accept that fact, the better. In the end, it comes down to us. We are the ones who have to take final responsibility for the flyers we print. What the merchandising department does, what the manufacturers want us to print—in the end it doesn't matter. It all comes down to us. And until we come to terms with that, we can't expect any mercy from the angry god we're trying to please. Do you understand?"

"Yes," Horiguchi said, nodding humbly. He couldn't help thinking that Kôjima had more than a touch of the strict, unforgiving god himself. But perhaps that was what Ishiei Stores had always lacked. It wasn't much fun when you were on the receiving end, but it was refreshingly straight and unambiguous.

And so it was decided that from that day on every one of the company's flyers would bear the signature of the head of the sales and promotions department. Another result of the day's events was that Horiguchi became a passionate convert to Kôjima's cause, five years after joining the company as a new university graduate.

"If you're going to have a brainstorming session, why not do it in the meeting room?"

Kôjima had arrived back at his desk in the sales and promotions department without anyone noticing. He raised his voice now in obvious annoyance. Clearly all of the shouting and laughter had disturbed him. The young employees fell into chastened silence. Everyone had forgotten that they might be disturbing others with their noise.

Horiguchi started to apologize, but caught sight of something in Kôjima's expression and said nothing more.

Motoko chose precisely this moment to tiptoe over to Kôjima's desk. Was she crazy?

"I have a favor I want to ask of you . . . ," she said haltingly.

Kôjima looked up at her without a word. It was plain that he wasn't in the best of moods.

"The members of the Kôjima Appreciation Society have a petition to make. We humbly request permission to visit you at home."

Kôjima was caught unawares. He said nothing. He looked uncomfortable.

"At the moment, the following employees are signed members of your fan club: myself, of course, as well as Misaki-*san*, and Kôda and Také from the development department."

Horiguchi couldn't believe her gall. But then he saw a spark of interest in Kôjima's eyes. What was going on? Was it mention of the good-looking Yoshiko that did it? Or Také? Or what?

"Thank you. You're very kind. If that's what you really want, I'd be happy to show you the sad reality of my lonely bachelor's existence."

"Really?" Motoko's eyes lit up.

"Let's fix a date some other time, OK? I'll call you and suggest a time."

"Fantastic. Thank you very much."

Motoko walked away glowing with contentment.

Kôjima sat quietly, his expression somber, lost in thought. He made a phone call and lost himself in thought again.

Horiguchi was concerned for him. He did not want to intrude, but Kôjima seemed sad. "Kôjima-*san*?" he said finally. "They're going to do something about that pillar."

"What's that?"

Horiguchi smiled at the open confusion on Kôjima's face. "The pillar at the new store in Shimo-Shinden. It was bent out of shape, remember?"

"Of course. And what about it?"

"Our guys looked at it, and it's not right—structurally, I mean. They said there's no way that roof should be held up by such flimsy pillars. They think probably the original construction work was shoddy and the ceiling started to buckle. So these pillars were added as a kind of stopgap, to give the roof extra support. Only one pillar is bent, but I think they're going to replace all of them with something sturdier."

"Good. I'm glad to hear it," Kôjima said, and seemed to slide back into thought.

"Is everything all right, sir?"

"What do you mean?"

"You just seem a bit down."

"Oh, it's nothing to worry about. Thanks."

"OK, sorry. Didn't mean to intrude."

"I've considered everything, and I can't think of any alternative," Kôjima began. "I'm not sure whether I should be dragging you into this, Asayama-*san*, but I don't know who else I can turn to."

"What is this about, Kôjima-*san*?" Asayama said.

"After you left the other day, Kameyama and I went to have a look around the clothing department. And the things we found out there—I haven't been able to get them out of my mind."

"Problems there too?"

"Well, not absolutely for certain, but it looks like there is bad stock—bad stock worth tens of millions of yen, just sitting in the storeroom."

"What?"

Kôjima broke it down for him, reminding him to say nothing until all was confirmed. Asayama was normally a jovial, good-natured character; it was rare to see his features clouded over the way they were now.

"That's not all. I really don't want to believe this either, but there might also be gross misconduct in the meat department. Maybe even embezzlement."

"Embezzlement?"

Kôjima proceeded to explain what he'd learned from Kameyama, and then recounted how Ishikari had reacted when he told him about it. He decided not to mention his suspicions about Ichimura.

"As far as the bad stock is concerned," Kôjima continued, "I'm going to take Ishikari to look at it tomorrow. If it really is bad stock, then we'll have to decide what to do about it."

"Will he be able to know for sure whether it is bad stock?"

"That's the big question."

"Do the people in the department know about it?"

"That's another big question. It's possible that they simply haven't noticed—as unlikely as that might sound. Or they might have been afraid to factor the unsold stock into their end-of-season accounts, so they held on to whatever they hadn't sold in the hope they could sell it the following season. And before anyone realized it, the pile of unsold stock mushroomed. That's one possible scenario."

"Yes, but only if the people in charge were really stupid."

"I know. But that way at least there wouldn't be any deliberate malice involved. The worst-case scenario is that someone has been keeping this bad stock back on purpose."

"It's hard to imagine anything like that happening without the floor manager Sugai knowing about it."

"Sugai? The pretty boy, you mean?"

"That's the one."

Kôjima's choice of words brought a faint smile to Asayama's lips, but he let it go. "Anyone else?" he asked.

"It's possible that all of the floor chiefs are in on it. That isn't to say they knew all the facts. Only the floor head and above have the power to get rid of stock and authorize discounts."

"What about the next level up—the store manager?"

"It's possible. But when I showed Manabe the bad stock, he didn't even seem to grasp what the problem was. Personally I think it's more likely that the head of clothing at the head office might know about it, even maybe someone even higher up."

"Really?"

"We can discuss this again tomorrow after Ishikari takes a look at the stock. I just needed to let you know what was going on."

"Well, I guess I'm glad you could tell me, even if it is pretty shocking news. But what about the stuff going on in the meat department?" Asayama asked. "I still can't believe it. Sashima may be a bit cheeky— insolent—but he seems to work hard, and he's funny, and everyone says he's got one of the best business brains in the whole company."

Kôjima didn't reply. Sashima had never struck him as amusing in the least. During Kôjima's training period at the center store, he and Sashima had gone out for drinks several times. There was no disputing that he was quick-witted, and he certainly had plenty to say for himself. Even so, Kôjima had never warmed to him. On the contrary, something about Sashima suggested the kind of person who would badmouth you as soon as your back was turned. Most of the staff Kôjima had met since joining the company had impressed him as honest, hardworking, and unpretentious people. Not Sashima.

"What do you think about starting checks on employees' bags?" Kôjima asked.

"We could do that, but it would only put the culprit on guard. I'd rather catch him in the act. Why don't we keep an eye on him. There's someone in my department I know I can trust. I'll tell him to watch what Sashima does every night on his way home."

Kôjima groaned. He didn't like the idea of one employee keeping an eye on another. It felt underhanded and dirty. Asayama, on the other hand, had no problem with the tactic. He'd gone from shock and helplessness upon first learning about the problems to a hunting dog that has picked up a scent. It was a sudden turnaround that surprised Kôjima.

"Of course we need to clear this up, but the worst thing we can do would be to wreck relationships and create a paranoid atmosphere in the company. Don't forget that."

What Asayama said next startled Kôjima: "Ichimura. The root of problem is Ichimura. The bad stock in the clothing department, the missing meat—I'll bet his dirty hands are pulling the strings in both places. This means war against the Ichimura faction! What we need to do is to form an anti-Ichimura alliance. Among company directors, we can count on Konno and Katsumura. Obviously, you would be head of the faction. If we band together, we can stand up to them. We have to be decisive and fight. We can beat 'em."

"What's come over you all of a sudden?"

"Listen, Kôjima-*san*, don't be naïve. There's no way the problem in the clothing department problems is going to be solved by having Ishikari go and take a look tomorrow morning. You should understand that right from the start. You mustn't expect him to resolve anything for you."

Kôjima was taken aback by Asayama's bluntness.

There was silence between the two men for a bit. Then Asayama spoke up: "This is what we'll do. Let's organize a secret meeting tomorrow night, and invite everyone we think we can rely on for support. We don't want to bump into anyone from the Ichimura faction, so let's arrange to meet somewhere in Tsunoura. This is a perfect opportunity—a chance to root out the Ichimura faction that is feeding on the company from the inside—like a parasite."

"But we don't know anything for certain yet. We don't have any proof that Ichimura is involved. We don't even have proof that anything is happening at all."

"It's beyond reasonable doubt. We've always suspected something fishy was going on—we just didn't know what it was. It's like Kitô said:

No matter how much profit we make, not one store has really gained the support of its customers. It's because of falseness in the company. And the source of that falseness is Ichimura. We should definitely invite Kitô to the meeting tomorrow, come to think of it."

"Wait a minute, Asayama-*san*, wait a minute," Kôjima said, holding his hands up in protest. "I'm not saying you're wrong. Maybe you're right. But you can't pin everything on Ichimura. And you've got to drop this idea of an anti-Ichimura faction."

"You won't last long in this company if you keep trying to be such a nice guy."

"Maybe not. But at least give me a few days. And at least give up this idea of trying to get people together tomorrow."

"All right, if that's what you want. But it will have to happen sooner or later—for the sake of the company. Don't forget that." Asayama's eyes were moist with tears.

Kôjima walked over to the telephone in the corner of the kitchen, but once again he couldn't get himself to lift the receiver.

He'd gone through the same pointless charade several times over the past hour.

The dining table seated six. But the only things on it now were the leftover dishes from the meal he'd just eaten alone. *I'll call after I've cleaned the place up*, he told himself.

He threw out the uneaten curry rice, put the lid back on the tub of pickled vegetables, and threw away his empty beer bottle. He couldn't summon the energy to wash the dishes.

Not that he was the cleanest or tidiest of men at the best of times. Newspapers and magazines were scattered on the dark blue carpet, and crumpled shirts and empty supermarket bags still lay on the floor where he'd thrown them. The furniture wore a coat of dust. The only things that were clean were the bottle of whiskey, the piano, and the stereo. You didn't need to be Sherlock Holmes to figure out how Kôjima spent his evenings.

Takako was supposed to join him in the autumn. She was pregnant with their second child, so there was a perfectly good reason why she had gone to her parents' home and left Kôjima to make the move to Sawabe on his own. But Kôjima couldn't help feeling let down.

Her morning sickness started about the time Kôjima started his new job in March—a month and a half after their big argument about his decision to change jobs. That must have been a dangerous time for Takako—a sudden shock might have caused a miscarriage. Kôjima regretted that, but Takako was still refusing to budge during the safest time of the pregnancy.

"I could come see you now, but I'd have to bring Kayoko with me, and then we'd have to go back almost immediately. And for the two of us, all that travel would be quite expensive."

This had been her response when he asked her to at least come take a look at the apartment. There was nothing more he could say. He understood her feelings perfectly well, but he wanted to hear her to say something positive: that she would come if she could. He would have felt better if she'd been desperate to come and he'd had to tell her it wasn't worth it. The result would have been the same, but he would still have felt better about it.

The truth was, he was lonely. And his loneliness was getting worse by the day. Today had been particularly bad. He was tired. He was stressed. His body felt stiff all over. He wanted to talk to someone. He wanted comfort. He wanted someone to massage away the stiffness from his body and his mind. And the only person who could do that was his wife.

Kôjima had walked over to the telephone with the intention of calling his wife and telling her how he felt. But then he worried that the sound of his wife's voice might just make him feel lonelier than ever, and he decided not to call after all. He had walked over to the phone and walked away over and over again; he was like a caged bear in a zoo.

Kôjima smiled grimly at the absurdity of his own behavior. He mixed himself a whiskey and water. He stood in front of the record cabinet and picked out a recording of Chopin nocturnes. A beautiful Japanese pianist smiled up at him from the jacket photo. Soft sweet music filled the living room. The Chopin seeped into Kôjima's weary soul and caressed his cares away.

The pianist's smile reminded him of Ishikari's secretary, Misaki

Yoshiko. A wave of embarrassment washed over him the likes of which he hadn't felt since he was a young man.

He drained his glass and closed his eyes. He wanted to sink as quickly as possible into the beautiful world of fantasy and reverie created for him by the whiskey and the music.

His body felt weak and woozy the next morning.

It was just after eleven when he walked over to the center store clothing department, Ishikari following grudgingly behind.

Kôjima passed quickly and silently through the sales area. He felt too worn out to talk to anyone. He had showered before coming in to work, but he could still smell the stink of alcohol oozing from his pores. He opened the door at the end of the sales area and entered the long storeroom he had visited with Kameyama only a few days ago.

"Good morning," Sugai said as Kôjima entered the room.

"Good morning," Kôjima replied, but the sight that greeted him in the storeroom struck him dumb. He ran his eyes along the shelves that lined the storeroom to the shelves along the walls to the shelves in the center of the room to the shelves farther back. The cardboard boxes that had been crammed to bursting in every available space were almost all gone; just a few remained. It was like a bad dream. The bad stock had vanished.

"What's wrong?" Sugai asked.

Kôjima felt dizzy, and instinctively steadied himself against a shelf.

"Is something wrong?" Sugai asked.

"This is it?" Ishikari said incredulously, waving a hand at the shelves.

"No. This isn't what I was talking about at all."

No trace of his hangover remained now. His brain was beginning to whir.

"What's wrong?" Sugai asked again.

Kôjima turned and glared stared at Sugai. "What have you done with the boxes that were on these shelves?"

"What are you talking about? Why are you shouting?"

"Answer my question: Where have you taken all the boxes that were here yesterday?"

"I don't know what you're talking about."

"Don't lie to me. You know what I'm talking about."

"What's wrong with him this morning?" Sugai asked Ishikari, like a man begging to be rescued from a lunatic.

"It's nothing, really. Mr. Kôjima just wanted me to come and have a look at the stock here."

"Please, feel free."

Kôjima ran over to the phone, preparing to call Manabe to confirm what he had seen yesterday. "I'm afraid Manabe-*san* isn't at the store today," said the voice on the other end of the phone.

"What? Is today his day off?"

"No," the woman replied. "He called to say there's been a death in the family, and he's taking a couple days off."

Weakly, Kôjima put the receiver back in place.

He felt caught in a web of conspiracy. Rage coursed through him. He heard a voice inside warning him: *Keep calm.* Unless he acted calmly and coolly, the situation would only get worse.

"I don't know what to say. Somehow, almost all the stock that was here yesterday seems to have disappeared."

"Don't be ridiculous. Surely there must be some mistake?"

"It's no mistake. I saw it with my own eyes."

"But that amount of stock couldn't just disappear overnight. It's impossible."

"I know. That's what I can't understand."

Suddenly, Ishikari burst out laughing as if the mystery had been solved. "I think I know what's happened. It's an easy mistake to make. I've had the same experience myself." Ishikari looked over at Sugai. "Is everything here the same as yesterday?"

"No," Sugai said in his usual nonchalant tone. "Not quite. I only heard about it this morning, but someone came from Arai Shôkai yesterday evening. They deal in women's wear, and they took away a load of merchandise we'd negotiated return deals for a while ago."

"How much would that have been?" Kôjima asked.

"Quite a bit. At least ten cases' worth, I'd say."

"There were far more boxes than that," Kôjima said. Suddenly, something occurred to him. "Where's the receipt for those returns?"

"The receipt? Just over here," Sugai said, walking over to retrieve it.

"I understand what's happened now, Ryôsuke," Ishikari said, a bright smile on his face. "It's easy to misjudge stock when you're new to the business. Sometimes it looks like there's more in the storeroom than you could ever cope with, while at other times you're convinced you've got the opposite problem. I was just the same when I started. I worried myself sick about it. I was convinced the store had too much old stock on its hands; I thought we were going to go bust at any moment."

Kôjima looked silently at the receipt Sugai handed to him. There was no point insisting on what he had seen. The argument would just go around in circles.

The receipt seemed to be in order. Kôjima turned it over in his hands, but his mind was somewhere else: What was the significance of this receipt? To prove that stock had been returned to the supplier the night before. A large truck would have necessary to carry away that much merchandise. Surely someone in the store would have noticed a truck that big being filled with that many boxes. So a receipt was like insurance; it was made specifically for this purpose. Kôjima was dealing with a pro.

"Who's responsible for the stock checks in this department?" Kôjima asked.

"We are," Sugai replied.

This meant that Sugai was in a position to bring merchandise in or out of the department whenever he wanted.

"Is that enough now, Ryôsuke?" Ishikari said, eager to leave. He always wanted to get these things over as quickly as possible—whether it was a meeting, a shop tour, a business negotiation. It was quite the opposite whenever the conversation was about a nonwork matter.

"Yes, thank you," Kôjima said. There was no point arguing further. He needed to think things through logically.

Apart from himself and Kameyama, only three people knew about the bad stock—Ishikari, Asayama, and Manabe the store manager. One of them had warned Sugai. It was possible that someone had overheard his conversation with Kameyama in the clothing department the other day, but he was pretty sure that nobody else had been around. And they had been speaking so quietly that even if someone had been there, they would have been hard put to pick up much of what they were saying. No, someone had leaked the news.

Asayama wouldn't do anything that would benefit the detested Ichimura faction.

Ishikari? It was quite plausible that the first thing Ishikari had done after his conversation with Kôjima was to call Ichimura. You could put a gag order on subordinates, but it was harder to keep your superiors quiet. The higher up you were in the hierarchy, the more freedom you had to act as you saw fit. Ishikari could well have decided to follow his own counsel and speak to Ichimura, who was on a business trip. But there wouldn't have been enough time for Ichimura to mobilize the whole operation.

So, most probably, it was Manabe. If Manabe got on the phone to Sugai right after talking to Kôjima and Kameyama, Sugai would have had plenty of time to arrange for a truck to come around that evening.

But it was hard to believe that Manabe was working with Sugai to keep the bad stock hidden. Everything Kôjima knew about Manabe suggested that he was honest and responsible. And the two men had been on good terms ever since they had gotten to know one another during Kôjima's time at the center store.

Even if the leak had come from Manabe, it didn't mean that he was necessarily in cahoots with Sugai. Perhaps he hadn't fully understood what Kôjima meant when he said he would deal with Sugai himself. Perhaps he had felt obliged to track Sugai down and ask him personally about the merchandise. But could it really be a coincidence that Manabe had taken two days off for a family bereavement?

Kôjima walked with a heavy step back to the head office.

"Everyone makes mistakes sometimes, Ryôsuke. Don't take it to heart," Ishikari said as he walked at his side. He sounded like a man consoling his little brother.

Kôjima was sifting through the new facts in his head: removal of the merchandise the previous night was a deliberate act, planned and executed. There was no coincidence involved. The urgency of the removal strongly suggested the merchandise was bad stock, without any commercial value. The central actors in the removal were Sugai as well as the Arai Shôkai trading company.

Kôjima's plan had been foiled, but he had gained a clearer idea of the adversary he was up against. Dealing with Ichimura was not going to be easy.

A sticky sweat oozed from his pores. It was caused by more than just the sun and the alcohol in his system.

SIX

EMERGENCY MEASURES

Ichimura appeared at Kôjima's desk the morning after the day the bad stock disappeared, a confident
grin on his pockmarked face.

"*Good mo-o-orning*," he sang. "I owe you an apology, Kôjima-*san*. Seems I caused you some trouble
while I was away."

Kôjima acted as though he didn't know what
Ichimura was talking about.

"The stock at the center store."

This took Kôjima by surprise. "How did you hear
about that?"

"Ishikari called me at my hotel the night before
last. I was out late, doing a tour of the local bars in
Gifu, but Ishikari's message said to call him when I
got in, no matter what time. So I called him at one in
the morning. He was worried sick." Ichimura perched
himself on the trash can by Kôjima's desk, the steel
canister crumpling a little under his weight. "Ishikari
was freaking out about the bad merchandise you
showed him in the clothing department, saying if it
was worth several million yen, we were going to get
killed. Pretty shocking news. So first thing yesterday
morning, I called Sugai to find out what was going
on. Turns out it was nothing to sweat over."

"What do you mean, nothing to sweat over?" Kôjima
was doing everything he could to maintain a calm
and polite surface. He wasn't going to show his cards.

"Most of the clothes you saw were returns waiting to go back to Arai Shôkai. Some were in storage for the summer and waiting to go on sale in the fall. So, no cause for concern," Ichimura said, his smile just this side of a smirk. "I checked everything out myself, and calmed Ishikari down. Everything's on the up and up, so no sweat."

"Ichimura-*san*, I'm sorry to have caused you so much inconvenience. Sounds like I've been guilty of a silly mistake," Kôjima said.

"Not at all. I'm grateful for your concern. I hope you'll continue to bring things to my attention whenever you notice something. Often that's the best way of finding new ways to improve things." Ichimura picked himself up and sauntered back to his office.

Asayama and Kôjima decamped to the reception room where they could speak privately.

There was no doubt in Asayama's mind that Ichimura had been hiding the bad stock. He wanted to put together an anti-Ichimura faction in the company to stand up to the guy.

"And what would you do with this alliance of yours?" Kôjima asked.

"For now, we could split the work between us, check out the various wholesale suppliers and monitor the calls of the Ichimura faction."

"Listen in on their conversations, you mean?"

"It sounds bad when you put it like that. But all the phones in the company are on the same line; it wouldn't be hard. Just need to stay alert."

Kôjima could say nothing. He couldn't find the words. Until a few days ago, Asayama had been a gentle, timid soul. Now he was proposing they use the office phone system to listen in on conversations, as though it were the most natural thing in the world.

Kôjima got up from his chair, not wanting to dwell on this faction business. "Manabe holds the key to all this. I'll talk to him when he gets back to work tomorrow. That should give us a better idea about what's going on."

"Kôjima-*san*," Asayama began, his tone of voice shifting. "I have great respect for you. Your intelligence, your knowledge, your openness to new ideas, and your honest, upright attitude. I know it's not polite of me to say so, but I think sometimes you're too forgiving.

You're naïve. You don't understand the way this supermarket world really works."

"What do you mean?" Kôjima could hear his voice betraying his emotions.

"I'm sorry. Perhaps I am going too far, but this is too important to be left unsaid," Asayama replied, gesturing to Kôjima to sit down. "Manabe is lying. That cockamamie story about a dead relative? It's a cover-up."

"We'll find out tomorrow. We'll have plenty of time to get tough once we have more facts. By all means, let's try and find who's responsible for manipulating things behind the scenes. But there's something else, something that we need to start on right away."

"What're you talking about?"

"The company is in a management crisis. We need to do something or we're all going to be pulled down in the swamp." Kôjima stood up slowly. "That there was a large amount of bad stock seems beyond any doubt. How much exactly we don't know, but the effort made to cover it up suggests it was plenty. Let's say tens of millions of yen. That would be equivalent to the company's operating profits for a whole year, and there's no reason to assume that the problem is limited to the center store. For all we know there could be comparable amounts of bad stock at the other stores."

"Right."

"And it's not just clothes. We could have the same problem with any other kind of nonperishable merchandise—anywhere in the sundries or durables departments, basically."

"That would be pretty bad."

"That would be a disaster."

It was possible that Ishiei Stores was already in the red. And not just in the sense that their losses were greater than their profits. In the worst-case scenario, the profits they thought they had been accumulating in recent years were fictitious too.

The majority of the company's shares were held by Ishikari Eitarô and the Ishiei Trading Company. In theory, the Ishiei Trading Company was there to provide financial support for the supermarket chain, but now that they had grown to ten stores, the offshoot was larger than the parent company. Almost certainly the Trading Company no longer had sufficient capital at its disposal to bail Ishiei Stores out if things got really bad. Although the company was not without physical collateral, the essential truth was that the bank continued to offer the company generous loans at low interest because they believed the financial reports.

"But we can't rely on bank loans for all the capital we need for the new stores. The banks are usually willing to loan about seventy percent of what can be offered as collateral. Even if we used all our land and property as collateral, it still wouldn't be enough. The company was lucky enough to acquire land at a low price several years ago, and until now the cash value of this land has been enough to secure us our loans. But that isn't going to be enough to cover this wave of expansion."

"Trust the banker to know the facts."

"The company is investing in several new stores at the moment. Five are under consideration, three of which are relatively small, more or less on the scale of the Shimo-Shinden site. But the other two are much larger—about the same size as the center store. The company doesn't have enough collateral to guarantee these new investments, and so as a kind of last resort there is talk of transferring a mortgage to cover costs."

"How do you mean?"

"It's the Tsunoura development I'm talking about. The way the system works is that the landowner provides the land and allows the building to be constructed on his land with guaranteed funds provided by the company. We're allowed to use his land as part of our collateral in order to raise funds from the bank."

"You can really do stuff like that?"

"As long as the landowner agrees, yes."

"But that would involve the landowner in a massive risk."

"As long as the company's doing well, the risk is small. But if the company went bust, the landowner would be in serious trouble too."

Asayama was no expert when it came to finance, but the significance of what Kôjima was saying was crystal clear. The bank loans and the permission to use the landowner's property as collateral both depended on the company's continuing good performance. If Ishiei Stores were no longer able to meet these requirements, everyone would be pulled under.

"At the moment we're doing everything we can to raise the extra capital on top of the transfer mortgage—leases and guarantees from Ishiei Trading and the owner, Ishikari Eitarô. But all of these things depend on good results. If we don't show good results, the next step is panic."

"Panic?"

"Panic."

The image that appeared before Asayama's eyes was creditors fleeing from the company like rats from a sinking ship. And one of the biggest rats would be Ishikari Eitarô.

"The banks will always take collateral, for sure. I know the criticism: *Banks don't trust anyone. They're only interested in protecting themselves.* But what the banks are really interested in are the business results of the company, and the character of the management. The collateral and the guarantees are really just a formality, a kind of checklist they have to go through."

Kôjima, pausing for a moment, smiled wryly at the sound of his voice. It was like a flashback to six months ago. If it hadn't been for Seijirô's job offer, he would still be at Saiwa Bank today, mouthing off about high finance from the comfort of his Osaka office.

"And that's why any downturn in the company's results would be catastrophic."

"Good grief. What are we going to do?" Asayama moaned. "That means everything's got to be kept top secret, doesn't it? It would be a disaster if the company's creditors or stockholders caught a whiff of any bad results. Any investigation into the bad stock has got to be kept absolutely secret."

"Yes, although in some circumstances it might be preferable to come clean to any creditors we can rely on to support us. But I'm getting sidetracked. I had something else in mind." Kôjima stopped pacing and looked directly at Asayama. "The really essential thing is to bring the company's performance into line with its published results. Keeping the bad stock problem secret is just a way to gain us time. Unless we can actually achieve those positive results, we won't solve any of our problems."

"You're right, of course. The only problem is, the way things are, there's no way that's going to happen in the foreseeable future."

This self-evident statement left the two men in silence.

Finally, Kôjima spoke up. "One thing we have to do, no matter how much bad stock is being covered up, is to make fresh produce profitable."

This seemed like a conundrum to Asayama—nonsense, in a way.

"Don't worry, I'm not about to start lecturing. What I'm thinking is this: if the clothing department's no good, at least we should still have the fresh food to fall back on. Ishiei Stores only has one outlet focusing on clothing and nonperishable goods—the center store. Clothing is becoming more important for two of the other stores as well, but for the other seven it only makes up ten percent of total sales. But at the moment even these stores are propped up by profits from clothing. They've somehow managed to muddle through using the profits they make from clothing and other goods to make up for the losses on fresh produce."

"I can't argue with that."

"If it turns out that the clothing department is losing money too, and the success we've been relying on is just an illusion, then this system isn't going to work for us anymore. Our only hope would be to make up for these losses by turning our fresh produce departments into profit centers."

"I know, I know. But easier said than done."

"I'm confident we can do it."

"What?" Asayama gasped, unbelieving. "What did you just say?"

"I said I'm confident we can get the fresh produce department back on track," Kôjima responded calmly. There was a smile on his face.

A mass of images whirled through Asayama's mind. The chaos of the fruit and vegetable supply markets, where outsiders were not welcome. The bullheaded fishmongers who lived in a world of their own. The smug butchers who could spot toughness in a cut of meat at a glance. Kôjima didn't know anything about these things. It didn't matter how brilliant he was.

But Kôjima continued to talk, oblivious. "I don't know anything about fresh produce, of course. I'm going to need the help of the pros like you. When I say I'm confident, I only mean I am confident I can do something if I get the help I need."

"You know I'll do whatever I can," Asayama said, half-frustrated, half-desperate.

"We'll need to get all the help we can from Kameyama. We should treat him as our mentor in this. I think we can probably learn the fundamentals of how to sell fresh produce from him. But there's something else we need as well, and maybe that's where I can help."

"What do you mean?"

"I think it might be better if I don't try to put it into words today. I need to think it over some more." Kôjima got up to leave, but stopped before he reached the door. "There's one more thing. If we're going to save the company from sinking, we need to stop the plans for the two new superstores where clothing will have to carry the bulk of the profits."

"Tsunoura and Mukoyama, you mean?"

"Right. Both of them are supposed to be about the same size as the center store. If it turns out that the clothing department isn't making any profit, then opening those two new stores could be suicide."

"But how are we going stop the plans at this late stage?"

"Who knows? We may not have a choice."

"Both sites have been formally approved by the board of directors, and even as we speak, the development department is negotiating purchase of the land."

"We'll have to think about it," Kôjima said, turning the doorknob. "The first step to do is meet with Manabe. The next step comes after that."

"This was pretty much all there was, I think."

Manabe's words left Kôjima in shock. The two of them were standing in the clothing department storeroom.

"Manabe-*san*, you can't be serious."

"Really, it doesn't seem a whole lot different from the other day," Manabe said.

"I can't believe I'm hearing you say this. The stock the other day filled these shelves from one end to the other. There was literally no space left on the shelves. And there were piles all along that corridor too."

"Really? I suppose it's possible, but then there was that return shipment to Arai Shôkai that reduced the amount of stock to more or less what we're looking at now."

"Then how can you say . . . Listen, Manabe, what's going on?" Kôjima said angrily.

Manabe's chiseled features were as expressionless as a Noh mask. He didn't turn to look at the cardboard boxes or the empty corridor. His eyes were fixed on the floor at his feet. Kôjima stared at Manabe's face, anxious not to miss the slightest flicker of emotion.

Manabe said nothing, remaining stone-faced.

"Why are you lying?"

Silence.

"Someone told you to lie to me. Who was it?"

"Nobody told me anything."

Manabe's normally powerful baritone fell weakly to the floor.

"Why are you lying like this? This is serious. The whole company could collapse if we don't find out the truth and draw up a strategy to deal with the bad stock."

"It doesn't matter what you say to me. I won't lie and say I've seen something that wasn't here." His voice was so low now that Kôjima could hardly hear him.

"Come on, let's take a little walk." Kôjima guided Manabe down the corridor. "You don't remember the boxes here—piled right up to the ceiling?"

Manabe traipsed along forlornly behind Kôjima. He raised his eyes briefly to look at where Kôjima was pointing, but lowered his gaze immediately and stared blankly down at the floor again.

"Manabe, we haven't known each other long. If someone you know better than me has asked you to lie, I can understand why you wouldn't want to let them down. But let me repeat myself. This is an extremely serious matter—far more important than your relationship with me or whoever it was who told you to lie about this. I need you to tell the truth about what we saw and to act as my witness to Ishikari. If you give a statement, Ishikari will wake up to the problem."

"I don't know what you're talking about."

Kôjima was speechless. He was tempted to ask Manabe about his two days off for a supposed death in the family. But what was the point? If Manabe was going to lie about the bad stock, he was sure to lie about that too. Kôjima walked out the storeroom feeling sick.

Out on the sales floor, clothes displays filled every available inch of space. There were racks of men's suits, each selling at around twenty thousand yen. Pricey items like this were something they'd only branched into this spring. The sales figures for clothing had been so impressive they decided to give them a try.

Beyond the suits was the men's casual wear department. Short-sleeved polo shirts hung against the wall, along with tennis and golf wear. Beyond this was the women's department.

Until a few days ago Kôjima had believed that the success of the clothing department had helped make Ishiei Stores profitable. It was a symbol of the company's growing prosperity and expansion. But the picture had changed drastically since then. Now it looked more like a pile of worthless rags—a bomb ready to go off at any moment.

"Will that be all?"

Kôjima wheeled around at the sound of Manabe's voice. He hadn't realized Manabe was still with him. "Yes, you can go now," Kôjima said. "But any time you want to talk, please let me know. Right now, I'm extremely disappointed and upset."

Manabe drew himself up straight and looked Kôjima straight in the eyes. He didn't say a word. He bowed deeply and walked away.

Downstairs, Kôjima walked through the fresh produce section, mulling over what to do next.

He bumped into Ôtaka, whose customary surliness seemed now to have turned to embarrassment. As he passed through the meat section, Kôjima thought of Také, the young man who'd been transferred to development. This led him to think of Motoko in development, who was friends with Také. That's right: he had to remember to invite the youngsters over to his apartment one night soon.

But first, Také. He needed to find out what had really happened with Také. There was the apparent embezzlement of meat, and next thing Také's sacked. Who engineered that? Disappearance of meat, the sacking of Také, now the disappearance of the bad stock. Was there any connection, any pattern, here?

Kôjima left the store and walked back to the head office, racking his brains: he could conceivably go straight to the company president Ishikari Eitarô. Who knew, he might actually do something radical to straighten out the company. But given the fact that Eitarô's heart had never been in the supermarket business in the first place, maybe he would decide to get out of the business altogether. And if he did that, where would that leave Kôjima?

Kôjima recalled Seijirô calling him into his office not long after he had finished his training at the center store. "This is Udagawa-*san*, from Toto Stores," Seijirô said, introducing him to a neatly dressed, expressionless young man in his mid-thirties.

"Pleased to meet you," Kôjima said.

"Likewise. We're always happy to have an opportunity to do business with Mr. Ishikari and his friends," Udagawa said, smiling. "I hear you've just joined the company from the Saiwa Bank?"

"That's right."

"A very daring change of career. Presumably you would have been set for life if you'd stayed there."

"That's what everyone keeps telling me, though it's not the way it seemed to me. Anyway, it wasn't a difficult decision to make. I think I was getting tired of life in such a big company."

"I know what you mean. In the past few years our company's been growing too, and somehow it's just not the same. But any successful company is going to turn into a big company eventually. I think we just have to resign ourselves to it, or we only make life more difficult for ourselves."

"You're probably right," Kôjima laughed.

He remembered the way he used to feel before hopes and good intentions were bludgeoned to the ground in the big corporation. You just had to learn to live with it, as Udagawa said. Obviously he was speaking from experience.

Udagawa's business card indicated that he was part of the planning division, and Kôjima asked him what kind of work he was involved in.

"All kinds of things. Planning . . . plotting and scheming. Call it what you like. I hardly know what I'm doing myself half the time."

Kôjima learned later from Ichimura that Udagawa was one of Toto Stores' operatives in acquisitions and mergers.

"The guy's a real pain in the ass," Ichimura said, practically spitting the words out. "He's responsible for the whole of western Tokyo and is always turning up at meetings and social events, schmoozing with the top management guys in all the small supermarket companies. He's got a huge expense account so he can hang out with the owners, takes them out to dinner, gets real buddy-buddy. Then sooner or later he'll spot his chance and try to get them to merge with Toto Stores. He's a con-man; no better than a pimp."

"So what's he doing talking to Seijirô?" Kôjima asked.

"Those guys have such a high opinion of themselves. Until a few years ago they were just another small supermarket chain like us. But then they hit it big—got lucky with their locations or something. And now they're one of the big boys, with sales in the billions of yen. As far as they're concerned, it's all about fighting for supremacy with the other chains. And the easiest way to win the game is to snap up as many other companies as they can. They'll do anything to achieve that end. One day they'll suddenly announce they're going to set up a new store right next to your most profitable outlet. Don't like the idea? Then how about a little merger?"

"But that's extortion."

"Precisely. But it works. Another chain surrendered just the other day."

"The law of the jungle: the weak get eaten by the strong."

"It's worse than that. You don't have to be weak to be at risk. They take you and make you weak first, then snap you up. It's more like a shark, gobbling up anything that crosses its path."

"And we could end up as prey too, if we're not careful."

"Right. In fact, it's a safe bet that Udagawa or some other parasite has his eye on us already."

In these circumstances, Kôjima now reasoned, it would be disaster if the president of the company lost his stomach for the business. So he could forget about going to Eitarô. But what other options did he have?

We need to form an anti-Ichimura faction. That was Asayama's idea of a solution.

It was no solution.

It was one of the reasons he had wanted to get out of the bank business. He'd barely gotten his foot on the first rung of the management ladder, and already some of his coworkers could talk about little else. It was like something out of a cheap business novel. And yet here he was, struggling against the temptation to form a faction himself. He was starting to feel that his problems would never be resolved unless he had a group to help and support him. Should he take Asayama's advice and try to unite people under his own leadership?

Manabe's denial forced Kôjima into a decision. He knew now that there was no room for optimism. Simply pointing out the company's problems was not going to be enough. Ishiei Stores wasn't equipped, or prepared, to deal with problems of this kind.

Kôjima was going to have to do it himself.

It was dangerous work. If he failed, he would be thrown out of the company, and if that happened he would have a wound that might never heal. Why take such an absurd risk?

He asked himself the same question over and over: Why should he be the one to risk everything to save the company? One alternative was to do nothing and just let things take their course. All he had to do was sit it out and devote himself to his job.

Even with several tens of millions of yen of bad stock on its hands, the company probably wouldn't collapse. So long as the company's creditors didn't find out the truth, there would be no problem. Even if the company was in the red and making cumulative losses, until it reached a critical level a supermarket could always make ends meet somehow. It was only when these measures stopped working that the company would go bust.

In a normal business it was difficult enough to balance the cash flow even when times were good. In a few cases companies had gone bust even while they were still technically in the black. But that could never happen to a supermarket.

A supermarket paid its suppliers six weeks after delivery. The merchandise itself was usually sold within a month after the supermarket received it from the supplier. This gave the supermarket a float of two weeks' worth of sales. On top of this, there was the amortized value of the company's real estate holdings—the buildings themselves and the equipment within them. This meant that even if a supermarket was taking a loss, it still had substantial capital in reserve. In other words, a supermarket would not go bust as long as its cumulative losses did not come to more than half a month's sales plus the amortized value of its real estate holdings.

Of course, this wasn't taking the burden of any new investments into account. But the essential point didn't change, so long as funds were raised separately for any new investments. Coming from a banking background, Kôjima had been struck by the way this system of trading based on daily sales worked. It was one of the advantages of receiving cash in hand on a daily basis.

But the system was open to abuse.

Even if a company accumulated unsustainable cumulative losses (the equivalent of half a month's sales plus alpha—or about 5 percent of the company's annual turnover), the fact that they were taking in money every day meant that the company would have no immediate lack of funds, and might appear from the outside to be in no trouble at all. In this respect, the situation was quite different from that facing other kinds of business, such as producers or wholesalers, for whom any operating losses automatically led to a commensurate shortage of funds.

If the management wasn't afraid of taking risks, all it took was a few simple manipulations of the figures on the balance sheets and they would be able to raise loans and even carry out aggressive expansion plans without the slightest protest from the company's creditors, even while making cumulative losses of anything up to 5 percent of their annual sales turnover.

Ishiei Stores could follow this course with impunity, even while it was technically in the red. All it needed was for the company's top executives and the people responsible for the company's debts and liabilities to come to an agreement to cook the books and publish inflated results. There was no real risk that anyone would see through the deceit. All they had to do was estimate the value of the company stock a little high, and they would come up with financial reports that any accountant would accept as fair and accurate.

It was perhaps thanks to this mechanism that the company was able to carry on unimpeded by the fact that it was carrying bad stock worth tens of millions of yen. There was an alternative: if they could take advantage of this mechanism to earn breathing room for several years, then the company would have enough time to find ways to solve its problems.

From a personal point of view, it would also give Kôjima enough time to find another job. . . .

But why did he have to be the one to find a solution to the company's problems?

He would be taking a huge personal risk. He couldn't explain his motives even to himself. All he knew was that he had to work to protect the company. If he shirked his responsibilities and ran away from the situation, he might as well not have quit his old job.

This was his castle now. This was where he had to work and fight, however meager his contribution might be, no matter how much fear and doubt raged inside him. If he ran away now, where would he go?

The first thing he did was to invite Kitô, head of development, to a meeting in the reception room. He asked Asayama to join them. He needed someone to back him up, and to persuade Kitô to help them out.

Kitô came into the room with suspicion written all over his face, like a man wary of walking into a trap. He sat and listened while Kôjima brought him up to speed, confining his account to the bad stock in the clothing department and its implications for the company. Kitô sat blankly through the recitation. That changed when Kôjima drew his remarks to a close:

"So, given these problems with the company, Kitô-*san*, this is what I'd like to ask of you to do as director of development. Do *not* proceed with the two new large properties. Stop the development of the Tsunoura and Mukoyama stores."

"That's the most outrageous thing I ever heard," Kitô sat up, his eyes practically popping out of his face. "I've just come from a meeting with the landowner of the Mukoyama site. After a year of diddling around, things are finally heading toward an agreement. You don't know how hard it's been, the hours, the money, the bullshit. And now I'm supposed just end it? Are you crazy?"

"Kitô-*san*, I'm utterly serious."

"You don't understand. I proposed the site a year ago, a whole year ago, and we've invested enormous amounts of time on it. We also have a lot of business relationships riding on this—down to *feng-shui*."

"What?" It was Asayama's turn to be incredulous.

"I'll tell you quickly, just to give you an idea of what we've been through. Our head office is located to the northeast of the landowner's house, which makes it inauspicious. It was a deal breaker for the land-owner. We almost had to scrap our plans until Kôda came up with a brilliant idea."

"To relocate head office?" Asayama asked.

"Almost. Instead of Ishiei Stores, the landowner agreed to lease the property to Ishikari Eitarô, and Ishikari will then sublease the property to Ishiei Stores. Luckily, Ishikari's house is in an auspicious location."

Asayama laughed out loud. "That's pretty dumb," he said.

Kôjima joined in the laughter. Privately, though, he was struck by the strange logic of the situation. From the landowner's point of view, it made all the difference in the world that the agreement was with Ishikari Eitarô and not Ishiei Stores. It was probably coincidence that the land-owner's superstition led him to insist on the safer option, but it was the kind of deal one might expect from someone who had seen through the façade and understood the truth about the company's finances.

"Anyway," Kitô went on, "since the guy's such a slippery character, we were trying to get the formal contracts signed the day after tomorrow, before he changes his mind again."

"So if you don't sign the day after tomorrow, then that's the end of the story," Asayama said casually.

"Gimme a break. After all of this, you can't just come and tell me to drop the whole thing, just like that. What do you expect me to do—just nod my head and shrug? Oh sure, no problem, no big deal. You can't expect me to back down like that. I mean, if the order was coming from the company president, or this had been formally decided at a board meeting then maybe, but . . ." Kitô trailed off, now looking beaten, ready to burst into tears.

"I understand it's a shock. And I understand you've got a right to be angry. I understand that, but I'm asking for your help. Is there anything you can do?" Kôjima's voice was seriousness itself. His eyes flashed as he spoke, and his whole body gave off an aura of strength and determination.

Kitô folded his arms and pushed his body deep into his chair. "If it's so important, why don't you hold a special board meeting?"

"You're not very quick on the uptake, are you?" Asayama piped up. "The guy who is the root of the problem is on the board."

"Well, we don't know for sure that—" Kôjima tried to interrupt.

Asayama ignored him and went on: "We're almost certain that the guy to blame for allowing all this bad stock to accumulate and then keeping the whole thing secret is on the board. In fact, it's fair to say that the ringleader of the whole plot is almost certainly a member of the board."

Asayama stopped short of mentioning Ichimura by name, but he needn't have bothered.

"All right, all right," Kitô mumbled. "That's . . . that's pretty bad." He looked exhausted.

Kôjima let a few moments pass. Then he asked, "What about the situation with the Tsunoura store?"

"How do you mean?"

"Have you exchanged contracts?"

"Not yet—not formally at least. Next week, if everything goes according to plan."

"Can you come up with a convincing issue so that plans for these two stores do not go ahead?" Kôjima said, practically begging.

"Listen, it's quite simple," Asayama said, completely reasonable on the surface. "All you have to do is rub the landowner the wrong way, and the guy will cancel the deal himself."

"But . . ." Kitô could not summon the words. He put his hands on his knees and lowered his head as if in apology.

"This is crucial for the future of the company," Asayama said. "The clothing department's in the red, and the whole company could go bust if we open two new superstores."

Kôjima didn't think that Asayama was choosing the most persuasive of arguments, but he couldn't think of anything better himself. He could see that what he was asking was outrageous. The plans had been formally approved at a board meeting, and now two members of the board were trying to get that decision reversed without any authority whatsoever. He and Asayama were the ones being unreasonable. But none of that changed the essential truth of the matter: opening two new superstores with the company in its current state would be like rowing a leaky, waterlogged boat into a hurricane.

"Don't give me an answer now. If the contract date for the Mukoyama store is the day after tomorrow, you have until tomorrow. I'm very sorry to have to ask you to do this, but, please, take this evening to think things over."

Kôjima smiled positively and stood up. "I'm sorry I had to call you in and throw something like this at you all of a sudden."

"I'm in shock, to tell you the truth," Kitô responded, and got up to leave.

Kôjima called him back just as he was about to open the door.

"One last thing. I've been meaning to ask you about it for a while, actually. What was the story with Také, the young guy who was moved to your department from the meat department at the center store?"

"That was pretty much forced on us by Ichimura. Why?"

"What reason did he give for wanting Také transferred?"

"He said Také wasn't really cut out for selling, didn't have the skills to become a really good butcher. But he said that Také was a good worker and it would be a waste to get rid of him altogether. Také might be better suited to a job that involved more thinking and planning, so he asked if we could give him a chance in our development. That was pretty much how it went."

"And how has he come on since he joined your department?"

"He seems fine. He's a little uptight, maybe, but he seems bright enough, and he's a hard worker. We're pretty happy with the way things worked out, actually. We found ourselves a good employee."

"Glad to hear it."

"Why are you asking? Is there something I should know about him?"

For a few moments Kôjima was lost in thought, and said nothing. Finally, with the air of a man who had finally made up his mind, he continued: "This is only a hunch, but I think young Také might have discovered what was going on in the meat department. I think he had to be transferred because he found out that the meat department chief was embezzling cuts of expensive meat."

"What?" Waves of shock ran across Kitô's face. It was almost painful to look at him.

"Is this true?" asked Asayama, who was hearing all of this for the first time too.

"This is just conjecture."

"But what is this talk about embezzlement?" Kitô asked.

Asayama filled him in on what had been happening. "We don't have any proof yet. We have someone keeping an eye on him, but there's no evidence so far."

Kitô groaned. A single thread linked the bad stock and the meat department in his mind: Ichimura.

Kôjima hadn't wanted to mention Také, but in the end he had no choice, and he had brought the subject up as a way of making Kitô realize the seriousness of the situation. His tactics seemed to have been more effective than he had dared hope.

Kitô was standing at the door, dazed.

"Take your time. Take the rest of today to think things over," Kôjima said as he showed him out. But in his own mind, he knew something wasn't right. Things didn't add up.

If Také really had discovered what was happening in the meat department, and if Ichimura really was the ringleader behind the plot, then why didn't he simply fire him? Why move him to a part of the company beyond his own authority and control?

Maybe they were mistaken. Maybe Také hadn't uncovered the embezzlement after all. Maybe there was another explanation.

"Why did you keep something so important hidden till now? If we get Také to make a statement, we can get to the bottom of things right away," Asayama said critically.

"But this was just speculation." Kôjima was struggling to bring order to the confused mass of thoughts running through his head. It was even possible that Ichimura knew nothing about what was going on.

"Let me have a go at Také," Asayama said. "This is getting more interesting all the time." Anyone watching would have thought he was relishing the whole situation.

The next person they called in was Konno, the director of store administration.

Konno had been the manager of the first Ishiei Store—the same store that after much extension and rebuilding was now the flagship center store. He had managed other stores after that, and was now a company director supervising the managers of the ten stores. He was one of the company's oldest and most loyal employees.

Some twenty years earlier, Konno had been an anxious young man with literary aspirations. After high school in Numazu, he studied literature at a university in Tokyo, where he soon fell into a dissipated, aimless way of life. Feeling he was wasting his time, he dropped out and went back home, where he helped in his father's sake shop, but the work was dull and offered no prospects for the future.

One of his wholesalers mentioned that a colleague was starting a supermarket business in Tokyo. Konno made further inquiries, and although he knew nothing about supermarkets, he was hired on the spot. His youth and readiness to learn were enough to see him appointed manager of the first Ishiei Stores supermarket.

The last twenty years had removed every trace of the dreamy, bookish youth he had once been. In its place was a somewhat chubby physique and a brassy realism. He was known to examine details meticulously from every possible angle. Given his personality, it was not surprising that he did not like Ichimura, who had joined the company many years after him and had risen to become the most powerful figure in the company. Konno did not have the popularity or track record to challenge him.

Konno listened thoughtfully to Kôjima's account, which again was confined to the bad stock problem; nothing was said about the meat department or any possible connection with Ichimura.

"The problem is that the bulk of it vanished without a trace overnight. The only proof that it was ever there at all is the testimony of the two people who were there—Manabe, the store manager, and myself. So Manabe is crucial, but for some reason I can't figure out, he's determined to stick to his ridiculous lies." Kôjima spoke slowly, keeping a close eye on Konno's reactions. "At the moment, there is no way we can prove the existence of the bad stock. And there's no point asking the Arai Shôkai people either, who allegedly took the stuff away. I assume they're in on the scheme and are helping to keep the bad stock hidden."

Konno listened in silence, nodding occasionally and murmuring his agreement. His face was absent of expression.

"I've given it some more thought," Kôjima went on, "and I've decided to give up trying to prove what I saw."

"What are you going to do instead?" Asayama asked Kôjima.

"I may not be able to prove the existence of the bad stock, but I think I should still be able to prove that the department's results are nothing like we've been given to think. I want to make a thorough on-the-spot inventory of the department, and calculate the precise value of the stock. If bad stock has been removed from the store, then the value of the inventory will be less than what you would expect. I expect we'll find that several hundred million yen or so is missing. Factoring that into the balance of payments will reduce profits dramatically. If we can show that the clothing department is underperforming, then we should be able to stir Ishikari into coming up with a plan to address the problem on a company-wide basis."

"That won't be easy," Konno said, speaking for the first time. "We generally take inventory once a quarter, but it's carried out on a departmental basis. So any stocktaking within the clothing department would take place under the supervision of the clothing department bosses themselves. So if things are as you say and Ichimura is concealing bad stock in the clothing department, then he would just jiggle the figures in the inventory as well."

"Wait a minute, Konno-san. I haven't said a word about Ichimura keeping stock hidden," Kôjima said.

"Of course it's Ichimura. This is all a big scheme of his. What other explanation is there? I just don't think you should put your trust in an inventory. It'd be like asking a thief to declare the value of the goods he's stolen."

"What would you suggest, then?"

"You won't get anywhere till you've got Ichimura out of the company first. That's what I think."

"But how would we do that?"

"You'd have to get him to take responsibility for the bad performance of the clothing department."

"And for that we need indisputable proof that the clothing department is actually losing money."

"I think just a statement from you would be enough. I mean, it's obvious enough to anyone that Ichimura is a source of evil."

"I don't think that's really true."

"But you're a cousin of the company president and its general manager. It should be easy enough for you to get someone like Ichimura sacked. He's not related to the family at all."

Kôjima tried hard to suppress the unpleasant feelings welling up inside him. Konno's suggestions were far too smug and self-righteous to be useful. But Kôjima knew that he would end up the loser if he got impatient and lost his temper now. Whatever happened, he needed to have Konno's support and cooperation.

"This is what we can do," Kôjima said. "We submit a joint proposal to have the responsibility for inventory-taking moved over to your department. Then we carry out the stocktaking ourselves."

This was the rationale they would push: Since the stock belonged to the company, it made sense that the whole process should be carried out by the store administration, which was ultimately responsible for operations at all of the company's outlets. This way the inventory would be more comprehensive, more centralized.

"I've read several books on stocktaking for small businesses," Kôjima said. "If you're willing to follow my lead, I will draw up a manual of new ways of taking an inventory."

"And what would I have to do in concrete terms?" Konno asked.

"All you have to do is put forward the suggestion at the next board meeting, saying that you want the responsibility for stocktaking to be transferred to your department for the next quarter. I will prepare everything else. We should probably have some kind of project team. You could act as head of the team, and I would be your deputy. So long as we can get approval at the board meeting, we're free to do what we want."

"But wouldn't Ichimura oppose the idea?"

"There aren't any reasonable grounds for opposing us. He'd be wasting his time. I think he'd be more likely to endorse the idea. And then, probably . . ." Kôjima paused. He realized that he had started taking it for granted that Ichimura was responsible too.

"And then, probably what?" Konno said, eager to hear the rest of Kôjima's plan.

"Well, if Ichimura really is responsible for the bad stock, then we can expect him to start putting all kinds of obstacles in our way when it comes time to put our new stocktaking system into effect."

"More than likely, I would say." Konno nodded enthusiastically. "I'd love to help."

"We're starting to get somewhere now," Asayama said. "Things are really starting to move. Who should we call next?"

"Next, my friend," Kôjima said with a smile, "is you."

"I should have known. Time to think of ways to improve things in fresh produce, is it?"

"Absolutely right."

Kôjima was obviously exhausted, but there was enthusiasm and excitement in his voice as he moved on to the next subject.

SEVEN

THE TYPHOON

Piles of vegetables and fruit littered the table in the employees' recreation room on the fourth floor of the center store.

Earlier that morning, Kôjima had summoned Ôtaka, the fresh produce chief, to his desk; Asayama was present. Ôtaka was given an assignment: to purchase a selection of produce from each of three supermarkets. Each store would have its own merchandising. He was to note how items were packaged and sold, and he was to purchase samples to bring back to the office.

Buying the produce was easy, but how was he supposed to remember everything in each store, Ôtaka asked. He didn't think his memory was good enough, and he didn't want to attract attention by taking notes.

"Don't worry. I've got something here to help you out," Kôjima said. From a drawer in his desk he brought out what for the time was a relatively small tape recorder. A microphone was attached to Ôtaka's collar, the cord leading under his shirt through his sleeve, where it connected it to the tape recorder, which Ôtaka would hold in a paper bag. "Let's try it out."

Ôtaka looked perfectly normal—just another man with a bag in his hand. If you looked closely, you could just about make out the cord dangling between his sleeve and the bag, but otherwise there was nothing unusual at all.

"All you have to do is talk normally, and the machine will record whatever you say." He gave a quick demonstration. "Cucumbers available in two-packs and three-packs; tomatoes in packs of three and four." He rewound the tape and played it back. The tape had captured everything perfectly.

"Ordinarily, these tape recorders come with directional mikes, which means they'll pick up sounds from whatever direction the mike is facing. The problem with that is that if the mike is not in the right position it won't pick you up. So yesterday I went and found a non-directional microphone. That means sounds from all directions will be picked up at the same level. Your voice will definitely be picked up, but unfortunately so will everything else. If you speak too softly, you'll probably be drowned out by all the background noise."

"But if you go around talking to yourself in a loud voice people will think you're a lunatic," Asayama said, laughing.

"I suggest you take someone with you," Kôjima said. "Someone you can talk to naturally as you make your rounds."

Kuroba Motoko happened to be passing by at this moment—on another of her little excursions through the office.

"Motoko would be perfect. Why don't you ask her?" Asayama said.

"I don't think we can do that," Kôjima said with a wry smile. Kuroba worked—theoretically, at least—in the development department, and neither of them had the authority to ask that she do this.

"Don't worry—I'll have a word with Kitô," Asayama said breezily, undertaking to speak to the head of development. And to Kôjima's surprise, it took Asayama no time to get Kitô's consent. The whole procedure was a million miles away from the labored way the hierarchy worked at Saiwa Bank.

Ôtaka and Motoko had known each another for a while, but they had never been close. And both were permanently single.

Nevertheless, the day turned out to be an enjoyable one for Ôtaka. It was always a nice change to have a young woman by his side, even if she wasn't someone he had any particular feelings for. And Motoko turned out to be an excellent assistant.

They had their strategy down within five minutes of entering the first supermarket. Motoko held the shopping basket. Ôtaka would pick out a packet of each of the produce on their list, and put it into the basket. Motoko would recite the different packaging available for this product, and Ôtaka would repeat the information into the microphone. They fulfilled their assignment like any other happy young couple shopping, then returned to the head office.

A glance at the array of produce laid out on the table showed how varied the merchandising of produce at the different supermarkets was.

Celery could be sold whole with the root, or as sticks. It could be packaged by the single stalk, or as several stalks together, in plastic bags, or bundled together with tape. The lettuces and cabbages all looked more or less the same in their plastic packaging, but upon closer inspection the outer leaves were shaped in a particular way in some, cut from the stem differently in others. And, of course, the quality of the produce varied significantly from item to item, from store to store. Ôtaka was fascinated. He had never noticed such variety before. He was supposed to be an expert—a veteran with more than ten years' experience in this line of work, and yet he felt as if he were seeing things for the first time.

"What's going on? You trying to set up a little extra business with all the stuff you can't sell on the floor?" It was Sashima, chief of the meat department. He was joking, sort of. "Oh, I know what this is. This is for the famous Fresh Produce Research Group meeting I've been hearing about."

"Mmm," Ôtaka responded with a sound like he was clearing his throat.

"You're really going for it, huh? What the hell are you going to do with all this stuff?"

"I'm not sure."

Sashima laughed contemptuously. "Well if *you* don't know, what chance has anyone else got?"

"Mmm," Ôtaka uttered again, not eager to continue the conversation.

"Asayama's been taken in by Kôjima's crazy ideas. And now we all have to go along with it."

"You're doing the same thing in your department?"

"Yeah. Tomorrow. We're supposed to go out and buy all the meat we can find and then compare it with our own stuff. Pretty dumb, if you ask me. A bunch of guys who can't tell the difference between a rump steak and a brisket if their lives depended on it. What a fucking farce. A waste. Those guys wouldn't know the difference between beef and pork." Sashima was getting more agitated as he spoke. "The whole thing pisses me off. Ever since Kôjima joined the company it's been the same old bullshit. What the fuck does he know anyway? If his cousin hadn't dragged him up here and made him an offer he couldn't refuse, he'd still be crunching numbers. All he's done since he got here is poke his nose into somebody else's business."

"Mmm."

"He screws up the flyers. And then he makes a big deal out of a few boxes of bad stock. What a fucking fool."

"What was the story with the bad stock?"

"Oh, he saw some boxes stacked up in the clothing department. Starts crying 'Wolf! Wolf!' Didn't know the stuff's supposed to go back to the suppliers. Can you belief that? Doesn't know the difference between a blouse and a pair of panties, and he's got the balls to send everyone into a panic. The problem didn't even exist."

Sashima stopped his rant to pick up a bag of grapes from the table. He ripped open the packaging and popped a few grapes into his mouth.

"Hey, we need that," Ôtaka cried.

"Whatever."

"Yeah, I guess company property doesn't mean much to you anyway."

"Screw you." Scowling, Sashima threw the grapes down onto the table. "This whole company's going down the tubes with this Kôjima jerk. Got to get him out of the picture. If we don't get Ichimura in charge quick, it's over. You better give us your support when the time comes, you hear?"

"Mmm." Ôtaka concentrated on arranging the produce on the table.

"Don't let Kôjima and Asayama talk you into anything," Sashima hissed and walked out of the room peeling a banana.

•　　•　　•

At seven that evening, the meeting was convened by Asayama and Kôjima. The group was asked to examine the produce Ôtaka had purchased during the day and rate them for quality, price, presentation, and packaging.

Ten young employees stood around the table, six from fresh produce sections at different Ishiei Stores outlets. Also in attendance were the produce buyers from the head office. The produce chiefs of each store had been invited, but since the meeting was taking place outside regular working hours, not everyone had been able to make it.

"Why is there a knife cut here?" Kôjima began, pointing to a nick in the base of a cabbage stem.

"Probably just a mistake," Asayama said.

"Hmm, but look, this one has a nick in the same place."

"There's no cut in this one," one of the young employees said, holding up a cabbage from Diamond Stores.

"Do you know why these nicks are here, Ôtaka?" Kôjima asked.

"There were cuts like that in the stems of all the cabbages at Kimura Mart and Coral Stores. So it's got to be done deliberately. I don't know why, though."

"Ah—" It was Shimakura, perhaps the quietest of the employees in attendance. He was shyly standing a little apart from the group.

But Kôjima heard his response and followed up, "Do you have an idea?"

"I . . . I could be wrrr . . . rong, but . . . ," Shimakura stuttered, "but I think that it ss . . . stops the cabbage from ggrr . . . owing."

"Aha!" Delight spread across Kôjima's face. "Of course. The plant keeps on growing even after it's been prepared for sale and put on display. That's why you sometimes see half-cabbages on display where the stem is sticking out where the vegetable has kept on growing. So this is to prevent that? . . ."

"I . . . I think so."

"Very good, Shimakura. Very good."

Shimakura blushed bright red and looked down at his feet. He couldn't say a word now that everyone's eyes were on him.

"They may have put those nicks in there to stop the growth, but it's a waste of time if you ask me," said Nakayama, the oldest of the produce chiefs. "Someone told me about that once. I tried it out, but it didn't make any difference that I could see. It just took more time."

"But if Kimura Mart and Coral Stores both do it, it must have some effect. Maybe we should think about it too," Asayama said.

"What's the point? It's a waste of time," Nakayama grumbled, unhappy at having his expert testimony doubted.

Kôjima stepped in. "Let's have a trial. I want to hear whatever opinions you have. Where there's a difference of opinion, we'll try things and see. The trial should help us decide one way or the other—and after that I want everyone to go along with the decision without any complaint. Agreed?"

This was the first meeting of the sort that Ishiei Stores had ever had, and many of the participants weren't sure why they were here. Probably some were wondering whether the meeting had any value, unclear what it was supposed to achieve. Kôjima hoped that involvement would come with time.

From cabbages, the group moved on to tomatoes. And then cucumbers.

"This is taking longer than I thought," Asayama said, looking at his watch. "Maybe we should divide into groups and spread the evaluations around."

Kôjima didn't like the idea. He wanted the entire group to look over all of the items together—at least for this first meeting. No doubt things would go more quickly if small groups examined just one or two items. But if that happened, then only Asayama and Kôjima would get to see the whole picture. The experiment would have no impact on the people responsible for doing most of the actual work.

"Can I say something, please?" Ôtaka said, stepping forward, a little hesitantly. "I had my doubts, but I really learned something today while I was going around buying this stuff. I saw all kinds of small things I never saw before." Ôtaka was not the most gifted speaker, but he was soldiering on. "Today I went to three different supermarkets: Kimura Mart, Coral Stores, and Diamond Stores. And—how can I put this?—all three of them had one thing that was the same. They had some kind of a philosophy, and you could see it on the sales floor. You could see the philosophy in the produce too. I mean, take a look at this stuff on the table."

There was total silence as the group listened to Ôtaka, whose sincerity was palpable.

"In my opinion, these sort of meetings are very helpful. I think we need to look carefully at each of the items we sell and think about how we want to present them."

Nobody said anything. What Ôtaka was saying made sense, but he had spoken so passionately that it was not easy for anyone even to pipe up and agree. Ôtaka, convinced that his message had failed, then plowed ahead: "I'm going to do it anyway. Even if no one wants to join me. To tell you the truth, it wasn't easy for me today. I didn't like what I saw. These people were in the same business as me, and at all three of the stores they were running a better department than mine. I said to myself: *I don't want to get stuck being second best.*"

"You're right, Ôtaka. That's the spirit," Asayama cheered. "All of you, please, join in and support what Ôtaka is trying to do."

There was a chorus of positive responses from several of the younger employees. Some had perhaps been too shy to say anything, but Ôtaka's testimony was so heartfelt, so convincing, that Kôjima thought he could feel a new sense of determination flickering inside them. They had taken the first crucial step.

For the first time in a long time, Kôjima felt happy inside.

"Kampai, kampai!" The *mama-san* raised her glass. She spoke the way she dressed: neither subtle nor refined.

Ôtaka and Asayama were sitting in the hostess bar where Asayama was a regular.

"Ah, sure. If you want," Ôtaka replied nervously, a little overwhelmed by the reek of perfume and the flash of cleavage as the *mama-san* squeezed in next to him.

"This one's still wet behind the ears," she said.

"Just like everyone I bring here," Asayama said. "Just like me."

The *mama-san* laughed heartily at that. "That guy the last time, yeah, real wet. What a lecher!"

She was talking about Konno, whom Asayama had invited along with Kitô. Konno had started talking smut with the girls, and once he got started, the scandalized laughter didn't stop. He talked about the red-light district before prostitution was driven underground, his experiences with foreign women, and the unspeakable things young people did on crowded subway trains. It wasn't clear where the truth ended and his imagination began, but he was so witty that even the most dubious and hackneyed of stories sparkled.

No way!

Oh my God! What happened next?

Stop, please—or I'm going to die laughing!

Konno soon had every girl in the bar huddling around him, leaving the rest of the clientele nursing their whiskey and sodas alone. Maybe this was the outlet for the man's literary aspirations.

"I'll bring Konno again if you like."

"No, thanks. Once was enough. People like that are no good for business," the *mama-san* said with a coquettish pout.

The night Konno and Kitô first heard about the bad stock problem, the two men, independently of one another, had called Asayama, wanting to talk. The three of them ended up going out for dinner, after which Asayama invited them to this bar.

Over dinner they had expressed their anxieties about what Kôjima wanted them to do. Kitô was particularly concerned. It would be a breach of professional duty if he canceled plans for the two new superstores without first putting the matter to vote at the next board meeting. If anyone found out what he was doing, he would be dismissed without appeal.

Asayama's response was straightforward. "I think you should do what Kôjima's asking."

"But what if he's wrong?"

"Kôjima has based his decision on what he thinks is the best for the company."

"But will he take responsibility if a problem occurs?"

"Yes, that's the real question," Konno interjected.

There was no breach of trust involved in the inventory issue. Konno was worried about contingencies. He would take over the stocktaking, but he didn't really have the confidence. And he'd be in serious trouble if he did what Kôjima asked, only to find himself without Kôjima's support if something went wrong. He didn't want to start climbing if the ladder was going to be taken away as soon as the ground started to shake.

"I guess what it comes down to is whether we can really trust him or not."

"Can you trust him? Absolutely. Beyond a shadow of doubt. If anything goes wrong, he'll take responsibility for everything. *That was my fault. Yup, that too. Sorry, I was to blame for that as well.* If the cat next door has stillborn kittens, he'll even take the rap for that too, if you want."

The two men were able to laugh at that.

Kôjima, said Asayama, was as responsible as a man could be. Nothing bad could possibly come from doing what he was asking. He himself was thoroughly convinced. And that is when he invited Konno and Kitô to the bar.

With the bar girls laughing behind them as they got into a cab, Kitô announced that he had made up his mind. "I'll do it. All or nothing. I'll trust the guy," he slurred.

Asayama made an important discovery that night: It didn't matter how persuasive Kôjima's arguments were. It didn't matter that he was related to the owners of the company. It didn't even matter how brilliant he happened to be. None of these things on their own could persuade anyone to act on his behalf. No one would do anything without the word of people they knew and trusted.

Asayama knew now what his role would be. He would be a supporting actor. An assistant. A disciple dedicated to ensuring that Kôjima's teachings reached the widest possible audience. He would be a loyal vassal devoted to the service of his lord.

When Kôjima suggested the Fresh Produce Research Group as a way to improve performance in the fresh produce section, Asayama spoke to Ôtaka before the first meeting. "We need you to play a central role," he told him.

"What do you mean? What do you want me to do?"

Now that the question was put to him so directly, Asayama wasn't sure how to respond. "I mean just, you know, speak out. Be positive about things."

Silence.

"Help him out if he looks like he's in trouble."

Silence again.

"If anyone objects, knock 'em dead."

"I don't think I can do that."

"That was a joke." Did the man have no sense of humor? "Just do your best," he said, without much hope.

But Ôtaka had stepped up to the plate and hit a home run. His impassioned speech inspired everyone and brought a much-needed sense of purpose and enthusiasm to the meeting.

"Thanks for what you did in the meeting today. I appreciate it," Asayama said. "Here, have another drink."

"OK."

"Enjoy yourself."

"OK."

"What about a song? That guy with the guitar can play just about anything you want."

"No thanks. I can't sing."

"Oh."

Asayama gave up and struck up a conversation with one of the hostesses. She wore heavy blue makeup around her eyes. The last time he was here, the three men had nicknamed her the 'Blue-eyed Panda.' The problem was, she wasn't much fun to talk to. He'd have been better off drinking with a real panda.

"Asayama-*san*?" Ôtaka spoke up suddenly, rousing himself from his drink. "Maybe I shouldn't be asking you this, but . . ."

"Go ahead, ask me anything you like."

"Do you think this new management strategy for fresh produce is really a good idea? I mean, do you think we should take this new strategy at face value?"

This strategy had been announced several days earlier at a special meeting of the fresh produce chiefs from all the Ishiei Stores' outlets.

Asayama had made the formal announcement, followed by explanatory remarks from Kôjima. But it was clear that the substance of the program was Kôjima's work.

"What are you talking about? All you have to do is follow the strategy as it's been laid out for you."

Ôtaka fell silent.

"Or are you saying you think something bad might happen if the strategy is followed?"

"Yes."

"I don't understand. Can you be a bit more specific?"

"Kôjima said it himself: 'The first thing is to resolve never to put anything on sale that isn't absolutely fresh.'"

"Right."

"The thing is, that's been said in the past too."

"Right. I've always said the same thing myself."

"But there was something else he said. 'If something's gone bad, throw it away. Don't obsess about preventing waste.'"

"Right."

"That's what concerns me. Is it really a good idea to throw stuff away as soon as it goes off?"

"Of course it is." Asayama said, although he could see what Ôtaka was driving at. If they started to throw more produce away, their profits were going to drop. Before long, they would be struggling to balance the books. *Everything in moderation; within reason,* he wanted to say, but deep down he knew that anything along these lines would be going against the true intent of Kôjima's message.

"And there's something else," Ôtaka said.

Asayama waited for him to continue.

"Standardization. I don't think it makes sense to try and make everything exactly the same across all our stores—at least not for fresh produce."

Asayama said nothing.

"We're supposed to set our retail prices at the levels provided by the head office. But as it is, we're already being undercut by some small vegetable stores. Sometimes, like when we've ordered too much of something, we have to sell at a lower price than the vendors can offer, even if it means selling for less than what we originally paid. If we had to sell everything at the prices given to us by the head office, we wouldn't be able to do that. That might affect our sense of how things are going on the sales floor, and could even have a detrimental effect on morale."

"It sounds as though you're suggesting that this new strategy is going to cause nothing but problems."

"Not at all." Ôtaka was frustrated at the way he was failing to get his meaning across.

"Go on. Take your time," Asayama said. He refilled Ôtaka's whiskey and added fresh ice to his glass.

"Kôjima knows all about selling fresh produce, I guess."

"I don't know about that. He always worked in a bank till he joined us. What would he know about selling groceries? I don't think he knows much about supermarkets or the retail business at all."

"I think he knows more than he lets on," Ôtaka said. He described Kôjima's special price seals and the remarkable effect of his experiment. "At first I thought he was just silly. *What does he know about anything anyway?* I thought. But I was amazed when I saw the results."

"Did you keep on using the seals after that?"

"No. We ran out of seals, and after a while everyone seemed to forget about them. But then today I saw the same seals on display at Kimura Mart and Coral Stores."

"You're sure they weren't just normal discount stickers?" Asayama was talking about the kind of discount seals that all of the supermarkets used to label items that were on special offer or whose price had been reduced as the items approached their expiration date.

"No, these were definitely being used in the same way as in Kôjima's experiment. At Kimura Mart they were called 'bargain seals'; they were called 'manager's recommendation' at Coral Stores."

"Hmm."

"I think Kôjima was really onto something. And when I went shopping for the fruit and vegetables, I saw that the sales floors at Kimura Stores and Coral Stores were organized according to something very similar to this new strategy Kôjima is trying to introduce here. So I'm willing to give the new plan a try. But I want to put my mind at rest about any questions before we actually get started. I mean, is it really a good idea to standardize everything? And does it really make sense to have all the retail prices fixed by the head office? I'm worried that that might affect the performance of the section chiefs."

"I see," Asayama said thoughtfully, looking over at the *mama-san*. She was not pleased to see them talking shop. "I'll let Kôjima know about your reservations. But for now do whatever you can to make the new strategy work. It's designed to make things better, not worse."

"OK."

Now that he said what was on his mind, Ôtaka relapsed into silence. Asayama could barely squeeze another word out of him all night.

The next morning, Asayama recounted this conversation to Kôjima.

"I knew that Kimura Mart and Coral Stores were using the seals. I would probably never have had the idea in the first place if I hadn't seen them there."

"Let's get some more stickers printed as soon as we can and introduce them into all our stores."

"I don't think that would be a good idea."

"Why not?"

"If we handed out stickers like that to our fresh produce chiefs now, you can guarantee they'd start putting them on produce that was about to go off. It wouldn't make any difference how many times we told them not to. Before we think about the stickers again, we need to get everyone used to the idea that we simply do not sell any produce that's not fresh, and make sure that everyone develops a sense of what real freshness means."

"How much time are you figuring on?"

"About a year, if we're lucky."

"A year?"

A distant look came into Asayama's eyes. A year could seem a long time or no time at all, depending how you looked at it. How much would their losses increase in that time if people started just throwing things away without worrying about the waste? The thought depressed him.

"I understand Ôtaka's concerns," Kôjima said. "Let me try to answer his doubts and put his mind at ease. Some of the kids from the office are coming around to my place next Monday. Kuroba is going to be there—the woman from development who helped Ôtaka with his shopping. I think I'll invite him to come too."

"Is your wife here now?"

"No. I'm still living like a bachelor, I'm afraid. But for some reason the kids want to come and have a look at my lonely lifestyle."

"Some guys have all the luck. You wouldn't be inviting all the young women to your place while your wife's away, would you?"

"Nothing that exciting, I'm afraid." Kôjima smiled as he jotted a reminder to call Ôtaka.

On the morning of the second Monday in September, a typhoon swept through the Kanto region.

The regular meeting of the board of directors was due to begin at nine thirty, but several board members were unable to get to work on time and the start of the meeting was delayed by an hour.

Kôjima spent the extra hour with Konno while he called all of the stores to find out whether they had sustained any damage. At the Kishimachi store, a fence had come down. At Iizuka, a signboard in the parking lot had blown over. At Higashi Motoyama, the loading and deliveries area was flooded. At the center store, the roof had sprung leaks; water wasn't dripping in, but blotches had appeared on the walls and ceiling.

"In this business you're really in the hands of fate," Konno remarked between phone calls.

Kôjima looked on with admiration as Konno dealt with one crisis call after another.

"I stress that nothing has been decided at this point, but I'm afraid we've come up against serious roadblocks regarding our plans to acquire land for the two new superstores at Mukoyama and Tsunoura."

It was Shinkawa, the director of nontrade business, who made the announcement. Immediately, voices were raised.

"What?"

"Why?"

"What's gone wrong?"

Ichimura said nothing, but stared open-eyed at Shinkawa in shock.

"As I say, nothing is decided yet. The development department is doing everything possible to make up the ground we've lost. But there is a big chance that we may not succeed in acquiring these sites. In the light of this, I suggest that we shelve our plans to recruit large numbers of graduates to work in these new stores."

The board had been discussing how many new staff would be needed. The numbers given in the report presented by Katsumura, who was director of personnel, had seemed unusually low, and it was only when someone had queried his numbers that Shinkawa made his announcement.

"What the hell could have happened to make us abandon our plans so suddenly?" Ichimura blurted out. "These were going to be brand-new superstores. I thought everything was cut and dried."

"I don't know any more than you, I'm afraid. Kitô-*san* was in charge of the negotiations for these projects. I don't know much about the details."

There he goes again. Shinkawa was notorious for avoiding responsibility at all cost.

"But of course as a member of the team myself, I have looked into the situation and found out the following: As far as the Mukoyama store is concerned, we received a request, out of the blue, from the landowner the day before the scheduled exchange of contracts, asking for a postponement. He refused to divulge his reasons, but according to Kitô it almost certainly has something to do with his horoscope or geomancy or something like that. At the moment I'm afraid we have no choice but to assume that the landowner has lost his enthusiasm for the deal.

"A similar thing happened with the Tsunoura site. Just before we were due to exchange contracts, the landowner submitted a number of outrageous amendments to the contract: he wanted an increase of both our deposit and our rent. He refused to accept any mortgaging of the security money due him, the effect of which would make it impossible for us to go ahead with our plans for a transfer mortgage on the site. He also wanted the right to ask us to vacate the land at any time.

When we told him that these terms were unacceptable, he said to forget the deal had ever been on the table."

This isn't looking good, Kôjima thought as he listened to Shinkawa's explanation. The Mukoyama story was straightforward, and left no room for dispute. The landowner had made up his (admittedly crazy) mind for reasons of his own. The problem was the Tsunoura story. It sounded too contrived, an obvious lie—a mess of not very convincing details Kitô had made up to answer any objections that might be raised.

"That doesn't make sense," Ichimura spoke up, menace in his voice.

Asayama and Konno blanched.

"It just doesn't make sense. Someone must be deliberately trying to attack the company." The wrinkles in his forehead deepened. His eyes narrowed, glinting with rage. "It's too bizarre. There must be something else going on." He drummed his banana-sized fingers on the table.

Asayama looked down to avoid his gaze. His knees were shaking uncontrollably. He started to recite a sutra under his breath. He had never had any religious beliefs, but he found prayer coming unbidden to him now.

Konno folded his arms and stared at the ceiling, trying desperately not to let the panic show on his face. His heart was pounding.

Ishikari looked anxiously at Ichimura.

Ichimura folded his arms, his stare fixed on the opposite wall. "Tell me," he said to Shinkawa, "have you met these landowners?"

"No, not myself, not yet." He was not feeling comfortable under interrogation. "Kitô has been dealing with the actual negotiations. I've left the day-to-day dealings to him. I didn't have the time to follow every twist and turn in the saga personally."

"But the purchase of land for these new stores is of vital importance for the future of this company," Ichimura began to expound forcefully. "This is an important matter—more than important enough for your personal involvement. Not just you, but that of the whole of the management team, from the president on down."

"You're quite right," Ishikari said. "I'd be more than happy to meet the landowners at any time."

This isn't going to do, thought Kôjima anxiously. If Ishikari and Shinkawa ended up going to talk to the landowners, then Kitô was certain to be exposed. Kôjima was confident that Ishikari wouldn't really go talk to the landowners, despite his protestations. There were few prospects he would enjoy less than a trip to negotiate with an unhappy landowner who wanted to back out of a deal. But Shinkawa might actually do it. The pressure from Ichimura might force him to go, even if it would be merely a face-saving gesture. And if he did go, he was bound to find out the truth.

Somehow he had to make sure neither Ishikari nor Shinkawa got anywhere near the landowners. What options did he have? Kôjima's mind was racing.

Shinkawa spoke up again. "It's no good. According to Kitô, the landowners are refusing to meet us. If they'd agree to a meeting, then everything would be simple. But why would they want to meet us again when they've already made up their mind not to go ahead with the deal? This isn't the first time this has happened. The first hurdle in any of these negotiations is always persuading the landowners to agree to a meeting. If they're not interested, you can't get them to sit down in the same room with you."

"Is that what Kitô said, or are you just assuming that?" Ichimura asked.

"He definitely said that. Definitely. This was such an important issue, so why hadn't I gone myself? I did want to go, and he basically stopped me. He told me it was no use—even if I did go, the landowner would just refuse to see me."

It wasn't pretty to listen to, but it was an effective enough way of diverting the responsibility onto someone else. Shinkawa hadn't spent so many years in the business for nothing.

It was at this point that Ichimura made his unexpected announcement: "I'll go see them myself. If they refuse to meet me I'll call on them at home. I'm going to get to the bottom of this."

"Of course. I'm sure they'll agree to a meeting if you go to see him yourself." Shinkawa looked relieved.

"I'm sure that's the best way out of this mess," Ishikari added. He sounded like an anxious baseball fan relieved to see the star pitcher stepping up to the mound.

Asayama, Konno, and Kôjima, on the other hand, were less pleased with this latest twist. Suddenly, things had gone from bad to worse. Kôjima racked his brains for ways to prevent Ichimura from going ahead with his plan.

Asayama had already made up his mind. Now that it had come to this, he had to do everything he could. He was prepared to fall on his sword by Kôjima's side. But making the decision in his mind was one thing—persuading his body to play along quite another. The shaking in his knees got worse.

Konno was consumed with regret. Why had he let Asayama and Kôjima talk him into participating in their foolhardy scheme? Unfortunately, he had already proposed Kôjima's new stocktaking system to the board. It had been the last item on the agenda before they moved on to the present debate. The proposal had passed unanimously, everyone delighted that his department was offering to take this tedious, time-consuming task off their hands. Even Ichimura hadn't raised any objections—as Kôjima had predicted. So Konno had made his first move as an active member of Kôjima's faction. Turning back wouldn't be easy now.

And now it was all but certain that Ichimura would find out what they had done. What was he going to do? He was close to panic. He could think of nothing. Except regret.

Ichimura stormed into the development department as soon as the meeting was over.

He ordered staff to give him the contacts for the two landowners, and called them right there and then. Both agreed to an appointment without fuss.

"Would you like me to come with you?" Shinkawa asked timorously.

"No. I'll go on my own."

Kitô looked on helplessly, his face drained of color.

It was just before sunset when the typhoon passed, leaving behind a beautiful cloudless evening. The last rays of sunlight blazed down through clear September skies.

The wind had swept the dust from the city streets, and the heavy rain seemed to have washed the buildings and trees of soot and grime. Sawabe, a drab, nondescript suburban city, now glistened in the sunlight.

Not long after the last daylight faded, five young people could be seen standing together in front of the head office of the Ishiei Stores supermarket company, about to go off in the direction of Kôjima's apartment.

Half an hour later, the party was underway.

"Please don't go to any trouble," Kôda called out from the other side of the sliding door.

"I'm just getting some ice out of the freezer," Kôjima called back.

Kôjima had turned down offers to help from Yoshiko and Motoko, and was now busy in the kitchen. He'd ordered food from a caterer, and had tried to choose snacks that didn't require preparation. But for someone like Kôjima, who had never had to do this kind of thing before, just getting the hors d'oeuvres onto plates was a job in itself.

He emptied a can of scallops onto plates he had unpacked for the occasion a few days earlier. Then he opened a can of tuna and added its contents to the plates. He squeezed out some mayonnaise. Then he added some cod roe—the best that Ishiei Stores sold. But try as he might, he just couldn't get the food to look good on the plates.

At least this effort was helping to distract him from what had happened in the meeting, allowing him to forget for a few minutes the seriousness of the situation. He hadn't wanted it to happen this way, but a confrontation with Ichimura now seemed inevitable.

Asayama had come to him as soon as the meeting was over. "This is terrible. Let's get together with Kitô and Konno tonight and discuss what to do."

Kôjima said he couldn't do it—the kids from work were coming over. But even if he'd had nothing going on, he didn't think an emergency meeting would help. He could think of no way to prevent

Ichimura from meeting the landowners. He had to brace himself for a face-to-face with Ichimura.

"You're too soft and naïve. You won't stand a chance."

Kôjima didn't want to hear it anymore. But maybe Asayama was right about coming up with a strategy to fight back.

He could talk to Ishikari and try to win him over to their cause.

He could get in touch with the landowners and ask them to go along with their story.

Or he could try talking to the company president, Ishikari Eitarô.

Perhaps he could talk to every member of the board separately and persuade them that he was doing the right thing. . . .

Kôjima didn't want to think about any of it now. He'd consider his options again in the morning. There was no sense obsessing and worrying about it now.

"Shouldn't we go in and help?" Yoshiko asked, a little nervous about the evening. She and Ôtaka had agreed to be friends after their disastrous date, but socializing at a company director's home was another matter.

"If that's what he wants, then leave him to it. No harm letting him wait on us for a change, right? Just relax and have a cigarette with me," replied Motoko, who was rummaging around in her handbag for cigarettes. "Want one?" she asked.

"I've got my own, thanks," Yoshiko said, pulling out a pack of cigarettes and a slim wine-red lighter.

"I've got a glass lighter someone gave me in my bag here, it's really cute. Want to try it?"

"Sure."

As Yoshiko lit up, Kôjima suddenly appeared in the doorway, laden with plates of food. "I didn't know you smoked, Misaki-san," Kôjima said.

"Just now and then."

"Come on, Yoshiko. You're a chain-smoker!" Motoko joked.

"Honest, I don't smoke very much," Yoshiko responded shyly, hurriedly stubbing out her cigarette.

"Don't mind me. Smoke as much as you like," Kôjima said, setting the plates down on the table.

Food and several drinks later, everyone was relaxed.

"Do you actually play that piano?" Motoko asked Kôjima.

"Sure. Not very well, but I can accompany someone if they want to sing."

"Wow, cool. Come on then, Také—sing something for us."

"I've got some songbooks here if you want to look through them," Kôjima said, bringing over a few from the piano and tossing them on the table.

Také, usually quiet and shy, didn't hold back when it came to singing. He flicked through the books till he found one he liked. "How about this one?" he said.

" 'The Song of the Shore'? Yeah, that's a good one."

Kôjima began to play, and Také sang:

> *Alone now on the sands*
> *I walk along the shore,*
> *Her love slipped from my hands*
> *And will come no more . . .*

His voice was soft, sweet, easy. No over-the-top *enka*-style posturings here. When he came to the end of the song, everyone cheered and he sang two more as an encore.

"You're really good, Také. The company's number one singer!" Kôjima exclaimed.

"No way," Také replied, a little embarrassed. "There's only one number one—and that's Manabe."

"Manabe? You mean the center store manager?"

"Right. You should hear him sing Russian folk songs—he's like a professional."

Mention of Manabe cast a sudden pall on the evening for Kôjima. If only Manabe would tell the truth about what was going on in his store, he wouldn't be in the mess he was in now.

Why had he lied?

He seemed like an honest, hardworking guy.

What was wrong?

Had someone gotten to him, threatened him?

"Actually, Manabe's been acting kind of weird recently," Ôtaka said in a voice that was almost a whisper.

"How do you mean?" Kôjima asked.

"Could be nothing, I'm not sure."

"I don't know. I've been kind of worried about him myself recently."

"No, it's really nothing. I probably just imagined it."

Kôjima was struggling not to show his impatience. Ôtaka knew something about Manabe, but he was being coy.

"What's wrong with you?" Kôda popped up. "Just say it."

"OK," said Ôtaka hesitantly, remaining quiet for a bit. Finally, he said, "I don't really know what's going on. He's upset about something. Something's bothering him."

"How do you mean?"

"He's got something on his mind. Never says anything. He used to always stop and say a few words when we saw each other, but now he doesn't even say hello."

"How long has this being going on?"

"Not long. I couldn't say for sure. A few weeks? I wondered if he was stressed about something. I even thought he might be having a breakdown. I went to his office a week ago, and he was sitting at his desk crying."

"Was there anyone else with him?"

"No, he was alone."

"I know what it is," Motoko said. "He's in love."

"Don't be stupid," Kôda told her. "Manabe's married with kids."

"Don't be so stupid yourself, Kôda. Maybe that's why he's so upset—he knows his love can never be requited."

"Hey, maybe you're right." Kôda sounded almost convinced.

"Anything else?" Kôjima asked.

"Well . . . ," Ôtaka began, then clammed up again.

"Come on—out with it. You can't start saying something and then just stop like that," Kôda said.

"No, really, there's nothing else."

"You're the one who's acting weird if you ask me," Kôda said—and with that the subject was closed. Kôda now announced that it was his turn to sing, and Kôjima sat down at the piano to accompany him.

"Stop! Stop!" Motoko screamed, running around the room with her fingers in her ears.

Everyone laughed.

Kôjima was disappointed not to have learned more. He'd try Ôtaka some other time, when there weren't so many people around. But at least he had learned that Manabe was worried sick about something. Maybe it was still possible that Manabe would lead him to the truth of the matter after all.

His guests were happily babbling away about something else now. Manabe had already been forgotten.

Ôtaka sipped his drink quietly, thinking about what he had almost let out to Kôjima and the group.

Sashima had dragged him to a bar where the pro-Ichimura faction had gathered. Only Ichimura himself was missing. Sashima went on at length again about the dangers facing Ichimura; he cursed Kôjima. Ôtaka had heard it all before. It was nothing new.

And then something happened that upset Manabe. He could normally hold his drink fine, but something set him off and he started to go wild. Ôtaka had had more than a little himself at the time, so he didn't remember exactly how it had all happened, but Manabe started to pick fights with people. And then he was shouting out all kinds of nonsense at the top of his voice, tears streaming down his cheeks.

I'm cursed! The devil's blood is flowing in my veins!

He was screaming so loud it wasn't easy to make out all the words, but Ôtaka was positive that was what Manabe said.

Ôtaka had almost told this story, but had he done so, he would have let slip the fact that he was attending meetings with people united by their hatred for the man who was now his host. Ôtaka resolved that he would attend no more of these meetings. From this point on, he was going to work hard under Kôjima's guidance and do whatever he could to make his department more efficient and successful.

Motoko had arrived at Kôjima's apartment that night with a plan.

She would deliberately forget something when the group left the apartment at the end of the party and then go back to fetch it alone. Probably she couldn't have said herself what she hoped to achieve by this. All she knew was that this was the best way to ensure that she and Kôjima ended up alone in his apartment late at night.

She went over the plan in her mind countless times over the course of the evening, the whole time acting as natural as she could, joining in the conversation and pretending to be having a great time. She began to feel hot and flustered; her heart was beating fast.

What should she leave? A handkerchief? Her cigarette lighter?

In the end she decided to leave her lighter behind. Who would want to have to deal with someone else's handkerchief?

Kôjima found the lighter in the corner of a chair almost as soon as his guests had left.

He remembered having seen it earlier in the evening. The scene flashed in front of his eyes again now: the bright flickering flame and the long white fingers of Misaki Yoshiko. He had had to look away when she raised the flame to light her cigarette. There was something about the scene that made her more beautiful than ever, and he had found all kinds of inappropriate thoughts coming to mind.

This must be Yoshiko's lighter, he thought. She couldn't have gone far. He could still catch up with her. He grabbed the lighter and hurried out of the apartment.

In the late night, a cool breeze caressed his skin. The sky was filled with stars.

He set off at a trot in the direction of where he'd overheard Yoshiko saying she lived, just on the other side of the first railroad crossing. It didn't take him long to find her. Under the glow of a streetlight in the distance he could make out Yoshiko's long hair and slender, feminine profile.

"Misaki-*san*!" he said, running up to her.

She turned around, a look of surprise on her face.

"I'm glad I caught up with you. You left this behind."

"What? But this isn't mine."

"What?"

"It's Motoko's."

"Oh. I'm sorry. I thought . . ." For a moment Kôjima considered asking Yoshiko which way Motoko would have gone to get home, but soon thought better of it. He didn't feel like chasing after her. He would never have left his apartment in the first place if he'd known the lighter was hers.

"Can I walk you home? Now that I'm here . . ."

"But . . ."

"Come on. Lead the way," he said with a smile, practically forcing her to accept his offer.

Yoshiko smiled back at him, and they set off side-by-side on the late-night street, a soft autumn breeze cooling their skin.

There was no moonlight, and in the long distance between street-lights, their path was dark.

When she was drawing up her plan, Motoko had considered all of the logistics.

Yoshiko lived in the other direction from her. There would be no problem there. But what about the three guys? What if they suggested going for a drink somewhere?

As it happened, she needn't have worried. She said good night as soon as they left Kôjima's apartment, and watched the three men go off together to find a cab. In other circumstances she might have been upset that they hadn't invited her to join them, but tonight it suited her purposes perfectly.

She walked slowly alone until she was sure the coast was clear, listening to the *click-clack* of her heels on the pavement. Then she turned around and made her way back to Kôjima's apartment. She touched her hand to her breast and felt the pounding of her heart.

And that's when it happened.

Kôjima came rushing out of the apartment building and ran off in the direction of the railway crossing. He didn't notice Motoko standing there just a few feet away.

Motoko understood at once what had gone wrong, and almost shouted out: *No, you've got it wrong. It's my lighter!* but she couldn't get the words out.

Kôjima had looked excited, eager, as he dashed off past her. She wasn't sure what to do. Should she wait for him here? He'd probably be back in a couple of minutes once he learned his mistake. Or should she just give up and go back home? Or should she follow him?

She followed him. She was burning with jealousy.

Kôjima was wearing a polo shirt. As he and Yoshiko walked together, his right hand brushed against her bare arm. Her skin was cool and smooth.

I shouldn't be walking so close to her, he thought. *I ought to move away.* But he discarded the idea almost immediately. It didn't seem fair to put such an abrupt end to the sweet sensation he was feeling from having touched her.

He tried to think of something to say. Something witty, interesting, amusing. He didn't normally have this problem. He could think of nothing. But he could feel the tension that had been building up in his chest for months beginning to melt.

They crossed the railway tracks, and the road forked.

"It's down to the right," Yoshiko said, breaking the silence at last. Her voice sounded dry.

The touch of a man's hand against her bare skin had sent waves of emotion running through her. The waves were still surging inside her. Her mind was a blank. Part of her wanted to get the moment over with as quickly as possible. But another part of her wished it could go on forever.

The road narrowed, and suddenly there were no streetlights.

When they got to her building, Yoshiko stopped. "It's here. Thank you," she said. She tilted her head slightly to the right and looked up at Kôjima. Her long straight hair drew lines on her face, pale in the darkness. "Do you want to come in for a coffee or something?" she said.

"Thanks. But it's getting late," he found himself saying, against his will. His eyes were on fire. He looked hungrily into her eyes, hoping to find fire there too.

He took her by the hand.

Yoshiko felt heat run through her body that she had almost forgotten existed. She stood still, unable to move. She felt as if she were about to fall over. She needed his arm to hold her up. Her eyes were still open, but she was ready to close them at any moment.

In the end he was the one who closed his eyes first. "No. Not now," he whispered to himself. "Good night," he said to her.

She felt his hand squeeze hers, and then he took his hand away.

He tried to fight back what he was feeling and leave.

"Kôjima-san."

"Yes?"

"Thanks for tonight." It didn't matter what she said. She just wanted to thank him. He had given her a sense of happiness she hadn't felt for a long time.

"The other way around. I'm the one who should be thanking you." Kôjima stood looking into her face for a few moments. "Good night," he said again. He was failing to calm his racing heart. He looked up at the sky.

It was full of stars. The typhoon had swept all of the pollution from the air. A sudden memory of the night sky in Nagano came to him.

"It's so beautiful," Yoshiko said.

For a while they stood together gazing up into the sky.

Everything else seemed to vanish—Ishiei Stores, Sawabe . . . There was only the vast unending brilliance of the stars, and the all-encompassing silence that surrounded them.

Kôjima bent down and touched his lips to Yoshiko's cheek. Yoshiko looked up, startled, only to see Kôjima's back as he walked briskly into the pitch-black darkness of the night.

•   •   •

Motoko felt her heart miss a beat at the sight of Yoshiko and Kôjima disappearing across the tracks together. She thought she was going to explode.

She hurried after them across the tracks until she came to a standstill under a streetlight where the road began to narrow. But this was not a good place to stand. It was too bright. She couldn't see them and she was running the risk that they would see her. She stepped quickly around the corner.

She looked on as their silhouettes joined and became one in the darkness in front of Yoshiko's house. Now they were holding each other close, embracing, kissing. She was sure of it. She felt hot. Sexual excitement ran through her. A man and woman embracing and kissing before her very eyes! And not just any couple—it was Kôjima and Yoshiko! She crouched down to the ground. Then she saw the two shadows separate. And before she knew it, Motoko was running as fast as her legs would carry her back down the road she had just come from. Tears were rolling down her cheeks. Had Kôjima gone into Yoshiko's apartment? What was going to happen? She shuddered with jealousy.

She found herself in front of her own building. By the time she had turned the key and opened the door to her apartment, Motoko was feeling waves of hatred and envy wash over her. That bitch had stolen Kôjima from her. "That should have been me in his arms!" she screamed.

Once inside, she slumped down onto the floor, and twisted open a bottle of whiskey.

What an idiot I am. They would never have gotten together if it wasn't for me.

A fresh torrent of tears rolled down her cheeks.

EIGHT

THE BUSINESSMAN

Two things made Ichimura Juichi stand out from the crowd: his ugly, oversized face and his uncanny sensitivity to other people's feelings, which he picked up like mental wavelengths from the air around him.

There were curiosity wavelengths, hovering like reconnaissance planes; anger wavelengths, remorseless and unbending, never stopping till they hit their target; and sympathy wavelengths, soft and flexible enough to encompass an object and wrap it in an embrace. Together, they made up the sum of what a person was feeling. Ichimura was acutely sensitive to these wavelengths, and used them to interpret what people were thinking.

He'd never tried to do it consciously. He'd never put any effort into it at all. Just like his big ugly face, this ability to act as a radio receiver finely tuned to the emotional signals of those around him was something he was born with. Like most people, he had assumed for years that everyone else was just like him, but over the years he began to realize that what he had was a special gift.

In college, his friends would be sitting around discussing something when suddenly one of them would lose his temper and start screaming. *So that's the kind of guy you really are, is it? You jerk!* And all hell would break loose. They were students, of course, and it didn't take long for good relations to be restored. What amazed Ichimura was how blind—or deaf—they were to the signals the other person was giving off.

The substance, or logic, of an argument almost didn't matter. Sometimes the other person was going to be persuaded by your argument; at other times he would flat out refuse to listen. You had to recognize the difference. And you did that by reading the emotional wavelengths given off by the person you were talking to. His friends got into fights because they put their faith in logic and reason instead of listening from the heart.

Ichimura experienced the same thing when he joined one of the large food wholesalers out of college. Unlike student arguments, fights with bosses and coworkers could cause real damage—breakdowns in the chain of command, major failures in the workplace. But people kept on repeating the same mistakes. Why were people were so insensitive to each other's feelings? Eventually, he figured it out. *He* was the freak. His sensitivity to what other people were feeling was preternatural. And it was this knowledge that gave Ichimura the confidence he needed to succeed.

From that day on, the word *businessman* was never far from Ichimura's lips. The true businessman was someone like him, ever sensitive to the signals given off by other people. The true businessman understood what other people were feeling, and was able to maintain good relations with them at all times. The true businessman could get people to do what he wanted them to. The image of the true businessman became an ideal, almost an obsession. If only there were more people like him in the world, there would be no more fussing and fighting over trivial things, and everyone would live and work together in peace and harmony.

Ichimura's talents as a businessman brought him professional success. At one stage, the company had been trying for months to expand into a rival's patch without success until Ichimura got involved. With him on board, anything seemed possible, and the company was able to obtain government licenses they would never have managed to get their hands on otherwise. One incident in particular astonished everyone who witnessed it. There had been a dispute over contracts, and one day the president of the company they were dealing with arrived for a meeting with steam practically coming out of his ears. After an hour and a half alone with Ichimura, he emerged with a contented grin all over his face. It was hard to believe it was the same person.

However, these same attributes could also lead to failure. Ichimura had been developing a partnership with a sub-wholesaler based in To-hoku. Rumor had it they were struggling. One day the president of the company, a man in his early sixties whom Ichimura trusted, threw himself at Ichimura's feet and begged him to act as guarantor for his liabilities.

The company needed a half month's extension on payments to get them through a crisis. With Ichimura's help he'd managed to scrape through six difficult months already, but now one of his creditors was threatening to pull the plug unless he could find someone to act as guarantor. He was begging Ichimura for help: he wanted him to guar-antee debts of twenty million yen for two weeks. There was no time to go through all of the proper channels, and even if there had been, it was unlikely that Ichimura would have felt the need to bother with the formalities. After all, it was only a half month. And he could feel in his heart that the old man sitting opposite him had never betrayed anyone in his life. Ichimura agreed to guarantee the company's debts and ap-plied his seal to the documents.

Five days later the company went bust, and the trustworthy presi-dent vanished without a trace. If the company had survived, this might have been Ichimura's moment of triumph. Instead, his gamble back-fired. Twenty million yen was a drop in the bucket compared to the contributions he had made to the company over the years, but in situ-ations like these, the balance sheet meant nothing.

And so it happened that Ichimura changed jobs and joined Ishiei Stores.

Recently, static had been disturbing the reception of Ichimura's finely tuned receiver. He'd first noticed it six months earlier; by now it was a constant irritation. His head throbbed from the loud, scratchy inter-ference.

Ichimura had been the central figure at Ishiei Stores for several years. From the outset, he knew he didn't have all of the skills necessary for running a company of this size. He wasn't good with numbers, he could have used a greater knowledge of economics and law, and his understanding of supermarket management was far from perfect. But he was convinced he could make up for these deficiencies. His inherent talents as a businessman would compensate for a lot; he might not be first-class management material, but he had what it took to make the grade.

He had his background in food wholesaling, but he hadn't been in his new job long before he realized that selling food was a different proposition from a supermarket's point of view. Clothing was something else entirely, something he had no experience in, but he decided to leap right in and meet the challenge by taking charge of the new clothing department himself.

"I don't know much about the merchandise we're selling here," he said, coming clean to his employees in the new clothing department. "When it comes to fashion, I'm clueless. But that's your job. You're young; you have plenty of time to learn. In return, I'll teach you the business end of things: how to read what the other party is thinking, how to negotiate, when to attack and when to defend, when to clinch a deal, how to read market trends . . . I'll teach you what it means to be a businessman."

Ichimura was true to his word. Several years later, the clothing department had become the company's biggest source of income. Ichimura was proud of this achievement, which had secured him a position of authority within the company.

Naturally, in a company with so many employees, not everyone was eager to accept his authority. He knew that some bore grudges, and secretly longed to see him fail, feelings that manifested themselves in an occasional moment's overt hostility. People like Konno, for example, the director responsible for store management, and Asayama, who was in charge of fresh foods. On the other hand, there were people who acted like loyal retainers, reporting anything untoward said behind his back. Men like Odagiri, for example, who was in charge of the groceries division.

Ichimura tried to maintain a certain balance. He was grateful for the respect he got and the authority to lead the company unhindered, yet he was open to criticism. But the interference in the mental wavelengths around him for the past six months was nothing so passive as criticism. It was aggressive, with a malice that seemed to grow stronger by the day.

At first he had no idea where the static was coming from, but gradually Ichimura came to realize that it was in some way connected to the only major change that had taken place at the company within the last six months: Kôjima. There were people who wanted to see Kôjima replace Ichimura as the figure of authority, and they had flooded the air with strong anti-Ichimura signals. It was possible that the signals had something to do with Kôjima's own scheming; Odagiri had suggested as much. A group of loyal young employees had banded together to stand up for Ichimura, which he thought was sweet if naïve—but maybe with their youthful sense of justice they were right.

But suppose Kôjima really did intend to dislodge Ichimura from his position; suppose he did manage to unite Ichimura's opponents and launched a full attack on him? Nothing could be more foolish. For one thing, Ichimura was perfectly ready to give up his position the moment there was someone better suited to lead the company. He didn't mind being number two or number three. He would happily serve the company in any way he could under a gifted leader. He didn't see himself as the pushy, power-hungry type.

But if Kôjima wanted to be number one, he was going to have to show some signs of leadership. Simply being related to the company's owners or having graduated from some fancy university wasn't enough. He had to earn his position by hard work. If not, well, that was a lot harder to forgive. How could Ichimura entrust the livelihood of hundreds of employees to someone motivated by nothing more than a lust for power?

Ichimura didn't have a clear idea yet what kind of person Kôjima was. No doubt he was educated and refined, his knowledge of the world deep and wide-ranging. Whatever that meant. Education and refinement alone were not much use when it came to supermarket management.

Kôjima had many attractive qualities. He impressed almost everyone he met as gentle, warm, and open-minded. And he was tall and handsome, and apparently popular with the young women at the company. But what was all this really worth?

It wasn't the job of a supermarket director to be urbane or to win a popularity contest. The job was all about leadership: a strong, forceful personality that could win the hearts and minds of the people out working on the supermarket floor. It didn't matter if he was uncouth, unrefined, not the best looking guy in the place. He had to be a leader who would sweat blood to get the job done.

He had to be a businessman!

Ichimura looked at his watch: twenty to nine.

He always arrived at work just after eight—a habit he had picked up before he joined Ishiei Stores. He never struggled to get up in the morning. Maybe his blood pressure was a little on the high side—but he had the perfect constitution for a man who had work to do in the mornings. He could get by on very little sleep—just a few hours a night if he caught up at the weekends. And he had a good head for alcohol.

In fact, he had had a lot to drink the night before. Sashima, chief of the center store meat department, had come over, and the two of them had been up till the wee hours, deep in conversation. It was the second time Sashima had visited Ichimura at home.

The first time was a year and a half ago—one afternoon when the store was closed for a holiday. Sashima squeezed his flabby, overweight body into an armchair and explained about the crisis he was facing. If Saijô Sakiko, a young woman who worked at the company, decided to press charges, Sashima could soon find himself on trial for rape. The facts were straightforward: Sashima had asked Sakiko out on a date, and then attacked and violated her in his car.

"She consented," he said. "All right, she did struggle a bit—but it was just an act. You know what they say: no means yes, right?"

"You idiot!" Ichimura stood up and shouted. His right hand shot up and slapped Sashima across his fat face. Sashima cried out in surprise. Ichimura grabbed hold of his hair and stared into his face. "You stupid goddamn jerk," he spat. And then there was the sharp crack of Ichimura's hand hitting Sashima in the face again.

Sashima tumbled off his chair.

"What the hell do you think this is?"

Sashima was babbling meaninglessly on the floor.

"What kind of an animal are you anyway?"

"I'm sorry. I'm so sorry," whimpered Sashima, who had never been hit by his superiors at work before. He was too young to have experienced that. "Forgive me." He was trembling.

"Get the hell out of here!" Ichimura screamed at him. "I don't want scum like you polluting my house. Get the fuck out—now. And don't ever show your face at work again."

"Please, forgive me. I'm begging you," Sashima whined. He could hardly form words. His teeth were chattering, and blood was oozing from the side of his mouth. "Please. Help me. I know what I did was wrong. I will never do anything like that again. I will work harder than ever to make up for it. I promise."

The rage and anger faded from Ichimura's body. And as his presence of mind returned, he began to appreciate how desperately the young man in front of him was begging for mercy. "Get back in that chair," commanded Ichimura.

Sashima stayed down on his knees.

"I said, get back in that chair," Ichimura repeated, his tone even sharper.

Sashima tried to pull himself together and kneeled formally in front of Ichimura. "Please, give me another chance," he said, bowing deeply and touching his head to the carpet.

There was heavy silence in the room. And by now it was clear to Ichimura that Sashima's remorse was genuine.

"I understand," Ichimura spoke at last. "You're still young."

From that day on, Sashima had been like a devoted disciple. For his part, Ichimura was happy that he had been able to rescue this promising young man from destruction. His life might have been ruined beyond repair—and all for one night of youthful indiscretion. Like a teacher who holds a special affection for his unruliest student, Ichimura had come to feel particular fondness for Sashima—like a father's love for a spoiled and disobedient child.

After a while, Sashima came to appreciate Ichimura's fondness for him. Ichimura had beaten him, and he had groveled on his knees, begging for forgiveness. There was probably no better way he could have become one of Ichimura's favorites. Ichimura was without doubt the most powerful figure in the company; Sashima made up his mind to make the most of his opportunity.

The second time Sashima had visited Ichimura at home was the night before. The subject of their conversation: the "plot" against Ichimura being orchestrated by the Kôjima faction.

According to Sashima, Kôjima had arrived at Ishiei Stores with his eyes popping with greed. Invited to join the company by his cousin, he had been shocked to find that the person with the greatest authority was not Seijirô or his brother but Ichimura. So long as such a powerful rival held sway over the hearts and minds of the company's employees, Kôjima had no chance of fulfilling his ambitions of running the company.

According to Sashima, Kôjima started to get jealous. That was why he had kicked up such a fuss over the mix-up with the flyers. He had used what happened as an excuse to introduce a new set of flyers—which just happened to bear his name. The whole thing was nothing more than a lame attempt to boost his own image—at the cost of massive losses for the company.

But no one was taken in by such a childish stunt. So Kôjima had come up with another means of attack—something more direct and effective. He would expose Ichimura's mistakes. Of course, these mistakes didn't really exist. Kôjima's strategy was to fabricate a whole catalog of failures, and use them to drive Ichimura out of the company. And now apparently he had come up with some story about piles of bad stock in the clothing department.

That wasn't all. A strange person had taken to keeping constant watch over the entrance to the center store. This was Kôjima's doing as well, of course, although Sashima was not sure what the person was watching for. But betrayal and treason and intrigue were everywhere.

"You think too much," Ichimura said, with little conviction in his voice. A lightbulb had just gone on in his head. Negotiations had suddenly broken down over two plots of land the company wanted for new outlets at Mukoyama and Tsunoura. Unconvinced by explanations at the board meeting, Ichimura had gone to meet the landowners himself, only to discover that, in both cases, it was not the landowners who had broken off negotiations, but Ishiei Stores.

Apparently Kitô, head of development, had approached the two landowners with a series of outrageous demands just as contracts were about to be exchanged. The discussion with the landowner of the Mukoyama site was relatively calm, but the landowner of the Tsunoura site was not so easily mollified. It was some time before he could be persuaded even to sit down and talk.

Upset by the day's revelations, Ichimura tried to get his thoughts in order. He had called the office on the spot and arranged a meeting with Kitô in the morning. The purpose of the development department was to obtain land for new stores. Why had the head of the department deliberately sabotaged negotiations? Was Kitô working as a double agent? Maybe he was about to move to one of the company's rivals, taking the information he had gained during his time with Ishiei Stores as a sweetener? It wasn't impossible, but Ichimura's meetings with the two landowners suggested otherwise. Neither landowner had stated it outright, but Ichimura's impression was that the plots of land were now to be purchased by two separate companies. In one case the land would be developed as a department store much bigger than the outlet Ishiei Stores had planned for. The landowner was more than happy with the way things had turned out.

And Kitô was still working for Ishiei Stores—which didn't seem to make sense if he was planning to betray them. There had to be another explanation, but what could it be? Who stood to gain if plans for the Mukoyama and Tsunoura developments collapsed? Both developments were for superstores—even bigger than the center store. Only a rival supermarket could stand to gain from the collapse of these negotiations.

Ichimura tried thinking things through the other way around. Who stood to *lose* the most? The clothing department, of course—the very same clothing department that was growing fast following its success at the center store. These two new stores would have represented an ideal opportunity for the clothing department to achieve even greater success. And who had come up with the plans for this great leap forward? Ichimura himself.

So someone was trying to prevent him from enjoying his biggest

189

triumph yet. Was it Kitô? If so, why? One thing was certain: if Kitô was involved, he wasn't acting alone. There was someone else behind him. And that was when the image of Kôjima came unbidden to Ichimura's mind.

Sashima's conspiracy theories had sounded crazy at first, but Ichimura couldn't deny that they were starting to make sense.

"I know you're not going to like this," Sashima went on, "but I have to say it: you have to get rid of Kôjima."

"What are you talking about? Why should I want to do a thing like that? I can't go driving people out of the company for no reason."

"But there is a reason."

Sashima paused and sucked his tongue dramatically. What he was about to say was the main reason he had come to see Ichimura tonight. "Kôjima is sleeping with Misaki Yoshiko, Mr. Ishikari's secretary."

"What? What are you talking about?"

"What am I talking about? Kôjima visited her at home this Thursday night, and . . ." Sashima paused, searching for the right expression. "And they became . . . intimate. They did it, I mean."

"Huh? How would you know?"

"There was a witness. Kuroba Motoko from development saw them. They were kissing right in front of her. Then they went into Yoshiko's house and that was the last she saw of them."

"Is this some kind of fantasy?" Ichimura couldn't make sense of what he was hearing.

"It's the truth. If you don't believe me I can bring Kuroba over and you can ask her yourself. Everyone at work knows about it."

"If this is true, we're going to have problems."

"What are you talking about? This is a perfect opportunity to get rid of that preening son of a bitch."

Ichimura sat in silence. If Sashima's story turned out to be true, he was going to have to do something about it. He couldn't just ignore it. "Let me think it over," he said.

"But timing is everything," Sashima persisted, obviously not satisfied by this response. "You know how it is with rumors like this. After a while they die. We have to strike while the iron is hot. This is the perfect opportunity to get rid of Kôjima."

"All right, Sashima. I get the idea. You've made your position quite clear. I don't want to hear you speaking about one of the company directors like that ever again. Is that understood?"

"But sir—"

"I don't want to hear another word. This conversation is over."

Kitô Jun'ya, head of development, was at Ichimura's desk by nine o'clock the next morning. Ichimura stood up without a word and led Kitô into a nearby meeting room. Ichimura gestured over at a chair, and Kitô sat down gingerly, his back straight and his hands on his knees. He looked like a prisoner awaiting judgment.

Ichimura spoke quietly. "I've met with the landowners of the sites at Mukoyama and Tsunoura. And frankly, I was astounded by what they told me. I think you owe me an explanation."

"I didn't think that developing new stores on those sites would be in the company's best interests, so I decided to make sure the plans didn't go ahead."

"Well, you succeeded. Why?"

"I thought it would not be in the company's best interests to open new outlets at those two locations."

"What? What do you mean? They were ideal locations. They met every one of our selection criteria. And you were the one who proposed the sites in the first place. You were the one in charge of researching the potential of those sites, and you were the one who suggested we go ahead," Ichimura said, trying to keep his cool.

Kitô made no reply.

"Your job is to help the company acquire new properties. You've been neglecting your responsibilities—even worse, you've been deliberately foiling the company's plans and making sure the developments didn't go ahead. If the company decided to fire you for gross misconduct, you wouldn't have a leg to stand on. I need an explanation."

Kitô said nothing.

"I think I have a pretty good idea how it happened."

Kitô looked up in surprise.

"This wasn't your idea. Someone told you to do it. If you tell me the truth now, I promise I will do whatever I can to make sure you don't lose your job."

Kitô looked down at the floor, still saying nothing. The color drained from his face. There was only one thought on his mind. As soon as Ichimura said he wanted to see him, he'd known what he had to do. Only one thing mattered: keep Kôjima's name out of it. If Ichimura found out that Kôjima had been working with him to sabotage the plans, Kôjima would lose his job too. And if that happened, the whole reason for doing this would come to nothing. If Kitô could ensure that he was the only one to be punished, there was a chance something good could be salvaged from the situation.

The inventory was due to take place at the end of the month; the results would be available two weeks later. When that happened, management would see that the clothing department they had thought of as the company's number-one earner was in fact in the red. Kitô would be congratulated for saving the company from disaster. Ichimura would be forced to resign, clearing the way for Kôjima to assume leadership of the company. At least, this was how Kitô hoped things would pan out.

Just one more month. So long as he could bear the indignity of having his name dragged through the mud in the meantime, things would be back to normal in just one more month. Kitô and Asayama had discussed it at length, and agreed that for now the best thing would be for Kitô to sacrifice himself so that no one could find out the truth.

Kôjima had been reluctant to agree. It wasn't right to ask Kitô to bear so much of the burden. He wanted to tell Kitô that if the pressure became too much, he should come clean about his involvement. They could always arrange an independent hearing with Ishikari and Ichimura and present the full story. But Asayama told him he was a fool. If the situation was so simple, that's what they would have done right from the outset. Asayama insisted that he and Kitô would work out strategy in private.

"Don't try this shit with me!" Ichimura suddenly shouted, slamming the palm of his oversized hand onto the table. The explosion came out of nowhere, without warning. Kitô was terrified. He felt a pain in his chest as though his heart were being squeezed in Ichimura's powerful fists.

"I'm sorry," he said instinctively. "Please, I beg of you. Wait till the middle of next month. If you can wait till then, you'll find out everything."

"The middle of next month? What the hell are you talking about?"

"Please."

It didn't last long, but for a couple of seconds Kitô thought he saw Ichimura hesitate. And it was enough to give him the energy to hold on. With a shock that sent shivers down his spine, he realized he had been on the point of confessing everything.

"What do you mean, the middle of next month?" Ichimura asked again, his tone harsh and insistent.

But Kitô said nothing. Ichimura's hand crashed down on the desk. He began to fire off one question after another, like arrows from a bow. Kitô shifted in his chair. *It's just a dog barking,* he told himself. *Just a dog barking.*

Ichimura asked him the same questions over and over again, but Kitô said nothing. Ichimura was livid. "All right, if that's the way you want it. Stay here. Don't set foot outside this room till I get back," he said and strode out of the room.

For almost an hour Kitô remained in his seat. Finally, Katsumura, the personnel director, appeared, a stern but good-natured look on his face. Kitô had been in the same position since Ichimura left the room. He hadn't even lifted his hand to wipe away the tears rolling down his cheeks.

Within a few hours, everyone at head office had heard the news that Kitô had been suspended and sent home. People who didn't know the details of the case gossiped about it, while those better informed said nothing and waited anxiously to see how events would unfold.

Among those in the latter group was Konno Yoshio, head of store management. The suspension had come as no surprise. Konno had been expecting it since Ichimura had announced that he was going to talk to the landowners. But he was shocked all the same when it actually happened. He was surprised that Kitô hadn't been fired for gross misconduct on the spot.

The fact that he had merely been suspended indicated that a final decision had yet to be made. And that meant that the investigation was still going on. Even now, the company—or, rather, Ichimura—was doing everything it could to uncover all the details. The thought was unnerving. Kitô would take all of the responsibility himself—at least that's what Asayama had said. But would Kitô be strong enough to stand up to Ichimura's questioning? Even if Kitô gave nothing away, the truth could still be exposed.

In fact, that was almost certainly what would happen. Ichimura would strike back. He had always been suspicious of people who didn't show him absolute loyalty. Konno knew that he himself could hardly have escaped Ichimura's notice. He was always making jokes and muttering things about Ichimura behind his back. People like him were going to be in Ichimura's line of fire, whether they were involved or not. Things were going to get nasty.

Would Kôjima stand up for him? He couldn't depend on it. Wasn't it more likely that Kôjima would be driven out of the company himself? Already there were rumors of Kôjima sleeping with Ishikari's secretary. It was hard to think of anything stupider he could have done, assuming the rumors were true. The situation was dangerous enough already. It would be like presenting Ichimura with more ammunition. They should never have made such a dandy their leader in the first place.

But there was still hope. Konno himself had done nothing wrong. The worst anyone could accuse him of was keeping quiet about what Kitô was doing, and he was confident he could come up with some excuse to explain that. His role was to carry out a thorough inventory and expose the true state of affairs in the clothing department. No one could describe this as a neglect of duty. But if Ichimura interpreted it as an act of aggression, it wouldn't make any difference whether or not he had been acting for the good of the company. Konno thought hard. What would Ichimura think? That was the important thing.

So long as Ichimura didn't see the inventory as something designed to undermine his position, then everything would be fine. What could he do to ensure this was the case?

Konno stood up. He would go and talk to Ichimura. He would remind him that responsibility for stocktaking had been transferred to his department. He would tell him that while he was grateful for this display of faith in his department, he wasn't confident they would be able to carry it out at such short notice. He would tell Ichimura he wanted to hand back the responsibility to the merchandise division, which had always done it before. He knew it wouldn't be easy, since the decision to transfer responsibility to his department had been officially approved at a board meeting, but . . .

He would throw himself at Ichimura's feet and beg for his help. He didn't want to lose his job like Kitô. He couldn't help thinking of his wife and children at home.

Ichimura was in a bad mood.

He had countless things to think about, and now Konno had turned up unannounced wanting to talk about stocktaking of all things. He was on the point of sending him away when he sensed that something was up. Because Konno never came to him for advice. Konno didn't like him, was always bad-mouthing him. And yet here he was, suddenly asking for help. Something was definitely up.

He turned toward Konno with a smile, trying to act solicitous. But no matter how hard he tried, he couldn't understand what Konno was saying. Responsibility for stocktaking . . . new procedures . . . end of the month . . . unprepared . . . unable to cope . . . and he needed Ichimura's support. That was it? Why would Konno come to him with this? What was the big deal? He said he wanted ask advice, but he didn't have any questions that needed answers. What was going on?

Ichimura looked closely into Konno's childlike face as he spoke and concentrated on the signals he was giving off. They were coming through loud and clear. Flattery, ingratiation, humility. Guilt. Remorse. What did it all mean?

Suddenly, the pin dropped. The inventory! That was what was behind Kitô's mumblings. *Wait till the middle of next month.* The results of this new inventory would be out in the middle of next month. Kitô wanted him to see the results. Once Ichimura had this crucial clue in hand, the mystery soon unraveled itself. The only thing this inventory would reveal was the true value of the merchandise currently in stock at the center store. But what possible problems could there be? Imagine the worst-case scenario, say, if the actual value of the stock turned out to be substantially lower than it ought to be, then . . . the company could be in deep trouble.

The machinery of Ichimura's mind started to turn, taking him back to when Ishikari Seijirô had called him during his business trip to Gifu the month before, distressed about bad clothing stock in the center store—bad stock to the tune of several hundred million yen. The next morning Ichimura had called Sugai, the floor manager, only to be told the bad stock didn't exist. As soon as he got back to the head office, Ichimura had gone to the center store himself; he had seen with his own eyes that nothing was amiss.

Apparently Kôjima was the one who claimed he had seen bad stock. Ichimura had spoken to him to reassure him that everything was fine, but something in Kôjima's expression suggested he still had his doubts. Maybe this was the connection with Kitô screwing up the contracts. "Tell me," Ichimura said to Konno, "this new stocktaking—how does it work, exactly?"

"It's going to be terrible," Konno said. "In the past there were two stages to the procedure: counting and checking. You count the amount of each item in stock, and then you check the numbers against the accounting records. Now we're supposed to do the whole thing twice, and compare the two results. In the past, one person did the counting—now it's supposed to be one person counting, another person writing the numbers down in a ledger. Then another team does the same thing again, and then they compare results. And they say we have to do everything all over again if there's the slightest discrepancy. And then we check the numbers against accounting—not once but twice."

"Who says so?" Ichimura asked.

A look of concern flashed across Konno's features. It was now or never. "Mr. Kôjima," he said.

"And he's an authority on stocktaking?"

"I'm not really sure. Apparently he used to supervise the inventory his bank used to carry out on companies they were investing in, but I don't know that he's an expert, necessarily."

Ichimura mulled these revelations over for a few moments. "But surely you won't have enough time to do all that, will you?"

"Excuse me?"

"How are you going to find the time for this new scheme that Mr. Kôjima wants to introduce? Even if you do it on a day when the store is closed, if you start first thing in the morning it will be the middle of the night by the time you finish."

"I know. That's the problem. But according to Mr. Kôjima, stocktaking is pointless unless it's accurate. Accuracy, accuracy, accuracy, accuracy. He's like a broken record."

Konno's flippant tone was making Ichimura scowl. Konno hurriedly rephrased what he had just said: "He really does seem to value accuracy above everything else, I mean."

"Of course. There's no sense in taking inventory unless you're going to do it accurately. Is he suggesting there were inaccuracies in the way stocktaking was done in the past?"

"Seems that way."

"For example?"

"Apparently he took part in stocktaking at the center store at the end of May, and he got the impression that the people doing the checking were getting their figures from the people doing the counting, and that everyone just wanted to get the whole thing over with as quickly as possible. He seemed to think there wasn't any real checking going on."

"There could have been a few negligent people involved, but he's not suggesting that the whole team was like that, is he?"

"I don't know. Maybe."

For a last few minutes something had been gnawing at Ichimura. It was the same kind of anxiety he had felt back when he was a student and showed up for an exam without having studied. Stocktaking was like that: he hadn't done his homework and as far as management was concerned, it was a terrible weakness for him. There were certain aspects of his job—allocating the company budget and organizing accounts among them—that didn't suit his character and talents at all. And stocktaking was up there.

He had taken part in stocktaking once, not long after he joined the company, and it was the most boring day of his life. It was time-consuming, required incredible attention to detail, and was unspeakably tedious. They had gone through the entire supermarket counting every single item. He understood that that was the only way to be absolutely sure of what you had in stock at any given moment, and you had to have accuracy, but still . . .

Something else started to gnaw at him as Konno complained about the new procedures. An uneasiness. Maybe he'd made a big mistake. Maybe there had been some miscalculation in the clothing department. Maybe . . . it was just about conceivable . . . maybe there really had been piles of bad stock. Maybe . . . Kôjima was right. . . .

These thoughts led to others, all of them pointing to the same conclusion. What had started out as a worst-case scenario was starting to look like fact. He thought about Kitô's reckless sabotage of his own work—and the way he acted under questioning, like it was a crime of conscience. He remembered the panic in Ishikari's voice over the phone when he had called about the bad stock. He could almost see the piles and piles of boxes of unsold clothing in the storeroom. . . . Was it really possible? Could it really be true?

If they carried out an accurate stocktaking, everything would be revealed. But Ichimura didn't like the idea of it happening at someone else's instigation and under someone else's control. More than anything else, he wanted to avoid having any unpleasant truths revealed by Kôjima and his faction, especially if this marked the beginning of their full-frontal assault on his own position.

"All right, Konno-*san*," he said. "I understand your position. I think the best way of dealing with this would be to let the merchandise department carry out the stocktaking as in the past, but have your department remain formally in charge. Leave it to me; I don't think there's any need for you to worry."

"That's a relief. I'm really grateful for your help," Konno said, as he got up, bowed and turned to leave.

As Ichimura lumbered out of the head office, he bumped into Kôjima coming in at the entrance. Ichimura was shocked by Kôjima's appearance. He looked haggard and worn out. His face, drained of color, had a claylike pallor. Ichimura thought to inquire after his health, but didn't get a chance before Kôjima hurried into the building, as though he were running away from something.

Ichimura could sense the rejection and hostility. But there was nothing he could do about it. He hadn't wanted the fight, but he wasn't going to back down now that Kôjima had started it. With a heavy heart, Ichimura made his way back to the center store. He wanted to have a good look at the stock in the clothing department.

If there was even the slightest possibility that the stocktaking was going to reveal unpleasant truths, he needed to make sure it took place under his own control. So long as he got his hands on the information before anyone else, he would have any number of options when it came time for an appropriate response. If necessary, he could earn himself some extra time by fiddling with the results a bit. If he could persuade the suppliers to play along they could even help manipulate the figures.

There was no sign of anything out of the ordinary in the storeroom on the second floor. Ichimura walked from one corner of the storeroom to the other. There was merchandise on the shelves, everything neat and orderly. He looked into a few of the cardboard boxes and checked on their contents.

"Is something wrong, sir?" came a voice behind him.

Ichimura turned round to find Sugai, the floor manager, standing, looking neat and trim in his company uniform. "No, there's nothing wrong." Ichimura smiled. "But I am supposed to be the director responsible for the clothing department, so I thought I'd stop by and have a look around. It's been a while."

"Thanks for coming by," Sugai said perfunctorily. His big brown eyes couldn't conceal a certain discomfort. He couldn't stand it when other people interfered in his business.

"You seem to be doing a good job. It's always so neat and tidy in here."

"Ah, not really."

Ichimura was always reminded of cats whenever he looked at Sugai. A bright, intelligent animal—but not one that would ever try to make friends with a human being. "How's business?" asked Ichimura.

"Not great. It's this warm weather. Impossible to shift autumn clothes when the weather's like this."

"Things will get cooler by the end of the month. We'll make up for it then."

"I hope so."

"Is Manabe around, by the way?"

"I saw him just a few minutes ago. Should I go look for him?"

"No, never mind. I'm sure I'll bump into him."

Slowly, Ichimura made his way up the staircase from the second to the third floor, and then took the public elevator up to the fourth floor. No sign of Manabe. He was about to go down to the food department, when he caught sight of the stairs leading up to the roof garden, and decided to go out for a breath of fresh air. He couldn't remember the last time he'd done that.

There were a few kids in the small children's play area, several mothers sitting on benches chatting. Things were quiet: it was early on a weekday afternoon. And there, standing by the chain-link fence on the other side of the play area, was Manabe. Ichimura was about to shout a greeting, but stopped himself. Something about Manabe's posture suggested weariness. Manabe didn't notice him, even when Ichimura walked over and stood beside him. He was staring vacantly out into space.

"Hello," Ichimura said at last.

Manabe turned to him in surprise. "Sorry, I didn't see you there," he said blankly.

"Lost in thought? What's up?"

Manabe said nothing.

"Are you all right? You don't look so great. Are you feeling sick or something?"

"No, I'm fine."

"You sure?"

Standing next to Manabe, Ichimura took in the view of the city as it stretched to the mountains beyond. There were new housing developments in the hills to the west. He could see the red and blue tiles of their roofs glinting in the September sunshine. Out there lived the purchasing power that supported the store. "You know, it's amazing," he said. "They're all our customers. The economy grows. People flock to the cities. Their income increases. But there aren't enough retail outlets to soak up all that new purchasing power. That's where we step in—to help them out. For a company like ours, the future is bright. There's no end to the opportunities ahead of us."

Ichimura was getting carried away, speaking with some force. But Manabe said nothing.

"Look how we've grown. Think back to the way things were four or five years ago. It's like a dream. Unbelievable. Back then the company was just a vulnerable little sapling. Not anymore. We've put down sturdy roots, and we're starting to spread our branches toward a glorious future."

Pause. But no comment from Manabe.

"The whole supermarket industry has a glorious future, but the outlook is especially bright for us. This area is going to see expansion on a massive scale over the next few years. Sawabe is becoming a part of the Tokyo commuter belt. No other supermarket chain has such a rich and fertile area to operate in. But it's not just our location. Things are looking good within the company, especially here at the center store. Getting a superstore like this up and running has worked wonders for us. Our prospects are better than ever. You agree, Manabe-*san*?"

Manabe didn't say a word. He didn't seem to have heard a word Ichimura said.

"Manabe-*san*, what's wrong? Something's bothering you. What is it?"

"Nothing. I'm fine."

But Ichimura could see pain, despair, self-loathing. He could sense a darkness that was sucking the light out of Manabe's soul. Manabe, who was always cheerful, energetic, optimistic.

"Come on, something's not right. Tell me what it is. I'll do whatever I can to help you."

"It's nothing,"Manabe said, looking at his watch. "I'm sorry, you'll have to excuse me. I have to go. If there's something you need to talk about, I can see you later." He walked off hurriedly.

Ichimura remained fixed to his spot, perplexed. He had no idea what the reason was, but Manabe was obviously not himself. He was deeply disturbed. Something at home? Or at work? And that's when the thought came to Ichimura: the bad stock?

He suddenly felt an undefined anxiety. Something had been going on that he knew nothing about. He didn't like it, and he didn't want to believe it, but he had no choice. Ichimura tried to think logically, running through the chronology in his mind. Kôjima claimed he had found bad stock. Sugai categorically denied anything of the kind when Ichimura called him about it. Ichimura believed him. When he went to check the storeroom the next day, Ichimura found nothing suspicious.

But assume that Kôjima's claim was right, then things started to look very different. All that bad stock: there one day, and gone the next. Someone had hidden it, gotten rid of it. If that was the case, then it had to be Sugai—or at least he was in on it. And Manabe knew about it!

Ichimura started to move toward the staircase, his pace increasing with every step. He walked faster and faster as he descended the stairs, keeping an eye out for Manabe. By the time he got to the first floor he was taking two steps at a time. He found Manabe by the cash registers.

"Would you mind stepping outside with me for a minute, please?" Ichimura said to him.

"I've got a meeting with the floor heads that's starting any moment."

"Do it later."

It was clear from Ichimura's tone of voice that this was not a subject for debate, and Manabe followed Ichimura to a coffee shop next to the store.

"Tell me, Manabe. About a month or so ago, you found a large amount of bad stock in the clothing department storeroom on the second floor. Am I right?" Ichimura went straight to the heart of the matter, watching carefully for Manabe's response. Suddenly, color rushed back to Manabe's face. It was as though the truth were trying to break through the lies and rise to the surface.

"Well?"

"No. I didn't see anything."

"There's no use lying to me. I can see it in your eyes. Come on—tell me the truth. What did you see?"

"Nothing. Really, there was nothing."

"Come on. That's enough."

Ichimura had to laugh. There was no getting through to some people. But Manabe just repeated the same answer. Ichimura kept at him with his questions. But Manabe stuck to his guns too. He had seen nothing. There had been nothing there.

The struggle went on for a half hour, the two men sitting across from one another like two kids having a staring contest. But still Manabe refused to give anything away. He sat motionless at the table, not even touching his coffee, and repeated the same words over and over again—even though it was clear from the expression on his face that he was lying.

"All right, I get it. You're not going to cooperate. You're sticking to your story no matter what happens. Suit yourself."

Ichimura left the coffee shop with Manabe. They went back to the store together and up to the second floor, where Ichimura saw Sugai.

"All right, you get back to your work," Ichimura said, finally releasing Manabe to go about his business. Ichimura did not want to let Manabe out of his sight. It would only take him a moment to call Sugai and warn him.

"Sorry to bother you, Sugai-*san*. Can you spare me a few minutes?"

Ichimura went back to the same coffee shop, this time with Sugai in tow. The procedure was the same as with Manabe. After gesturing in a friendly manner to Sugai to take a seat, he sat down opposite him and got straight to the point. What did he know about the bad stock in the clothing department?

"As I've said all along, there was never any such thing," he said. Unlike with Manabe, Ichimura could sense no wavering or uncertainty. *Why are you bringing that up again?* Sugai seemed to be saying. Ichimura didn't have much to work with.

Sugai responded to all of his questions with a short yes or no. And his answers came without a moment's hesitation. He never stumbled, never got flustered. Ichimura could feel Sugai's big brown eyes staring right back at his own ugly pockmarked face the whole time. Sugai even managed to finish his coffee.

"All right. Get back to work," Ichimura said at last. There didn't seem to be much reason to drag the conversation out any longer. Sugai bowed his head politely and walked out of the coffee shop.

Ichimura sat deep in thought as he watched Sugai leave. Regret and remorse struck at his breast. He should have kept a closer eye on things. He should have looked at the merchandise more carefully. Why had he always neglected stocktaking? His one big weakness had crept up behind him and bitten him in the ass.

Ichimura got back to the office to find a message saying that Ishikari Seijirô wanted to see him.

"Have you heard these rumors about Kôjima and my secretary?" Ishikari asked.

"I've heard what people are saying, of course."

"This is turning into a real mess. What should I do?"

"Why do you need to do anything?"

"Come on, be serious. The whole company's talking about it. I can't pretend I don't know what's going on."

"Have you checked the facts with the people involved?"

"Not yet. But it must be true. Kôjima's living apart from his wife—and besides: No smoke without fire, right?"

"Well . . ."

"I'll have a word with Kôjima and see what he has to say. We may have to transfer him to Ishiei Real Estate until the fuss dies down."

Ishiei Real Estate was a property management company that belonged to Ishikari Eitarô. Aside from its day-to-day business, it was also used to help the family out of scrapes and embarrassments—from avoiding taxes to providing a refuge for loyal employees who had outgrown their usefulness. It was the perfect place to put Kôjima out to pasture after the scandal he had caused at Ishiei Stores.

But at the moment Ichimura wanted nothing to do with it. He had more important things on his mind.

NINE

THE SHIMO-SHINDEN STORE

The official opening of the new Ishiei Stores outlet at Shimo-Shinden took place at nine thirty on a Thursday morning toward the end of September. After a few words from the company president, there was a congratulatory message from the head of the local retailers' association and an address by the new store manager, followed by a heartfelt recitation of the Businessman's Pledge by all the new employees.

Ichimura had put together the Businessman's Pledge about five years ago, and it had been recited at official openings and other major company functions ever since.

> *We will value the customers' feelings above all other things.*
>> *We will never lose sight of the bottom line.*
>> *We will never raise our voices in anger.*
>> *We will . . .*

There were seven statements, all in the same vein. The employees chanted the pledge in unison and then, on a signal from the store manager, punched the air and cheered at the top of their voices, shaking the walls of the new store. The ceremony closed with the employees bowing in a line at the entrance, and loudly chorusing the words they would use to welcome every customer from that day forward: *Thank you for visiting Ishiei Stores!*

Nearly a hundred women were waiting outside. They had started to gather a half hour before the advertised opening time, clutching flyers promising big bargains to commemorate the grand opening. They had been watching the ceremony through the windows with mounting excitement, but now that the employees had turned and started shouting and bowing in their direction, something close to embarrassment seemed to have overcome them.

A young woman snipped a ribbon with a pair of scissors, and the Shimo-Shinden outlet was officially opened. The waiting was over, and the crowd of women surged like the tide into the store. Each customer seemed to have a particular product in mind—lingerie (20 percent off), pots and pans (specially priced); panty hose (two pairs for fifty yen)—and there was no stopping them.

The girls at the cash registers waited nervously for the first onslaught. The company had shipped in extra support from other outlets to help with the cashiering. Workers from the head office were also there—Kuroba Motoko was helping out with the bagging. And before long, there were lines in front of every register. The store was full of people, and still more people kept coming. It was an amazing sight.

As the first hour passed, the hardcore bargain-hunters were replaced by the simply curious. Horiguchi Gen, head of sales and promotions, made his way around the store, eavesdropping on what customers were saying:

I can't believe it! You'd never know it was the same place.

What happened to the place that used to be here?

Well, things are a whole lot brighter in here now, that's for sure.

Horiguchi felt both relief and gratification. He had stopped by the night before to make sure everything was ready and ended up getting stuck in a torrential downpour. It had something to do with the mountains, one of the workers told him. "It'll be pouring around here, and clear in Tokyo." So he was overjoyed this morning to wake up to beautiful clear blue skies stretching as far as the eye could see. The company had decided to acquire this new outlet on the recommendation of

Kôjima, whom Horiguchi greatly admired. That was enough in itself to make him eager to see the store succeed.

And now, listen to this crowd of customers!

Even the day before the grand opening, there were some in the company who thought chances of success in such an out-of-the-way location were touch-and-go. But if they could continue to attract customers like this, then signs were good. Of course good figures on opening day were no guarantee of long-term success. But a store that did badly on its first day of business was guaranteed to fail.

Horiguchi headed for the fresh produce work area. He wanted to talk to Ôtaka, who had come over to advise the new section chief and help out with the usual opening day chaos. Horiguchi was going to have to choose his words carefully.

"How's it going?" he asked.

"Things are selling OK, but we're not putting any good stuff out there yet. It's all just junk like this," Ôtaka replied, holding up the cucumbers he was wrapping. None of them was straight.

"How about the new toy?" Horiguchi asked, gesturing toward the big refrigerator in the corner. It was the keep-fresh "regenerator" that had been left unused by the store's previous owners.

"I'm still not sure how you're supposed to use it, to be honest," Ôtaka said, stopping what he was doing and following Horiguchi over to it.

The regenerator was more like a large refrigerated storeroom than a standard walk-in refrigerator. Stepping in, they found it cool, but not uncomfortably cold. Some kind of cylindrical machinery on the shelves was giving off vapor with an occasional *whoosh*ing hiss.

"Does it really work? Does it really bring dead vegetables back to life?" Horiguchi asked.

"Sort of seems to. Spinach and stuff definitely gets crisper after it's been in here. You can take stuff that's started to wilt, give it a rinse, put it in one of these big square baskets, and after a while it's as fresh as anything," Ôtaka said, pointing to rows of fresh-looking spinach inside a basket.

"Fantastic. With new technology like this we should be able to transform the fresh produce section into one of our strengths. Was it Kôjima who showed you this, by the way?"

"Not exactly . . ."

"Listen," Horiguchi said, suddenly getting serious, "you've heard the rumors about Kôjima?" It was time to get to the point.

"What? No, I haven't heard anything," replied Ôtaka. But his expression told a different story.

"You must have. I'm sure you wouldn't take them seriously, but it's really making things awkward for him."

"I'm sorry to hear that. But you know the old phrase—no smoke without fire."

"Don't be stupid. I know who started the fire."

Ôtaka was tight-lipped.

"This whole thing was started by Kuroba Motoko," Horiguchi went on angrily.

"I don't know what you're talking about."

"Just don't get taken in by gossip and rumors, that's all I'm saying. People have been acting weird around Kôjima ever since the rumors started. It's making it hard for him to do his job. And he's also been really upset by the change in your attitude recently. He was hoping you'd help him out with his research groups."

"How can I trust a man who would do something like that?"

"Listen to you. You obviously believe every word of that garbage."

"How could I not? I heard it from someone who was right there when it happened."

As Horiguchi struggled to reason with Ôtaka, workers came into the regenerator several times, wheeling out fresh produce to be put on display. Apparently the produce was flying off the shelves.

"Horiguchi-*san,* as you can see, we're a little busy right now," said Ôtaka, eager to end the conversation.

"All right. But remember—there's no truth to the rumors. It's a bunch of lies. I'm going to have a word with Kuroba myself."

Ôtaka didn't say anything. He didn't know what to say. And even after Horiguchi left, the conversation continued to haunt him. Ôtaka had believed what Motoko had told him. She had seen the whole thing herself.

Just when he had changed his mind about Kôjima, thinking he was an OK manager after all, along came this story to throw cold water over his enthusiasm. It was pretty clear that Kôjima and Misaki Yoshiko liked each other. But now they were sleeping together! That wasn't right! Ôtaka had given up any hope of making Yoshiko his wife since she had flat-out turned him down, but that didn't mean he was completely over his feelings for her.

The morning after the party at Kôjima's apartment, Kuroba Motoko had come to work a bit overheated. As fate would have it, Yoshiko was the first person she bumped into. "Did you have a good time last night?" Motoko asked, and a flustered look of panic and embarrassment crossed Yoshiko's face. Motoko hadn't wanted to believe what she had witnessed on the dark sidewalk. But given Yoshiko's response, it had to be true.

She told Ôtaka, who immediately stopped being cooperative with Kôjima. Kôjima couldn't help noticing, and no longer asked Ôtaka for help. The atmosphere at the research meetings became strained and uncomfortable. It was a shame, Ôtaka agreed, but Kôjima had brought it on himself. At least that is what he had thought—until now, with Horiguchi trying to convince him that the rumors weren't true. But if that were the case, that would mean Motoko had lied.

Impossible. Motoko could be brash, but she wouldn't tell lies to hurt someone.

Ever since the day they had gone together to buy produce for the first of Kôjima's research meetings, Ôtaka had seen Motoko in a different light. He had even started to think that she would make someone a good wife. They had gone out on a date once. Nothing special—they had simply spent a few hours in another's company—but Ôtaka nevertheless had pleasant memories of the evening.

That was when she had told him about Kôjima and Yoshiko.

Ôtaka forced himself to stop thinking about all this, and went back out onto the sales floor. It was seething. The aisles were filled with people. Just finding what you were looking for and getting it to the cash register was a struggle. Exhausted women were throwing items randomly from the shelves into their baskets.

"Welcome to Ishiei Stores. Bargain prices!" Ôtaka heard his voice rise from his throat of its own accord.

Kôjima stood next to Asayama and looked on at the commotion across the street.

"Looks like a roaring success," Asayama said, a smile on his wrinkle-heavy face.

Kôjima stood in silence, also smiling.

"Thanks to the sales plan we ran," Asayama went on. "That 'Bright New Future' campaign was a good idea. It's really helped shake off any associations with the bad old Ogawa Stores days."

Kôjima still said nothing.

"No one can deny that your ideas are working. You were the one who persuaded the board to open a store here, and your research group has been coming up with some impressive results too."

Kôjima looked at Asayama in surprise. This was news to him.

"I don't mean visible results in terms of sales yet. It's too soon for that. But the attitude of the people has really changed for the better. Several of the store managers have told me about the big difference they've seen in the department heads taking part. There was one funny story," Asayama said, beginning to laugh. "The head of the fresh fish department in the Nakasu store is this guy named Ôsawa. One day, the store manager was walking by when he heard Ôsawa talking loudly in the staff recreation room. 'The only way to make sure is to stick your finger in. Sometimes you have to lift her up a bit to get it in properly.' The store manager stormed into the rec room and started freaking out, 'This may be the recreation room, and but that doesn't mean you can talk smut like that in my store—especially with ladies present!' Turned out Ôsawa was lecturing his workers on how to clean and fillet a fish!"

"So what did the store manager do?"

"Well, he had to apologize, of course. He told me it was the first time he'd ever heard Ôsawa talk about anything besides sex, baseball, and mah-jongg!"

Kôjima laughed.

"It's funny," Asayama went on. "Attitudes toward the research groups seem to be quite split. Most of the employees think it's a great idea, but there are a few—not many, but a few—who don't want to help out at all, who actually want the groups to fail. And then a few others who don't care one way or the other."

"Let me guess who the ringleader of the uncooperative group is. The chief of the meat department at the center store?"

"Sashima. How'd you know?" Asayama said, quite surprised.

Sashima was leader of the meat-section meetings. The way he behaved at the meetings, you'd have thought there was no one more helpful or more receptive to new ideas. How had Kôjima guessed that underneath this façade he was not merely uncooperative, but deliberately trying to sabotage the meetings altogether? Asayama had only found out the previous day from a meat-section chief at one of the other stores.

"Wild conjecture."

"No, can't be. Did somebody tell you?"

"Nobody said anything. But if Sashima really is manipulating the price of his cuts and taking the best stuff home, then it figures he would be opposed to something like this."

"You're quite the cunning detective, I have to say."

"It's simple. The idea of these meetings is to go through all the fresh food items we sell, comparing them to similar items at other supermarkets, and try to find better ways of processing, packaging, and managing them."

"Right."

"If we keep these meetings going, we'll eventually have a pretty good idea what kinds of products we want to be selling. Not an idea that's been pushed on people from above, one that the employees came up with themselves. And because they came up with it themselves, they'll want to work hard to put it into practice. And they'll pressure their colleagues to act in accordance with the standards they've all agreed on. Ultimately, these meetings could act as a kind of positive social force within the company. But once things are up and running, it will be almost impossible for anyone to manipulate his department for personal gain. Which would mean the end of Sashima's little shell game. And that's why he wants these meetings to fail."

"But why act so cooperative, then?"

"Good question," Kôjima said with a wry smile. "He could be trying to work himself into a position of leadership, so that he can twist the findings to suit his own purposes. Or maybe he's pretending to go along with things for a while so that he can suddenly to turn round and reject the whole thing."

Kôjima hadn't been looking well lately, and Asayama had been hoping to cheer him up. This conversation seemed to energize him a bit, but Kôjima had a lot on his mind. Kitô had been suspended. The research groups weren't going as well as he'd hoped. And then there were the rumors.

Asayama had been worried about them too; they still showed no sign of fading away. He had decided to bite the bullet and had gone to ask Kôjima about them directly. Kôjima denied everything, and Asayama believed him. But the rumors continued. If anything, they seemed to get more lurid every time he heard them.

Kôjima had opened up to Asayama. He was in pain about what Yoshiko was going through. He knew that for her every prurient gaze, every suggestive remark, was like a dagger to her heart. "It's my fault. I should have been more careful, and now I've caused her all this misery. I wanted to apologize—but how? There was no way I could talk to her about it at work, and if anyone saw us talking together outside the office it'd start off a whole new slew of rumors. In the end I called her at home late one night and apologized. She said she wanted to quit the company. But I told her that would be the worst thing she could do. It would just add fuel to the fire and make people believe the rumors even more. I told her she should try to carry on. I could hear her crying."

"Everything will be all right in the end. If there's no truth to the rumors they'll just go away after a couple of months. And in this case, you know exactly who started the rumors. The first thing to do is to put Kuroba Motoko right."

"Sure, but how can I do that? How I am supposed to prove that nothing happened?"

Several days after this conversation, Horiguchi had gone to Asayama about what was going on.

"I know who started the rumors," Asayama said. "Kuroba Motoko. Is there anything you can do to ask her to stop them?"

"Kuro-*chan*? I might be able to talk her. She's a pretty bright kid. Why would she do a thing like this?"

"Who knows what goes on inside a woman's mind," Asayama said.

"Could it be jealousy, do you think? *Hell hath no fury like a woman scorned. . . .* "

Asayama longed to see Kôjima back to his old self again. No army ever won a battle led by a general who was depressed. For now, he would put all his efforts into restoring Kôjima's morale.

"For now, everything hangs on the results of the stocktaking at the end of the month. One thing's for sure: it's going to open everyone's eyes to what's been going in the clothing department."

"Not necessarily. In fact, there's every chance things won't go the way we expected at all," Koijima said, his voice flat.

"Why?"

"I have a feeling Konno doesn't want to play ball anymore. And the people from the clothing department have been showing an unusual interest in developments recently. I'm starting to suspect that after all our efforts to get the store management department put in charge, we're going to end up having the guys from merchandising running things just like they always have."

"Ichimura's counterattack, do you think?"

"Could be. He's certainly showing an a lot of interest in how we're planning to carry out the inventory."

Normally Kôjima defended Ichimura whenever Asayama and the others talked about him as the villain, but today he seemed to have made up his mind that Ichimura was indeed interfering with their plans. Perhaps the gradual accumulation of incriminating evidence was becoming too much even for him.

"That sneaky damn badger," Asayama said.

"The first thing is to make sure that this stocktaking is absolutely accurate. And if that fails, then . . ." Kôjima swallowed his words.

"Then . . . ?"

"If that fails, there's only one option left. We have to confront Ichimura face-to-face. I would make sure Ishikari was present when we did that. Ichimura's not stupid, though; he'll probably just explain the whole thing away. If that happens, I will hand in my resignation."

"But . . . you shouldn't even be thinking about that."

"I wish I could resign right now, to tell you the truth. I made up my mind that this was where I wanted to be, but for some reason the company isn't ready to accept me. I'm trying my best, but all I seem to do is cause problems. I'm just getting in the way."

"Don't say that. Plenty of people want you to stay."

"Really? Then why are they all saying such awful things about me?"

Kôjima looked down at the floor, and Asayama noticed tears in the corner of his eyes.

It was late at night, and Ôtaka's Toyota Corolla was speeding down the highway toward Sawabe. There were few cars on the road at this hour. Huge long-distance trucks were making the most of the deserted roads.

Kuroba Motoko sat in the passenger seat next to him.

For the time being, silence reigned.

Until a few minutes ago, Motoko had been telling him about her conversation that afternoon with Horiguchi. Horiguchi had wanted to know the truth behind the rumors about Kôjima and Yoshiko. Motoko told him the rumors were true. Where was the proof? he wanted to know. She had seen it with her own eyes. How, where, when? What were the precise details? He had pressed her so hard that Motoko started to lose her temper. This only made Horiguchi even angrier.

"And what happens if you're wrong?" he said.

"I'm not wrong."

"There are two people's lives at stake here. Don't you realize that?"

"Of course I do."

"These rumors are making Kôjima's position impossible, you know."

"What do you want me to do about it? He's only got himself to blame."

"That's what I'm trying to find out. Are you absolutely sure you saw what you think you saw?"

"I know what I saw."

The conversation went around in circles like a cassette tape on a permanent loop. They had gone over the same ground again and again through the lunch hour. In the end, Motoko refused to budge an inch, and Horiguchi stomped off angry and frustrated.

"Well, you can't help what you saw," Ôtaka said now, gripping the steering wheel tight and staring ahead.

Motoko said nothing as the car cruised silently through the night.

"Don't back down now. Never mind how much pressure Horiguchi puts on you. I hate that. Just because they're in a position of authority, doesn't mean these people have a right to twist the facts. For all we know Kôjima was the one who told Horiguchi to quash the rumors in the first place. Don't give in. Don't let them browbeat you into submission. If that's how they're going to come at us, we have to stand our ground and fight back. I believe you. I'm on your side. What you saw is what you saw—no matter what anyone else says."

"That's the thing, though," Motoko said after a while. "I'm not so sure anymore."

"What are you talking about? I'm on your side. I'll stand by you. You can't let yourself be beaten down by pressure from a schmuck like Kôjima."

"It's not that. I'm trying as hard as I can to remember exactly what happened. But the harder I try, the less clear it all becomes."

"What do you mean?"

"That night. I mean, I was pretty sure I saw them embracing. But it was dark, and I couldn't really see too clearly."

Suddenly a truck streaked by with a loud blast of its horn. Ôtaka had lost concentration for a few moments and his car had to swerve to get back in his lane.

"But Kôjima did go into her apartment?" he asked.

"That's what I thought. But I didn't actually see it happen. My head was spinning after what I had seen, and I went home before anything else happened."

"Wait a minute," Ôtaka said. "Just wait a minute." At the next side road, he turned left then pulled over. "You'd better tell me what actually happened," he said.

Motoko said nothing.

"Tell me the truth. Did you just make the whole thing up?"

"No way. First I saw Kôjima come rushing out of his apartment, practically skipping along the sidewalk with excitement. They were walking along like lovers, really close together. Then they stopped and stood in the dark together by the entrance to Yoshiko's apartment."

"And then what happened?"

"I could feel it. I really could. I could feel them burning with passion for one another," Motoko said as she started to cry. "Then, when I asked Yoshiko about it the next morning, she turned bright red. So it was like proof."

"All right, I understand. There's no need to cry." Ôtaka was confused. How was he supposed to deal with a woman when she started crying?

"But I didn't actually see it. It was too dark. I don't know whether he actually went into her apartment or not. But the way they were acting, nothing would surprise me. That's all I said." Motoko was sobbing now.

Ôtaka sat helplessly waiting for the tears to stop. He caught sight of a building out of the corner of his eye, its flashing purple neon sign blazing like a beacon in the night. It was shaped like a European castle. A love hotel.

"Come on, that's enough of that kind of talk. Never mind other people. They can look after themselves."

Motoko had stopped crying now, but still she said nothing.

"Let's not worry about it anymore. It's time we started thinking about us. About you and me."

"What?"

Motoko looked up to see the castle shimmering like a fairy tale. She could hardly move her lips to speak. It was all so sudden. But perhaps deep down, a part of her had always known it would come to this.

The car moved quietly thought the deserted streets.

Neither of them said a thing.

The car continued its ascent up the slope, a little faster now, and slid into the hotel parking lot.

Horiguchi Gen was furious. So Motoko had seen Kôjima and Yoshiko from behind, and somehow sensed "flames of passion burning between them." And now it had come to this. How someone could spread such rumors based on nothing more than a fantasy was beyond him. Women were like children—unpredictable and hard to handle.

After the Shimo-Shinden store closed its doors for the day, Horiguchi hitched a ride in a car heading back to head office, cursing womankind under his breath the whole way, a look of disgust on his face. The car was in Sakuradani before he knew it.

"Anywhere around here's fine," he said, and got out just off the main road. It was a ten-minute walk home. But he wasn't ready to go home yet. He wanted to go someplace to decompress. He needed a drink. He hardly ever went out for a drink alone, but tonight the circumstances were different. He remembered a bar he had gone to not far from here about a year ago with Sugai, the clothing department floor manager at the center store, who lived in the area.

As he expected, no one in the bar remembered him. "I have been here before, actually," he said to the *mama-san,* feeling for some reason a need to explain his presence.

"Oh? Who were you with?"

"No one in particular. Actually, I'd rather just be by myself tonight."

"Please yourself. Make yourself at home," the *mama-san* said, drifting off to tend to her other customers, a professional smile on her lips. Taking that as their cue, none of the other hostesses felt the need to pay Horiguchi any attention either.

Sitting alone, he drank three highballs and munched absentmindedly on peanuts and *sembei.* He had forgotten how hard it was to feel comfortable in a bar where they didn't know you. He would have been better off going home and drinking there. He was getting up to leave when he heard the door open and the voice of the *mama-san* calling out a greeting.

"Sugai-*san!* Long time no see!"

Horiguchi spun around and saw the *mama-san* welcoming the very man he'd been to the bar with once before. Sugai was nattily dressed as ever in jeans and a crisply pressed shirt; with him was Manabe, the manager of the center store. Horiguchi was about to call out to them himself, but apparently they hadn't seen him in the dark. They slid into a booth not far from where he was sitting, their backs to him.

They were just feet away, but Horiguchi knew that the moment for making his presence known was gone. For some reason, he didn't feel like going home anymore. *Just one more*, he thought, and ordered another double highball.

"It's cheaper by the bottle," the hostess serving Sugai and Manabe was saying.

"All right, we'll take the bottle then."

With the bottle of whiskey placed in front of them, Manabe and Sugai sat hunched close together, talking in low voices. There was a closed, self-contained air about them, as though the last thing they wanted was to be interrupted. And for some reason Motoko's claim about Kôjima and Yoshiko—that she had sensed the flames of passion between them—came to his mind. It was just like her to say such a stupid thing. And yet . . . *flames of passion* . . . Maybe it could look like that from a certain point of view?

Horiguchi sat in silence, turning his thoughts over and drinking his way through a couple more highballs. If Manabe and Sugai hadn't left the bar themselves, Horiguchi would probably have carried on drinking till he fell off his stool. He stumbled out into the late-night streets, his feet unsteady.

"Flames of passion? What bullshit. It doesn't make any sense," Horiguchi mumbled out loud now, spitting the words as though this could help sober him up. What the hell had those two been talking about so seriously anyway? And what about those weird nicknames they were calling each other? *Man*, was it? And *Guy*?

Weird talk. He had never heard anyone call them by these names before.

It was just after six on the day of the Shimo-Shinden opening that Ichimura turned up unannounced at the center store with Konno in tow. Ichimura went straight to store manager Manabe's office and asked him to call in Sugai, the clothing department manager.

Sugai appeared five minutes later, and Ichimura leaped to his feet the moment Sugai shut the door behind him. Ichimura stood in the middle of the room, his large frame dominating the space around him. The other three men sat, waiting for him to speak.

"Manabe, starting tomorrow morning, I want you to move to the Kuwahara store for a while," Ichimura said in his low, penetrating voice.

Manabe stared back at Ichimura in silence.

"The store manager there, Taniguchi, is going to be on sick leave for a while. I want you to cover for him."

Manabe was quick to pick up on what Ichimura was really saying. Taniguchi had been in a car accident and had suffered severe whiplash, and the word was he wasn't going to be back at work for some time. But there was something else going on; he could smell it in the air.

"Mr. Konno," Ichimura continued, "has agreed to keep an eye on things here at the center store while you're away. I know this is abrupt, but I want you to tie things up and hand over everything to him today. You can start work in Kuwahara tomorrow morning."

"There's no way I can hand over everything in such a short time."

"I'm not asking for a formal transfer. I just want to make sure that the stocktaking preparations won't get in the way of our other work here. You're still manager of the center store."

But for how much longer? Manabe couldn't help feeling that before long he would no longer be able to call himself manager of anything. On the face of it, he was only moving from one store to another, but there was a huge difference between the two stores. The center store was a superstore, the company's pride and joy; the outlet at Kuwahara was a decrepit old place with a sales area of less than 3,500 square feet. This could mean only one thing: a demotion.

"And as for you, Sugai," Ichimura said, "I want you to move to the clothing department at the head office starting tomorrow."

"Of course," Sugai replied politely. But his eyes were flashing with hostility and resentment.

"Your successor will be Kishiwara-*san*. From now on, you are relieved of your responsibilities as floor manager. This is effective immediately. I don't want you to touch any work-related documents in your possession from this moment on. You can remove any personal items from your desk and locker in the presence of Mr. Konno, and then I want you to leave the store right away. You are to report for work at the head office tomorrow morning at nine o'clock sharp. Is that understood?"

"Not entirely."

"Not entirely? What do you mean?"

"What is the reason for this? I can only assume you're accusing me of having done something wrong. You're treating me like a criminal."

Ichimura turned his fierce, pockmarked face toward Sugai. "We don't have to give reasons for moving people. You just do as you're told. If you really want to know the reason, why don't you examine your own conscience?"

Sugai's huge dark eyes were fixed upon Ichimura for several seconds. Then, with evident effort, he wrenched his sculpted features to one side, and did not look at Ichimura again.

Handing over responsibility to Konno was the hardest thing Manabe had ever done in his life. It wasn't that Konno was making things difficult for him—in fact, he was being almost painfully considerate. The problem was Manabe himself, and the way he felt inside. Everything he had lived through over the last six months came back to him in a flood of disjointed images. He was unable to concentrate.

He was overwhelmed. He felt as though he were being dragged down into the depths of hell. He felt despair and resignation. What could he do about things now anyway? But beneath everything there was yet a faint sense of pride—he'd really lived through something now.

He thought of his wife and their two daughters. He'd practiced this moment a hundred times in his mind. He'd seen it coming. He ought to have been resigned to his fate by now. But now that it had actually happened—now that he was face-to-face with the reality of it—he found that his heart was torn apart by a grief and confusion more profound than anything he had ever imagined. He sighed heavily.

"Try not to worry about it too much," Konno said. "No one is blaming you. Even Mr. Ichimura is mystified how you managed to get caught up in all this. I'm sure there were reasons—mitigating factors and circumstances we know nothing about. Why don't you just tell me the truth?"

But Manabe said nothing.

"It doesn't have to be now. Come see me any time you like. Or Mr. Ichimura. You'll feel much better if you get it off your chest and tell us the truth. We want to do whatever we can to help. We know you're not the kind of person who would ever do something really bad like this on your own."

"I'm sorry, I've done nothing wrong. I'm not hiding anything, and there's nothing on my conscience."

"Suit yourself. But Mr. Ichimura told me to say he would always be ready to listen to anything you wanted to say."

Finally, the handover was complete. Konno suggested going for a drink together, but Manabe shook him off and hurried back to Sakura-dani alone. Before he did anything, he had to talk to Sugai, the only person in the world who would understand what he was going through.

"I've been expecting you," said Sugai as he opened the door. The words were like a balm to Manabe, more comforting than ten thousand words could have been from anyone else.

Sugai turned as he stepped out the door and called back into the house, "I'm just popping out for a bit."

"Don't stay out too late," a voice called back. Sugai lived with his mother. Manabe had met her once; even in her fifties, she was still an attractive woman, and her voice retained a youthful sparkle.

"Where to? The country place?" Manabe asked, as the two men set off together.

"I need a drink first," Sugai replied. "I'm about at the end of my tether."

They set off side-by-side in the direction of their regular bar. As he listened to the sound of their shoes on the pavement, Manabe thought back sentimentally on everything that had happened so far. The story was surely at an end now.

TEN

GONE FISHING

The phone rang and rang; there was no ignoring it.
Finally, Ichimura Etsuko, wife of the Ishiei Stores
director, climbed wearily out of bed. At this hour—
the clock read just past midnight—it had to be either
a wrong number or an emergency.

"It's for you," she called back into the bedroom.
"Someone from work. Says his name's Manabe."

Ichimura rose sluggishly from bed and stumbled
over to the phone.

"Manabe?"

"I'm sorry to call you this late, but I need to apologize for something."

Ichimura said nothing.

"Crimes have been committed in the clothing department. Embezzling, gross misconduct. The ringleader is Kishiwara, the new floor manager at the center
store. It's him and Sashima—the meat department
chief. Sugai and I went along with it too."

Ichimura came to with a jolt. "Go on," he said.

"I'm sorry. I don't know what else to say. There
were reasons why Sugai and I cooperated. We had no
choice. But what we did was wrong—nothing can
change that. I'm ready to face the consequences. I sent
you proof of what's been happening via the office
mail this evening. It'll be on your desk tomorrow
morning. Well, I guess that's all I . . ."

"Hold on, hold on. I don't know what you're talking about. Come see me in the morning and we'll talk it over. But I'm glad you decided to come clean. I'll make sure it is taken into consideration."

"Thank you," Manabe said, then said nothing for a few moments. "OK, I'll come see you in the morning. Good night." The call was over before Ichimura could say anything more.

Ichimura put down the receiver slowly, a shiver running down his spine. Manabe wasn't going to come see him in the morning. Manabe was thinking of something else: death.

Ichimura picked up the receiver again and dialed Manabe's home number. A sleepy voice came on the line; it was Manabe's wife.

"Is your husband home?"

"No. He's gone fishing."

"Fishing?"

"Hmm. He's crazy about fishing these days. I think he went with Sugai-*san*."

"Sugai?"

"I think so. Why, is something wrong?"

Kôjima could hear the phone ringing through his bedroom door. He was in bed, but not asleep. He hadn't had a good night's sleep in a long time. But something more than his usual insomnia was keeping him awake tonight. He was thinking about the evening he had just spent with Misaki Yoshiko. She was so bright and cheerful, so full of life. He could still see her lovely smile. It was hard to believe she had lived through such an unhappy marriage. Was that unshakable cheerfulness of hers something that came naturally, or was she just putting on a brave face to the world?

He had thought a long time before finally asking her out for dinner. He wanted to apologize for the misunderstanding that had caused her so much embarrassment. More than anything, though, he wanted to relax over a meal with an attractive woman again. It had been a long time. Of course it was out of the question for them to meet anywhere near Sawabe, so they arranged to meet in Shinjuku. After dinner they went for drinks at a bar on the top floor of a high-rise hotel and just talked and talked. They seemed to have a natural understanding of one another, and the hours sped by.

Kôjima saw her clear white skin every time he closed his eyes. He was in his mid-thirties and hadn't been intimate with a woman for months. The images that danced before him now were torture. He was about to get up and fix himself a drink—the only dependable way of getting to sleep—when the phone started ringing.

He picked up the receiver and heard a series of pips. Whoever was calling at this hour was doing it from a pay phone. Then he heard Manabe's voice.

"Kôjima-*san*, I'm sorry to disturb you so late at night, but there's something I need to apologize for . . ."

Kôjima said nothing.

"You know the business about the bad stock in the center store clothing department? Well, it really was there. Everything was exactly the way you said it was."

Kôjima couldn't believe what he was hearing. He'd been waiting for Manabe to say this for so long, but now that it was finally happening it didn't sound real.

"I lied to you. I have no excuse. I had no choice, though; there was nothing else I could do. But I didn't want to leave you in the dark. That's why I'm calling now."

A premonition ran through Kôjima's mind: Manabe was about to do something awful. "I understand. But what . . . why—"

"I'm sorry. There were various things, private reasons . . ."

"I don't mean that. I mean why tell me now?"

Manabe was silent.

"Where are you calling from?"

"I'm in a phone booth."

"Where?"

"I'm sorry. Forgive me . . ." Manabe fell silent.

"Hello? Hello?" Kôjima shouted desperately into the receiver, afraid he was about to get cut off.

After a few seconds Manabe spoke again. "I have a favor to ask. Will you listen to what I have to say?"

"Of course. I'll do anything I can."

"Thank you," Manabe said, then went on slowly, thoughtfully, as though pondering each word: "I know that people are going to talk . . . about what's happened tonight, and about what happened in the past. And sooner or later, I'm sure you'll find out the truth. . . . But the truth is the one thing I never wanted anyone to know. Please help keep the truth hidden. If you knew what it was, I believe you would understand."

"I won't forget what you've said. But I have no idea what you are talking about."

"That's all I can say for now."

"But what is this truth you keep talking about?"

"You'll find out sooner or later. Probably by tomorrow evening—or is it already today? By tonight, then. Probably Sashima will say something."

"I should ask him, you mean?"

"I guess."

Kôjima was trying hard to keep Manabe talking. He was clutching the receiver as if holding on to a lifeline.

"All right. But about the bad stock . . . Come into the office tomorrow morning—I mean, *this* morning—and tell Mr. Ishikari what you've just told me. My word won't count for anything. Everyone knows I'm a complete ignoramus when it comes to the clothing department." Kôjima was starting to ramble, but he was desperate to keep Manabe on the line.

But Manabe was in no mood to go along with Kôjima's flippant tone. "I've forwarded all the relevant documents to Mr. Ichimura. You should go talk to him in the morning."

"Does he know the truth behind all this?"

"Not yet. But he will soon."

Kôjima said nothing.

"Thank you. I'm very sorry for all the trouble I've caused you. Especially asking such a selfish favor of you now, after everything . . ."

"Hello? Manabe, wait. Wait a minute. Don't hang up. Don't get any stupid ideas into your head. Hello? Where are you calling from?"

"Good-bye, Kôjima-*san*. Don't let my family ever find out the truth. Please."

There was the sound of line going dead.

·   ·   ·

Ichimura went back to bed, but he didn't stay there long. He was pacing nervously when the ring of the phone echoed through the house again. Was it Manabe calling back?

He ran over to the phone. It was Kôjima. They had to talk, urgently, he said; it sounded like Manabe was in trouble.

"I'm worried too. I'm wondering if I should call the police," Ichimura said.

"He's desperate that no one should find out the truth. What is he talking about? That's what he kept saying over and over."

"The truth? Must be something to do with what's been happening at work. He was going on about some embezzlement scam in the clothing department. That's probably what he meant."

"Could be," Kôjima said. "But somehow it doesn't add up. He sounded despondent. If you don't mind, I'd like to come and talk this over with you right away."

"I've got a car. Why don't I come see you?"

"Good. I'll be waiting."

Thirty minutes later, in the living room of Kôjima's apartment, the two men were deep in discussion.

They couldn't imagine what truth Manabe was so desperate to keep hidden. The embezzlement scam in the clothing department didn't seem like reason enough for someone to kill himself. Besides, no company wanted bad publicity; the company was more likely to deal with the matter quietly, not wanting to broadcast the problem. And why would Sashima know the truth? What connection could the chief of the meat department have to whatever had been going on in clothing?

Any secret a man would give his life to protect must have something to do with his reputation. Maybe he was having an affair that his wife didn't know about? But Kôjima and Ichimura would have to expose his secret if they had any hope of saving his life. Was that the right thing to do? It was easy to claim that nothing was more precious than a human life, but things weren't always so simple. Maybe a person's freedom of will was even more important than life itself.

Then there was the hard-nosed realism to consider. It would be a disaster for the company if the police got involved at this stage. The reputation of Ishiei Stores would take an almighty battering if it was revealed that employees had been defrauding the company of vast sums of money. No one would ever trust the company again. Ichimura was the first to express this concern, and Kôjima had to agree.

There was the wild hope that if they did call the police, they might be able to stop Manabe's car at a highway tollbooth or somewhere, but as the minutes ticked by—at a time when every second was vital—the less likely it became that they would take any action at all. By the time they reached their decision not to contact the police, it would have been meaningless to make the call anyway.

Manabe's car raced along the coastal highway. The road twisted and turned as it followed the jagged coastline, but at this time of night there was hardly any other traffic.

Next to him in the passenger seat was Sugai.

Until a few moments ago Sugai had been staring out at the street-lights whizzing past and the black seething ocean beyond, but now he leaned back his seat and shut his eyes tight. He was worn out from the time they had spent at their country place, and he soon fell into a deep, carefree sleep. Manabe, though, was wide awake, alert as he had ever been. He felt no hint of tiredness, not the slightest doubt or hesitation. He had done what he needed to do. He had thought it through many times, and always arrived at the same conclusion. There was no other choice.

Of course, you could always daydream about what might have been. He might have lived a totally different life if he had never met Sugai. But for Manabe such a life was impossible now. His life had been incomplete until he met Sugai and fallen in love. Once that happened, Manabe had no choice but to follow the path he had chosen—no matter where it led. Until the night it happened he could never have imagined such a thing. Until then he had been utterly straight, living an utterly straight life. Married, with two kids. A real Mr. Average—that's what everyone around him believed. He had believed it too. Until that night . . .

It had happened six months ago, at the end of March, in San Francisco. It was the first night of the overseas trip they had been sent on as reward for their contributions to the success of the center store. The impact of the events of that night had been so profound that Manabe expected every detail to be etched indelibly in his memory. For some reason, though, he didn't remember much about it at all.

The time they had spent together was sweeter and more precious than anything Manabe had experienced in his life, and by the time he realized what was happening they could no longer bear to be apart. To put it in crude terms, Sugai seduced him. But then Manabe discovered something within himself he had never known existed, and had been dragged into a world of forbidden pleasures from which there was no return. From that night they started calling each other "Man" and "Guy"—nicknames in English based on their Japanese names that served as a secret language for this forbidden world.

After their return to Japan they had struggled to find suitable places to meet. They didn't like the idea of visiting the love hotels that catered to homosexual men, and took to meeting in secret in the recreation room at the center store. It was there that Sugai told a shocked Manabe about Kishiwara and the embezzlement ring.

"Are you one of them, Guy?"

"No way," Sugai replied with a laugh.

"Then why haven't you told anyone?"

"Why? You really don't get it, do you? Conventional ideas of justice and morality don't apply to people like us. As far as the rest of the world is concerned, when you fall in love with another man you've moved into a dark, shadowy underworld. You know and I know that world is a beautiful place—but those idiots will never accept that. The tragedy for people like us is that we're more sensitive, more refined than most other people, and yet we have to keep the truth hidden all our lives. It's not fair, it's stupid, I hate it, but we have no choice. Because if people ever find out, it's over."

Manabe said nothing.

"That's why the people who live in our world reject the whole establishment thing. What the hell do we want with the establishment? The laws of the establishment are rigged to hurt us."

"But that doesn't mean you should look the other way while somebody defrauds the company."

"Why don't *you* expose them if that's the way you feel?" Sugai said in his routine blasé manner.

Manabe had no response.

Sugai explained how the scheme worked. It involved a wholesaler for the clothing department; he had set himself up as a company to make things look legit, but basically it was a one-man operation. The people on the Ishiei Stores side would issue payment to him for items they had never ordered, or they would "lose" the invoices for things and pay for them twice. What clued Sugai in to what was happening was the unusual number of "missing" invoices. Kishiwara and the wholesaler were dividing the money between them.

Manabe thought this unconscionable. For several uncomfortable nights, he lay in bed mulling over the right thing to do. And then he decided: he would report the crime to Ichimura.

When he told Sugai this the next time they met in the recreation room, he was totally unprepared for Sugai's response, and it broke his heart. Sugai was entirely opposed to the idea, almost like a man possessed. They didn't often fight, but they did now. Sugai usually considered it beneath him to get into an argument, but he clung to his position vehemently now. And Manabe countered in kind. Soon, it became a shouting match, and that was when the road to destruction opened up in front of them.

It was well after closing time, and Sashima had come back to the store to heist some beef. Surprised to hear loud voices, he crept to the door of the recreation room and listened in to everything they were saying. It didn't take him long to figure out the nature of the embezzlement scheme—and the nature of their relationship.

Nothing could have pleased Sashima more. Using this new information as blackmail he was able to bring the scheme under his own control.

Manabe and Sugai had no choice—either cooperate or get exposed. With the store manager and the floor manager on board, there were virtually no limits to what Sashima could do.

Forced into colluding with the plot, and then the cover-up, Manabe and Sugai found solace by fleeing deeper and deeper into their own private world. Before long, this secret world was their only reason for living. They took to creating a separate life in an apartment Sugai had rented in Sakuradani. They filled it with furniture and appliances like any young couple starting out life together: bed, dinner table, television, stereo, air conditioner . . .

They called it their "country retreat," and thanks to their cut of the proceeds from the embezzlement scheme, they were able to fix up the apartment nicely. But they found their desperation growing. They felt trapped, stuck, dragged down. Was there any way they could have prevented this catastrophe from happening? Or was this the inevitable fate that had been lying in wait for them since the day they had fallen in love? And how long would it be before they came to the end of the road?

They were trapped in a world of crime, where everyone lived in fear of being caught. But instead of persuading people to wash their hands and come clean, this fear only pushed people to grab as much as they could while it lasted. Cynicism was the order of the day. Distinctions between perpetrator and victim, ringleader and accomplices, became blurred. It was like a game—but it was a game without rules, where the stakes got higher with every round.

It had been two years since Kishiwara had chosen Shimoda, managing director of the Arai Shôkai Women's Wear Wholesalers, as his accomplice. Kishiwara was working as floor head in the clothing department at the Higashi Motoyama outlet when he caught Shimoda in the act of removing merchandise from the stockroom, claiming they were items for return. Despite his impressive title, Shimoda was a seedy little man in his early thirties. The color drained from his face when he realized he had been found out.

Kishiwara decided to ignore the crime, and from that day on, Shimoda was his poodle. The cozy relationship between Shimoda and Kishiwara worked perfectly, and the volume of merchandise supplied to Ishiei Stores by Arai Shôkai Wholesalers grew by the day. Shimoda soon introduced Kishiwara to other accomplices.

The beauty of the arrangement was that it allowed them to balance the books by moving merchandise from one link in the chain to the next, giving them a place to hide bad stock on a short-term basis. The bad stock Kôjima happened upon in the center store in August had been delivered there with the collusion of Kishiwara to create fictitious sales for wholesalers needing to balance their books at the end of the month. This had significant advantages for Kishiwara too. Besides the kickback he received, reporting large orders at a high markup allowed him to increase his margins and keep the department's summer losses from becoming public knowledge.

Each time Sugai told Manabe about the latest scam, Manabe's blood boiled. Sugai was only passing on what he had heard, but for some reason he always seemed resigned to it.

"How can they do that!" Manabe shouted angrily one day in their Sakuradani apartment.

"Don't get so twisted out of shape about it," Sugai said. "It's the name of the game: earning some yen without working for it."

"That's what I hate. Working for a living—it's a basic rule of life. Anything else is just wrong. It's like, so, un-Japanese!"

Sugai laughed out loud.

"What's so funny?"

"You sound like something out of one of those old left-wing textbooks. You must be the last person left in Japan who believes a person's lifestyle should reflect how hard he's worked. Although if you said people should be paid according to age and position, you'd find plenty of people who agreed with you."

"Doesn't it come to the same thing?"

Sugai laughed again, even louder now. "You're sweet. If everyone was like you, Japan would be a wonderful place to live. It's not. The world is not the way you think it is."

"And how would you know?"

"Come on, Man. What about university entrance exams—what do you think that's all about? Why do parents drive their kids to study, study, study? One reason—so the kids will be in a position one day to make money by sitting on their butts instead of actually having to work for a living. Can you think of any other explanation?"

"You're overstating things."

"What does it matter anyway? There's no sense arguing about stuff like this."

Manabe agreed about that. He had to admit that there was something subversively true about Sugai's argument. What he said about the examination system had never occurred to him before. Maybe it was true that ultimately there were only two kinds of people in the world: those who sat around with their heads full of big ideas, and those who worked themselves to the bone and never got anywhere in life.

The real problems started when you got people in the latter category who continued to believe, despite everything, that they had a natural right to a life of ease. These were the ones you had to watch out for; they were the ones who caused all of the trouble.

But that didn't make what they were doing right. Manabe knew that perfectly well; he was just trying to make himself feel better. Destruction would come in the end. He didn't doubt that for one instant. But what would they do when it finally arrived? Assuming he and Sugai were not prepared to separate, did they have any other options? Could they, for example, move to another company?

It wasn't an impossibility. But it was hard to see them finding lasting happiness in this way. They would be swept along by the river of life, they'd hit some jagged rocks along the edge, cracks would appear in their relationship, and eventually they would split up. Manabe had gone over this in his mind more times than he could recall. At first, he had taken it for granted that their life together would go on; the question was simply what they should do next. But before long, he could only wonder whether they'd have that luxury.

If they were found out, he would die. That was it. There—his mind was made up. All that was left was to find a way to die that would cause the minimum of fuss to those left behind, and the least amount of pain to Sugai and himself. After months alone with these thoughts, an image began to form of the place where they would die. It was at a bend in the road he and Sugai took when they went fishing. One quick turn of the steering wheel and the car would go spinning into space, to be dashed into pieces on the rocks far below.

As they sped along the coastal highway, Manabe thought about the phone calls he'd made to Ichimura and Kôjima before leaving Sakura-dani. Had that really been a good idea? It had been his habit for as long as he could remember to reflect on the events of the day before he went to bed at night. He had always been honest. He was sure he had done the right thing. He had been right to pass on the documents to Ichimura, and he had been right to ask Kôjima for help in keeping the truth a secret. This way was best for his wife and their two daughters too. Not many kids had fathers who were homosexual, but plenty of kids had fathers who had died in a car accident. At the thought of his family, self-reproach stabbed his heart. He should never have married. Why hadn't he realized that before it was too late?

They were nearly there now. Sugai was next to him, asleep, his hands behind his head on the headrest. Manabe hadn't discussed this with Sugai. He was sure he would not object. But of course even Sugai was not immune from the natural fear of death. He was sure he was doing the right thing in saying nothing to him now. Together they would leap toward a beautiful death. He was sure that was what Sugai would have wanted.

Manabe started to sing a Russian folk melody. Quietly, his clear baritone voice described the scene: a sunlit field of grass, and the handsome beloved with soft, dark eyes. Memories flooded his mind. He noticed with surprise that tears were rolling down his cheeks. What was he so sad about?

The curve was approaching fast. Manabe slammed his foot down on the accelerator and turned the steering wheel sharply to the left. The car crashed into the barrier at the side of the road and began to spin wildly. There was a horrible ripping crunch, and the car came to a stop, its back tires hanging over the edge of the cliff.

Something was keeping the front tires on land. Seconds went by. Whatever had been supporting the front wheels snapped, and the car lurched backward. Illuminated by the headlights of an oncoming car, it bucked like a stallion and with its nose pointing to the heavens slipped backward off the cliff and into the darkness.

As the oncoming car screeched to a halt, there was the sickening sound of the stallion crashing to pieces on the rocks below.

The news that Manabe and Sugai had been killed in an accident in Higashi Izu arrived at the head office just after the start of work. Katsumura in personnel took the call from the police, and came rushing into Ishikari's office as soon as he got off the phone. Ichimura and Kôjima were in Ishikari's office five minutes later.

Together they had been going over the documents Manabe had sent Ichimura.

"I don't understand," said Ichimura, shocked by the discovery that Kishiwara Takao was the ringleader in the clothing department scam. "He has bags of talent, always seemed diligent and hardworking, popular with the kids . . ."

Of course, Ichimura had appointed Kishiwara as head of clothing at the center store to take the place of Sugai, who had been their prime suspect at the time; and now he had to come to terms with the fact that Kishiwara had been the chief culprit all along. It was no wonder he was in shock. Manabe's letter named the wholesalers and suppliers who had been complicit in the scam, and included copies of several invoices as proof. There was no room for doubt. He was clearly telling the truth. Among those named as coconspirators was Sashima. How had that happened? How had someone from the meat department ended up implicated in a scam in a completely separate department?

Ichimura and Kôjima had been trying to make sense of these revelations when Ishikari called Ichimura into his office.

"I'm bringing Kôjima with me," Ichimura said. Ishikari was reluctant at first, but Ichimura insisted.

"This is terrible," said Ishikari, clearly distraught. He had known

Manabe and Sugai personally. His fingers trembled as he fumbled for a cigarette, and his face was drained of all color.

"In a way, this was a near escape for us," Ichimura said. "If the accident had happened a few days earlier we would never have found out what was going on at the company."

"What do you mean?" asked Ishikari, perplexed now.

"Manabe came to see me last night. He told me everything about the embezzlement in the clothing and meat departments at the center store."

"Please, Ichimura-*san*. What on earth are you talking about?"

"Apparently he'd known about it for three or four months. He should have told me about it right away, of course, but he chose to cover up for his colleagues. In the end he seems to have gotten caught up in the scheme himself. He was supposed to be the store manager, but he chose to overlook the embezzlement when he found out about it, and ended up going along with it himself."

Kôjima was stunned by what he was hearing. How smoothly Ichimura was able to come up with these fictions! Even Kôjima found the story believable—and he knew that most of what Ichimura was saying was made up! It was obvious what Ichimura was trying to do: convince Ishikari that Manabe's death was an accident. He had been forthright about the embezzlement—it was going to have to come out sooner or later, after all.

"But that would mean . . . that maybe Manabe's death wasn't an accident. It could have been suicide."

"I don't think so," Ichimura said without a moment's hesitation. "Manabe had his regrets all right, but he didn't choose to become part of the scheme, and he certainly wasn't lining his own pockets. He regretted his actions, but I don't think it would have caused him to take his own life. When I saw him yesterday he looked relieved to have gotten it off his chest at last, and was looking forward to his fishing trip. Besides, if he wanted to commit suicide, why take Sugai with him? It doesn't make any sense."

"I suppose. There wasn't any suicide note or anything?"

"We haven't checked yet, but I doubt it. He didn't know he was going to die."

Ishikari seemed satisfied.

Ichimura went on: "There's a chance the police will want to ask us some questions. I think it's best that we keep quiet about what's been going on in the company recently. We don't want them getting any ideas. And besides, our reputation would take a nosedive if people found out the police were investigating us."

"You're right. We mustn't say anything," said Ishikari, nodding sagely, an expression of boundless wisdom on his face.

Investigations started that same day. Ichimura and Kôjima called in the people involved in the scam one by one, and confronted them with the evidence. They weren't in a position to conduct a full-blown investigation, and their results were mixed, but they did manage to get admissions from most of the major players.

Shimoda was willing to admit that he had helped Kishiwara with his schemes, but then added, "If the guy I'm selling to practically forces me to do it, how can I refuse?" There was a strained smile on his features.

"The fact remains: you helped yourself to huge amounts of merchandise from the company, none of which appears on any invoice. The least you can do is compensate us for what you took."

But Shimoda wasn't going to be pinned down that easily. "No way. The stuff I took was junk—no commercial value. Sugai asked me to take it off his hands, so I did it as a favor. It wouldn't cover what I spent on transport. I should be the one demanding compensation from you."

"That's too bad. In that case, we'll settle for you returning the items themselves."

Shimoda laughed out loud.

"What's so funny?"

"I'm sorry. You really don't get it, do you? When I say the stuff was junk, I mean it. I sold it to a junk dealer for next to nothing. Look, I'm telling you the truth. This is so dumb. I'm the one who's the victim here. Take me to court if you don't believe me."

"If you sold it on, you should be able to show us a receipt."

"No problem. I'll bring it with me next time I come. I'll bring a receipt for the truck that came to collect it if you like."

• • •

Sashima was called in next.

As soon as he saw the evidence, he turned red in the face and screamed: "Those fucking queers!"

Suddenly, Kôjima understood everything. This was the truth that Manabe had been desperate to keep hidden. Kôjima turned to Sashima when their preliminary investigation was over. "What you've committed is a crime. If we go to the police, you'll do several years in jail. And the conviction will stay on your record forever. You'll never work in this business again."

"Please, I beg you; it was like temporary insanity."

"Come on. Be serious. It went on for months. We know what a depraved character you really are."

"Please—"

"But I'm ready to cut a deal with you."

"A deal?" A flash of hope crossed Sashima's features.

"That's right—a deal. I want you to promise never to say a word to anyone about Manabe and Sugai. If you keep your promise, we won't report you to the police. But if I hear one word about them, I promise, the cops will be knocking on your door."

Sashima looked at Kôjima in amazement. He had heard about the accident. The two queers were dead. What did it matter what people said about them now?

"I know why you're looking so surprised. They're already dead, so what difference does it make, right? But even dead men have their dignity—and I want to make sure that Manabe and Sugai keep theirs intact."

"All right. I promise I won't say anything. But Kishiwara knows about them too. What if he talks?"

"Then we'll tell Kishiwara the same thing. Let me repeat: If I ever hear any talk about Manabe and Sugai—it doesn't matter when—I will go straight to the police."

"What if someone else—?"

"There is no one else."

ELEVEN

THE OWNER

Ichimura sat in the sauna, counting down the seconds: 120, 119, 118, 117 . . . Nine minutes down, two more to go. At 110°F, sweat was pouring out of his body, and the dry air singed his nostrils when he breathed. He looked down at his body—this body that had supported him through thick and thin all his life. Not once had it let him down—not even after sleepless nights spent working, or drinking, too hard. But the sight of it now only depressed him.

He'd never felt this way before. He'd had his failures—of course he had. It was a failure that had led to him joining Ishiei Stores, but that hadn't felt like defeat. If anything, it was more like sacrifice. This time it was different. Everything he'd devoted years of his life to building up had been shown to be worthless. He had been stripped of his illusions.

He felt rage when he thought about the crimes committed against the company—when he thought of Kishiwara and Sashima, those poor bastards Manabe and Sugai, and all of the rest of the sleaze— but the rage soon faded, to be replaced by a deep sense of despair. He could still hear the snotty response Kishiwara had given him under questioning: *You can never have too many markdowns or inventory evaluations.* It was pure cynicism, but Ichimura got the meaning right away: the more markdowns in the balance books, the better your chances of keeping hidden any losses from missing merchandise. And over-reporting the inventory during stocktaking did the same trick.

Inevitably you ended up with "plus losses," when the actual value of a company's inventory exceeded the amount recorded in the books. Logically, it was something that should never occur. But it was easy to get sucked into the fantasy of it. It meant you didn't have to deal with bad news. You could fool yourself you had good news instead. The problem at Ishiei Stores was that too many people were prepared to listen to nothing but good news—and Ichimura now realized he was one of them. When he might have suspected cooked inventory, he had been only too happy to ignore it.

Kishiwara was just more upfront—and unrepentant—about the whole charade. The realization sank Ichimura's self-image: Kishiwara, the cheeky prick, had seen through him and sensed his weakness so easily. That was supposed to be Ichimura's strength.

He was disgusted with himself. He looked up at the clock. He'd ended up sweating in the heat longer than he meant to.

Ichimura pondered his options as he wandered home. As Kôjima kept emphasizing, they would only know the true state the company was in after an accurate inventory was carried out. But the ways things looked now, it was only a question of how dire the situation turned out to be. Ichimura had been the dominant figure in the company for the past seven years, the person responsible for the company's results, however good or bad they turned out to be. If things were really bad, wasn't it his duty to bite the bullet and resign?

Unless there was some way to keep the facts from coming out? That's what Odagiri and Matsuo wanted him to do. Ichimura didn't like the idea. But Matsuo, far less submissive and ingratiating now than Ichimura was used to, was quite insistent. "Resign? That would be stupid," he said. "Who's in charge of this company? Ishikari Seijirô. Let him or his brother take the responsibility."

"But everyone knows I'm the one who's really in charge."

"That doesn't mean you should resign. Besides, who would take your place?"

"You two would still have a job, don't worry. And Kôjima would still be here. After all, Ishikari and his brother brought him in to take over the company one day, right?"

"This is no joking matter," Odagiri said. "What use would a self-satisfied little punk like him be? Sure, he talks a good talk, but can he really walk the walk?"

"Watch it, Odagiri. Don't badmouth people like that."

"All right, so you accept responsibility and you resign. That's great. Great for you. You make a noble exit, and that's that. But what about us? We've always regarded you as the true founder of the company, and we've always looked up to you. If Kôjima takes over, the people who suck up to him score points, and us, the ones who stay loyal to you, we become second-class citizens. Is that what you want?"

Ichimura didn't say anything. There was probably some truth in what Matsuo said. He hadn't actively encouraged the group that had sprung up to support him, which counted directors as well as managers among its members. In his head he knew it was divisive and should be suppressed—but part of him was warmed by the adulation. He rather liked the idea of a pro-Ichimura movement. The problem was that it was an anti-Kôjima movement.

"If you resign, I'm resigning too," Matsuo suddenly said.

"Me too," Odagiri piped up. "I don't want to work for someone who cost the company millions over that lame screwup with the flyers just so he could make himself look good."

"We understand how you feel," Matsuo went on. "But there's no reason for you to resign. Leave it to us. We'll sort things out. Everything will be fine."

"The most important thing," Odagiri said, "is that you shouldn't sacrifice yourself."

It was a nice sentiment, but the warmth of it had turned cold for Ichimura. Six months ago, Sashima—that lying thief—had thrown a party to mark the forming of the pro-Ichimura group. Kishiwara was there too. So were Manabe and Sugai. They had all sung his praises and signed a pledge—in blood, no less—to stand by him through thick and thin. And now these very people had caused the problems that were threatening to destroy his career.

His mind was made up. "No more cover-ups, no more fudging. I'll consider my future once I've seen the results. I'm sorry that my negligence has caused you so much inconvenience. But I can't go along with what you're suggesting. I will cooperate with Kôjima-*san* and find out what state the company is really in. And if you want what's best for the company, I suggest that you do the same."

Ichimura's tone had made it clear to Odagiri and Matsuo that his position was not up for debate. But he realized now that he was not so sure himself. It was all very well saying that he was prepared to take responsibility, but where would he go if he did resign? He could probably use his contacts to find a job somewhere, but not one that would pay anything like the money he was making now. A pay cut would be no joke at this stage in his life. There was the mortgage to think of, and the kids' education and the household expenses. Resigning now would mean tough times for the family.

Was what he had done really so bad? True, he had failed to notice the embezzlement going on under his nose. And true, thanks to his halfhearted inventory management, the company's positive results over the past few years would probably soon be revealed as bogus. But had he really committed a crime? Wouldn't it be fairer to say that the whole saga was the inevitable consequence of the way the company had grown? Certainly if Ishiei Stores had remained the way it was when Ichimura joined the company—with just two or three outlets and no superstores selling clothing and other nonperishables—then this disaster would never have happened.

Did that mean it had been a mistake for the company to expand? Not at all. They had started out small, they grew, they branched out, they were now a force to be reckoned with. The whole industry was full of praise for what the company had achieved. And whose efforts had made it all possible? His! No one else could have done it. He had built another man's castle from nothing, and just because of some minor collapse in one of the outer walls, he was expected to get on his horse and ride off into the sunset? It was preposterous.

Ishikari Seijirô, the managing director—how would he react if Ichimura handed in his notice? He had an idea. And Ishikari Eitarô, the company president—how would he react? This Ishimura knew for

241

sure: if Ichimura resigned, taking responsibility for the company's problems, Eitarô would shut up shop and run for home. Just the sound of the word *embezzlement* would be enough to make him break out in a cold sweat. He'd be so mortified if he found out the truth, he wouldn't want anything to do with the business. No: whatever happened, he couldn't be told about this.

So it was impossible for him to resign—even if he wanted to.

Ichimura made up his mind. If the stocktaking confirmed that the company was awash in red ink, he would hand in his resignation to Ishikari Seijirô. The likelihood was that Seijirô would refuse to accept it. But the gesture itself would be enough. Time would mend the rest. There was nothing to worry about. He wouldn't have to cause his family any hardship. Everything was going to be fine. All he had to do now was to put his energy into working with Kôjima to rebuild the company.

He realized that he was almost skipping back home. What a simple creature he was. He stopped and smiled at himself. The cool air felt good against his skin.

Ichimura and Kôjima began to work in tandem—with the same goal in mind.

Special teams were organized to reevaluate the planned stocktaking project. Even now, nobody knew exactly how much the company had lost to embezzlement (the thieves themselves didn't know how much they had taken). And they were more than likely to unearth plenty of bad stock that had nothing to do with the scam at all.

Two departments in particular were in urgent need of a thorough investigation: clothing and sundries. Another team was put together to look into the fresh foods department. This team would discover significant amounts of bad stock in the various fresh foods sections. In several stores they found freezers full of unsold tuna and whole haunches of Japanese beef long past the point of being suitable for human consumption. Just the items left abandoned in the freezers had to be worth several million yen, at the very least.

The team looking into the sundries department found items that had been featured in special promotions many years past, now languishing unwanted and unsold in warehouses and storerooms. There were jars, pots, portable gas stoves, bicycles, furniture, birdcages, musical instruments, toys, and games—even hula hoops and dolls. Some items had been popular so long ago that seeing them again now was like taking a trip back in time.

As a result of these preliminary investigations, the formal company-wide stocktaking was postponed until the end of October. Meanwhile, Kitô Jun'ya, who had been suspended for his part in blocking attempts to acquire land for two new stores, was reinstated as director of development.

The alliance between Ichimura and Kôjima was a source of consternation for a few diehard supporters on both sides, but in general people were relieved to see the two men pulling in the same direction.

In due course, the stocktaking took place under their joint leadership, according to the methods that Kôjima had devised. The results were released two weeks later. There were unexplained losses in the clothing, sundries, and fresh food departments totaling eighty million yen, plus a drop in inventory value after reevaluation of more than 110 million yen. Ichimura stood in stunned silence when Kôjima showed him the figures. He had been bracing himself for bad news—but this was a nightmare.

Once the new figures were taken into account, the company stood to take a loss for fiscal year 1969. The original projections for the year were for sales of 3 billion yen, and profits equivalent to two percent of that total, or 60 million yen. They were now heading for a loss of at least 130 million yen. But the bad news didn't stop there. If, as seemed likely, profits had been overestimated too, then the company couldn't count on making the 60 million yen budgeted for either. They could well be looking at a loss of something closer to 150 million yen.

The company's assets at the end of fiscal year 1968 were a little over 100 million yen, including 20 million yen in capital. Ishiei Stores was operating with debts of more than 50 million yen.

•   •   •

With unaccustomed humility, Ichimura went to see Ishikari Seijirô the morning after the results were released.

He stood before Ishikari's desk and bowed deeply. "I've let you down. I haven't lived up to the trust you put in me. Please accept this," he said, solemnly handing a white envelope to the company's managing director. Written on it were the words *Letter of Resignation*.

"What is this? What the hell's going on?" Ishikari looked at Ichimura with something close to fear on his face.

"For years I have done what I could for this company," Ichimura began. "I've dedicated myself to Ishiei Stores as though it was my own. I always believed that I was of some use. . . . But recently, I have come to understand that this belief was nothing but a foolish illusion. I thought my presence here was for the good of the company, but in fact I was only doing it harm all the time."

"Ichimura-*san,* what on earth are you talking about?"

"The results of the stocktaking were released last night. We revalued the inventory in every store, and we came out with huge losses."

"Big enough to cancel out our profits for this quarter?" Ishikari asked. *This could be serious,* he thought.

"Worse than that. More than all the profits we've accumulated until now."

"You mean . . ."

"We're in debt. Serious debt."

"What are you talking about?"

"The details are in the figures here. I had no idea. I'm so sorry. I feel sorrow and shame." Ichimura bowed his head low. Remorse and humiliation washed over him. His eyes stung as he struggled to keep the tears from flowing.

Ishikari devoured the figures on his desk, running his finger down the columns of numbers. Ichimura watched him turn pale as the gravity of the situation sank in. "I can't believe it. This is terrible," he said.

"I have let the company down. None of this would have happened if I had been more diligent."

"What are we going to do? Are we going bankrupt?" Ishikari slumped in his chair. "You can't quit now, Ichimura-*san.* Please. You know how much I depend on you. If you go, I'll have to go too."

"Thank you, but really the responsibility is mine. You need to stay and help rebuild the company. I probably shouldn't be saying this, since I'm the one who caused the problems in the first place, but I'm confident that Kôjima-*san* will be able to make up for all the damage I've done."

"Kôjima? What are you talking about? Because he's my cousin? Because he used to work in a bank? Is this a joke? What makes you think he can take your place and rebuild the company? You're not really suggesting I should entrust the future of the company to a man who can't even be left alone with my damn secretary?"

"No one believes that story anymore. It wasn't true in the first place. Kuroba admitted it."

"What? So it was all a lie?"

"I think she got carried away, that's all. Thought about things too much and leaped to conclusions. It never happened. At least she had the courage to admit it."

"But where there's smoke there's fire, no?"

"Not in this case."

"Well, it doesn't matter. The fact that the rumors have stopped doesn't mean Kôjima is ready to take over your position. Let's sit down and talk about this," said Ishikari. "He's not been here long; he doesn't know enough about the business yet," Ishikari went on.

"You're right, of course. But his natural abilities more than make up for his inexperience. I've worked with him a fair bit since the embezzlement came to light: investigating the thefts, reevaluating the bad stock, directing the stocktaking. And I must confess I've been very impressed. He's got an extraordinary mind. So he gets a bit carried away at times, but that's just his age. He's a bit idealistic too sometimes. But he's smart, and he pays attention to detail. He's much better suited to management than I am."

No final decision was reached by the time Ichimura stood up to leave. It was at this point that Ishikari asked him to take back his letter of resignation.

Ichimura refused. "I'm very sorry," he said again, bowing deeply and walking out of the room.

• • •

Thirty minutes later, Kôjima was sitting in Ishikari's office.

Ishikari explained that Ichimura had resigned in the wake of the ruinous stocktaking results. "And these figures . . . What are we going to do, Ryôsuke?" he asked beseechingly.

Kôjima had to avert his eyes. He couldn't bear the sight of Ishikari's face.

"This can't be happening. It doesn't make sense. It's like a bad dream. There must be some mistake—right, Ryôsuke?"

"I'm afraid not," Kôjima replied. "It's not a mistake. It's the truth. Unfortunately, it's the truth."

Ishikari bit his lip like a child who has been scolded for misbehaving. He was struggling to contain his emotions.

"There's only one thing we can do," Kôjima said. "We need to talk this over with your brother and come up with a strategy for building the company up again."

Ishikari looked back at Kôjima, stunned. "Talk things over with my brother?" he said. "About this? I can tell you right now what he would do. He'd sell the whole company to Toto Stores at whatever price he could get."

"How do you know?"

"Previous experience."

Eitarô had come close to selling the company three times in the past, Ishikari said. The first time was not long after he founded the company, when he had tried to offload it to the wholesaler friend whose idea it had been to expand into supermarkets in the first place. He had been assured that the company would make him easy money, but all he saw were losses. But his friend wasn't interested. The second time was when P., managing director of the parent Ishiei Trading Company and a close adviser to Eitarô, died suddenly of a brain hemorrhage. When Seijirô and Ichimura joined the company, he decided to wait and see how things developed. The company started to turn a profit, and Eitarô's ideas about selling had been forgotten for a while.

The third time was more recent. After the success of the expansion at the center store, Eitarô thought the time was right to get out of the supermarket business once and for all. "We could make a killing if we sold now." Ishikari wasn't sure how serious he had been, but Eitarô had mentioned Toto Stores as a potential buyer. But apparently he hadn't taken the idea any further.

"How does your brother really feel about the company? Doesn't he want to see it grow?" Kôjima asked.

"Of course he does. But far more important for him is to avoid too much risk. That's the way he is. He's obsessed with making a profit. Not surprising—he's a businessman. For him, Ishiei Stores is just one part of his business assets: nothing more, nothing less. His assets are more important to him than anything else—don't get me wrong. But running the company is not a dream come true. There's nothing romantic about it for him. It's just money. It's a way of investing his capital—and he measures it in terms of profit and loss, safety and risk. It makes sense, if you think about it."

Kôjima said nothing.

"I think he looks at the future of the company in a completely different way from us. How likely is it that Ishiei Stores will be able to hold its own against the competition, for example? Some of the big chains out there are racking up sales of a hundred billion yen a year. Ishiei Stores has a strong customer base, in spite of all its problems, which he still knows nothing about, of course. But what about later on, when the competition gets serious? I think my brother worries about these things more than we realize."

"But what good does worrying do? All you can do is to try your best to secure your position before the serious competition starts."

"Right. That's how you would look at things as an employee manager who was taking the continued existence of the company for granted. Might as well give it everything you've got. If things don't work out, you'll cross that bridge when you come to it. But that's not the way the owner looks at it. For him, the only thing that matters is the safety of his investment."

Kôjima understood perfectly what Ishikari was saying. But what did it mean in practical terms?

"What I'm saying is that if we tell my brother what has happened," Ishikari went on, "the company will disappear forever. Is that really what you want?"

"I want to avoid that at all costs."

It was turning out to be a strange conversation. Ishikari seemed to be treating Kôjima like he was the man in charge. He was discussing the future of the company so objectively and dispassionately anyone would have thought it didn't affect him personally at all. "We need to come up with some good ideas. I don't think we can just go at the problem head-on and hope for the best."

Kôjima said nothing.

"I think we should just carry on the same as before. It's only since we started digging around for bad stock and revaluing the inventory that everything's gone to hell. All right, so some of the stock estimates were a bit slapdash—but that isn't a recent thing. It's always been like that. And the company's been fine till now. Things today are not so different from the way they were yesterday. What makes you think things will be different in the future?"

Kôjima was astonished. He didn't know what to say. He was a man who couldn't rest until he had checked that every detail was correct. An approach like Ishikari's was unthinkable for him.

"So that's what we need—some good ideas."

He was musing over things at home later that evening when the telephone rang.

It was his mother-in-law, calling to tell him that his wife had given birth to a boy. "At least come and see his little face," she said.

"I can't, I just can't right now. There are huge problems at work."

"You don't have time to come and see your own son? That supermarket job is really taking over your life. At least try to think about Takako from time to time."

Kôjima put the phone down, feeling dark and lonely.

"November fifteenth," he said out loud. The least he could do was to try to remember his son's birthday.

The next day Kôjima called together a select group of the company's directors: Konno, who had been in charge of the stocktaking; Asayama, fresh foods; Odagiri, groceries; Matsuo, clothing and sundries; and Shinkawa, accounts.

"The situation could not be more serious," he began. "As a result of the recent stocktaking, we know that the company is suffering huge losses—more than enough to swallow up all our capital. Mr. Ichimura handed in a letter of resignation yesterday, accepting responsibility for what has happened."

This was the first anyone had heard of Ichimura's resignation, and a buzz ran around the room.

"So far his resignation has not been accepted, but I understand he is determined to quit. Yesterday I had a meeting with the managing director, who has asked me to do what I can to resolve the situation. I thought it would be a good idea for him to talk things over with the company president, but Mr. Ishikari believes that if his brother finds out about the losses, he will divest himself of his stock in the company. It's unfortunate, although it's natural enough that an owner would think that way. After all, his managers have let him down," Kôjima said. His tone was resolute. He went on: "I've thought this through carefully, and my personal opinion is that, despite the possibility that the president might act to sell the company, the best way to proceed would be to be open and forthright and tell him everything."

"Do you mean to say you don't care if the company gets taken over by one of the big chains?" Matsuo asked in a loud voice that cut through the noise of several conversations that had erupted in the room.

"Of course I don't want that to happen. But it's not our decision to make. The only one who can make that decision is the owner, Ishikari Eitarô."

"Then you might as well just hand the company over to one of the big chains now."

"We don't know that for a fact. It's possible he will decide to stick it out."

"You can't take that chance," Matsuo said vehemently. "I hate to have to say this, but the president knows nothing about the supermarket business. If we tell him what's been going on, we're finished."

Matsuo's point seemed to be shared by everyone in the room. No one was willing to criticize the president openly, but they all agreed that Ishikari Eitarô was not likely to put his employees' interests first.

"So what should we do?"

Kôjima had spent the night thinking about that very question and had come to no satisfactory conclusion. He asked the five directors what they thought, then stood listening on in silence for the next thirty minutes as debate filled the room. And then he spoke up again: "From what I hear, none of you think we should discuss the situation with the president. But no one has come up with a better idea of how to get through this crisis." Kôjima looked slowly around the room. He'd hardly slept for days, but his eyes glinted with resolve as he spoke "As far as I can see, there's only one way we can navigate our way through this crisis. It's not the kind of thing we'd normally want to find ourselves caught up in, but if we're determined that it's what we want, it might just work."

A heavy silence filled the room.

"We need to keep the truth from the president. That buys us time to come up with a strategy for getting the company back on the rails within the next few years. In other words, for the next five years, we have to feed the president misleading reports of the company's performance while we work to get the figures back into the black. With any luck, we should be able to bring the true figures in line with the reports within five years."

"Is that really feasible?" Matsuo asked.

"It might be. We should be able to produce financial performance reports that almost nobody would detect as fakes. Working in the supermarket industry, we have several factors in our favor—no working capital, and large amounts of merchandise and fixed assets. It wouldn't be easy to check the accuracy of our reports just by looking at the figures. So long as everyone here swears to keep this strategy absolutely confidential, I am prepared to take responsibility for drawing up the reports."

This was a defining moment. Kôjima's offer of self-sacrifice seemed to stir the rest of the group into action.

"Improving the way the company is run will be much more difficult. You could say that if we were capable of this we would never have found ourselves in this mess in the first place."

"It was impossible to get anything done with Ichimura in charge," Asayama grumbled, bringing on stares from Odagiri and Matsuo.

Kôjima ignored this and continued, "That doesn't mean we can't succeed. All we really need to do is improve the performance of the three fresh food sections—produce, fish, and meat. If we can get these to start turning a profit, that would probably be enough."

"Impossible," Odagiri said. "Those are the weakest departments in the whole company. Things are so bad that the old-fashioned grocery stores in the area are doing better than ever."

"That's not fair," Asayama replied.

"Look, there's no denying that things in fresh foods are pretty bad at the moment," Kôjima said.

"So you're on their side too, huh?" Asayama muttered.

Kôjima raised his voice. "What this means is we have plenty of room for improvement. And we know how to do it too. We can save the details for another time. For now, we just need to agree to keep the facts from reaching the owner. As for the rest of it, all I can do is ask for your trust."

Kôjima was putting his neck on the line. For a few moments, there was silence. People looked at one another uncomfortably, reluctant to commit themselves. Finally, Konno spoke up. "This way of improving things you just mentioned. Is that anything to do with these research group meetings you've been holding?"

"Yes. I think that's one concrete way of improving things."

"I think that's a good idea. The kids who've been taking part are full of praise for the scheme. You want to keep it up till you've changed the whole approach of the young people working in the stores, is that right?"

"Something like that, yes."

"Well, I'm with you," Konno said. "Anything's got to be better than leaving things the way they are now."

"There you go again," Asayama muttered. But deep down he was happy. He knew that Kôjima was gaining people's trust. And the research meetings to which Asayama had devoted so much energy were also beginning to serve their purpose.

For a while the directors spoke among themselves. The general direction they were going to take was already clear. Now it was just a question of talking things over till they reached a formal agreement. Finally there was a succession of voices declaring support for Kôjima.

"I'm happy to leave it to you."

"I can't see any alternative."

"Let's go ahead and do it. We can't just let the big chains gobble us up."

Only one person, Shinkawa, disagreed. "I agree that we need to strengthen the fresh foods department," he said. "And I certainly don't want to see the company sold. But I don't think it's a good idea to give misleading performance reports to the president. That's the same as cooking the books."

"We know that much," Asayama said. "But this is a crisis. This is no time for scruples."

"But cooking the books is a criminal offense. You can go to jail for it. And as directors we're the ones who would be held responsible."

"Only if the company brings a lawsuit. But we'd be doing it because we want to save the company. Who's going to sue us? As long as everyone in this room agrees, no one else need ever find out."

"I don't like it. I'm responsible for the company accounts. That means I'll be the one responsible for cooking the books. I don't want to go to prison at my age."

"No one is asking you to take all the responsibility yourself."

"I don't want to do it."

"Still trying to act like a Boy Scout at your age?" Asayama shouted.

"I don't like it. It doesn't matter what you say—the director in charge of accounts shouldn't be publishing faked performance reports. You have to understand. I've worked in accounts all my life. Everything we do depends on submitting accurate, factual reports. It's the fundamental rule that underlies everything we do. Telling an accountant to falsify his figures . . . you might as well ask him to kill himself." His voice cracked as he spoke. He hung his gray head low, trembling with emotion. "I am a dull, cowardly man, I suppose. But I've been doing this job as honestly as I could for forty years. Maybe I've not been much use to anyone—maybe I've just been getting in everyone's way all these years. But not once have I ever issued a false report—not here, and not where I worked before either. If I had to do it now, my whole life would be a lie."

A heavy silence descended on the room. Minutes went by that felt like hours. Then Shinkawa stood up.

"I'm sorry," he said. "I can't be part of this. Forgive me. I won't tell anyone what was said here today. But any reports that I'm responsible for will continue to be accurate and truthful. And now if you'll excuse me . . ." Without waiting to hear anything further, Shinkawa opened the door and walked out of the room.

"He's just running away from his responsibilities," Konno mumbled.

"This is pretty bad," Asayama said, looking over at Kôjima.

There was tension on every man's face.

"It's all right," Kôjima said quietly. "I spent years in a bank, so I can understand how an accountant might feel about these things. The main thing is that Shinkawa has shown himself to be on our side."

"Really?" Matsuo asked uncertainly. "I thought he said he was going to continue to put the true figures in his reports."

"I think what he meant was that if we are going to change the figures we should do it before it reaches his department. And I agree—that's the best way to do it."

"You really think that's what he meant?" Matsuo's face was a study in amazement.

"It's going to be all right," Kôjima said again. "Now, there's one more thing I would like to get your agreement on. It's about Ichimura."

Everything in the room grew still. Ichimura's name had a special significance. He had held sway over the company for so long that almost everyone had some kind of vassal-like relationship to the man. You loved him or you hated him.

"If Ichimura resigns, the president is bound to realize that something is happening. And then our plans will collapse. I suggest we ask him to reconsider and persuade him to stay at the company."

"But he's the one who got us into this mess," Asayama said.

"What happened to the idea of taking responsibility for your actions?" Konno added.

"Certainly Ichimura should not be allowed to escape responsibility for his mistakes. But for now it is more important that he should stay with the company until this present crisis is resolved. We don't want to have to fall on our swords with him, do we?"

"Well, when you put it like that . . ." Reluctantly, even Asayama and Konno had to agree.

And with that, the discussion was at an end.

Kôjima was on his way back to his desk when Matsuo hurried behind him and whispered, "You're quite a guy, Kôjima-*san*. At first I thought you were just another theory wonk, but you really understand people."

"What are you talking about?"

"Come on, you don't have to pretend. Ichimura is a lucky guy."

As he watched Matsuo walk away, Kôjima realized that the goodwill people were showing him was based on a misunderstanding. Even Odagiri, the unofficial head of the Ichimura faction, smiled contentedly at him as he walked away. That couldn't be helped, he supposed. The next thing to do was to talk to Ichimura, he thought as he sat down at his desk. He felt tired, but he couldn't afford to put it off. He had to get Ichimura to take back his resignation before word of it reached Ishikari Eitarô.

For a while Ichimura was firm, refusing to listen to Kôjima's arguments. But in the end he agreed to postpone his resignation.

A new age had begun for Ishiei Stores, and Kôjima was in charge.

TWELVE

SUBTERFUGE

Ten-pin bowling was the latest craze. King's Bowling was the third alley to have opened in Sawabe in as many months, and it was so popular you often had to wait hours to get a lane. That the Ishiei Stores development department had been able to hold a party there at all was thanks to Kôda Kôtarô, who was friends with the manager. Kôda was a bowling nut, and his passion for the sport had reached almost absurd proportions.

He was dressed in full bowling drag, and had a ball inscribed with his name. And tonight, he was on fire. He had started with two spares, but he had followed that with five strikes in a row. Kuroba Motoko was bowling in the next lane. She started jumping and screaming when Kôda got his third consecutive strike, attracting the attention of everyone around. By the time he got his fourth, everyone was watching, and when he knocked down his fifth, a huge cheer went up.

"It's not even his party, and look at the way he's carrying on," Kitô Jun'ya muttered. He had recently been appointed head of clothing, and one reason for tonight's party was to send him off in style. He was in the lane next to Kôda, but was having nothing like the same success. He staggered up to the line and dropped the ball clumsily at his feet with a *thud*. More often than not, it ended up in the gutter.

Kôda, on the other hand, kept racking up the points. A remarkable transformation came over his lumpy, unathletic frame each time he stepped up to bowl with determination written on his face. He began his approach, began his swing, and let the ball go, watching as it homed in on the gap next to the center pin, only to veer away slightly at the last moment, leaving one pin standing. The crowd groaned.

"Too many people watching," Kôda muttered as he waited for his ball to come back through the chute.

But in fact it was something else that had broken Kôda's concentration. Midstride, he'd caught a glimpse of Matsuo in one of the other lanes, and that had been enough to throw him off. Matsuo had been appointed head of development, and Kitô, who'd been running development, was switching jobs with him at clothing. It was a major reshuffle, but for some reason the transition was to be completed in just three days. And to make matters worse, Matsuo had announced at a meeting on his first day that he had hired the Teikoku Kôeki Company as prime contractor for all new construction projects.

"It's stupid," Kôda objected. "You don't know anything about construction yet. Appointing a trading company as prime contractor won't save us anything. They'll just take a cut of everything and drive up costs."

Matsuo wasn't convinced. "A big trading firm like that has all the assets we need: personnel, capital, information. A second-rate supermarket chain like ours can use that. We'd be foolish to pass up on an opportunity like this."

But Kôda wasn't ready to give in. "Kitô used to work for a trading company himself before coming to development here. But he never hired Teikoku Kôeki for any construction project."

"I'm sure Mr. Kitô had his reasons. I have mine."

"And how come you refer to us as a second-rate company? What about Teikoku Kôeki—they're the ones who are second rate! If it's personnel, capital, and information you want, why not go to one of the old *zaibatsu* conglomerates?"

"There is nothing second rate about Teikoku Kôeki, I can assure you. I've dealt with them for years. They have years of experience in the business."

"That may be true for clothing. That's how they started, right? As fiber wholesalers in the Kansai. But construction? First I ever heard of it."

"Look, I've made my decision. Stop arguing with me."

In the face of this brusque retort from the new department head, Kôda backed off and shut up. Ishiei Stores was a small company where everyone knew each other by sight, but apart from that the two men were virtually strangers.

Kôda raised the subject at lunch with Také later that day. "Doesn't it seem weird to you?" he asked.

"Maybe Matsuo thinks he knows more than he does. The development business has rules of its own." It was six months since Také was shifted from the meat department to development, and already he was speaking like a true construction man. There was less of the naïve student about him now.

"For sure. But I'm starting to wonder if there is more to it than that."

"What do you mean?"

"Come on. It's not like you to be so slow. You were the one who sniffed out what Sashima was up to."

"You think there's something funny going on?"

"I don't know. But it smells kind of fishy, don't you think? No, not 'kind of'; it fucking stinks. Here's how I see it: Matsuo was on the take from Teikoku Kôeki when he was in clothing. Then suddenly he gets moved to development. What's he supposed to do? He can't keep placing bogus clothing orders with them. So he tries to do the same thing with construction costs."

"Clever," Také mused. "He bumps up construction costs by appointing Teikoku Kôeki as primary contractor, and funnels the extra money into his embezzlement projects."

"There are two projects under negotiation at the moment: the store at Hanaoka Kamimachi and the one at Onohara. If the estimates for those two projects come in way higher than expected, then we'll know."

The two young men felt a rush of excitement. This could be something really important. They'd heard about the scandal in the clothing department, of course. For some reason, though, nothing much seemed to have been done about it yet. Kishiwara and several members of his team had lost their positions; and Sashima was no longer making himself obnoxious in the meat department. They'd heard rumors that Ichimura was going to take responsibility and resign. But no real action had been taken. One thing had changed, though, as a result of recent events: The words *misconduct* and *embezzlement* were now at the forefront of everyone's mind. Before long, anything that looked even the slightest bit mysterious was being described as "misconduct" or "embezzlement."

A week later Také came rushing up to Kôda. His face was flushed with excitement. "Just as we thought," he said.

"What are you talking about?"

"The rise in construction costs since Teikoku Kôeki came on board. Don't tell me you've forgotten?"

"As if I could."

"All right. Just relax. Calm down."

"What are you talking about? You're the one who's freaking out."

"No, I'm not. Well, maybe a little bit. I tell you, this is serious stuff. Forty million extra for the two jobs!"

"Forty million?" The blood drained from Kôda's face. He could hardly imagine that much money. And it was all being filtered through Matsuo's pocket. "What's Matsuo saying about this?"

"He hasn't really said anything yet. Only the usual line about costs going up and how much safer he feels with a proper trading company involved."

"That makes it even more suspicious," Kôda said. "I'm taking this to Kitô."

Kôda hadn't done that yet—this conversation had taken place in the morning—but when he saw Matsuo out of the corner of his eye, his concentration on knocking down ten bowling pins was just a little shaken.

"So what's the difficulty?" Kitô said.

"It's going to cost the company an extra forty million yen. You don't think that's shocking?"

"I'm sure there's a perfectly good explanation for it," Kitô said, and that seemed to be the end of the matter.

Kôda could hardly believe what he was hearing. "I know that the price of materials has been going through the roof recently," he persisted. "But not like this!"

"Sure," Kitô said, puffing on his cigarette. "But a rise in the price of materials isn't the only reason why construction costs go up. We'll just have to hope that the profits we make as a result of having Teikoku Kôeki on board will compensate for the higher costs."

"But—" Kôda started to protest, but then stopped. Something wasn't right. Kitô was supposed to be a Kôjima supporter, and Matsuo had always aligned with the Ichimura faction. What was going on? Kôda came into his own at times like this. He brought his conversation with Kitô to a conclusion as soon as he decently could, and decided to speak to Kôjima instead. Other people might have held back until they had more evidence, but not Kôda. He had taken to referring to Kôjima as his "big brother" a while back, and liked to think of himself as his loyal apprentice. Bringing something serious to his attention would be like a dream come true.

At first, Kôjima just mumbled. Then he looked up slowly and grinned at Kôda. It was such a good-natured smile that Kôda couldn't help smiling too.

"I'll be upfront with you," Kôjima began. "There are reasons for what's happening. But I can't tell you what they are, even though you have come and asked me to my face. It's kind of like a company secret. As you have guessed, both Matsuo and Kitô know about it. But it is not misconduct or embezzlement or anything like that. I can promise you that much. I'm afraid that's all I can say for now. Can you be satisfied with that for the time being?"

"Yes, of course," Kôda said, bowing to authority he respected. He was about to walk away, but decided to push his luck with just one more question. "Why did Teikoku Kôeki suddenly get involved?"

"That's enough for now," Kôjima answered brusquely. His voice was no louder than normal, but it was definitely less lighthearted.

Kôda bowed and left.

• • •

Shinkawa came out of Ishikari Eitarô's office. He had just briefed the president on the company's performance for November. The figures all seemed to be in order, and there hadn't been any awkward questions. But these visits were starting to get him down.

Shinkawa knew that the figures were not what they seemed to be, but there was nothing specific that he could point to as suspect. He didn't feel he could ask Kôjima what was going on—not after he had walked out of the meeting and told them he wanted no part in their scheme. The only thing he knew for sure was that the stocktaking figures that had formed the basis for September's accounts contained fabrications. As a result of the inventory reevaluation, the estimated value of the company's stock had fallen dramatically, with large unexplained losses as well. It was this that had led to the emergency meeting of all the directors concerned. But here the official accounts for September showed a performance that was only slightly more sluggish than usual.

Shinkawa didn't raise any questions, but it was apparent that the results of the recent stocktaking had been doctored. Time had been short, so it was unlikely that Kôjima could have done anything too involved. Commercial value had been reduced for only a few items, which led Shinkawa to conclude that the thoroughgoing reevaluation of stock had not been included.

He looked back over the trends in stock turnover for the past few years. The turnover rate should have slowed down along with the increase in bad stock. As expected, he found that stock turnover in the clothing department had started to fall off a year ago, and had slowed dramatically in the last six months. And it was in a board meeting precisely six months ago that Ichimura and Konno had assured him that it was quite normal for clothing and sundries turnover rates to drop when you opened a major outlet like the center store. When the turnover for high-priced items was as quick as it was for cheaper stuff, that was when you started to worry.

He should have been more persistent then, he realized; he might have been able to nip the problem in the bud. It was too late now. But what were Kôjima and the others planning to do? There was a limit to how much they could achieve by continuing to overvalue worthless goods. Taken too far, that would start to affect their cash flow. In order to restore the company to good health, they were going to have to revise the estimates on their bad assets at some stage. And in order to make up for the massive reductions that would bring about, they would need to start making money somewhere else.

Shinkawa looked carefully at the monthly accounts. For October and November the net profits were more or less as expected. The clothing and sundries departments were doing well, and continued to make up for losses made in the fresh foods departments. In this respect, nothing had changed. But when he examined the figures more carefully, he noticed a new trend starting in November. The amount of stock had started to shrink. He looked over the gross profit calculations for the month. There was an extra five million yen worth of reductions, most of it coming from clothing and sundries.

They had obviously revalued some of the merchandise. This was good. But something wasn't right. In spite of all the reductions, the final figure given for gross profit was holding steady. The key was the markup. For clothing, this was an unbelievable 40 percent. Autumn was one of their most successful times of year, but even so, this was way too high. So this must be where they were giving themselves a boost. But that still didn't explain things. If you increased your prices by 10 percent, you would expect your sales to go down. Here, the opposite was the case. The fall season clothes were selling well, and sales for November were up on the previous year too.

Shinkawa was of two minds. Part of him preferred not to ask too many questions, but another part was desperate to know the truth. In the end, his curiosity got the better of him, and he approached Kôjima. "In the past the company generally sold things at a markup of just ten percent, so you still had room to put prices up without affecting sales? Is that how you managed to keep profits steady and carry out reductions on old stock at the same time?"

"Whoa—are we being investigated by accounts already?" Kôjima asked, half in jest.

"No, of course not." Shinkawa gave a noncommittal laugh.

"Listen, we're not charging higher prices than before. If we did, sales would go right down."

"That's what I thought. But then how come the markup has increased so much?"

"Hard work and better buying by the purchasing department."

"Really?"

"I've talked to the people in the merchandise department, and this is how we're going to do things from now on. We're concentrating on the purchasing side. If we work hard at it we should be able to get good terms on the merchandise we buy. And then, by running careful, well-timed special offers on the merchandise we've already paid for, we should end up with a new, up-to-date range of clothing in stock. That way, we can have high markups and good reductions, and still achieve more or less the same profits as before."

"I see. I'll explain it to the president in my next meeting."

Shinkawa was able to do so in good faith. He almost believed it.

Kôjima pounced on the monthly balance sheet for November as soon as it arrived and devoured it like a man going over a long-awaited letter. He already had a good idea what the figures would be, but still felt an agitated excitement that logic couldn't calm. One glance through the figures was enough to reassure him that he was headed in the right direction.

If the truth about the dire straits the company was in could be kept from its president, then Kôjima could concentrate on making the company strong again—to the point that performance actually tallied with the fictitious figures. Thanks to the knowledge and goodwill of Kameyama Tsurunosuke, president of the Banrai Stores chain, he had a good idea of how to go about dramatically improving performance in specific practical ways. Fresh foods was foremost in his mind, and the fresh foods research meetings were critical to this strategy.

In his heart, he was bubbling over with enthusiasm and excitement. *Let's really go for it! Let's turn this company into the best fresh foods retailer in the country!* That would mean they'd have to come up with a fresh foods department that was even better than Kameyama's. But Kôjima was up for the challenge.

Kameyama's first visit to Ishiei Stores was a watershed moment for

Kôjima, and he and Asayama had subsequently visited Banrai Stores to see how things worked there. Kameyama showed them around, laughing and smiling and sharing bits of retail wisdom; he gave them copies of documents they might otherwise have assumed were company secrets. His generosity and kindness brought tears of gratitude to their eyes. But as they were being shown round Banrai Stores, an idea popped into Kôjima's head.

Banrai Stores was a revelation. There was a fantastic range of fresh produce on display, all of it in excellent condition. There were shimmering assortments of sashimi and well-trimmed slices of beef designed to whet the appetite. There was a host of processed foods on display and a rich array of imported goods. The whole store gave off an air of quality and class. The effort that went into this on a daily basis was obvious. There were far more staff than at Ishiei Stores, and the employees seemed much better trained. Everyone seemed to know exactly what part he was supposed to play—like well-drilled soldiers in an army. But—and this was the idea that kept popping back into Kôjima's head—things could be even better! Imagine how much more smoothly everything would run if the IE philosophy were introduced to this kind of business!

IE stood for "industrial engineering"—a system of business management that had grown out of the scientific management methods developed by Frederick W. Taylor, an American engineer and the founder of scientific management. Industrial engineering aimed to apply knowledge from mathematics and science in order to improve productivity and efficiency in the workplace. These days it was practically taken for granted in the manufacturing industry, where it had been achieving impressive results for years, but in the retail sector no one seemed to have even heard of it.

Kôjima had first encountered IE when he was researching a large steel manufacturer for Saiwa Bank, and had not forgotten its impact. He resolved to apply the theories of IE to Ishiei Stores.

It was at a second Banrai Stores outlet that Kôjima was struck by a realization that caused his heart to pump with excitement. Just like the first Banrai store, this one was incomparably better organized than any of the Ishiei Stores outlets, and much more vibrant. But he couldn't help noticing that the meat and fish were cut slightly differently here, and that the food displays were different from the ones he had seen earlier. Kameyama explained that this was due to the fact that there were different butchers and fishmongers working in each store. Obviously everyone had their own way of doing things.

It occurred to Kôjima that there would come a day when it was no longer possible to manage a company like this effectively if the number of stores continued to increase. It was all very well leaving it to the individual butcher or fishmonger to decide how he wanted to do things—no doubt they knew what they were doing. But in terms of management, you couldn't have a large supermarket chain made up of several hundred butchers and fishmongers all doing things their own way.

In order to create an effective chain of stores, where quality standards could be relied upon across the board, you would have to lose the individuality. But by using the IE philosophy, you could get rid of the individuality without losing the knowledge and expertise. You could standardize techniques and still keep skills at the same high level. And if he could achieve that, then Ishiei Stores could become the only supermarket chain to combine a high level of skills with a chain-store approach to management. In other words, Ishiei Stores could become the number one supermarket chain in Japan!

Kôjima's next step was to put his ideas into concrete form, as his New Strategy for Fresh Produce Management. That was three months ago. A lot had happened since then, but little by little his ideas seemed to be producing results. The fresh foods research groups had ground to a halt when the rumors about him and Yoshiko surfaced, but now that the rumors had faded and Ôtaka had rejoined the group with renewed enthusiasm, they were starting to reap dividends.

Kôjima was starting to feel confident. He was convinced that over the next five years he would be able to lay the foundations on which the company would rise to preeminence as a supermarket chain. But before any of this was possible, he had to keep on producing faked performance reports. What was his best way forward? For the monthly statements immediately following the stocktaking, he had no choice but to pretend the disaster had never happened. The company had to return the estimates to their original levels and add fictitious stock to the accounts. Kôjima was amazed by how easy it was to do. All you had to do was add a few zeroes to a column in the inventory and the rest took care of itself. Until another thorough inventory was taken, the deception would be almost impossible to detect.

It was so easy that for a while Kôjima was tempted to think he could carry on doing things this way indefinitely. But he soon realized that if they carried on like this, their turnover would soon become abnormally low. Anyone who knew anything about supermarket accounting would know right away that the figures had been meddled with. The previous accounts were full of figures representing stock that didn't exist or would never serve any useful purpose, and although these figures had not been deliberately concocted, they did mean that turnover for the past year was already low. But no one at the company was likely to notice anything, and the Sawabe Sôgô Bank, which dealt with most of their accounts, suspected nothing. But this grace period would not last forever. As the listings of supermarket companies on the stock market increased, and as financial reports were made public, more attention was going to be paid to the figures. Sooner or later those chickens would come home to roost.

Kôjima knew he had to come up with a way of disguising the truth that was both more subtle and effective than simply padding the figures. "I never thought I'd need to be so creative in a supermarket," he laughed to himself. One thing was certain: he needed to come up with some extra profits from somewhere. He could either enter lower operating costs into the accounts, or higher profits. Adding zeroes to the stock figures was one way of lowering the operating costs, since things that would normally be put down under operating costs were omitted from the accounts, but there had to be other, less gross ways of reducing operating costs.

You could reduce personnel costs, for example, by fictitiously reassigning employees to another company for a period. If you moved fifty Ishiei Stores employees to affiliate Company A, then as far as the accounts were concerned, Ishiei Stores was better off to the tune of fifty annual salaries—say, by fifty million yen or so. Of course that would mean that Company A was in the negative by fifty million yen too, but if Ishiei Stores provided them with funds equivalent to this amount, the fiction could hold water. Of course, you would need to get the CEO of Company A on board first, and perhaps provide him with an honorarium for his inconvenience, but since Ishiei Stores had appointed him to this position in the first place, it was hard to see this being a serious obstacle.

Kôjima had gone down the list, crossing out each wild idea in turn, and had ended up deciding to bump up the numbers in the profit column—hardly the most foolproof of alternatives—when Matsuo casually came by and suggested the Teikoku Kôeki Company. Teikoku Kôeki had been doing business with the Ishiei Stores clothing department for more than a decade—surely they would be prepared to cut the company some slack? "They've started branching out into construction and real estate," Matsuo began, "trying to get in on the action while the economy's booming. They've been struggling, but I'm thinking we could help each other."

"You mean we could hook up with them for new store construction?" Kôjima asked. "Not bad. We could put in an order with them of two hundred fifty million yen for a job that's really worth two hundred million. They don't finish it within the contracted time, and they have to pay us back fifty million yen for breach of contract. That way, we would be able to shave two hundred fifty million off our accounts here, and get fifty million in the plus." Kôjima's eyes started to sparkle. "I think it might just work."

"Yeah, could be fun."

"But wait," Kôjima said thoughtfully, as though to himself. "If we did it like that then the fifty million yen would be nonoperational earnings. That would look suspicious right away." He sat quiet and thought it through some more. "No, it's all right. There's a way we can do it, and make sure the money gets taken as operational earnings."

His face full of optimism again, he began an enthusiastic explanation of what he had in mind. They would inflate the construction costs as much as necessary—say, by fifty million yen. At the same time, they would appoint Teikoku Kôeki and its subsidiary wholesalers as sales agents for Ishiei Stores. This would mean that they could recoup the fifty million through reduced prices or rebates or something else. In this way, the money would come in under normal operating profits.

"That's a great idea. Almost too good. If we don't lose anything at all, our profits will just go up and up."

"But we're bound to lose something. Construction costs will be higher than before, so the costs of repaying our debts and the interest on our loans would go up too."

"But that wouldn't be too much, would it?"

"Let's see—fifty million yen would mean an increase in our monthly payments of about six hundred thousand yen per month."

"We should be able to cope with that."

"The question is whether Teikoku Kôeki will dance with us."

"They'll dance. I'll talk to them if you like."

They called in Kitô and put the finishing touches to their plan.

Matsuo and Kitô visited Teikoku Kôeki, and within a week they had an agreement.

"You're going to have some explaining to do when this comes out," Matsuo said amusedly to Kitô as they worked out the details in Kôjima's office. "You've always said you should never hire a trading company as a contractor."

"I've got an idea," Kôjima said unexpectedly. "How about Matsuo moves to the development department, and Kitô—you can take over as head of the clothing department? It might be the best thing under the circumstances."

"You want me to become head of clothing?" Kitô gasped.

"Well, the clothing department was the center of the embezzlement scandal, so it would make sense to move Matsuo-*san* to another department. If neither of you objects I'll suggest it to Mr. Ishikari the next time I see him," Kôjima said.

In between settling on this subterfuge and putting it into practice, Kôjima was destined to live through another period of worry and uncertainty. It was clear that the easiest thing to do—if not the most prudent—would be simply to tell Ishikari Eitarô the truth.

He was tossing this idea around when, suddenly, it occurred to him: he would ask Misaki Yoshiko for her opinion. Surely she would have a fair understanding of Eitarô's character. She would have a better intuition of how Eitarô would respond to the truth. And besides, it gave him a perfect excuse to ask her out for dinner again.

A few days later, in a private room at an exclusive restaurant in Shinjuku, Yoshiko considered Kôjima's question carefully for a few moments, and then replied, "I'm sorry. I don't really know him that well."

"Never mind. I'm sorry to have bored you with something so dumb," Kôjima said, smiling. He could feel himself being drawn in by Yoshiko's lustrous skin and the gentleness in her eyes.

"But," Yoshiko started to say, as though she had just remembered something, "I don't know if this is the kind of thing you mean . . ."

"Please. Every little bit helps."

"I don't know if I should even be saying this. But there is one thing I found out about him that came as a bit of a disappointment to me. He doesn't care about his employees."

"Why do you say that?"

"I don't remember exactly when it was, a while ago anyway, but several managers from the fish department came to his office for some reason. After they left, I went into his office to clean up, and Mr. Ishikari said to me, 'Can you smell the fish? Can you smell it? I can't stand that stink.' Once he mentioned it, I had to admit I could smell something. But the expression on his face was so unpleasant, it was full of disgust and contempt, and I've never forgotten it. It made me think he didn't really like those men, or any of the people who worked at the company. He didn't have any respect for them. And that he didn't like company either. Or even the idea of a supermarket."

Kôjima had heard enough. He knew now what he had to do.

An awkward silence came between them in the taxi back to Sawabe. It was hard to believe that they had been talking and laughing together just ten minutes ago. Here they were, a man and a woman alone together in the back seat of a taxi, acutely aware of one another and the situation they were in. As the taxi moved onto the highway, Kôjima took Yoshiko's hand.

"I hear your wife's moving to Sawabe soon," Yoshiko said.

"In the New Year," Kôjima replied, his voice dry and strained.

Their hands fell apart, and they didn't touch again until the taxi pulled up outside Yoshiko's apartment.

THIRTEEN

PROMOTION

Four years later, in January 1974, the reception room at Ishiei Stores' head office was filled with the machine-gun laughter of Kameyama Tsurunosuke.

"*Ga ha ha ha!* I can't wait to see what it's like. All the talk is that it's a whole new store."

"There's still a long way to go," said Kôjima and Asayama, practically in chorus.

"The atmosphere here at the head office has definitely brightened, I must say. Things were a bit stale the last time I visited, all those years ago. But there's a real twinkle in everybody's eyes today."

"We've still got plenty of problems, believe me," Kôjima said, blushing. "We've been struggling with things going out of stock recently. It's been chaos—just when we were starting to get back on track."

"Oh, it's terrible, isn't it? But it shouldn't last long. Normally it means your customers are trying to anticipate price increases, and a few items sell out for a while. True, this time's a little different."

"Well, the sooner the chaos dies down the better."

Chaos was the only word for it. War had broken out in the Middle East the previous October, and Japan, like other oil-importing countries, was feeling the pinch. Fear that supplies might run out had sent people into a state of panic. The first things to disappear off the shelves were toilet paper and detergent. Both were bulky products, both were cheap, and both were mass-produced; for these reasons Ishiei Stores, like most retailers, kept only small amounts in stock. Once customers started stockpiling these items, they vanished from the shelves.

Reports in the media led to the suggestion that businesses were hoarding goods to drive up prices, leading crowds of angry customers to lay siege to stores across the country. At Ishiei Stores, customers pounded on storeroom doors at two locations, demanding access to the store's "secret reserves." In fact, no such reserves existed—but that didn't stop irate customers from vowing to meet every company truck and inspect the deliveries.

The effects of the oil shock were not limited to the relationship a supermarket had with its customers. The relationship with suppliers was turned upside down too. Overnight, wholesalers were vaulted into a superior position. In the past, they had always been looked down upon; suddenly they were in the driver's seat. Supermarket buyers now shuffled ingratiatingly before them, bowing and serving them tea.

This reversal of the wholesaler-retailer relationship had far-reaching repercussions. Wholesalers were more than happy with things the way they now were. With the vulnerability of markets exposed, they were free to gouge the supermarkets for everything they had.

One of the most aggressive wholesalers was the Ishiei Trading Company—the parent of Ishiei Stores, and also owned by Ishikari Eitarô. Within a week of the oil shock, Eitarô had reshuffled his team, moving his best people from sales to purchasing. At the first board meeting he had attended in several months, he announced that Ishiei Trading would name its prices and decline to do business with anyone who did not meet them. "The oil shock has altered the commercial landscape in Japan. Supply cannot keep up with demand. Suppliers not only can but *must* dictate terms, so that stock is not depleted and stability is ensured. This will have a huge impact on profitability and growth, and Ishiei Stores must adjust to this new reality, just like any other retail marketer. There may come a day when Ishiei Stores has nothing left to sell."

"May I say a few words?" Kôjima interrupted. "Most of the things we sell are everyday essentials. There might come a time when some things are harder to keep in stock and we struggle to provide the same range of choice—but I find it hard to believe the day will ever come when we have nothing left to sell at all. There'd be a riot if that happened."

"So you say," said Eitarô with a grimace. "And yet here we are running out of daily essentials like toilet paper and detergent. This oil crisis has shocked us into the need to do things differently. Of course we would prefer a surplus—but there's no room for complacency in this game. No one would disagree with that."

Kôjima heard the same argument countless times in the weeks and months that followed. People's reactions were split down the middle— they either interpreted the current climate as a golden opportunity or as a harbinger of a bigger disaster around the corner. Kôjima just wished things would get back to normal.

"The real problems will come once this has all blown over," Kameyama said. "This situation won't last forever. When it comes to an end, that's when the retail market's going to hit the buffers with a bang."

"Some of the weaker companies will struggle to survive."

"Indeed. You were lucky you managed to get your house in order before this crisis hit."

"I hope so," Kôjima replied.

As they toured the center store, Kameyama was astounded by the new fresh produce displays.

"You did it! I can hardly recognize this as the same place. I wasn't expecting this."

"It's all thanks to you," Kôjima said, bowing his head low. "If you hadn't come to see us back then, we'd still be selling rotten meat and wilting vegetables today. We owe you a great debt of gratitude."

"What are you talking about? This is all the result of your own hard work." His plump *daruma*-like face crinkled as his gentle eyes looked up at Kôjima. "And I bet it wasn't easy."

Kôjima found it difficult to reply. He was overcome with emotion, fighting back tears. Kameyama knew what it was like before, and he could see what it was like now. He understood what Kôjima had gone through.

"So, how many stores do you have now?" Kameyama asked.

"We've just opened number fifteen."

"That's tremendous! It must be tough keeping everything in order when you get that big. We're working on our eighth store now, and we're struggling to keep on top of everything. It's hard to maintain the quality we like."

"I know exactly what you mean," Kôjima said, feeling both humility and pride.

From the look of contentment on Kameyama's face, you'd have thought there was nothing in the world he liked better than touring supermarkets.

"Are you still up for taking a look at our latest pride and joy, Kameyama-*san*?"

The fifteenth store in the Ishiei Stores chain had opened a month earlier on the outskirts of a town called Yuki.

Kameyama was shown the fresh produce section first, and he was unprepared for what he saw. "Kôjima-*san*, this is utterly amazing! How on earth did you . . ."

Kameyama's rapture was interrupted by the approach of Ôtaka Seizô, the deputy store manager.

"Do you remember who this is, Ôtaka-*san*?" Kôjima asked, gesturing toward Kameyama.

"How could I forget? I still have nightmares about him coming around and filling up his basket with substandard produce."

"Yeah, you got a real shock that day," Kôjima said with a laugh. "I hope the knives aren't full of nicks and scratches at this store!"

"Don't worry. We've learned our lessons well!"

"Ôtaka is married now, Kameyama-*san*. He's just become father to a baby boy."

"Congratulations! I bet the baby looks just like his mother!"

"How'd you know that?" Ôtaka shrieked. The baby really did look like his mother, who was Kuroba Motoko. And just like his mother, the baby was full of character.

"*Ga ha ha!* Come on, Ôtaka-*san*—everyone knows that baby boys always look like their mothers."

Ôtaka beamed, an innocent happiness filling his heart.

"But this really is splendid, Kôjima-*san*," Kameyama said.

"We've still got a long way to go," Ôtaka said, barely able to contain his pleasure.

"What I find most impressive," Kameyama went on, "is the way the fresh produce departments here and at the center store look to have identical standards. You can't get them completely the same, of course—the sales area is a different shape and size for a start, and the display cases are not the same. But you've managed to standardize just about everything else—from the order of your displays to the packaging and presentation of each piece of merchandise. It sounds easy, but I know how hard that is to do. And yet you've succeeded. Brilliant! I assume all your stores follow the same guidelines?"

"More or less," Kôjima answered, gratified that Kameyama had noticed.

"But how are you able to train all your employees so well? I get the results I want only with employees I train myself, but it's almost impossible to get the same standards with the new employees. They argue about everything. We have seven stores, and it's getting hard to control the standards."

"Tell Mr. Kameyama about the fresh food research group, Ôtaka-*san*."

Ôtaka explained briefly how the research groups worked and how they had developed. Kameyama listened attentively.

"Kôjima-*san*, that's wonderful," Kameyama said, genuinely impressed. "It looks like it's my turn to learn from you."

"Not at all," Kôjima protested, but he couldn't hide the emotion in his voice.

One evening several days later, the directors and department heads of the company were gathered together in a Sawabe restaurant for a New Year's party. This was being held to make up for the annual end-of-year party, which had been canceled because of the oil-shock shortages. But there was another reason for holding the dinner, which only a few of the directors knew about. It was being held to mark Ishikari Seijirô's retirement and Kôjima's appointment as his replacement.

Ishikari was leaving the company to fulfill his long-cherished dream: establishing a calligraphy school that would open soon in a modern two-story building tucked away in an old section of town. Kôjima's appointment as his successor on the other hand, had come as a surprise. Ichimura, long regarded by almost everyone in the company as the heir apparent, had turned the job down when Ishikari offered it to him. "Be serious," he said. "I should have resigned four years ago for the mistakes I made. You and Kôjima saved my career. All I want is to be able to use my talents to work for the good of the company. Kôjima should take over."

"But he's still young. He's only thirty-seven."

"Plenty of people his age are at the top in this business. He may be young, but he's proven himself to be a strong and able leader. Look at how the company's results have improved over the past four years."

Ishikari wasn't sure what he should do, so he asked his brother for advice. Eitarô's response surprised him: "Kôjima sounds like the best choice," he said. "Let's go with him." With his brother on board, Seijirô knew everything would be fine.

When Seijirô approached him about the job, Kôjima was surprised but grateful. He was humbled by the support—and the deference—Ichimura had shown him, and was determined not to let anybody down. He was pleased to accept the new position.

Asayama had come over to pick up Kôjima at his desk. "Ready to go to the party?"

"Sure."

The restaurant was no more than a five- or six-minute walk from the head office. Kôjima shivered and hunched his shoulders against the cold. It was the chilliest day of the winter so far.

"I just saw the preliminary results for December," Asayama said. "Profits look like they'll be more than one hundred million yen. Not bad!"

"We're finally starting to achieve good figures. With any luck we won't have to cook the books next year."

"Everything's gone according to your plan."

"Only because everyone has been so helpful. This oil-shock panic must have helped to boost sales for December, though. So I'm a little bit worried about the comedown once things get back to normal. But it wasn't just good luck that achieved these results. It was hard work. So we should celebrate. Long may it continue."

"You saved the company," Asayama said.

"No: we did it together. This is our fortress, right? We have to defend it when it comes under attack. And what's really great is to see fresh produce making a profit. You've really worked hard for this, Asayama-*san*. We couldn't have done it without you."

Despite the cold winter air, the hearts of the two men were warmed by pride and happiness.

Ishikari Eitarô got to his feet as soon as the party was underway and announced the immediate promotion of Kôjima to general manager.

A buzz rose from the crowd. Kôjima watched the expressions on people's faces as Eitarô spoke, hoping that the response would be positive. He needn't have worried—people were surprised, but pleasantly so. They gathered around him as Eitarô finished speaking, reaching out to shake his hand.

"Thank you for your support. I'll do my best," Kôjima said, bowing as he shook hands and accepted their congratulations.

"Best of luck, Ryôsuke. I can feel safe in the knowledge that I've left things in your capable hands," Ishikari Seijirô said. He looked as if a huge weight had been lifted from his shoulders.

"I'm looking forward to working with you, Kôjima-*san*," Ichimura said, squeezing Kôjima's hand so hard it hurt.

"Hey, why so uptight? Why aren't you saying anything?" Asayama shouted in his excitement. "Three cheers for Kôjima-*san*! *Banzai banzai banzai!*" the group roared along with him. "And now," Asayama shouted, "let's toast our new general manager! *Kampai!*"

Asayama grabbed a glass and knocked back several large swigs of beer. Kôjima was a bit worried by this. Asayama didn't usually drink much, and it probably wasn't a good idea for him to lose control completely. But before long, Kôjima was drawn into the party spirit himself, spurred on by an unending succession of congratulatory toasts.

They drank. And then the singing started. Ichimura sang an old folk song.

> *Raise high your cup*
> *And fill your plate*
> *Let's drink and sup*
> *And ce—le—brate!*

It was a little-known drinking song from Miyagi prefecture, but sung in Ichimura's deep husky voice, the song had a poignancy to it. Kôjima stood up to sing too. He wasn't much of a singer, but he managed to get through an old nursery tune and was cheered for his efforts. In between songs people chatted among themselves; every so often the talk would be punctuated by a shout. And then Konno stood up and sang a lewd song that reduced the crowd to hopeless laughter.

The party was in full swing when Katsumura came up to Kôjima and whispered that Asayama was drunk and had Ishikari Eitarô cornered.

"You're the company president, and I just want you to know. I think you're doing a great job. I mean it, really. I didn't realize it before, but I see you in a new light now. You knew the whole time. You just didn't let on. You knew that Kôjima was the hero. He saved the company from ruin. I'm really glad to know you know," Asayama said.

"And tell me, Asayama-*san*, have all the losses been taken care of now?" Eitarô was going along with Asayama, but he was stone-cold sober.

"Don't worry about a thing. It's all gone. Disappeared. *Poof!* Like I told you. Everything has gone according to Kôjima's plan. He did such a good job. It's unbelievable," he slurred.

"So you overpaid Teikoku Kôeki and had them lower their charges to compensate, did you?"

"*Wash'un thadda grade eyejeer?* Who else but Kôjima could have come up with something like that?"

"A great idea," Ishikari Eitarô said, his voice now quiet and restrained.

"But don't worry about all that now. It's all over now. I just wanted you to know how brilliant he is. I mean, sure, so we pulled the wool over your eyes for a bit. But only because we love the company so much. We wanted to fight for the company, even if it meant breaking the rules and acting like the bad guys. So that's what we did. *Fish'un dada mazey fin to do?*" His words were starting to come out garbled, but it was going to take more than that to hold him back now. "But you knew. You knew all along, right? You knew all along, you were just pretending. You were watching the whole time! That's why you know he's the best. That's why you promoted him to managing director, right? I'm so happy. Here's to the new boss, here's to the success of the company, and—most of all—here's to the company president, because you had the balls to make the right decision. Where is Kôjima-*san* anyway? Hey, where'd the new managing director go?" he said, stumbling a bit as he turned around.

"He's right next to you," Ishikari Eitarô said, his eyes fixed on Kôjima, who had come up to the two of them. "Asayama-*san* has been telling me all about your hidden talents. My own vision and judgment also came in for more than their fair share of praise."

Kôjima had nothing to say. He'd tried to restrain Asayama when he heard what he was saying, but Ishikari Eitarô had stopped him with a stare. It was too late now anyway. Kôjima felt no trace of intoxication. He knew that things were beyond his control now. All he could say was, "I'll explain everything to you tomorrow."

Ishikari Eitarô turned without a word. He stepped quickly through the crowd and left the party. Kôjima thought about going after him— but what was the use? All he could do was wait to see how Eitarô reacted and then formulate his strategy.

Almost nobody noticed what had happened. Kôjima and Katsumura stood motionless, while Asayama himself lay passed out on the tatami. In the background, Konno's song was entering yet another ribald verse, accompanied by raucous cheers and applause.

FOURTEEN

COLLAPSE

The morning after the party, Kôjima arrived at the office earlier than usual and went directly to Ishikari Eitarô's office without stopping to put his coat in his locker. He was about to knock on the office door when Misaki Yoshiko came out holding a tray. "Good morning," she said, cheerful as always.

"Is the president here yet?" Kôjima asked.

"He's in a meeting with his brother." Kôjima knew at once what they would be talking about. "How did he seem?"

"Excuse me?" Yoshiko looked up at him, puzzled. She obviously hadn't understood his question.

"Never mind. Can you call me as soon as his brother comes out? I'll be at my desk."

"Of course," Yoshiko replied. "Is something wrong?"

"It's nothing, I hope. Thanks. I'll be waiting for the call." Kôjima returned to his desk, leaving Yoshiko mystified. It was more than an hour and a half later when Yoshiko called.

"The managing director has left the president's office, but Mr. Shinkawa is with him now." She sounded sorry to be the bearer of bad news.

"Did you tell him I was waiting?"

"I did. But he asked me to send Mr. Shinkawa in first."

"It's important that I see him next. Call me again when Shinkawa leaves, OK?"

"Sure." Kôjima was about to hang up when Yoshiko started to speak again. "I hear congratulations are in order? You're being promoted to managing director? I'm really happy for you."

"Thanks. But nothing's fixed yet."

Yoshiko fell silent for an instant. She could tell there was something wrong, but she didn't feel it was her position to ask what it was. "I'm sure you'll be a big success. I'll let you know as soon as Mr. Shinkawa comes out."

He hung up. It had only been the briefest of conversations, but Kôjima was grateful for Yoshiko's concern.

Kôjima waited at his desk. Asayama and Katsumura came by, Asayama apologetic, Katsumura worried sick. At eleven, Ichimura stopped by, hurrying over as soon as he heard the news.

"I'm going to tell him everything," Kôjima said. "I'm sure the president will understand. Most of our problems are behind us now anyway, so maybe it's good that it happened like this. He had to find out sooner or later."

The phone rang. It was Yoshiko. "The president says he'd like a word with Mr. Ichimura next. If he's there with you, please let him know." Yoshiko's voice was soft and low; something wasn't right. "I told him you were waiting. He said he'll see you later."

Kôjima understood what was happening. Ishikari wanted to talk to all of the other people involved before he spoke to Kôjima. He could hear the words now. *I can't trust you anymore.* He struggled against the urge to run upstairs and force his way into the president's office.

Kôjima couldn't get any work done. He closed his eyes and sank down into his chair. From time to time someone would stop by to congratulate him on his promotion. There had been a steady procession of people all day. He got to his feet and thanked each one of them with a smile, but deep down the constant coming and going of well-wishers was only making things worse. The kids from sales and promotions stopped by around midday to invite him out for lunch, but Kôjima turned them down. He had lost his appetite.

"Let's have a party soon to celebrate," they said as they left.

As it turned out, Kôjima didn't get to see the president at all that day. According to Yoshiko, almost every other member of the board was called in. Several of them stopped by to see Kôjima after their own meeting was over, but he still knew nothing beyond the fact that Ishikari had been quizzing each of them about the falsified accounts. Everyone agreed that Ishikari hadn't seemed particularly angry about Kôjima's involvement. But who knew what he was really thinking? After he had spoken to Konno, the president had put on his coat and gone home.

"He said he wants to see you in his office first thing tomorrow morning," Yoshiko said.

"Thanks." Kôjima went back to his desk and cast his eye over the documents on his desk, but he knew he was wasting his time. There was no way he was going to get any work done feeling like this. The other directors had all gone home nursing their own private thoughts. It was already night.

On his way out of the office, he bumped into Horiguchi from sales and promotions. Horiguchi was soaking wet.

"Is it raining?" Kôjima asked, surprised.

"Sleet. It's going to start snowing any minute. It's been raining the last two hours over at Shimo-Shinden."

"You've been out in this?"

"Looks like it's going to stick. Tomorrow's the first day of the sales but the manager says if the weather stays like this, they won't sell a thing."

The manager was Kôda, who had been moved from development to the Shimo-Shinden store. He would still crack jokes and fool around given half a chance, but his hard work was never in question. People said he had a knack for knowing what his employees were thinking.

Kôjima went back into the office for an umbrella. By the time he got outside, the sleet had turned to snow. Snowflakes danced through the air. In the bright glare of the streetlights, it looked as though the sky was turning to powder. Kôjima hurried home, the fingers of the hand holding the umbrella rapidly turning numb.

•　　•　　•

281

"Is it true you were the ringleader of a plot to doctor the company accounts?"

Kôjima had been looking forward to getting his thoughts in order once he got home. A sudden accusation like this from his wife was the last thing he needed.

"Who told you that?"

"What does it matter who it was? So it's true?"

Kôjima couldn't think of anything to say. He stared back at his wife and said nothing. One of the director's wives must have told her what was going on. But Takako was right: it didn't really matter who it was.

Takako had been against the idea of Kôjima leaving the bank and joining Ishiei Stores from the beginning. But she seemed to have a change of mind once she moved to Sawabe after giving birth to their son, Tomoyuki. It didn't take her long to realize that being the wife of a company director was a better deal in all kinds of ways to being the wife of a middle-manager at a bank.

Sawabe was not a big city, and Takako was soon joining the other directors' wives in their friendly clublike get-togethers. Her status within the group rose as Kôjima climbed the promotion ladder at work. The apartment was much bigger than the one they had lived in before, and they were better off financially. She had never admitted it in so many words, but it was clear to Kôjima that she was happy with her new life.

Kôjima wasn't too thrilled about the hangers-on that had attached themselves to her, especially not when he learned of the rumors and gossip they were passing on, but he was pleased to see that she had come to terms with his job. He had brushed her early objections aside and forced her to move; he didn't know how long he would have been able to stand it if she'd been really unhappy.

One of these hangers-on must have told her about the company accounts. Now that he thought about it, it surprised him that the story hadn't leaked before. The gag order had been effective. But now that the company president had found out, one of the directors must have revealed all to his wife, probably in an attempt to establish his own innocence.

"So, is it true?" Takako asked again.

"It's true," Kôjima said.

"You . . ." She was surprised that she had managed to get the truth out of him so easily. "I don't believe it. What exactly did you do?"

"There were reasons."

"What reasons? And what happened to all the money?"

"Money? What are you talking about?" Now it was Kôjima's turn to be taken by surprise.

"You don't have to play the innocent with me. That's what it's all about, right? What did you do with the money? How much was there? Where have you hidden it? Or did you hand it all over to some young slut?"

"Slut?"

"What else would it be? Mrs. Ishikari said that's what it must be, and she was right."

"The president's wife? So that's who you heard all this from?"

"Yes. So you see, it's not just idle gossip."

"I see. And what did she tell you, exactly?"

Ishikari's wife had called Takako sometime that morning and invited her to lunch in Tokyo. Takako had thought this a bit strange— Ishikari's wife had never done anything of the sort before—but she'd been happy to accept the invitation. They met at Shinjuku station and set out for Ginza. They were sipping coffee at the end of lunch in a French restaurant when Ishikari's wife brought up Kôjima's involvement in a plot to doctor the company accounts.

"I don't know how to put this," Mrs. Ishikari said, "but do you think there's any chance your husband has been . . . up to something behind your back? Does anything come to mind?"

"How do you mean?"

"Another woman. You have to be careful, you know. Take your eyes off them for one minute and they'll be at it in no time. It's the nature of the beast. And your husband's quite an attractive prospect. He's young, good-looking; he has a good job. I bet they can't leave him alone."

"I don't think so. He would never do anything like that."

"You want to be careful. It's a mistake to think that it would never happen. Even if your husband isn't interested, the world is full of wicked women."

Takako said nothing.

"I trust you," Ishikari's wife said to her. "I don't think you were in league with him, trying to make off with company money. But you can never trust a man." Mrs. Ishikari gave a fake laugh and looked suspiciously into Takako's eyes.

Kôjima now understood what Ishikari's strategy was. Ishikari would interview the other directors himself, while his wife went to work on Takako. It showed an absolute lack of trust in him. This was no good. This was no good at all. Pretty soon there would be nothing left to discuss.

"So why don't you tell me the truth?" his wife was saying.

Kôjima tried to explain why it had been necessary to falsify the company accounts, struggling against the despair that was welling up inside. He went into some detail about how they had done it, even though he realized she was probably not following much of what he was saying.

"If that's the truth, you're an absolute fool. And if it's a lie, then there's no hope for you," Takako said when Kôjima was done, bursting into tears. "How could you be so stupid? What are you going to do now?"

Kôjima didn't know the answer to that himself. Right now he couldn't think beyond tomorrow morning and his meeting with Ishikari Eitarô. He would have to see what happened and then decide what to do once the meeting was over.

Was he absolutely sure there was no other woman involved, Takako asked again. "Enough! It's just like I told you," Kôjima said. For once the strain was starting to show in his voice. A long and pointless argument broke out, and the night grew late.

"I'm going to bed," Kôjima announced suddenly and carried his bedding into the guest bedroom. He opened the window to try and shake off some of the sadness weighing on his chest. There was snow on the windowsill, and a gust of wind sent snowflakes swirling into the room.

He tried to focus on something, but from so high up he could hardly make out the city below him at all. It looked as though the city was in for one of the biggest snowstorms in years. He shut the window and pulled the curtains, then got into bed and closed his eyes, hoping for sleep.

Kôda got to work at eight thirty as usual, even though he had left home fifteen minutes early. He had allowed extra time because of the snow. As he'd expected, the bus was late. Everything happened slower than usual when it snowed.

"We won't do much business in this," he muttered as he made his way from the bus stop to the store, kicking out at the snow underfoot as he walked. They had put flyers in the day's papers advertising special discounts and promotions, but they would be lucky if anyone showed up in this.

"Morning," he called out as he made a circuit of the store. He did the same thing every morning, just to check that everything was in order and that everyone was present. Checking that the employees were clocking in on time was one of the store manager's most important tasks. Often a part-time worker would ask for the day off, and often someone would call in to say her child was running a fever. Kôda felt sure that several children were likely to be diagnosed with "fever" on a day like today.

Kôda made his rounds. As he moved from the fish section to the meat section he heard a loud creaking noise that stopped him in his tracks. Everyone in the meat section had their heads turned up toward the ceiling.

"What the hell was that?" Kôda waited for the noise to come again, but he heard nothing. "Maybe the store is going to collapse. We might all be crushed to death in an avalanche of snow."

"Please sir, don't tempt fate," the meat chief said with a wry smile.

"Don't worry, you'll be all right. It's only God's favorites that die young. But then, who knows? You're such a defective creation there's no guarantee he won't take you out of circulation."

"You're terrible."

Kôda left the meat section with a laugh. He may have been joking as usual, but the noise he had just heard had set off a chain of anxious thoughts in his mind. Kôda went outside and walked around the store. He pushed and kicked at the outer walls and pillars, but found nothing unusual. It wasn't really possible that a heavy overnight snowfall could cause the building to collapse, was it? It seemed inconceivable. And yet . . . something wasn't right. It was just after the start of the morning meeting at nine forty-five that Kôda remembered the pillar.

That was it! When they bought the store from Ogawa they had discovered that one of the main pillars in the building seemed to be buckling under stress. Kôjima had asked the development team to run a check on it. The conclusion, if he remembered correctly, was that the builders had installed a slightly bent pillar; it was almost certainly nothing to worry about, but it would be replaced anyway.

Kôda went to look at that pillar now. It was about a twenty-centimeter square pillar. They *had* replaced the old one, hadn't they? For some reason he couldn't be sure. Maybe they had never replaced the damaged pillar at all, but had merely tacked a façade onto it. He heard the same creaking sound again. Was it just his imagination, or was the noise louder now? It seemed to go on for longer too. And this time it was followed by a loud thud, like the sound of something falling. There was no doubt now where the noise was coming from: above the sales area, toward the center of the store.

Kôda looked at his watch. It was ten o'clock. Opening time. If there was any risk of an accident, it would be madness to open the store. But in the end, he decided to go ahead and open the doors as usual. Half a dozen customers rushed into the store. There *was* a sale on, after all—snowstorm or no snowstorm. But not long after, the fresh produce chief rushed up to him in a panic.

"Come quickly! There's snow falling into the work area."

"What? What are you talking about?"

"Snow is coming in through a gap in the ceiling."

Kôda ran to the fresh produce work area and looked up. Through a rent in the ceiling he could see the sky! Some of the ceiling tiles had shifted, and snow was falling into the store.

"This is not good." No sooner had Kôda spoken this than he heard the creaking sound for the third time, louder still, and accompanied by an even heavier thud.

Kôda hurried out onto the sales floor, where several customers stood looking worriedly up at the ceiling. Everyone knew that something was wrong. But no one knew what to do.

"Scary," an elderly lady in front of the meat sales area said with a laugh.

"A little bit of snow and the whole building starts to shake—that's no good," the other woman said. They both laughed as though it were the funniest thing they had ever seen.

They were still smiling when dust began to fall on their upturned faces and the roof fell in, bringing nearly a foot of overnight snow with it. There was a thundering crash, and the lights went out. Next came the splintering crash of a thousand things shattering into pieces, of metal being crunched and flattened—and then the screams of terrified people.

Kôda was sprawled out on the floor. The roof had crashed into the gondolas, and the force of the collision had sent the displays flying into Kôda, who now lay half-buried with the debris. He tried to stand, but couldn't move. His right foot was trapped. If fire broke out now, he was finished. Around him was total commotion.

"Kôda-*san*? Kôda-*san*? Are you there?"

"I'm over here," Kôda called back in the loudest voice he could muster. He felt a searing pain in his ankle.

Kôjima had been talking to Ishikari Eitarô for nearly an hour. Kôjima sat with his hands on his knees, attempting to explain why he had done what he had done.

Ishikari sat slumped deep in his armchair, nodding occasionally as he listened but otherwise expressionless. He didn't ask any questions. Kôjima was almost disappointed by this—he had come equipped with written notes—but after Eitarô's interviews with the other directors he probably had a pretty full picture of the situation.

He didn't have much to say in response to Kôjima's apology either. "There's nothing we can do about that now. Just be sure it doesn't happen again." That was all.

Kôjima struggled to understand the significance of this. Was he forgiven or not? It could be taken either way. "I'm going to speak frankly," Kôjima said, deciding to be more forward. "If you can forgive me for what I did, I'd really like to be given another chance. I will turn Ishiei Stores into the number-one supermarket chain in the country. Over the last four years I have put all the foundations in place. All we need to do now is to keep moving forward."

Ishikari listened quietly, his chubby face tilted to one side. He was nodding his head, but Kôjima wasn't sure how well he was making himself understood.

"I'm convinced we can turn this company into the first real supermarket chain in Japan. When I say a 'real' supermarket, I mean a supermarket chain that's run efficiently, making full use of the latest scientific methods. One that wouldn't leave the management of its fresh food sections to individual butchers and grocers with their own ideas of how to run things."

Ishikari Eitarô continued to listen in silence.

Kôjima hadn't intended to go this far, but once he started he couldn't resist the urge to make sure his views as fully understood as possible. "We're starting to see bigger chains growing up all over the country, some of them with sales of more than one hundred billion yen a year—but as retailers of food and provisions they are neglecting the most important thing of all."

"You mean selling fresh foods self-service style, right? I prefer selling fish and things face-to-face at a counter. It's more personal that way," Ishikari interrupted—but without any real interest.

For all Kôjima knew, he might only have spoken up to stop himself falling asleep out of boredom. "Well, it's something to do with that, I guess. Retail is like any other business in the sense that it involves goods and services. But unlike production companies, retail businesses have never put the way they handle those goods on a scientific footing. In the production industry, scientific management, a system created by a man named Taylor in the U.S., has been in place since the start of the twentieth century. It was out of that trend that the theory of industrial engineering was born. I've tried a series of experiments along with some of the employees here, and I think we've established that the theory works quite well for supermarkets. In fact, I'm convinced that it would be almost impossible to create a large supermarket chain without it."

Kôjima was choosing his words carefully, but he could feel frustration and anxiety mounting inside him. He felt that Ishikari wasn't taking in what he was saying at all, and was merely listening to the sound of his voice as it got louder and louder. "Please try to understand," Kôjima said. "We didn't want to worry you by letting you find out the company was losing money. What good would it have done if we had told you? And so we were guilty of some creative accounting in order to hide the facts from you—for four years. But our motives were never personal gain—we did it for the benefit of the company, and for the benefit of the people who work here. No one walked away with an extra yen. And now the problems have all been dealt with. Not only that—even though our annual sales are still relatively small, in terms of the way we're running the business now I truly believe we have laid the groundwork for the company to succeed as a chain. Please give me another chance." He had no option but to hope that Eitarô would understand. Tears welled in his eyes as he spoke.

This poignant moment was shattered by a loud knock on the door and Konno burst into the room without waiting for a reply. "We've just had news that the roof at Shimo-Shinden has fallen in from the snow," he blurted out excitedly.

"What?!" Ishikari and Kôjima said almost in unison.

"We don't have the details yet. The store manager is trapped under the fallen roof. Apparently several other people are trapped too."

"Customers?" Kôjima said, getting to his feet.

"I don't know. I'm going over there right now."

"I'm coming with you," said Kôjima, who then looked over at Ishikari Eitarô. "If any of our customers are injured, we're in deep trouble. We can finish this conversation another time."

Ishikari said nothing, but as Kôjima was about to leave the room, Ishikari called out to him. "A real supermarket chain?" he sneered. "You mean one where the roof doesn't collapse on the customers?"

His words pierced Kôjima to the heart, but he hurried out of the room without saying anything.

Alone in his office, Ishikari Eitarô held his head in his hands and heaved a heavy sigh. "I hate this. You never know what's going to happen in this business. You put up a building and let people come and go as they please, and they start selling more things than any man could keep track of. Anything can happen. It'll be food poisoning next." He shook his head slowly from side to side, then spread his hands wide and shrugged his shoulders, the way he had often seen French movie actors do. It was a habit he only indulged in when he was alone.

For Kôjima, the day was one long nightmare. Things at Shimo-Shinden were even worse than he had imagined. The people trapped under the falling rubble had been freed and taken to hospital by the time he and Konno arrived, but pandemonium reigned at the scene. The accident seemed to have driven half the staff out of their minds. Five people had been seriously injured, and seven others had suffered more minor injuries. Two female customers were among the more seriously injured (the others were all employees, including Kôda, the store manager).

Kôjima and Konno visited the injured at the hospital. The two customers were a mother and her daughter; the daughter was in critical condition. She was unconscious, and the doctors couldn't say for sure that she would pull through, or what the effects of her injuries might be if she did. The mother had broken her right arm and her left ankle, and she had sustained extensive cuts and bruises all over her body. Awake, she cried in pain, but at least she was out of danger, unlike her daughter, whose husband sat watching over her in tears, beside himself with grief and anger.

Kôjima could do nothing but apologize and bow. His interviews with the families of the three injured employees were no easier. They seemed reluctant to criticize the company in Kôjima's presence, but he could feel their resentment whenever they looked in his direction.

A formal verdict on what had caused the accident would have to wait until the police finished their investigations, but the facts seemed straightforward enough. The immediate cause had been the storm—or rather, the fact that the roof had been unable to withstand the weight of the accumulated snow. The main question was one of responsibility. Who was going to take the blame for putting up a building that had proved incapable of standing up to a mere foot of snow? That Ishiei Stores would be charged with criminal negligence seemed more than likely.

Kôjima returned to the store to take another look at the situation. The building itself was still largely intact. The only evidence that an accident had taken place at all was the broken glass in the storefront windows. But once you passed into the dim interior, the chaos and destruction were horrific.

Snow continued to fall heavily, but that hadn't deterred the crowd of gawkers. There were people standing all around the perimeter of the store, forming a kind of human fence. The store itself had been roped off, and as Kôjima was climbing over the rope, an employee hurried over to inform him that the police were conducting interviews in the coffee shop across the street.

Kôjima arrived to find Ichimura, Matsuo, and Kitô already there. Kitô had been called in as the former head of the development department; he seemed to be doing most of the talking. Kôjima took a seat and listened. The basics of what had happened were clear. One of the pillars in the center of the store had snapped under stress. This had caused greater stress on the other pillars, causing them to buckle; eventually the roof caved in. It would have been no surprise to learn that the bent pillar had caused the problem, except that Kôjima was certain the pillar had been replaced when Ishiei Stores took over the store. He had seen the new pillar with his own eyes.

"They never replaced the old pillar," Ichimura leaned over and said quietly, noting Kôjima's bewildered look. "They just covered it up with another layer of plaster."

Wrapping up the meeting, the police asked Kitô for the name and particulars of the builders.

"Didn't you check to make sure?" Kôjima asked Kitô once they police had gone.

"By the time we took possession of the building, the old pillar had already been plastered over, so there was no way we could tell. We did send someone over while the work was still going on, but there was no negative report. But it really comes to the same thing—we failed to make sure the job was done properly."

Kôjima nodded, but said nothing. The way the company was run in those days, it wasn't hard to imagine how it had happened: No system was in place for checking what was going on and filing an official report. The day-to-day work could have been done by a bunch of students, and no one would have thought anything odd about it.

The biggest problem was not responsibility or criminal liability, Kôjima now thought, but compensation. He knew the company had insurance to cover injury, but this seemed a less clear-cut case. He'd have to go over the policy this evening as soon as he got back to the office.

And when he did, Kôjima heaved a sigh of relief. They company was fully covered. Kôjima picked up the phone to call Ishikari Eitarô to tell him the news.

"Thanks for letting me know," Ishikari said. But that was all Kôjima could get out of him. His voice was flat and empty of emotion. He didn't want to talk to Kôjima at all.

Kôjima sat at his desk, exhausted. He was getting ready to go home, when the phone rang.

It was Takako. "Why didn't you call me?" she said. "Didn't you get my messages?"

"There's been a terrible accident."

"I know. It's been all over TV. What are you going to do?"

"What *can* we do? I feel terrible about the people who got hurt, but we can't do anything about it now. It's happened."

"And this was the store you pushed the company to acquire?" she asked, her voice with a critical edge.

"Who told you that?"

"So it's true. You're beyond help," she sobbed. "I went to see Mrs. Ishikari again today. I wanted to find out what was going to happen after everything you've done. Then the phone rang about this accident. I didn't know what to do. It's just too terrible. All I could do was apologize and come home."

Do I really didn't need to hear this? Kôjima thought, grinding his teeth.

"I don't know what to do," she started up after a pause. "You don't call me, and then when I do finally get a hold of you, you just lose your temper and fly off the handle . . . I'm going to take the kids and go back to my parents' place and talk things over with them. Kayoko will miss a few days of school, but that can't be helped."

"Are you leaving right away?"

"Tomorrow morning. I already called my mother. We'll be back on Sunday—Kayoko has to be back in school on Monday."

"I see. Do as you please," Kôjima said, and hung up the phone.

An emergency board meeting was called the next day to discuss a strategy for dealing with the aftermath of the catastrophe. Despite requests from Kôjima, the company president Ishikari Eitarô chose not to attend.

The meeting began with a report from Katsumura on the latest news from the hospital: the condition of the critically injured young woman had improved, and her doctors now expected her to make a full recovery. The announcement brought huge sighs of relief, but beyond this there was nothing significant to report. The meeting lasted an hour and a half, but all it achieved was to confirm what most of the board members already knew. Yet there was no doubting the seriousness in the room. There may have been small personal differences between them, but it was clear they all wanted the same thing now. They were longing for someone or something to free them from their collective anxiety.

The false reports had been exposed, the roof had caved in, and the president of the company had stayed away from the meeting. This did not bode well. Was Ishikari Eitarô intent on unloading his stock in the company? Would the company be hung out to dry? Could anything be done to stop him?

"I will talk to the president," Kôjima volunteered. "The company is in good shape at the moment—at last—and I don't think this accident will hurt us too much financially. I don't think there's any real reason to worry. I'm sure I'll be able to make the president understand."

• • •

Kôjima first went to see Ishikari Seijirô, who ushered him into his office with a smile. Seijirô had moved to a new office on the second floor, but the layout and decor of the room were identical to his previous office. The framed piece of calligraphy still had pride of place on the wall. *Follow Heaven, abandon Selfishness.* Only the expression on Seijirô's face had changed: he looked happier and more relaxed. He had the air of a gentle, mild-mannered scholar.

"The board is convinced your brother is going to want to wash his hands of the company after the recent events. I'm worried too. I need to talk things over with him as soon as I can, but I wanted to sound you out first."

"Well, I share your concern. Eitarô really gave me hell over those faked accounts. I think that's what finally pushed me to retire and pursue my dream of a calligraphy school. It was only right that I should take responsibility. To tell you the truth, with that freak accident in Shimo-Shinden and everything else that's happened, things couldn't get much worse for me right now."

Kôjima found himself biting his lip, suppressing a rush of anger. Seijirô's resignation had nothing to do with taking responsibility for the faked accounts. He was trying to pass it off as some kind of noble sacrifice, but Eitarô had found out about the accounts at a party held to celebrate Seijirô's retirement. Kôjima decided to swallow his irritation and overlook what Seijirô had said; he needed him on his side.

"What do you think your brother's feelings are at the moment?" he asked.

"I couldn't say. Let's try and discuss the situation with him over the next few days."

Kôjima leaned forward. "I want to be absolutely honest with him, clear up all the ambiguities. The doctored accounts for one thing: the whole thing was my idea from the start. I brought it up, I developed the plan, and I carried it out. Every one of the company's directors knows that. You know it yourself," Kôjima said, looking Seijirô directly in the eyes, although Seijirô averted his gaze.

"Next, the Shimo-Shinden store. It's been so long I don't remember all the details myself, but I was the one who argued that the company should acquire that property. Several of the other directors were against the idea—Ichimura in particular, as I recall. I think people backed down and let me have my way because I had just joined the company and argued so passionately in favor of the idea. You must remember it."

"I vaguely remember something of the kind. But . . ."

"You're going to tell me that has nothing to do with the accident, but I disagree. A manager is responsible for all the results of any course of action. All the consequences of a decision are the responsibility of the person who made the decision—even things that no one could foresee, including freak accidents and sheer bad luck. If the company headquarters crumbled in an earthquake, we wouldn't expect the gods to answer for the damage, or some catfish under the earth to take responsibility on our behalf. A manager's responsibility is total. And that means that I am responsible for the collapse of the roof at Shimo-Shinden."

Seijirô was bewildered. Even if you admitted that managers were responsible for the unforeseeable consequences of their decisions, the fact that Kôjima had argued in favor of buying the site at some meeting years ago didn't make him individually accountable for what happened at Shimo-Shinden. But he understood what Kôjima was saying: If Eitarô took the view that Kôjima was behind the recent bad news, then they had no alternative but to use the fact for their own benefit.

"I will take responsibility for what's happened," Kôjima declared. "I will resign. In return, I want you to talk to your brother and persuade him to allow Ishiei Stores to carry on as an independent company."

Seijirô said nothing. He shook his head thoughtfully, picked up a cigarette from his desk, and lit it with a large crystal lighter. He inhaled deeply, stood up, took a few paces around the room, then stopped to stub out his cigarette in the ashtray. He lit another cigarette almost immediately. Finally, he spoke: "I understand how you feel. But that's enough. I'm sure my brother will be satisfied just to hear that you have thought things through and come to that conclusion. You can't always take responsibility, even when you want to. It's simply not possible for one man to take responsibility for the whole management of a company, not even if you spend the rest of your life apologizing. The important thing is that you want to accept responsibility, that you're willing to do it. So as long as the will is there, no one can ask for anything more. Do you see what I mean? Isn't that the truth?"

"No, I don't think so. Maybe you're right; maybe it is impossible to accept responsibility for everything. The people who were injured in the accident are not going to get better suddenly just because I resign, and what we did with the company accounts is not going to change either, regardless of anything I say or do. But the responsibility is something we have toward society as a whole. It's important for people to know that Kôjima was the one at fault for what happened, so that they can wipe the slate clean, put the past behind them, and concentrate on working toward the future."

"You say that, but who would lead the company if you left? I can't do it. I don't want anything to do with running a company again ever in my life."

"Ichimura could do it. He's the only one who could do it. I know he's made a terrible mistake in the past. But he wasn't doing anything wrong; he was just careless. He has a keen business mind, but he bases everything on his relationships with people. He's not so good at thinking things through in an ordered, scientific way."

"But that's a fatal shortcoming, Ryôsuke."

"There's certainly no way the company could have carried on under the kind of leadership he was providing back then. But a lot has changed in the past four years. I think what happened opened Ichimura's eyes to his own weaknesses, and he's rock solid today. The most promising thing is that all the directors have really joined hands, and there's a system in place now that allows people to cooperate and work together well." Kôjima was picking his way carefully. He didn't want Seijirô to miss a single word of what he was saying.

"Ishiei Stores today," he continued, "is not the company we were four years ago. The people in charge of running our stores are the fifteen store managers. The people in the merchandise department choose the products and send them out to the stores, based on customer demand. It's not as though there's one person—me, or anyone else—running around issuing instructions and controlling everything.

There's a system in place, staffed with well-trained personnel. They're almost like the physical embodiment of a system of thought—the company philosophy made real, in people and things. As long as the company doesn't lose sight of that philosophy as it continues to develop, then Ishiei Stores has a bright future ahead of it.

"If the company's main directors—Katsumura, Asayama, Matsuo, and Kitô—give Ichimura their support and help to train and develop the various middle management people—the store mangers and the people on the merchandise side of things—then everything will be fine. I'll be heartbroken if I can't be a part of it, but if the alternative is to see Ishiei Stores disappear altogether, then I'll just have to learn to come to terms with it. We've put too much work into building the company and strengthening its foundations to see it fail now."

Kôjima waited for a reaction from Seijirô, but none came. "You understand what I mean, don't you?"

"No. To tell you the truth, I don't think I understand it at all," Seijirô said. His voice sounded deflated, his honest answer like a last resort. Then he smiled the smile that Kôjima had liked so much as a boy—slightly sadder now, but the same smile nonetheless. "Maybe that's why I could never run the business myself. Clearly the stores are much better now. My wife definitely thinks so; she does all her shopping here now. And I've heard the same thing from our customers. But that doesn't mean we can just carry on the same way forever. There are chains out there with more than a hundred stores already. And what's going to happen after the current shortages come to an end? It's impossible to know what the future holds for the company. That's what worries my brother. It's your confidence I find more surprising, to be honest. But I understand the way you feel, and I will do my best to help you persuade my brother you're right. But where will you go if you do leave the company? You can't go back to the bank after all this time, surely."

"That's not an option. At the moment, I have nothing lined up."

"Then the whole thing is just nonsense. What about your family?"

"We'll manage somehow. We have the apartment the company very generously gave us, so we don't have to worry about paying rent. We should be able to manage for a while."

Kôjima had rehearsed this line, and he said it straightforwardly—even though it was a lie. He had decided to separate from Takako. The apartment was his only real asset, and he was planning to give her that and everything else he owned. He wanted to provide enough for the children's upbringing and education, but he had no desire to continue in a loveless marriage. Ishiei Stores had not accepted him and all that he represented. If he was ending his connection with the company, then he was prepared to end his association with Takako, who had also failed to accept him for who he was.

Ha! Seijirô would be astounded if he told him the truth. At this very moment, Takako was probably on the bullet train, speeding her way back to her parents. She said she was going for a few days, but Kôjima didn't believe it. She wasn't coming back. A husband who had failed was worthless to her.

"Look, Ryôsuke, just forget about resigning. Let's talk things over with my brother early next week. I'm sure there's a perfectly good solution. I'll do what I can to persuade him to allow the company to continue and to keep you as managing director."

"I'll be grateful for anything you can do to make sure that the company survives. But please, stop referring to me as the managing director. I never received official notification of my promotion, and it's getting embarrassing hearing everyone refer to me as the boss wherever I go."

Seijirô gave a carefree laugh, and the meeting was over.

Kôjima was on his way home when he heard a woman's voice calling his name. He turned around to find Misaki Yoshiko standing behind him.

"Misaki-*san*, what are you doing here?"

"I've been waiting for you."

"What?"

"Everyone's in a coffee shop just around the corner."

"Huh? Who's everyone?"

"Ôtaka-*san* and his wife, Horiguchi-*san*, Také-*san*. We went to see Kôda-*san* in hospital."

Kôjima had been so pleased to see Yoshiko that he was disappointed to learn that she wasn't alone, but he was happy to go back with her to the coffee shop. "What's this all about?"

"Well, we were all talking about everything that was going on, and we decided we absolutely had to talk to you. We called the office and found out you'd just left, so we figured you had to pass by this way sooner or later."

"You mean you've been standing out here in this weather?"

"Only for a couple of minutes. I've got plenty of fat reserves under my skin, so a bit of cold weather is not a problem." Yoshiko smiled, seeming as young and carefree as a college student.

"Well, sure, I don't mind. I'd only be sitting at home alone anyway."

"Your wife isn't here at the moment?"

"She rushes back home to her parents the moment anything comes up." Kôjima had tried to convey the situation without saying outright what was going on, but Yoshiko didn't say anything in reply. Did she understand? Was it just his imagination, or was there was a slight change in her expression?

They arrived at the coffee shop, to be met by smiling faces.

"Kôjima-*san*! You made it!"

"We've been waiting for you. Come and sit down!"

"I knew he would turn up if Yoshiko was the one waiting for him," joked Motoko, sitting with an infant in her arms.

"You're as dumb as ever," her husband mumbled to her.

But the cheery atmosphere faded almost as soon as Kôjima sat down. Horiguchi, speaking for the group, began: "We've been hearing rumors about the company being taken over by one of the big chains. We couldn't believe it was true, but everyone keeps saying the same thing and we're starting to get worried. That's why we wanted to talk to you—we want to know the truth."

Kôjiima looked at the young people around him. There was freshness in their faces, honesty and innocence. They had played important roles in the drama of his life over the past four years. It was thanks to them, thanks to the fact that they had all banded together, and thanks to their efforts and hard work that Ishiei Stores had achieved so much. How could anyone think about selling a company that had such wonderful people working for it?

"So what's really going on?" Horiguchi asked.

"Well, the rumor's not true," Kôjima said.

"Really?"

"Really."

The group looked as though they didn't entirely believe him, but he could see relief in their eyes.

"I'm not the company owner," Kôjima went on. "The only one who can decide whether to dispose of the company is the owner. Personally, I think we can trust Ishikari Eitarô not to sell."

"That's good to hear," Ôtaka began, "because four or five guys in suits showed up at the head office in a limousine today. With all the rumors that have been going around, we started thinking maybe it was Toto Stores coming to check us out. We'd rather be dead than get taken over by a company with such rotten fresh produce. So what if they take in hundreds of billions of yen a year."

"You shouldn't believe everything you hear," Kôjima said, smiling.

They were going in the same direction, so Kôjima ended up walking Yoshiko home. They walked side by side, their shoes bumping up against the piles of shoveled snow. And then Kôjima started to fantasize: *If she'll still have me now that I'm penniless, this is the woman I want to be with.* The thought seemed to take over all others.

Would Takako agree to a divorce?

A husband for her was just a machine that provided her with money and food. As long as she could be guaranteed the lifestyle to which she had become accustomed, what further need could she have for a husband?

But actually, Takako took the social side of her life seriously—and in this respect a husband was probably quite important to her. He could already hear her screaming and crying and going on about how divorced parents ruined the employment and marriage prospects of their children. Certainly, he felt sorry for the kids. He wasn't worried about their future job prospects, though, or their ability to find a suitable spouse once the time came. But thinking about them growing up without a father made him sad.

Still, was that reason enough for him to suffer the rest of his life in a loveless marriage?

"Are you sure it's all right?" Yoshiko asked as they approached her apartment, turning her face up him.

"What's all right?"

"The company, I mean. Everyone's been talking about it."

"The company will be all right," he said, feeling slightly ashamed. He had forgotten all about it.

"Good night, then."

"Good night."

And they went their separate ways.

The evening had another surprise in store for Kôjima. He was about to turn the key to his apartment when the door opened from the inside. It was Takako.

"What are you doing here? I thought you went to see your parents."

"I changed my mind," she said, turning away and shutting the door behind him. He had only caught a glimpse of her face, but she looked exhausted. It looked as though she might have been crying.

"What's wrong?" Kôjima called out to Takako as she got the evening meal ready.

"I couldn't go. How could I? Kayoko didn't want to miss school, and Tomoyuki had a fever."

"Is it bad?"

"No, it was just a low-grade fever, but I was worried it would get worse," Takako said, her back to him.

Kôjima sat at the table and skimmed the evening paper. "You could have had the doctor give him an injection or something," he said. Suddenly, the chopping sounds stopped and the atmosphere in the room grew heavy.

Kôjima looked up from the newspaper. Takako's shoulders were shaking, and she was crying silently. He stood up. "What's wrong?" he asked.

Takako ran from the room without a word, flung herself into a chair in the living room, and started to sob.

"Come on, what's wrong?"

"You *want* me to go back to my parents. You don't love me anymore."

"What are you talking about? You were the one who wanted to go away for a while. I would never have said it otherwise." Kôjima was mystified. Was she trying to pick a fight?

"Of course I could have gone if I really wanted to. But I didn't. What good would it have done anyway? Kayoko started crying about how she didn't want to miss school, and I was standing there trying to take Tomoyuki's temperature, and that's when I realized that *this* was my family. Even if you did fake the accounts at work, even if you did cheat on me, even if you did quit your job, you and the kids are my family. I thought about it all day, but I kept coming to the same conclusion. This is my family, this is my home, this is where I belong. And then you come home and act like I shouldn't be here."

Kôjima hadn't been expecting this at all. "I'm sorry," he said. "I was being inconsiderate. I didn't mean it that way." He put a hand on her shoulder. "Come on, pull yourself together and get dinner ready. If you don't want to cook, I don't mind having one of those cans of curry."

Takako's words lingered in Kôjima's mind and in his heart, seeming to wash away the ill feelings he had been harboring toward her. Why is man such a simple creature? Things weren't clear in his mind, and he wasn't sure how to rationalize what had just happened between them, but one thing was certain: his plans for a divorce were off. Was this what was meant about children forming an unbreakable bond between their parents? Or was there some other explanation for it? Time would tell.

Takako wiped the tears from her eyes, and the chopping sounds resumed.

FIFTEEN

IDENTITY

A tense, heated atmosphere dominated the meeting room. For two hours, debate had raged about the best way to commemorate the company's fifteenth anniversary, which was coming up in March. Representatives from each of the departments were in attendance. As head of sales and promotions, Horiguchi was acting as chair, and he was starting to worry that the two opposing points of view would never be reconciled.

The groceries and clothing departments were in favor of a massive three-week sales campaign. What customers wanted, they said, was low prices—now more than ever in the aftermath of the oil shock. The best thing they could do was to offer as many discounts as possible. They needed to keep customers happy; happy customers were repeat customers.

"But that would cost us a fortune," Horiguchi said with a grimace. But the groceries and clothing people weren't prepared to back down. They knew that what they were advocating would have its cost, they said—everything had its cost—but look at the figures for February. They were sunk, and the company was already failing to meet its targets. Customers were bleeding from the recent price hikes and were staunching the wound by holding tight till things improved. March looked like being a repeat of February. The only way to persuade customers to start spending again was to offer low prices—and not the halfhearted reductions they usually offered, but lower prices than anyone had seen in the greater Tokyo area for months. Soy sauce and sugar for hundred yen. Panty hose at fifty yen for two pairs. Tofu for ten yen a *cho*. Blouses for 480 yen.

The fresh foods department had the opposite view. The company would be insane to do anything so rash. Who would these sales attract? Bargain hunters and bottom feeders—hardly the kind of customers Ishiei Stores was looking for. Ringing up losses to appeal to fickle customers just to boost sales and meet monthly targets was not the way to go. The company would be better advised to offer superior service and quality. Inflation was tough on the pocketbook, but their duty was to offer customers unbeatable value for their money.

"Not that simple. It's easy to talk about top-quality produce and unbeatable service, but is that really what we're offering our customers?" a groceries representative asked sarcastically.

"Of course it is," the three fresh produce reps chorused.

"Great, but your department isn't carrying the store. Bulk selling of the major brands is what keeps us in business."

The argument was getting more heated. Despite the awkwardness he felt at having to play monkey in the middle, deep down Horiguchi was gratified. Not too long ago, such a passionate exchange of ideas about the store would have been unthinkable. Decisions about marketing strategy had been taken within the respective departments and carried out in the most unimaginative of ways. The newly consolidated approach had injected new energy into the company's efforts. The occasional disagreement about strategy was a small price to pay.

They were having a tough time of it recently, though; that much was undeniable. Total sales for February were off more than 10 percent of their original projections. To be off by 10 percent was unheard of. The profits they had made during the oil panic would be swallowed up within a month or two at this rate. And underlying everything was an anxiety that was shared by everyone in the room. They knew the president of the company was mulling over the collapse of the roof at Shimo-Shinden; they'd all heard the rumors about the company going up for sale. Good results were more important now than ever—the survival of the company was at stake.

Some of the guys in middle management seemed to take it for granted that so long as the money kept coming in, the company was safe. "We're talking greed here," one manager said. Horiguchi wasn't sure how greedy a man Ishikari Eitarô was, but the opinion did seem reasonable. He glanced at Kôjima, who had been sitting next to him, listening to the arguments. It was time for him to make a decision.

Kôjima rose from his seat, and the room quieted down. "Thank you, everyone, for your suggestions. I really appreciate the effort you're making here. I've been sitting here listening to your arguments, and this is what I think. I know it's not without risk, but I want to go with the fresh foods proposal, for the reasons you've just heard. I want the people in charge of the various fresh foods sections to compile a range of products that will really make our customers happy. At the same time, I want everyone in the groceries and clothing departments to come up with the most attractive special offer items they can. However, I have an additional request." Kôjima paused, as everyone sat, intent on his words. "I don't want us to run out of any of the items on special offer. And I want to do away with the idea that specials are limited to the first one thousand customers. What do you think?"

There was an outbreak of mumbling. "We can't do that," one of the representatives from the groceries department said. "If we get rid of the restrictions, we'll have no way of knowing how many we'll sell. We could end up losing a fortune."

"And it's out of the question for the clothing department. It's just not possible for us to have unlimited amounts of each product in stock—the nature of the merchandise doesn't allow it," the clothing representative said. "I'm sure the same is true with sundries, right? Products you only buy to sell at a special price . . ."

"All right. I know that. And that's fine," Kôjima said, interrupting with a smile. "I didn't mean everything. I'm talking about regular items you would expect to have on the shelves at all times. Soy sauce, coffee, mayonnaise, sugar, detergent, toilet paper. Isn't it possible to run a special offer on these kinds of items without running out?"

"I understand what you're saying," Horiguchi said, "but if there were no limits at all, that would destroy our profits." A chorus of agreement could be heard around the room.

"But that's the whole problem," Kôjima said. "What good is a special offer if it's only available to a small proportion of our customers? Can we really claim to be offering cheap prices? I don't think so. I think maybe the prices we're offering are too cheap. Maybe we should try to make sure we have enough of each item to supply every customer who wants one, and then set the price at a reasonable level that the company can support. These prices might turn out to be a bit higher than the ones we've offered for anniversary sales in the past. They might even be higher than the regular special offers we run throughout the year. But if that's the case, then so be it. Obviously we want to sell things as cheaply as possible, but there are limits to how low we can afford to go. It might sound harsh to say this, but the sale prices we've been offering in the past have been bogus."

"OK, but then we won't be able to offer any really attractive prices."

"But does that really matter? So maybe a few customers will complain—especially the hardcore bargain hunters—but if we follow through with our strategy, I have the feeling most of our customers will realize that we're offering better value for money in the end, since the items on special offer will never run out and they can always be sure of finding them in stock."

"Are you telling us to sell high?" one of the groceries representatives grumbled.

"Not at all," Horiguchi interrupted. "Sell as cheap as you can without running out of stock."

"Right," said Kôjima. "It will involve a bit of work, but I want the people in the groceries department to negotiate really hard with our suppliers to get the best possible prices we can. It's an ongoing process. Good prices are a supermarket's mission. All I'm saying is that we should attach a condition—no running out of stock."

The groceries representative scratched his head, uncertain.

"Once this period of shortages is over, it's back to reality again," Kôjima continued. "We won't survive that by offering sham bargains that are purely for show. If we're going to sell cheap, we have to do it honestly—by which I mean, we have to offer prices we can afford even if every one of our customers takes us up on the offer. That's going to take hard work: choosing the right suppliers, setting up distribution and information systems, developing well-thought-out sales promotions, and so on. But if everyone in the company comes together and devotes themselves to the job, we could really become the customer's best friend."

Kôjima's words seemed to bring the debate to a close.

But not everyone was happy. "All right, let's go with the 'sell high' philosophy," someone was heard to say.

"Please don't call it that. People will get the wrong idea," Kôjima spoke up immediately. "It's an 'honest discount' philosophy, if anything."

"Sorry, only kidding. The idea is to offer a fair deal to all our customers, right? If that's what it is, we'll do it."

"That's right. An equitable fair deal for all our customers."

The head of fresh produce burst out laughing. "For a moment there I thought you said an 'inedible fur seal'!"

And so at last an acceptable strategy was agreed upon, and before long the words *equitable discounting* were on everyone's lips. That same evening, a solitary loser at a mah-jongg parlor near the head office was nicknamed the "head of equitable discounting," while another group of workers took to settling their bills at the local bar by means of "equitable payment." Jokes like this helped the new concept spread throughout the whole company, and before long a new idea began to seep into the corporate culture.

Horiguchi was relieved that Kôjima had intervened to steer the debate in the right direction, but couldn't help feeling a little uneasy when he thought about it later. Kôjima's decision was based on a sound argument, and he had no doubt that the strategy was the right one—but it was one that was not likely to be effective right away. In the short term, in fact, things were likely to get worse before they got better. What if the customers reacted negatively to their decision to do away with rock-bottom prices? The anniversary sales would be a failure, and the results would look worse than ever. And if that happened, the specter of a takeover loomed.

"Don't worry about it," Kôjima said with a laugh. "I trust Ishikari.

But even if he was wavering, as everyone says he is, he wouldn't let his decision be influenced by a temporary downturn in the company results. It's not as simple as that. If he's in any doubt, it's about the long-term outlook for the company. About whether the company can survive. I think I can say that for a fact. And if that's the case, then I'm confident that I can persuade him that he has no need to be concerned. Which reminds me," Kôjima's face suddenly brightened, "I had a call just before the meeting from Kameyama-*san*. He asked if we would take on some of his employees for training at Ishiei Stores. You know what that means?"

"Banrai Supermarkets are famous for the high quality of their fresh foods. If they're asking us to take on trainees, then that must mean that we're reaching a pretty high level as well. But . . ."

"You don't seem convinced."

"I'm not."

"Come on—we may still have a few problems, but you can't deny that things have gotten a whole lot better."

"But we're still not up to the standards of Banrai Stores. I think Mr. Kameyama may be overestimating us."

"But what he's interested in is not the level of each individual store. It's the chain as a whole. Banrai Stores are looking to move to a more standardized way of running their business, and I think they want to learn from us how we do things, since we are managing fifteen stores at a relatively high level. Keeping fresh foods standardized across a whole chain is no easy matter."

"I guess so."

"Hey, you should have more faith in us!"

Kôjima's face beamed with confidence and conviction. Horiguchi knew he could trust him.

The following Sunday afternoon, Kôjima was invited to Ishikari Eitarô's house in the Meguro ward of Tokyo. A cold February wind gusted down the streets of the exclusive neighborhood as he made his way nervously toward Ishikari's address.

He knew that what he was about to hear would decide not only his own future but the future of the whole company. He thought he knew the role he was going to play in the drama. Ishikari, the president, was worried about the future of the company, and Kôjima's job was to allay his fears: the company was strong, it would survive, it needed Eitarô's support. But what was the best way to convince him? If he could just get Eitarô to open his heart to him, Kôjima would have all the room he needed to convince him.

Ever since the disaster at Shimo-Shinden, the members of the board had been agitated, unsettled. Asayama, wracked with guilt, couldn't stop apologizing for the way he had spilled the beans about the phony reports in a moment of drunken exuberance. "Forget it. It's all in the past," Kôjima tried to reassure him. "He would have found out sooner or later."

But Asayama refused to listen, going on to wring his hands about a host of other issues. He worried that something terrible was going to happen. He worried about the reemergence of the Ichimura faction. He worried about blame and unfairness. He worried. . . .

Kôjima couldn't help being aware of undercurrents of ill feeling. Asayama had credited him with saving the company, a feat—Kôjima knew—he had not accomplished alone. Everyone had done their part—Asayama, Odagiri, Matsuo, Konno, and Ichimura, no less. He could never have done it on his own.

"Maybe. But then no one person should have to accept the blame for the problems either."

If he resigned, then perhaps everything would get back to normal. The thought of this helped Kôjima relax. In a way, it didn't matter. He'd joined Ishiei Stores nearly five years ago. Even if all his work ended with a whimper, his efforts would not have been in vain. Ishiei Stores was back on its feet. If people united behind Ichimura now, there was no reason why the company shouldn't survive and prosper. And as for himself? Had these past five years been a waste? Not at all. He had experienced things he would never have known had he remained cocooned at the Saiwa Bank. He was a different person now.

But how he longed for someone to understand him! The image of Kameyama came into his mind. There was Asayama. And Katsumura, and Horiguchi, and Ôtaka and his wife, and Manabe (dead now, of course), and Yoshiko. And Ichimura, Odagiri, Matsuo, and Konno—they had understood him too, had they not, at least some of the time?

He had nothing to fear. If Ishikari Eitarô refused to understand him, all he had to do was to stay faithful to himself. He turned a corner and arrived in front of Ishikari Eitarô's house.

He walked through the big stone gate and made his way to a porch distinguished by thick decorative pillars. He rang the bell. Ishikari's wife came to the door almost immediately.

"Thank you for coming," she said. "We've been expecting you."

What did she mean? Who was there? He had thought it'd be just the two Ishikari brothers and himself. He looked around as he took off his shoes, and saw several pairs already lined up neatly by the door. He was about to ask who else was there, but Ishikari's wife was already sashaying back into the house. Kôjima followed her into a sitting room where the group was waiting.

Kawano, head of personnel. Yoshii, store manager at Kitamoto. Toda, one of the buyers in the clothing department. And Takamura, who had joined the company about a year ago. He knew them well enough, but wasn't particularly close to any of them. For a few moments he couldn't understand why they were here. It was the presence of Takamura, the new employee, that tipped him off. They were all related, either by birth or marriage, to Ishikari Eitarô. He struggled to conceal the unease that washed over him when he realized what had brought them all together.

"Why the long face? Come have a seat," Ishikari Eitarô said. It was the first time Kôjima had seen him smile since he had learned about the falsified accounts. The red knit shirt he was wearing made his belly look even rounder than usual. Seijirô was sitting upright on the sofa next to his brother, a faint smile on his face. Kôjima looked over at him inquiringly, but Seijirô just gave an awkward laugh.

"My brother thought it would be better this way, Ryôsuke," he said.

"I didn't know it was going to be a party," Kôjima said, trying to make light of his own anxiety.

"Never mind, Kôjima-san," Eitarô said. "Just sit down and relax. We're not at work now."

Kôjima was offered a chair, and he sat in it. Tea and snacks were served, and everyone made small talk.

Once the ice was broken, Ishikari Eitarô cleared his throat and began to speak: "As you all know, it was fifteen years ago, in 1959, that I founded Ishiei Stores and branched out into the supermarket business. It's been an eventful fifteen years, but thanks to everyone's hard work, we've managed to survive in a business where cutthroat competition is the norm. It's been touch-and-go at times, but today the company is bigger and more successful than ever."

Where was this leading, Kôjima wondered. He swallowed hard and concentrated on what Eitarô was saying. He closed his eyes and listened intently to every word.

"Everyone has been doing really well, but if you look at the bigger picture, it's not all plain sailing. Several things make the future look unpromising for a business like ours. The supermarkets that got into the stock market early are getting bigger and bigger all the time. They're making some amazing profits, and more and more companies are following their lead. And then there's this oil shock. And once the crazy prices calm down, there will be stagnant demand. At Ishiei Trading we can barely shift anything at all, and the people we supply to are worried sick. They say there's no guarantee that even the big chains will still be around in a few years from now. In the light of this, I've been trying to decide whether Ishiei Stores really has what it takes to survive in the long term. What are the chances? Fifty-fifty, forty-sixty? Or even lower?"

Kôjima struggled against the impulse to shout out: *It's 100 percent certain to succeed!* He found his heart was racing.

"In situations like this you've got to keep a cool head. So I went back to the basics, and tried to think things through from first principles. I listened to other people's opinions too, of course. And in the end, I made up my mind." Eitarô scanned the faces around him, as if trying to gauge their reaction. "I think we can agree on one thing: the essential thing for a supermarket is to sell cheap. Discount prices. There's no other way of doing it."

Kôjima was on the point of speaking out again. Hundreds of counterarguments were galloping through his mind.

But Eitarô cut him off before he could get the words out of his mouth. "Wait a minute, Ryôsuke. Listen to what I have to say first. So what means can we use to achieve that end? I think it goes without saying: volume, the power to buy and sell in bulk. A large number of stores. High sales. What matters is the scale of the business, in other words. Am I right, Ryôsuke?"

"That's certainly one aspect of it," Kôjima replied.

"It's the most important aspect. Think about it. Fifteen years ago, the retail industry was abuzz with talk about the so-called distribution revolution. What was the basic principle back then? I recently dug up some of the old notes I took at the seminars I attended around the time I started the company. *Building a chain of stores. Scale merits. Fixing prices.* It all boils down to one thing: scale. Making sales of ten or twenty billion yen isn't enough. You need to sell a hundred billion yen. A trillion yen."

Ishikari's voice filled the room. He cleared his throat and went on: "At Ishiei Stores, we did well. We worked hard and we grew. From nothing we have built up a chain of fifteen stores, with sales of fifteen billion yen. But what happens next? How long till we reach sales of a hundred billion? Even if we open three stores a year, it would take nearly thirty years. And how long until we take in a trillion yen a year? You're not going to tell me to wait another three hundred years?

"So after much thought, I've come to a difficult decision. We have to pull out. Even if we struggle on, the future is clear. There is more to life than continuing the fight. I'm convinced that we'd be better off joining forces with one of the big players now, while we're still in good health. With their help we can acquire the ability to sell in bulk, and that would put us in a much better position to fulfill the first duty of any supermarket—selling cheap. We might only be able to make a minor contribution, but isn't that the best we can do? Isn't that preferable to carrying on the way we are now, and selling off later on somebody else's terms? Wouldn't our employees be much happier that way too?"

"You're making a terrible mistake," Kôjima burst out, unable to contain himself any longer.

Eitarô turned toward Kôjima, scowling like a child whose favorite toy has been torn from his grasp. "What do you mean?"

"Things aren't going to stagnate. On the contrary, things should get better every year. Of course it will take some time before we are achieving sales in the hundreds of billions of yen. But not thirty years. Once we reach a certain point, the pace of growth will accelerate."

"How can you be so sure? How do you know that things won't stagnate?"

"Because Ishiei Stores is already well on the way to becoming the first supermarket chain in Japan with real know-how."

"I'm glad to see you're so proud of where you work, but let's not get too carried away. There are chains out there achieving sales in the hundreds of billions of yen every year—and yet you'd have us believe that Ishiei Stores, with a mere fifteen stores to its name, has discovered some kind of perfect system that has somehow eluded all our rivals?"

"But it's a fact. You keep talking about supermarkets with huge sales, but none of those companies are really *supermarket* chains. They are discount department stores that have been converted into chains. A supermarket's business is concentrated on fresh foods, on providing regular customers with the ingredients they need for their daily meals. It's a part of the day-to-day lives of its customers. You need all kinds of different knowledge and expertise to make a chain of supermarkets work—starting with a standardization of quality. We discussed this the other day."

Ishikari Eitarô folded his arms, scowling still. He did not look happy at all.

"I'm sorry, but there are a few more things I'd like to be allowed to say," Kôjima continued. "Big stores are big stores. They are not supermarkets. If these companies wanted to set up a chain of supermarkets, they would have to work just as hard as the department stores did when *they* wanted to start supermarkets. A chain of supermarkets requires a particular kind of knowledge—you don't just snap your fingers and it appears. You have to work at it. It's taken Ishiei Stores five years just to get close. And if it took us that long when we were a company of just ten stores, it would probably take at least ten years for a bigger company with dozens or hundreds of outlets to make a similar improvement—even if their management people were blessed with remarkable leadership skills. And there would be the risk of profits going down in the meantime. I don't think many of the big companies could afford the effort it would take."

"I don't understand what you're trying to say," Eitarô said. "The big companies have more workers, and probably better people too, than we have. You can't even compare them. They have masses of capital and all the savings they need to develop any way they need to, and then some. Tell me, Ryôsuke, is there really anything you can't do if you have all the money and human resources you need?"

"The important thing is the quality, the nature of the company—the climate or the culture, if you like. The know-how of a supermarket chain is not like know-how in a big production company. You can't illustrate it in a blueprint. There are manuals, of course, and in a way I suppose they are similar to the blueprints in a production company, but you need something more than that. You have to draw up a separate manual for every type of merchandise—meat, fish, vegetables, fruit, processed foods, and then make sure that every one of your employees absorbs and understands the information contained in those manuals. And then the company as a whole needs to pull together as one great unit and follow this strategy together."

"But, Ryôsuke, what you're saying is obvious," Eitarô responded, then looked around the room to see if anyone else had something to say.

Nobody did. Kôjima continued, "It may sound obvious, but putting it into practice is not easy. You need to get all your different departments pulling in the same direction without conflict of interest—merchandise, store administration, and development, for example, as well as all your nonoperating business departments. It's like a highly evolved organism. But unlike a living organism, each one of its cells is made up of human beings with their own ideas and emotions—just to make matters more difficult."

"But that's true of any company. Even the big supermarket companies must operate in just the same way. Otherwise there's no way they would be able to manage so many stores."

"But that's not how it is. At least not for the supermarket chains."

"How can you be so sure? You don't know anything about any store other than this one, surely." Eitarô's tone of voice was brusquer now. Irritation was bubbling over inside.

"I can tell from looking at their stores," Kôjima said, determined to make himself heard. "Two stores within the same chain that are obviously run according to completely different philosophies. Good stores and bad stores within the same chain. Everything is different, depending on the store manager and the section chiefs. That is not what I would call a chain."

"Don't talk such nonsense," Eitarô said, laughing contemptuously. "All that means is that Ishiei Stores is bad at business, and the big stores are good at it. Once there are a certain number of stores in the chain, of course they are going to differ in terms of their location, their customer demographic, and the state of the local competition. Why insist that they all need to be managed according to exactly the same standards? The big supermarkets know that. That's why they do things differently."

"I'm not saying all the stores need to be run in a uniform, standardized way. I'm just saying that the basic principles should be the same. Otherwise there is no way you can create a large supermarket chain. At the moment I don't think any of the so-called big stores have managed to achieve it."

"And Ishiei Stores has? Thanks to the sage pronouncements of our all-knowing sensei, Mr. Kôjima?"

"Please. It's something we all achieved together." Rather than anger, Kôjima suddenly felt an unbearable sadness weighing down on his chest. How could he make himself understood?

"Ryôsuke," Seijirô spoke up, "I understand how you feel. But it's already been decided. My brother has made up his mind."

"What?! What do you mean?" Kôjima was in shock. He felt as if someone had clubbed him on the back of the head.

For a while, the room was utterly silent. Eitarô looked searchingly at Kôjima. The president's face was like that of a ferocious carnivore and a mischievous little boy at the same time. It was his natural face, stripped of any ornament and pretense.

"How could you . . . ," Kôjima muttered to himself. There was only one way the sentence could have finished, but he couldn't get the words out. As if superstitious, he wanted to avoid confirming the worst by putting it into words.

Nobody spoke. Kôjima struggled to keep his breathing under control.

He looked at Eitarô and tried to speak to him with his eyes. *It's your turn to respond now.*

Surprisingly, Eitarô was smiling. "Enough with the scary face," he said, his own wild expression now gone now. "It's just like Seijirô says. I've made my decision. I'm going to leave it to the experts. Let's leave the supermarket business to the supermarket professionals. I'm the president of a wholesale company, and you're a banker. Even Seijirô doesn't really know anything about supermarkets. And from what I've heard even Ichimura goofed pretty badly a few years back. Although I have to say you managed to cover up for him pretty well."

"But who are the professionals? Is there really such as thing as a supermarket professional? You don't even know the difference between a big store and a supermarket. A real supermarket chain doesn't even exist in Japan yet."

"You know Dominant Stores, right?" Seijirô said. "The biggest supermarket in northern Japan."

Kôjima knew the name well. They were one of the major chains specializing in big stores, with their main base in northeastern Honshu. The owner and president of the company, Kuji Hideo, had built his vast enterprise on the humble foundations of a small general goods store. He had moved into supermarkets during the late fifties and early sixties and had achieved massive growth on the back of Japan's big postwar boom. He had wiped out his rivals and ate small companies like Ishiei Stores for breakfast.

"Kuji has been looking out for an opportunity to expand into the Tokyo area for some time. Eitarô has known him for years through the trading company. And so things kind of worked out perfectly for both parties, from what I understand."

"Right," said Eitarô, taking up the thread of the story. "According to Kuji, the end is near for supermarkets that focus on food products. Supermarket growth has already come to a halt in America, and things are beginning to stagnate here in Japan too. Kuji says trying to make money from food was a flawed idea from the start. If you start making big profits out of food, your customers are going to start complaining. There'd be a riot. Even your food wholesale business doesn't make much, he said. And I had to admit it was true. He floored me. What could I say to that?"

Eitarô was trying to make light of things, but Kôjima was not amused. His head was swimming. He wanted to scream out his rebuttal.

American supermarkets had been growing for fifty years, and it was only recently that their growth had flattened out. Things are different in Japan, where real supermarkets have only been around for a few years.

The reason why some Japanese supermarkets are struggling is that they have no competitive strength in fresh foods.

It's absurd to say that making a profit from food would cause riots.

Building up a superior supermarket chain is completely different from buying up people's daily necessities in bulk and selling them at inflated prices. Customers need to be happy and satisfied, and that's how the business makes its profits.

But it was too late now.

"Kuji offered us a good deal. An equal merger. Of course the company will be known as Dominant Stores, but they're in a different league from us in terms of size, so there's not much we can do about that. He's agreed to take on all our employees. And he's going to make Ishiei Trading Company his supplier for processed foods throughout the Tohoku region. That will allow the trading company to expand into the northeast. We couldn't hope for a better deal."

Once Eitarô had announced the sale of Ishiei Stores to Dominant, the look of the rest of the group in the room became considerably less relaxed. And when Eitarô went on to say that all the company's employees would be taken on by Dominant, there was a bit of fidgeting. Suddenly everyone was interested in how his own position would shake out.

"But don't worry," Eitarô added with a smile. "I'm not going to leave you in the lurch. You'll all be looked after, either in the Ishiei Trading Company or at Ishiei Real Estate. That's what I wanted to tell you today. But if anyone decides that they'd rather stick with Ishiei Stores through everything and wants to become an employee of Dominant Stores, then I won't do anything to stop them."

"I'm staying with Ishiei Stores," Kôjima said. The words had popped out, unbidden. He stood up from his chair, without knowing himself where he was going or what he was going to do.

"I will follow the same path as the rest of the company's employees," he said.

"Ryôsuke, are you serious? You shouldn't let your emotions get the better of you. You might regret it. Besides, I haven't asked Kuji to accept management too. I don't know what he would say."

"If he doesn't want to take me on, then I'll have to accept that. But either way, I won't be joining the trading company or the real estate company. I could never choose that path. What about all the people who trusted in me and worked hard for me and believed that I was leading them in the right direction? How could I possibly sell them off to a big supermarket company and then escape myself?"

"Ryôsuke, for heaven's sake, stop being so melodramatic. I haven't sold out the company's employees. All I've done is to release my holdings in the company's stock."

"It amounts to the same thing."

"No, it doesn't. I'm sure the vast majority of the employees will be much happier working for one of the big companies than continuing to work for a small firm with an uncertain future. Plenty of people would love to find work with companies like Dominant Stores."

"How can you say such a shameless thing?" Kôjima screamed. He was quaking with uncontrollable rage. "Is that why you've been running the company for all these years? I feel sorry for the people who have worked so hard all these years for a company run by someone like you. If they'd been loafing, maybe they wouldn't care. But you really can't imagine what the last five years have meant to them, can you?"

Kôjima stood up to his full height and spoke down to Eitarô, still on the sofa: "Five years ago standards at the company were low. If things had carried on like that the company would never have survived. But your employees realized what was happening. They worked hard to make up for lost time. We studied other stores, came up with ideas, listened to the opinions of consultants and industry leaders. We swapped ideas and by a painstaking process of trial and error, we finally succeeded in creating the prototype for Japan's first true supermarket chain. If Ishiei Stores continues to increase the number of its outlets and continues to develop, the company's profits will grow and grow. For you, the company is like a goose that lays golden eggs. Are you really proposing to sell that goose now for a handful of coins?"

There was a flash of interest in Eitarô's eyes. But it only lasted a moment. "Enough! Enough, you liar!" Eitarô screamed. He pulled himself up from the sofa and launched himself at Kôjima's chest, his fat arms flailing. It was so sudden that Kôjima failed to get out of the way, and fell backward into his chair. Now it was Eitarô who stood towering over Kôjima—their positions reversed from a moment ago.

"The goose that lays the golden egg? Cut the crap, Ryôsuke. After all the deceit and tricks you've played, you've still got the balls to talk to me like that? If you weren't family, I'd happily turn you in to the police. You have no right to claim my assets and property in any way. It's my company, and I'll do what I like with it. If you don't want my help then fine, go do as you please. You fly off with the goose that lays the golden eggs if you want. Either way, the contract formalizing the merger will be signed tomorrow morning. After that, an announcement will be in the papers. It's already decided. This is a fait accompli. Do you understand?"

Kôjima felt something click inside him. Suddenly his anger and excitement drained away, and he felt strangely lucid and relaxed. "I understand," he said. "But I would still prefer to stay with Ishiei Stores, if you'll allow me my own foolish notions."

Kôjima stood up slowly and bowed to everyone present. Then, shaking off Seijirô, who was trying to hold him back, he walked out of the room and out of the Ishikari residence.

A cold wind was still blowing. It was early on a Sunday afternoon in February, and the streets were empty. There was something eerie about it. Kôjima walked hurriedly up the road he had come down, heading back toward the station.

He was in a daze. He hadn't given any thought to where he was going, but as he stepped onto the train back to the suburbs, he realized that he was on his way back to the head office of the company that, after tomorrow, would no longer be his. From that moment, Ishiei Stores would cease to exist, its outlets and employees sold like chattel. It was like a body awaiting a brain transplant.

What was his hurry? This was just a bump in the long road he had to walk down. Why not go to Shinjuku and wander among the crowds, or kill time in a coffee shop? Or if he was really concerned about what was going to happen tomorrow, why not go to a bookstore and look for ideas on what to do next? But in the end Kôjima stayed on the train until he got off at Sawabe.

He walked down the main street from the station and turned the corner by City Hall. The two-story Ishiei Stores building stood ahead of him. He walked up the stairs and opened the glass door. There was a low counter, over which he could see the entire office, the office he had grown so used to. As he stood there, he was overwhelmed by emotion, and could not hold back his tears.

"Kôjima-*san,* what's wrong?" He heard a voice at his side. He lowered his eyes and turned; it was Misaki Yoshiko, looking up at him anxiously.

"It's nothing. Something in my eye."

"I hope you're OK," Yoshiko said, and disappeared with a quick bow, having discretion enough to know when questions were not welcome. *This is where I met her for the first time,* Kôjima reflected. *New Year's, five years ago.* The memories came bubbling up like a stream. He saw the faces of all the people he had known and worked with—the very people who would be sold off in the morning.

But this was a capitalist society. There was no sense in getting emotional about mergers and acquisitions. There was nothing wrong with the fact that companies were bought and sold. If a company couldn't achieve the results, you couldn't complain when it got sold. Probably it was better to be sold to a company with able leadership than to struggle on under incapable owners and managers.

But Ishiei Stores wasn't like that. The years of hard work were finally beginning to bear fruit, and the company had started to take its first steps toward a brighter future. And now the company owner—a man who knew nothing of supermarket management—was breaking the whole thing up, smashing it to smithereens. How could such a thing be allowed? It was a crime. It made no sense. It was unforgivable.

Was it right that an owner should be free to sell out the people who had devoted five years of their lives to rebuilding the company?

"Is it cold out?" said a voice behind him. It was Asayama, putting on his coat. "I'm thinking of going over to the Yuki store. I got a phone call from Ôtaka, the store manager. Apparently we're not getting anything like the number of customers we originally planned for, and to keep the sales area looking good he's having to offer big reductions or else he's left with piles of waste at the end of the day. Ôtaka got that done, but now they're running out of stock. I was thinking of going and talking things over with them."

"I'll come with you, if you don't mind."

"Do you know anything about Dominant Stores, Asayama-*san*?" Kôjima asked after they'd been on the road for fifteen minutes. He felt much calmer now.

"Dominant? From up in the northeast? Sure, I know them."

"What kind of company is it?"

"Pretty much a one-man band, I think. They say Kuji rules with an iron fist. In another life he'd have been the kind of man to lead an army to conquer the world."

"Have you ever been in one of their stores?"

"Sure. He runs a tight ship. Clean, polite, hardworking staff. Their strengths are in clothing and sundries, I think. But they're just a discount department store, really. At least as far as the fresh foods department is concerned, we beat them hands down. Why the sudden interest?"

"Oh, it's nothing. I heard a rumor yesterday that they were moving into the Tokyo market, that's all."

"Well, I don't think we have anything to worry about. Dominant is basically a big-store chain—like I say, as far as fresh foods are concerned, they're nothing to write home about. They shouldn't cause us any problems." Asayama took his left hand off the steering wheel and made a *V* for victory. "As far as supermarkets go, we've no one to fear. No matter who muscles in on our territory, we'll be fine."

Kôjima said nothing and tried to return Asayama's smile. But a wave of despair ripped through him and took him completely off guard. It was all over. Ishiei Stores was just an illusion now. An illusion, a mirage. The fifteen stores, the head office, the people who worked there, the merchandise, the service, the customers—all of it was just a big illusion. It would disappear in an instant, like a rainbow vanishing from the sky. And once it was gone, it would never come back again.

He fought to control his emotions, and shut his eyes to stop the tears from falling. Asayama mustn't see him crying. He turned and pretended to look out the window, but could see nothing but a blur.

"It's funny," Asayama went on, oblivious. "In the old days, if someone was in trouble at one of the stores, we'd just mumble about it. You know, what the hell is that guy up to over there? But we'd never actually go and look. Whereas now whenever there's a call from one of the stores I'll drop everything and go see right away."

That's why the company is better now, Kôjima wanted to shout, but his lips couldn't form the words and he continued to gaze vacantly out of the window, grunting by way of a reply.

The despair was overwhelming. He was consumed by self-pity. It would be the height of foolishness to get on a boat when he knew it was about to sink. But what alternatives did he have? He didn't want to escape to a cushy new job at Ishiei Trading Company, just because he happened to be related to Ishikari Eitarô. Was there no third way?

He could probably find a job somewhere. If he asked for help, Kameyama could put him in touch with a supermarket company somewhere. Or if he got in touch with his superiors from his banking days or wrote to some of his old college professors, someone would probably find him an opening somewhere. But was that the right way forward? He didn't know why, but the answer was no. An emotion that seemed to exist of its own accord kept pushing him in the direction of Ishiei Stores, even if it did mean climbing on a sinking ship. That's why he'd had his big bust-up with Eitarô. But it didn't matter how many clever words he spat out—it was all going to be over in the morning.

Maybe Eitarô is right, he thought. *Maybe I am allowing my emotions to get the better of me.*

But what was this emotion that was pushing him to stay on at Ishiei

Stores? What was this emotion that seemed so certain of itself? It was . . . a kind of narcissism. But why should staying at Ishiei Stores be narcissistic?

The question went around and around in his mind like a Zen koan. Exhausted, he leaned his head back against the headrest and closed his eyes.

By the time they got to the Yuki store, the winter sun had slipped over the horizon and the area was enveloped in darkness. The parking lot was almost deserted and the brightly shining store loomed massive in the darkness.

"Damn, it's cold," Asayama said. His breath rose in front of him like smoke. "Look at the stars. That tells you how freaking cold it is. Come on, let's get inside before we freeze." Rubbing his hands together and hunching over to warm himself, Asayama headed toward the store, but after a few steps he realized that Kôjima wasn't with him.

He was standing next to the car, looking up at the store, deep emotion in his eyes.

"What's wrong? You feeling all right?" Asayama asked, walking back to him.

"It's so beautiful," Kôjima whispered.

"What's that?"

"It's beautiful. This is the dream I had five years ago. And now it's here, shining in the darkness."

"It does look nice. Especially at night," Asayama said.

"That's me."

"What?"

"That's what it means." Kôjima was speaking louder now.

"What's wrong, Kôjima-*san*? What are you talking about?"

"Don't you think the store looks a bit like you too, Asayama-*san*?"

"Huh?"

"I'm not trying to be deep about it or anything. I mean, that's just the feeling I get. See, you can see the fresh vegetable displays by the entrance. The green of the cucumbers, the red of the tomatoes. You were the one who put those colors together. See that poster hanging down over the main fruit and vegetables aisle? I made that. Everything in this store, we created it all—all of us, working together. This is me. This is you. It's all of us. Do you see what I mean?"

"Well, sure. I guess."

"It is, though. Just look at it. All of it. The idea of building such a big store out here, the kinds of products we lined the shelves with, what prices to sell them at, the materials used for the walls and floors and ceilings, the color of the paint, the music—even the attitude of the people working there—we created it all. No one else could have done it the way we did. So Ishiei Stores is me and you—it is the people who created it."

Asayama was nodding silently, but he didn't have a clue what Kôjima was talking about. It didn't seem to matter to Kôjima, who kept on chattering dreamily to himself, until he suddenly stopped talking and took off at a trot toward the store.

"Kôjima-*san*! What's wrong?" Asayama said, running after him.

Kôjima stepped into the entrance, then stopped to take in the whole store. Starting with the fresh fruit, he walked slowly through the aisles. He examined each section carefully, occasionally stopping to pick up an item. He straightened a few POP flyers that had been knocked out of place. Suddenly he ran back toward the entrance. *What's he doing now?* Asayama wondered. *Is he finally losing his mind?* Kôjima returned with a shopping basket and began to remove substandard items from the displays. He seemed to be enjoying himself so much that Asayama didn't have the heart to disturb him, and just followed on silently behind him.

Once they had completed a circuit of the store and arrived at the cash registers, Kôjima turned around to look back at the route they'd just taken. Asayama did the same. Several customers were doing their shopping, standing in front of the displays, and picking up an item for a closer look. It was a scene of perfect harmony and balance.

"You can see how satisfied the customers are, can't you, Asayama-*san*?"

"Huh?"

"Look—reflected on the floor there."

"Oh, I get it," Asayama said. "I remember now. You were talking about that. You said we should polish the floor. Polish it so that the customers could see their reflections in the floor. You said if we did that we'd see our customers' satisfaction reflected there too."

"You remember," Kôjima said with a smile.

"I thought it was pretty far-fetched at the time, to tell you the truth. But you were right. When our floors were grubby and dirty, we couldn't see their satisfaction—because there wasn't any."

"Right. But they're not satisfied because this is Ishiei Stores. It's because the floors are polished, and they can find what they want when they want it and at a price and quality they like. It's because they're satisfied with the way the company is being run. It doesn't make any difference to them what the company is called, or who holds the company stock."

"What?" Asayama said, increasingly befuddled by Kôjima's philosophizing.

Kôjima paid him no mind: "And the things that are making the customers satisfied—all of it was developed by the people working at the company, starting with you, Asayama-*san*. We can identify with it; it's part of us, we are one and the same. What's important from the customers' point of view is not Ishiei Stores, but us. Don't you think that's true?"

"Uh, sure. You mean that lovely young woman over there and the pretty girl standing behind her, you mean they love us?"

"Yes. Yes, of course they do," Kôjima said, taking Asayama's joke at face value. "Asayama-*san*, I want you to remember what I have just said when tomorrow comes. If you can't remember it all, then come and ask me about it and I'll tell you again."

"Sure, but . . ."

Ôtaka, the deputy store manager, was hurrying toward them from the back of the store, a broad smile on his face. As he and Asayama walked to meet him, Kôjima chuckled. "He's looking pretty happy for someone who's been complaining he doesn't have enough customers."

Asayama followed along behind Kôjima, a broad grin on his face.

It was nearly closing time.

EPILOGUE

More than a week had passed since the announcement of the merger. The financial newspapers and industry journals had covered events in depth, heralding the merger as the beginning of a new era of amalgamation and consolidation for the industry.

Kôjima had been too busy since the announcement to feel sorry for himself. He was rushed off his feet with preparations for the transition, explaining details to employees, and meeting with journalists.

The company was in a state of excitement. The change was so extreme that excitement provided a way for employees to cope. It was like the tension you find among bereaved family members at a funeral. But the excitement soon vanished, to be replaced by emptiness and dejection and ennui.

At home in the evening, Kôjima retired to his bedroom without saying a word to his wife, without a bite to eat. He was sitting with a bottle of whiskey when the doorbell rang.

It was Asayama and several members of the former fresh foods research groups, fifteen in all. The visit was spontaneous, and they'd arrived unannounced. Kôjima showed them into the living room.

Some squeezed onto the sofa; the rest found a place on the dark blue carpet. Kôjima was overwhelmed by awkwardness. Ishikari Eitarô had made the decision to sell the company, but Kôjima felt responsible to these people. He had assured them that such a thing would never happen, and now he had let them down. There was nothing he could say.

He had seen them at work after the announcement was made. He'd apologized that his own efforts had not been enough to prevent it from happening. They'd all been perfectly understanding, and said *shôganai,* it couldn't be helped, but Kôjima felt a stab to his heart every time he heard the words. He wished they'd curse him to his face. And now here they were in his apartment. They could say what they wanted. Maybe if they vented their anger, he would be able to come up with something positive to say. But how could he, after he had let them work themselves to the bone only to be cut loose without warning? He stood in front of the group in silence.

Asayama spoke first: "Sorry for barging in like this. But they insisted on being brought to see you."

All right, Kôjima thought. *Say what you need to say. Get it off your chest. Hit me, punch me, knock me to the ground.*

Ôtaka Seizô spoke up from the center of the young crowd. "Do you know what we've been doing this week, sir?" he asked.

Kôjima looked at him dumbly. He couldn't believe how cheerful he was acting.

"We were all pretty shocked when we heard that we were going to be taken over by Dominant Stores. It felt like someone was snatching a jewel from our hands. But we checked things out. We divided the work up and ran an analysis of Dominant's stores, and we've discovered that things don't look so bad."

Ôtaka had taken charge of the project. Two days after the announcement of the merger, he drew up four teams of three members each—one from fruit and vegetables, one from meat, and one from fish—and set out to study Dominant's stores region by region. Ôtaka himself was in one of the teams. He had finished his report today.

"All four teams reached the same conclusion. If we can get our system introduced into Dominant's stores, we believe we can make great a big difference to the new company's performance. Dominant would win its battle against the competition, and would make huge profits."

Ôtaka continued to speak with a seriousness that made Kôjima think back to the very first of these research meetings, five years ago, when he had declared that he didn't want to spend the rest of his life working at a second-rate store. He was more polished now, but no less convincing.

"The fresh foods at Dominant are at roughly the same level as ours were five years ago. It's like looking at a living fossil, after the hard work we put into moving ourselves forward. They deal in anything that makes them money, claiming to be responding to customers' wishes, and the range of items in stock shows no evidence of thought or planning. The freshness of their produce is bad, and they don't even seem to be aware that they are selling substandard produce."

Ôtaka paused, looked around the room, then continued: "And everywhere you look there are staff shouting out how cheap everything is. Someone's obviously told them that the first principle of supermarket sales is to sell cheap. I believe we can salvage something from those miserable Dominant fresh produce sections and turn them into something we can be proud of. That would bring increased profits to Dominant, which has stores all over the country, and it would enrich the lives of the people who live near one of their outlets. It might even have some influence on other companies, and drag up the level of supermarket fresh foods sections all over Japan. This could be the start of a retail revolution. It would be a huge achievement—something we could never manage if we spent our whole lives in a small company like Ishiei Stores. I—no, *we*—want to give it a try."

Kôjima was struggling to understand what Ôtaka was saying. It occurred to him that they were trying to comfort him or cheer him up somehow. But no, that wasn't the case at all. Ôtaka was completely serious, and he meant every word he was saying. The reports were lying in front of his eyes: "Problems with the Fresh Foods Sales Areas in Dominant Stores"; "Defects in the Internal Management System as Inferred from the Condition of the Sales Area"; "Suggested Program for Effecting Improvements."

They had used the same technique at Ishiei Stores and the results were undeniable. If they were allowed to try it again, then it was almost certain that Dominant's sales would be vastly improved.

But the real question was whether such an opportunity would be given to employees of a company that had just been absorbed in a merger. It wasn't out of the question, but the chances weren't good.

"It doesn't matter what you think," Ôtaka said, as though he had read Kôjima's mind. "If you hadn't come along, Ishiei Stores would have disappeared a long time ago. And we would have gained nothing from our experience there. But in fact we won the battle; we created a great supermarket. And we can do it again. Maybe it won't be this time, but there's bound to be somewhere in Japan where we can put what we've learned to good use. This isn't just empty talk. When I look at Dominant Stores, I feel more convinced than ever. Will you help us, Kôjima-san? Will you be our leader? That's what we've come to ask today."

Of course, Kôjima wanted to say. *Of course I'll help.* But his heart was in his mouth, the words wouldn't come out, and tears were starting in his eyes. He wanted to go around the group and hug each one of them.

Still, Kôjima wasn't sure how to respond. But about one thing there was no longer any doubt: this group of young employees he had trained had grown up to be even bolder and braver than he was himself. Before he had thought out his answer, Kôjima found himself making a speech that was so dull and practical that it bored even him. And yet it was perhaps the most appropriate response he could have made:

"You decided to undertake these surveys on your own initiative, but we will recognize them as official company surveys. You should put in claims for expenses tomorrow. The next thing is to carry out more thorough investigations. I've only flipped through your reports, but I can tell that the content isn't quite there yet. First, the reports are too emotional. There is too much subjective language. I've always said the most important thing when compiling a report is to start with concrete facts. I want you all to come and see me first thing tomorrow morning." Suddenly, Kôjima was feeling relaxed. "And tomorrow we'll organize a group that will revolutionize the way supermarkets are run all over Japan!"

"Let's do it!" Asayama shouted.

The entire group joined in, and a wild chant shook the walls of the Kôjima living room: *Let's do it, let's do it, let's do it!*